The Apo

War of t

A Zombie Tale by Peter Meredith

Fictional works by Peter Meredith:

A Perfect America
The Sacrificial Daughter
The Apocalypse Crusade War of the Undead: Day One
The Apocalypse Crusade War of the Undead: Day Two
The Apocalypse Crusade War of the Undead Day Three
The Horror of the Shade: Trilogy of the Void 1
An Illusion of Hell: Trilogy of the Void 2
Hell Blade: Trilogy of the Void 3
The Punished
Sprite
The Blood Lure The Hidden Land Novel 1
The King's Trap The Hidden Land Novel 2
To Ensnare a Queen The Hidden Land Novel 3
The Apocalypse: The Undead World Novel 1
The Apocalypse Survivors: The Undead World Novel 2
The Apocalypse Outcasts: The Undead World Novel 3
The Apocalypse Fugitives: The Undead World Novel 4
The Apocalypse Renegades: The Undead World Novel 5
The Apocalypse Exile: The Undead World Novel 6
The Apocalypse War: The Undead World Novel 7
The Edge of Hell: Gods of the Undead Book One
The Edge of Temptation: Gods of the Undead Book Two
Pen(Novella)
A Sliver of Perfection (Novella)
The Haunting At Red Feathers(Short Story)
The Haunting On Colonel's Row(Short Story)
The Drawer(Short Story)
The Eyes in the Storm(Short Story)
The Witch: Jillybean in the Undead World

Forward

This is the story of the third day of the apocalypse as seen from the perspective of those who fought on the front lines of the Quarantine Zone and by those who were trapped within. Although there are easily ten-thousand stories from that time, few give us as full an understanding of the dire nature of the emergency as those depicted within these pages.

I have assembled a short list of the pertinent individuals mentioned within and they are as follows:

Dr. Thuy Lee—Lead researcher at the R & K Pharmaceuticals Walton facility. Using the innovative and inadequately tested Combination Cell Therapy, she discovered a cure for cancer, however her work was sabotaged resulting in the subsequent apocalypse. She is currently on the FBIs most wanted list.

Ryan Deckard—One-time security chief at the Walton facility, now a desperate survivor trying to find a way out of the Quarantine Zone

Chuck Singleton—A cancer patient and one of the few people to leave the Walton facility alive. He was late for the beginning of human trials and thus was not infected by the deadly Com-cells.

Stephanie Glowitz—She too is a cancer patient and one of the few people to leave the Walton facility alive. She was also late for the beginning of human trials and thus was not infected by the deadly Com-cells.

Dr. Samuel Wilson—Oncologist at the Walton facility. One of eight people to survive the destruction of the Walton facility.

Anna Holloway—As a front, Anna worked as a research assistant at the Walton facility. In truth she was as a corporate spy for a competing pharmaceutical company. She is in possession of a stolen vial of Com-cells and on the run in southern New York state.

Lieutenant Eng of the People's Republic of China—Eng is a spy and saboteur. In his undercover role as a research assistant, he made changes to the Com-cells which had worldwide repercussions.

John Burke—A cancer patient who received only sterile water during the Com-cell trial. He believes that he is immune to the deadly effects of the Com-cells.

Courtney Shaw—A state trooper dispatcher who oversaw the initial quarantine zone around Walton.

PFC Max Fowler—Once a soldier in the 42nd Infantry Division, he is now simply one of many thousands struggling to survive on the wrong side of the line.

Marty Aleman—Chief of Staff of the President of the United States. He sees himself as a "king maker," and runs the country using the president as a figurehead.

Jaimee Lynn Burke—Aged eight, she is the daughter of John Burke and the first person to escape the quarantine zone. She is thought to be partially immune to the Com-cells. She has become a deadly, unfeeling, sweet little killer, living and feeding in Hartford, Connecticut.

Chapter 1 The Hunger for Life

1–2:06 a.m.
Hartford, Connecticut

Jaimee Lynn remembered her name, at least her first name, and she had a firm image of her father's face. She also knew she was from a place called Arkan-na-sas or Arkarassis or something like that, and at the very edge of her memory, where everything was quickly becoming grey fog, she recalled the part she had fought for in the school play when she had been in the fourth grade.

She had played a tea cup, and there had been rainbow streamers hanging from the rafters, and there had been a mean boy who had pinched her bottom in front of everyone and had thought that was so funny that he had pointed at her and got his friends to laugh along.

But how long ago that was, she had no idea. It seemed like maybe it had been two years since the fourth grade, but it might have been ten. Numbers were somewhat of a mystery to her, while time consisted of either "now" or "before."

A lot had happened "before," and it was all a blur. There had been a funeral with her mama in a box, and a hospital that burned up and there had been a cat that had got all stiff and wouldn't meow or nothing. And there had been an ambulance with lights that turned the night dizzy, making everything two different colors: red then white, red then white.

And there had been blood. A shiver ran up her back at the thought of the blood. It was always so agreeably hot. She loved it hot. When it was cold it, it tasted like soup that had been left out to congeal and it made her stomach go icky. Jaimee Lynn would never drink cold blood. Never, ever, never…unless she had to. Unless there weren't none other.

Thankfully there was lots and lots of blood around, nice and hot and clean. There was blood in the people who were in all the houses and buildings. She was in a city full of houses and buildings, but she had no idea what the name of the city was. Arkanasas, maybe? She didn't know and she hadn't spent a moment caring.

All she really cared about was blood, hot and coppery. She cared even though she wasn't hungry yet and wouldn't be for a few hours. Her belly pushed out the front of the white gown she wore as if she had a baby growing inside of her stick-thin body. It was a blood-baby if it was a baby at all. Her belly sloshed liquid when she rolled over.

She was full and sleepy. Her eyes were heavy and her brain was addled. Her limbs seemed far away; maybe ten feet away or maybe nineteen. She didn't know and she didn't care. She was too sleepy to care about inches and miles and all that.

What she really wanted at that moment of fullness and contentment was to be cuddled. Even before that school play about the tea cup and the rainbows, and maybe even before the ambulance with its lights, she remembered being cuddled.

It must have been a thousand years ago, back before that rotten boy had pinched her. It was long ago and that was for sure, and it had been her mother who had done the cuddling. Her mother had been the color of gold, like wheat or a sunrise. And she had been soft.

Jaimee Lynn thought nothing could ever be so soft, and yet there was a brown woman with thick yarn for hair, lying not three feet away. She lay sprawled out with most of her insides spilled out on the ground. She was growing cold, but for the moment she was warmer than the grass where the *pack* lay in knots like cats in a sunbeam.

The pack were Jaimee Lynn's children, sort of. They were ugly. Some were missing parts and pieces. One little girl was missing most of her hair. It had been ripped out in great chunks and her head looked like pinkish hamburger, except where the bone showed through white as chalk. It was ugly and she was ugly.

There was another boy who was missing one leg from the knee down. He moved around like some sort of pale spider on two hands and the one remaining foot. He was surprisingly quick.

One kid didn't have a face and Jaimee Lynn didn't know if it was a boy or a girl, though it didn't matter all that much to her. She wasn't going to play with it no matter what it was. *They* were different. The other kids were all gross and stupid and couldn't even speak except for a few words like "hungy" or "mama," and everyone knew that even little babies could say those words.

Jaimee Lynn looked down her nose at them as they slept. The blood made them slow, like ol' hounds, and she knew they wouldn't budge for a few hours. They wouldn't roll over or scratch themselves or nothing. They would sleep like rocks. It was dangerous to sit out like that, though Jaimee Lynn couldn't remember why.

Remembering was hard, especially when she was full and sleepy. She was full, but cold and all she could think about was that the brown woman had soft, soft cheeks and that she was still warm. There was steam lifting up from her guts. Jaimee could smell the heat. It was a coppery sort of smell. She crawled to the woman and snuggled up into those warm guts, pulling a flap of skin around her like a blanket.

It was almost perfect, and she felt a bit like a baby herself, especially as she pulled the woman's arm around her, taking her soft brown hand in her small white one. She brought the hand to her face, put the thumb in her mouth, bit down savagely and then fell asleep, sucking gently on that thumb, drinking sips of blood like a baby would from a bottle.

2–The Capitol Building, Hartford, Connecticut

In the dark of midnight, Jaimee Lynn slept, not realizing that all around her Hartford was being fortified to keep out creatures just like her. The people were building tall walls and digging deep ditches not realizing that they were trapping themselves in with a pack of monsters whose numbers were growing.

Even as Jaimee Lynn sucked on that thumb, there were others whom she had eaten off of who were coming back to life as the unholy virus began replicating and regenerating. Organs and bone and skin grew back just enough for a semblance of life to return. Only the brain did not regenerate. These others came back as half-formed, flesh-eating monsters who knew only eternal hunger.

For the moment, the people of Hartford were oblivious to the danger in their midst. Certainly the governor of Connecticut, Christine Warner, had no clue even though her office stood only four miles from where Jaimee Lynn Burke had been feeding all day.

The governor, safe behind bulletproof windows, drank cup after of cup of the blackest coffee. Her nerves were wired and yet she yawned endlessly as she waited for the latest reports.

So far, news had been sketchy on every front. The last she had heard, the Rhode Island border to the east was closed, being held by a scattering of police and local firemen who had their trucks heeled over, blocking every route into the state. Things were tense but, so far peaceful.

The same couldn't be said of the border with Massachusetts to the north. Already there had been over thirty deaths—'murders' is how Christine referred to them. The boys up in Massachusetts weren't playing around. The border bristled with guns and men with itchy trigger fingers.

Christine had already been on the phone with her counterpart in Boston and had dressed him down, letting him know that she held him responsible for each death. It was after two in the morning and yet she had a squad of lawyers preparing briefs on behalf of every family who'd been affected by the violence.

It felt like a waste of time, but she needed to do something. She needed to occupy herself, or her eyes would slip up to the big map on the wall. It showed quite clearly that her state was hemmed in on three sides and worse, it showed the smattering of forces she had guarding the western border.

Her shoulders slumped and her chin dropped, but, as if the map were a magnet, she glanced up again for the tenth time that hour. All she had were a few thousand part-time soldiers holding back a horde of zombies a hundred thousand strong. She had seen footage of the unrelenting fury of the horde and it was sickening. The endless mob roared over everything in its path, killing and feeding like piranha.

At first contact, her soldiers had broken and fled. They had rallied and formed a new line, but that had been shattered by sheer numbers, and so too had the third line and the fourth. There were always too many of the beasts and too few soldiers, and that was partially her fault. For the last six years, she had grumbled over the cost of the National Guard units and until the day before, she had seen them as an unnecessary drain on the budget. Happily, she had stepped on their requests for greater spending because, well, who knew *this* was going to happen?

Who could have known a zombie apocalypse was even possible?

Now these weekend warriors were all she had. Four nearly useless militia companies, two companies of engineers, a medical support group, and an infantry battalion that was spread dangerously thin over seventy-five miles. At least she hoped she still had them. There had been only a few frantic messages from the front in the past couple of hours.

The last, a blunt response of: "We're holding, so stop asking. If you want to help, send all the reinforcements you can and stay off the damn radio!" Although terse and rude, the answer had been reassuring to the governor simply because there had been such authority in the way the woman spoke. There was a refreshing lack of fear in her voice; she'd been all business.

But that had been thirty-three minutes before.

Warner hit a button on her phone. "Carla, get Arnold in here!" she barked. Carla then barked at her own assistant, an unpaid intern named Charlotte.

Charlotte who at one time had bragged to everyone who would listen about how she was helping to sculpt the future and that she was 10an integral part of this or that piece of legislation when all she ever really did was fetch coffee and take lunch orders.

Now, she regretted having taken the unpaid position. While she was virtually imprisoned in Hartford, her family and friends back in Putnam, had slipped across the border into Massachusetts. That had been the day before, after Carla had placed a number of discreet calls, warning everyone she knew to get the hell out of Connecticut before it was too late.

Those had been illegal calls. No one was supposed to know how poorly the border was defended. "We can't be the cause of a large scale panic," the governor had said.

"Well, fuck that," Charlotte replied, under her breath as she hurried to the bathroom to begin texting and calling everyone she knew. If she could have, she would have left as well, but the doors were being watched and the guards were stopping people from leaving.

Fear rippled throughout the building until a lower floor window had been kicked out and everybody with any sense had fled. Charlotte had been stuck in another of the many long and boring meetings and before she knew it, the place was empty—

by then it didn't matter. The borders were closed and the capitol building was as safe as anywhere else in the state.

It was safe, but scary as hell. Charlotte found herself hurrying through the empty halls of the expansive capitol building searching for General Arnold and it was no lie to say that she was freaked out. Her steps echoed in the shadows, coming back to her as if they belonged to someone else—perhaps to one of *them*.

No real news from the western border in the last two hours meant an army of zombies could even then be creeping past the barricades the citizens had put up around the city. In Charlotte's mind the zombies were insidious and sly, slipping through culverts or sewers to sneak up on the unwary.

The ugly image made her hurry, holding her arms drawn in, seeing ghosts in every shadow until she practically screamed when she caught sight of a leering pale face in a nook of the kitchen. It was General Arnold hunched over a half-eaten turkey sandwich with a cup of very Irish-smelling coffee at his elbow.

The assistant to the assistant of the governor reverted to her snooty pre-zombie mentality in an instant. Charlotte raised an eyebrow at the smell of alcohol. "*She* would like to speak to you, sir," she said, trying not to look down her nose at the general's rumpled uniform and bloodshot eyes.

He had been on the phone, which he quickly covered up. "Tell her I'll be right there." To Charlotte, he sounded somewhat like a teenager being ordered to "hang up the phone," by an overbearing mother.

General Arnold waited until the girl and her snide look left before turning back to the phone. Holding a hand over his mouth, he asked: "Are you still there?"

"Yes…but you know I can't work the boat. I don't know the first thing about sailing."

"It has a motor. You know that, Bea. All you have to do is turn the damn key and point the boat where you want it to go. When you get to the marina, *don't* talk to anyone. And don't call your sister; she's safe where she is."

"She's in Bridgeport and that's even closer to the New York border than I am. I could pick her up on the way. It's not tha…"

General Arnold's grip on the phone turned his knuckles white. "Beatrice!" he hissed. "You cannot tell anyone. If they catch me, they'll throw me in jail and that's if I'm lucky. They could shoot me you know, and you too, so please, do not tell anyone, do you hear me?"

He waited until she mumbled a reluctant: "Okay," and then he sped through a quick class on how to operate the fifty-foot yacht, spelling everything out for her. It wasn't difficult and yet, Beatrice had become more and more helpless during their forty years of marriage until now she could barely balance a checkbook and if she ever had a flat tire, she would come unglued.

"Get the boat and work your way east along the shore until you get to Old Lyme," he said, spitting the words out faster now. He'd been gone too long. He'd be missed. There'd be questions. "You remember how to get there?"

"It's right after that Outer Bar Channel thing, right?"

"That's right. Now listen, don't try to dock the boat. Stay just off the Outer Bar and don't let anyone get near. Things are getting hairy along the coast; boats are being stolen and people killed, so don't let anyone near."

"Oh, Milt, I don't think I can do this."

The general felt a spike of pain in his temple and wondered if Beatrice had finally given him the aneurism she'd been hoping to kill him with for the last twenty years. "You can if you want to live. It's as simple as that. Call me on my cell when you get close and for God's sake don't call anyone else."

"Oh, Milt," she said, again. She wanted to be reassured, but he didn't have time. After a quick goodbye, he hung up and then ran for the stairs. He couldn't arouse suspicions; he couldn't be late or say the wrong word. From everything he'd read and heard in the last twenty-four hours, he knew Connecticut was doomed. The disease spread too easily, the politicians were too spineless, and the soldiers too unprepared for this sort of fight.

He wasn't prepared either. Twenty-five years earlier, he'd been the commanding officer of an infantry battalion in *Desert Storm*; he been a hard man. Then, somewhere in the last fifteen years of pushing papers and saluting at parades, he'd gotten soft in the middle and had lost his nerve.

Firm leadership might have been able to save the motley force surrounded on the western border, but he was no longer that man. He was a frightened man who needed to buy time for his getaway and so he rushed into the governor's office with an agenda. "I'm sorry about the delay, I was on the phone with the command post."

There were six people in the office, all suck-ups who were too afraid to take a stand on anything. They all looked to the governor. Warner raised a penciled eyebrow. "And?"

"They are looking for orders to retreat to this north-south highway." He pointed at a spot on the map. "Here outside of Torrington. That's only thirteen miles from the Farmington River, the eastern most edge of Hartford." This much was true, at least. Although the military channels were a mess as everyone with a damned radio was blathering for all they were worth, the one overriding cry had been a call to retreat.

"Can General Collins hold that line?" Warner asked, not realizing that Collins was a cold corpse with a hole in his head.

They hadn't heard from Collins in two hours, which scared her to no end and increased the that had been stress building up and up inside of her. She had aged a great deal in the last day and a half. Where before her beauty had been considered timeless, now the years seemed to have stacked up on her almost overnight. Her hair was uncharacteristically flat and dull, and her makeup had worn away to reveal the sixty-year old woman beneath.

Looking at her made General Arnold wonder what he looked like. He turned from her to stare at the map. On its flat surface, he saw all sorts of possibilities—none of them good. If the few thousand men who were left, fell back as they wanted to, it would shorten their line, giving them more firepower per mile—in fact, if they fell back to a line that was even closer, one that ran from Bristol in the north to New Haven in the south, it would free up probably thirty percent more men...but that would move the zombies even closer, only nine miles away.

It would be so close that the civilian population would be able to hear the battle raging, and boy then there'd be panic. With the borders closed, people would flee in the only direction that was left open to them; they'd go south to the ocean. Every boat would be swamped by sheer numbers, his own included. Arnold couldn't have that happen.

"I say they hold in place," he said, forcefully. "They may be cut off and surrounded, but they would become the focal point of the fight. They'd be like a magnet for the zombies." Warner looked stricken by the idea and so he reassured her: "They are being resupplied and reinforced by a swarm of Blackhawks. Trust me, they could conceivably fight for days in this manner."

Right up until one person got infected, and then the 360-degree perimeter would implode in hours, he didn't add.

Warner stared at the map; the zombies were already so close and the idea of letting them get even one step closer made her stomach jitter. "But how do we know that none of the Infected Persons are getting around them? There could be ten thousand of them coming right at us for all we know. Without an actual line, we'd never know until it was too late."

"Trust me, we'd know," Arnold said. "With all the flights going back and forth, we would know. The pilots use infrared; they'd know if a large enough group was heading our way. Besides, like I said, with all the shooting and all the commotion, the soldiers are the main focal point for the zombies. From what I gather through my channels, Collins is attracting every one of those creatures in a hundred mile radius. We should be safe."

Again, they'd be safe right up until some poor soldier got splattered with blood and then they'd all be "dead" in hours. After that, the zombies would head east to Hartford and how many of them would still be wearing helmets and armored vests? How on earth do you kill an armored zombie?

And what would happen if the soldiers disobeyed orders and retreated? What if they broke out of the throng of undead that surrounded them and came racing to Hartford? Who could stop them from tearing down the flimsy wall that had been thrown up? There'd be blood in the streets and anarchy.

That's why he had to get away in the next few hours even if he had to kill to do it.

"I say we try to get some sleep," he suggested. "There's nothing more we can do tonight and we should be as ready for whatever tomorrow brings." Reluctantly, the governor agreed.

3— The Quarantine Zone

Sleep was a luxury few could afford outside the heavy stone walls of the capitol building. On the outskirts of Hartford, the people toiled like ants, fortifying their city. Using every available piece of construction equipment, they dug tremendous ditches and behind these they created a wall out of a mishmash of items.

They emptied three different lumber yards and eight mega hardware stores of every scrap of wood. From two nearby quarries and three granite wholesalers tons of stone were heaved into place. Entire neighborhoods lost their trees when they were felled by men and women, some of whom had happily claimed the mantle of "tree hugger" just two days before.

The wall was immense and fantastic but it wasn't the only project that the people of Hartford set for themselves. They also demolished bridges, tore up roads and cut railroad tracks.

Their efforts were so prodigious that getting out of the city was nearly as difficult as getting in, though for the moment, almost no one but General Arnold was even considering leaving. The outside world was just too frightening, and now that the walls were going up so quickly, most people were beginning to feel, if not safe, at least safer than they had been.

Deep in the Quarantine Zone, sleep was even harder to come by. For Ryan Deckard, the only sleep he could foresee was the moment he put a bullet in his own head, something that was fast becoming a possibility.

His little group of six was nearly done in. What felt like hours before, he had watched Thuy disappear in the last helicopter leaving the trooper station. It had hurt to see her go, but it wasn't something he allowed himself to dwell on. He had pushed aside the pain, taken a deep breath and charged out the back door of the station. From that moment on, he had been running for his life and fighting for others' lives. He was thirty-eight, fit and strong. He could have left them all behind; he could have left them to choose between suicide or being eaten alive.

But it wasn't something he could do.

The only one besides Deckard who had any real chance was PFC Max Fowler. He was young and strong, and what was more, he could shoot his M16A2 like nobody's business. If he got lucky, he stood a chance. The others simply weren't going to make it. Chuck Singleton, a tough-as-leather good ol' boy, had tumors riddling his lungs which made breathing an arduous chore. He wheezed like a broken accordion and was so loud that the zombies could track him by sound alone.

Chuck was a tough one and a gamer, and yet the real reason he dropped further and further behind was that he was weighed down by Stephanie Glowitz, who stumbled and veered side to side as she coughed up what looked like bits of grey lung. He promised not to leave her and told her so over and over again.

All through that dreadful night, he had coaxed her along, but he knew the truth as well as she did. At one point, he had said: "Say the word, darling and we can sit for a spell."

She knew exactly what he meant. Sure, they would be able to sit and try to catch their breath, but for how long? A minute? Perhaps two? And then what? There would be no getting up again, they both knew it. Their muscles would seize, and the cancer in their lungs would allow only sips of air, just enough for a few last murmured words of love.

And then Chuck would kill her.

He had promised he would and she knew she could trust him in this. If there was one thing in this new world of monsters and constant death and misery that she had faith in, it was that Chuck Singleton loved her enough to put a bullet in her brain.

She certainly didn't trust herself. She would hesitate and make excuses and put off the end until the beasts were on top of her. It would be a nightmare death. Chuck would do it right. He would hold her and whisper words of love in her ear and she would die knowing the fullness of his love.

But she wasn't ready to die just yet. Doggedly, she ran even though it felt as though her feet had been cast in cement. She ran despite the pain, because there was still a chance. There was always a chance. What if they could get away at least for a little while? What if she and Chuck could enjoy this new love as God had meant them to?

She ran, stumbling and slewing right and left. She ran, sweat in her short brown hair and glistening on her pale face, wishing she could throw away the useless gun in her hands and the pack on her back. She ran for love and yet she was barely running. Her meandering, faltering steps were more of a haphazard jog.

Still, she kept ahead of Dr. Wilson who lagged far in the back with zombies nipping at his heels. The middle-aged oncologist had a slab of gut hanging over his belt that jiggled with every step and his once brown face was now a shade of grey. He looked like he was on the verge of a heart attack; if he hadn't had one already.

The only exercise he'd had in the last fifteen years was his bi-weekly golf outings, and even then, he had an electric cart to haul around his golf bag, along with his fat ass. The entirety of his exercise consisted of walking that fat ass from the cart all the way to the ball and back again. If the ball ever went into the rough, he broke a sweat searching for it—this was as close to jungle warfare as he had ever come.

Now, Dr. Wilson regretted the endless cheeseburgers and millions of fries he had consumed at the clubhouse after his "exercise."

Exhaustion slowed everyone including the German Shepherd, Sundance, who had his tongue hanging halfway down to the ground as he padded along, his nails scraping endlessly on the asphalt.

They were so far gone that they were nearly too done in to fight, which was okay with Deckard. Fighting was the last thing he wanted to do.

They had blasted out of the ring of zombies surrounding the trooper station, or rather, Deckard, Chuck, and Fowler had blasted out. When Deckard had seen Stephanie's atrocious shooting, he had put his hand on the barrel of her M16 and pressed it down so that it pointed at the dirt. Although she had been going full bore, rocking her weapon for all she was worth, she had accomplished little beyond poking holes in the forest.

"Save your bullets," he had said, trying his best not rip her a new one for wasting precious ammo. "Don't shoot unless they're right on you, okay? And then only head shots, okay?" A minute later, he'd said the same thing to Dr. Wilson, who had only slightly better aim—he was *almost* hitting the zombies.

Now, hours later, those first few minutes still played on Deckard's mind and stoked his fears. As they had rushed out into the night, there had been zombies tied in the trees, as if on leashes. They had been placed there to pen the humans in, to keep them from escaping. Although these zombies had been easily shot down, the ramifications scared the crap out of him.

He could deal with normal zombies. They were mindless feeding machines that didn't have the mental capacity to tie their own shoes…if they even wore shoes. Frequently, they came without pants, their parts flopping around as forgotten as the rest of their old lives.

And yet there were some, mainly the child zombies, who could think and who could plan and plot. Some part of their underdeveloped brains allowed them to "think" through the virus eating them alive. Unfortunately, the thoughts always concerned death and the need for more blood. As they ran, Deckard kept a sharp eye out for these little beasts, knowing that they were a hundred times more dangerous than the others.

Deep into the night, he pushed his little group along, keeping just ahead of the black-eyed beasts. His one hope was to come across a fully fueled Humvee just sitting in the middle of the road waiting for him to drive it away to safety. But all that lay ahead was more pavement, and more forest on either side, and more zombies coming up out of the darkness. They were on a road that went, well, if he was to be honest, he didn't even know what direction he was traveling and he didn't have time to stop at a gas station or poke around in one of the many crashed cars littering the road for a map.

He could only press onward and hope.

A sound from behind caused him to glance back. Doctor Wilson was whimpering between gusts of breath as one of the faster zombies had its rotted hand stretched within inches of snagging his collar.

"Oh…shit…Deckard…please…" Wilson gasped.

"Take point," Deckard ordered Fowler. He stopped and shouldered his rifle, pausing to let the others run past, trying to calm his own breathing. It wasn't easy, seeing the mass of undead surging after them.

They were fearsome things, made all the worse by the dark. In the light, one could see their deformities, the chunks that had been eaten out of them by those who had fed off of them, creating them. Frequently, they were missing fingers and hands, faces and bellies. And yet, they still came on, so hungrily it was unnerving.

In the dark, they looked and sounded like a host of demons.

When Wilson was twelve feet away, Deckard caressed the trigger of his M4, sending a bullet just over Wilson's right shoulder and into the black, spored-eye of a zombie who had been inches from getting hold of the doctor's white lab coat. It went down in a tumble, piling the ones closest into a tangle of scabbed arms and legs.

He shot another, dropping it, upsetting another cadre, creating another stumbling block. Slowly, Wilson lumbered by, his breath rasping in and out. Deckard fired four more times, making sure each shot counted for more than just one of the beasts. Only when he had caused enough chaos to give them some running room did he turn to catch up. As he pulled even with the doctor, he took Wilson's rifle from his numb fingers and slung it across his own back.

"Just keep going, it'll be okay." Deckard told him, though why, he didn't know. Nothing was going to save the man. They had another twenty miles to go before they got to the edge of the zone and once there they'd have to fight their way to freedom. Wilson wasn't going to make it another two miles, and as for fighting, he couldn't hold his own against the weakest of the zombies.

"I…need…my…gun," he rasped. "Just…in case." There was fear in his deep brown eyes. Deckard knew all about that particular fear. They all did.

"It won't come to that," Deckard lied to him. "Just keep going and you'll be fine." They would all keep going but to where, and for how long, none of them knew.

Chapter 2

1—2:44 a.m.
The Edge of the Zone, West of the Hudson

Up to this point, Private Ginny Kinna had held her own. She had her mask and her MOPP gear and her gun—to her it was and always would be a gun and the bullets that went in it were bullets. It wasn't a "weapon" and the bullets weren't "rounds" no matter what her drill sergeants always said.

She had her gun and her bullets and so far, everything had been okay. Her unit was a "support battalion," meaning they rarely went into the field, and almost never fired their guns. Because the 250th was what the infantry called REMFs—*Rear Echelon Mother-Fuckers*, they had been placed on the long perimeter across the wide river in what everyone thought of as the safest location.

There hadn't been a single zombie within a mile of Ginny and that was a very good thing, and not just for her. It was good for the nation as a whole, because in the two years she had been in the New Jersey National Guard, she had never actually qualified with the M16A2, or any other gun for that matter.

In basic training, after two miserable attempts in which she failed to hit anything beyond fifty meters, she had quietly been given a waiver. When she went to qualify with the 250th Brigade Support Battalion, she didn't think she had shot her gun any better and yet they pinned a little badge on her Class A uniform. No one pretended she was a marksman, then again no one had said a thing when she consistently failed to knock down target after target.

This same sort of 'look the other way' attitude also occurred when she failed her P.T. test time and again. It was usually the running that got her and so her platoon sergeant let her do what they called an *Alternative Aerobic Event* which consisted of her walking for two and half miles. It wasn't as easy as it sounded since the "event" had taken place on a warm day in March and part of the walk was uphill.

When there were complaints from the other soldiers, it was explained that since Ginny was a dental technician, she wasn't going to be marching off to war anytime soon. It was unfortunate that she wasn't a good dental tech, either. She had chosen the MOS because she figured that it would help her get a job in the "outside" world, only she hadn't counted on the smell.

It was a bit of a shock to her just how badly a decayed tooth could stink. In fact, many of the people who came into the clinic had the most awful breath. After she had gagged one time too many, she was relegated to record keeping, which amounted to little more than fetching records and putting them back where they belonged in alphabetical order. About half the time, the "Ps" ended up with the "Rs" and the "Ns" were frequently interspaced with the "Ms."

Ginny Kinna didn't belong in the National Guard. She could only just manage her job as a cashier at the Piggly Wiggly. The other soldier didn't think she could be trusted as a school crossing guard. To be blunt, most people thought she was possibly the worst soldier they had ever seen. In truth, she shouldn't be blamed. She found herself sitting against a tree with her M16 across her lap, staring out into a zombie-filled night simply because political correctness was a greater force in government than was common sense.

She would have been drummed out ages ago were it not for the quotas that had to be filled. Not that there weren't poor soldiers among the men. Far from it. In fact, there were half a dozen men who were on the line almost puking drunk, a number of them were balls-to-the wall high as could be, and others so scared they were on the verge of deserting.

And yet, Ginny was the very weakest link. She wasn't "considering" running away at the first sign of a zombie, she was planning on it. She wasn't even technically on the "line." Her squad leader had sat her down in the middle of the field in front of her, crouched beside her and tried to explain what a listening post was; however the moment he left, she had backed away, fearing that she was too out in the open.

Now, sitting up on the edge of a forest, she couldn't even see Sergeant McMullen who was supposed to be up and to her right, while PFC Garcia on her left was nothing but a distant orange glow as he chain-smoked Camels.

She was afraid and didn't know what she would do if one of the zombies came her way. More than anyone, she knew she didn't deserved that little badge they had pinned on her chest and now her life could hinge on being able to shoot straight. It was a terrible thought and one that made her want to pee so badly it was beginning to hurt.

At two in the morning, with clouds hanging low overhead, she couldn't take it anymore and slipped away, back into the forest where the old growth was thick and the brambles and nettles kept catching her feet, tripping her up. There was so much dead timber that she feared she would either fall and break her neck or accidentally shoot herself.

Eventually she found a secluded spot and undid the buttons on her "camy-pants' as she thought of them, and squatted. The relief was immediate and the flow like a river. She was just marking the fact that the bottom of her right boot was going to get pee on it when there came a crack of twigs somewhere in the forest in front of her. In an instant, her heartbeat revved, her mouth went cotton-dry and the flow of urine stopped immediately. Her bladder forgotten, she sat in her awkward, ungainly squat, listening as the sly noises came closer and closer.

Snap...crack...crunch—the noises were getting closer and louder. Ginny was frozen in the worst position possible, a puddle between her splayed feet, her pants down around her ankles, her heart whamming in her chest, her gun just out of reach.

Snap...crack...crunch. It was a zombie, she knew it. Her eyes were huge and wet, the only thing shining in the night. She was sure that they were like twin lamps bringing the monster right at her, and yet she couldn't blink. She found it impossible to shut her eyes or move at all; she couldn't even breathe.

Ginny felt frozen by her fear, petrified by it. She could picture herself still in mid-squat when the zombie found her. *Snap...crack...crunch*, so close now! So close that she couldn't take it anymore.

With a garbled scream, Ginny jumped up and grabbed for her gun, her hands wooden and fumbling for the trigger. Thirty feet away there was a shadow creature—the zombie! It had to be one of them, and instinctively she felt the need to kill it. In spite of her horrible predicament, she actually felt like a real soldier as she hefted her gun up to her shoulder, sighted and pulled the trigger.

The trigger didn't budge! For two wasted seconds she stood there with her pants around her ankles, staring at the gun, her mind a complete blank. She could think of nothing better than to press down harder on the trigger as if the reason the gun wasn't blasting out lead was in the weakness of her finger.

22

She was still uselessly squeezing the trigger when the shadow moved. It was coming for her! A scream built up in the back of her throat and she was just about to throw away the gun so she could yank up her pants and book it out of there, when her thumb brushed against something on the side of the gun.

Just like that it clicked in her fear-addled mind what the problem was: she had left the gun on safe! With a sob, she flicked the lever to three-round burst and then started pulling the trigger. She had no idea how many times she fired, and she had no idea if she hit the creature.

All she could see were weird orange blobs and all she could hear was a ringing tone that blotted out everything else—the monster could have been three feet from her for all she knew. That thought spread panic through her until she was helpless against it. She ran—for all of two steps, before the pants around her ankles tripped her up and sent her sprawling.

With one hand scrambling for the dropped M16, and the other hitching up her camy-pants, she took off in a mad sprint through the dense forest, certain the beast was right on her tail. It felt as though the creature kept reaching out to grab her and she ran, bouncing back and forth as the trees snagged her clothes, torquing her around, changing the direction of her flight until she was going at right angles to where she thought she was going.

Finally, the strap of her gun got hung up on a branch and was ripped out of her hands. She only looked back for a second as a weird gobbling sound erupted from her throat and then she ran some more.

Who knows how far she would have run if a root sticking up out of the ground like a demon's claw hadn't tripped her up and sent her face first into the dirt. She was cut and bleeding, tears in rivers coursed along the lines of her cringing face. Her pants were down below her bottom and her pale ass was like a beacon.

Sergeant McMullen could see it from forty yards though he didn't know what he was seeing until he came closer. He came creeping up, going from tree to tree, his heart going a mile a minute after his near miss. Three minutes before, the air, inches from his head had whispered to him with the passage of Ginny's bullets and he was still shaking from it.

"Ginny?" he called. Everyone else was *Private this* or *Sergeant that*, but Ginny had always been Ginny. Even Captain

Hauber had called her Ginny four hours earlier when he had whispered to McMullen: "Keep an eye on Ginny. Don't let her get into trouble."

McMullen was surprised it had taken this long for her to do something stupid. "Ginny? It's okay. It's Sergeant McMullen. You're safe."

"Sergeant M-McMullen? Where's the za-za-zoombie? There was one chasing me. I-I heard it."

He eased to the next tree, keeping it between them. He didn't know that her M16 was lost somewhere in the forest. "That was just me. I was coming to check on you when you freaked out."

"That was you?"

"Yeah," he answered. She began blubbering, her face in the dirt, her white ass pointed up at the clouds. McMullen didn't know what to do. Had this been any other soldier, he would have torn into him, screamed into his face, and, at a minimum, there would have been Article 15 charges pending.

But this was Ginny and the brass somewhere north of brigade level had made it clear that the 250th had a gender issue. The company was disproportionately male, to which Sergeant McMullen had only rolled his eyes. He wanted to scream: *Of course it's disproportionately male, It's the Army!*

Instead of screaming, he followed orders and that meant coddling dead weight such as Ginny instead of cutting her loose. "Hey, why don't you pull up those pants of yours? There you go. Now we can talk like…"

A noise in the brush had him turning, rifle up, eyes squinting into the dark. Someone or something was coming their way. For a moment, his fear ramped up, and he gripped his M16 with too much force, causing the tip to wobble. "Get up," he hissed to Ginny, who was only lying there trying to work the buttons on her pants.

She looked ready to bolt and McMullen wondered if he wouldn't be far behind her; he was the first to admit that he wasn't the hardest soldier in the unit and the internet videos of zombies eating people had him scared half to death. "Get behind me," he whispered. For once, she was quick to obey an order and he felt her nails digging through his shirt.

The sound in the forest came closer and he was on the verge of shooting when someone whistled a double note. Immediately, he sagged with relief—zombies did not whistle. "Who is that?" McMullen asked, pitching his voice low.

"It's Garcia and I have Orson with me. Is that you Sarge? Did you see one of them?"

McMullen shook off Ginny's claws and hurried forward to explain the mishap, thankful that it was Ginny who had screwed up and not one of the other soldiers. Ginny could get away with murder and he didn't think anything would come of the mishap.

He was wrong.

"Hey, where's your weapon?" Garcia asked Ginny a moment later. They all gazed around, expecting to see the M16 lying in the dirt.

"I…I lost it," she admitted. All three men groaned. A lost weapon was an infraction that ranked just short of mutiny in the army.

The sergeant was now closer to losing his temper than when he'd been getting shot at. After a steadying breath, he said: "We'll find it, don't worry." They did find it, eventually. The black M16 blended perfectly with the black shadows of the black night and it was an hour before it was discovered when Garcia kicked it quite accidentally.

He knew the man-made sound of boot leather on plastic, and whispered: "Thank God," as he lifted it out of a bush. "Got it," he said in a whisper that was only slightly louder than the chatter of night insects all around them.

During the search, they had all snuck around doing their best to keep quiet since there was no telling if a zombie might show up. In fact, while the four of them had been searching, a lone zombie, black-eyed and grey-skinned, had wandered right down a dirt trail that McMullen was supposed to have been guarding.

Its name, before it had been a zombie, was Simon Moyer. Once a Sunday School teacher and an all-around good guy, he was now a diseased hunk of walking death afflicted with a perpetual hunger. He had been attracted to the sound of Ginny's gun, but when the sound had ceased, his little zombie brain got lured on by a light that burned brightly in the dark night.

The light was miles away, but distance meant nothing to the creature and in three hours, it was eleven miles beyond the western edge of the zone. It strolled right down the main drag of a little town called Burlington, which was only a three hour walk to the New Jersey border.

Since Burlington had been deserted hours before, dead Simon just kept walking and walking and no one had a clue that the Zone had been breached once again.

2— The Connecticut Bubble

On the long sloping hill in front of him, *things* moved, in fact, to Specialist Jerome Evermore it seemed as if the hill were alive and undulating toward him. There were ten thousand bodies on the slope leading up the hill and many were still alive. They were chewed up, bullet-ridden, shredded creatures that could not possibly still be alive. And yet, they were, and worse, they were coming for him.

He had been at it all night long, not just fighting to hold the line but fighting for his very life. And now his ears rang and his hands were numb. He was exhausted and dulled from the endless battle. The world, running with blood and covered in diseased flesh, stunk of death, and fire, and the acid smell of spent gun powder.

What lay in front of him was a horror that he had trouble believing was real, while on either side of him men cried in the dark; they were going mad, their minds broken by fear and the insanity they had just witnessed.

Jerome felt as though his own madness wasn't far off. "Just gotta make it until the sun comes up," he whispered. For the last hour, if he had to speak it was in a whisper. *They* could hear if you were too loud and then they would come by the dozens, causing the fight to flare up again, hard and sharp.

No, Jerome kept very quiet and as still as possible. All around his feet were mounds of brass shell casings which made a strangely merry sound whenever he shifted his weight. He made sure not to move even though his legs were stiff as a corpse's and his back made popping sounds whenever he bent or twisted.

The monsters acted as though they too had been stunned by the ferocity of the battle and the ear-shattering noise of the explosions and machine gun fire. They lolled in the soup of their dead comrades, recuperating and turning blacker by the second. In Jerome's mind, this was what hell had to look like.

Twelve feet away a man suddenly spasmed, falling among his own piles of brass which tinkled a merry tune. "Cramp!" he hissed. "Jerome, I got a cramp. Help me."

For a second, Jerome wondered if the man, Sergeant Daggins, a tank commander who acted as if he were naked without sixty-eight tons of metal wrapped around him, was looking for a massage or something equally strange, but then Jerome saw that the movement on the hill had shifted.

The beasts were coming for Daggins. They had heard the human sound and their hunger erupted. Some moaned, an awful sound, and some wailed a frightful sound that always made Jerome want to run away as fast as he could.

Those creatures that had healed enough to walk, pushed themselves up and staggered forward. Those that couldn't walk, crawled. There were hundreds of them. Too many for Daggins to take on alone, even if he had been physically and mentally ready.

Jerome grabbed up his stash of six magazines and shifted left, hunkering low, until he was next to the whining sergeant. "Hush up, damn it," he hissed. "You know they can hear you."

"They're coming! And my leg! Son of bitch!" He was desperately kneading the back of his thigh with both hands, a grimace that was half-pain and half-terror on his face.

Without regard for rank, Jerome grabbed the sergeant's collar and pulled him close. "Keep whining and I'll plug you myself. Now work out the muscle and I'll take care of these. Just tell me you have some smoke?"

For a moment, the pain and terror was swept from Daggins' eyes as a dark look of suspicion gleamed there. No one knew how long they'd be able to hold out. No one knew when the line would suddenly cave, but everyone knew it would be every man for himself when it finally did.

At first, the helicopters had come one after another in long lines, filled with men and supplies, firing their guns until they went dry. But then the copters had stopped coming and the ammo dump had gradually shrunk. There were now twenty-two hundred people within the perimeter of what was being referred to as "the Connecticut Bubble" and the bullets were going fast. With supplies dwindling, the men had begun hoarding everything they could get their hands on and not just bullets, they also stashed food, water and grenades, especially smoke grenades, which tended to confuse the creatures.

Jerome had two stashed beneath one of the piles of brass back at his battle station. "Do you want help, or not?" he asked. The closest beast was six yards away, stumbling upwards through the piles of dead.

Daggins nodded, desperately. "Yeah, I have two, but only use one, okay? Don't waste it." There was never any guarantee. Sometimes the wind took the smoke and blew it back in their faces, sometimes the smoke went straight up, caught by some unguessable vortex. The only answer when that happened was more bullets and more smoke.

"Just work that knot out quick," Jerome replied and then centered the sights of his gun on the zombie's chin. He aimed low because at this distance the round would "jump up" a good three inches when it left the barrel. He pulled the trigger and the beast flopped, black blood and gunk shooting out the back of its head.

As it slithered down among the rest of the dead, Jerome was already sighting on another. He wanted to wait until he saw the "whites of their eyes," but there were just too many of them; he'd be overwhelmed if he went that route. He had to take the chance on wasting ammo, which to him was an unforgivable sin.

With a pull of the trigger he knocked another down and then another. His shoulder began to ache where the butt of his M4 banged into him for the five hundredth time that night.

The magazine emptied quickly and there were still an untold number of the monsters coming. Jerome's fear, which had been on him all night, like stink on shit, began to ramp up. He cleared the edge of the hill of the zombies and then whispered: "Gimme the smoke!"

Daggins was still gripping his hamstring with two hands. He took one off long enough to toss over the grenade. Jerome didn't waste a moment, pulling the tab and setting it nose first to point down the hill. In a second, plumes of dark smoke billowed out, covering the hill, hiding the monsters from sight.

The two soldiers hunkered down, Jerome with his gun out, Sergeant Daggins, just sitting there, his cramp apparently forgotten. They waited, hoping that once again the smoke and the sudden silence would confuse the zombies enough to stop their attack.

Jerome inched up just over the top plume of smoke to watch the beasts as they tried to work out the unexpected turn of events. Some simply stood in puzzlement as the smoke rolled over them while others kept going, only now they didn't have a destination in mind or a purpose, really. The sound drawing them on was gone and so they wandered. With the steepness of the hill, they tripped or stumbled back down, gravity pulling them away from the peak of the hill.

"Thanks," Daggins whispered, his voice trembling. "That was close."

"Just hang on until morning," Jerome replied. "It'll get better." Somehow the rising sun would end their nightmare; he had the concept implanted in his head and to him it was a fact.

Daggins burst his bubble. "No it won't be better, it'll be worse. With the sun up, *they* will be able to see us. We won't be able to take a leak without them seeing. And they will be stronger by then. They heal, like ten times faster than we do. That's what everyone is saying."

Jerome was stunned by the simple logic. He crept back to his spot on the line, almost overcome with a sudden depression. "It has to get better," he mumbled to himself, just as an echoing gunshot rippled the air. He waited for a second one or a slew of them, but it was just the one and it made his depression all the greater. Someone had just killed themselves.

3— The Connecticut Bubble

Dr. Thuy Lee, a Mensa-level genius with two doctorates, found herself running ammo…when there was ammo to run, that is. She had started out as an assistant to PFC Cindy Austin, who had been hauling around magazines all night long using a little red wagon she had found the evening before when she and a dozen other soldiers had been running for their lives. Although everyone else had simply thrown away their masks, helmets, and MOPP gear, in order to run faster, Cindy had kept hers out of fear that she would have to pay for them later.

The army was always making threats about the cost of missing gear coming out of her paycheck and, as she barely had a hundred dollars in the bank, she took those threats very seriously.

She had come across the wagon in the front yard of some abandoned house in an abandoned neighborhood and had dragged it along for eleven miles with a swarm of zombies chasing after. When her little group had found the command post, she had cried real tears of joy and then, an hour later, she had cried in fear when they were surrounded and making their final stand.

As a trained soldier, she could shoot as well as any of the men, and yet when the call came for all hands to stand on the line she had eagerly given up her gun to a staff sergeant who had lost his. She could shoot and she could fight, but that didn't mean she wanted to. With the wagon she could help while at the same time keeping the monsters as far from her as possible.

For two hours, she had hauled load after load of heavy ammo magazines around in a wide circle. But then Thuy came along and made her stop. "I'm the one in charge around here," Cindy had said; she was after all a private first class and this Asian woman was a civilian and in this new world, a private outranked any civilian. "We'll use the wagon, it's easier."

"It is easier and it's also the cause of about ten deaths an hour," Thuy replied. "In case you didn't know, the wheels on that thing squeak loud enough to be heard from one end of the perimeter to the other. And they are getting louder. Haven't you noticed that there are flare ups in the fighting every time you pass by? The creatures are attracted by the sound."

Cindy glanced back the way she had come and saw the soldiers closest to her were firing, while the ones further back were hunkered down, trying not to be seen by the trickle of zombies still coming at them. "Oh," she said, not liking the idea that zombies had been following her around all night simply because of the stupid wagon. "But...but I need it. The ammo is too heavy for me lug around."

It took Thuy all of five minutes to fashion a two-person yoke out of discarded tent canvas and a pole. Together they could carry four times as much ammo as the red wagon and they could do so without making as much noise. They also didn't need to follow along in the same circular rutted track that Cindy had created after two hundred trips around the line with her wagon. They could go from point to point from a central hub so that they weren't so visible to the zombies.

The effect on the battle was immediate and gradually the firing slowed all along the line, and only just in time. Every time they went back to the supply point, the stacks of ammo crates dwindled.

Eventually the supply sergeant stopped them altogether. "No more. They're just going to have to make do with what they have." Thuy challenged what she thought was an asinine order and the sergeant pointed up at the night sky. "You haven't noticed? There hasn't been a chopper come by for almost an hour."

Both Thuy and Cindy were exhausted from the long night and the hard fight and in truth, neither had noticed. Now, they both looked up and only saw the heavy, dark clouds hanging over them.

Thuy was the first to collect her wits. "But the soldiers need the ammo. How can they defend themselves without it?"

"I'm only telling you what I was told," the sergeant answered. "The orders are for us to save what we have, just in case."

Thuy and Cindy shared a look. "Just in case of what?" Cindy asked. The sergeant replied by shrugging which Thuy interpreted as: *Don't make me say the obvious.* There looked to be about two-thousand rounds left, enough for a mass-suicide event or a mass execution.

It was a sick thought, as well as a logical one. Not only was a bullet in the head better than being eaten alive, it also would prevent the person from "coming back" to eat others and further spreading the disease.

Cindy went green, looking at the few remaining crates of ammo. Thuy touched her shoulder as a big sister might and said: "Maybe I can do something. I have a friend who knows how to get things when no one else seems able. She'll get us some ammo, I'm sure of it."

Truthfully, she wasn't sure of anything. Surely Courtney had to know already how dire their supply situation was. If so, what the hell was she doing about it? And what was she doing about sending choppers out after Deckard and Chuck and the others they had left behind at the trooper station?

Just thinking about Deckard hurt her heart and she was an anxious bundle of nerves when she ducked into the communications tent. A second later, she about nearly hit the roof.

Courtney was sleeping!

The bushy-haired dispatcher lay slumped over a table, her cheek resting in a puddle of drool, a radio next to her head spitting out what seemed like endless questions from a thousand frightened voices. Thuy reached out a barely controlled hand to shake Courtney awake, but before she could, one of the dispatchers who had lived through the debacle at the trooper station stopped her.

"Let her be," the woman hissed. "She hasn't slept in two days and besides she's had it tough."

"Oh, *she's* had it tough," Thuy said, her eyes flashing, making the other three women in the dim tent lean back from the expected explosion. Seeing as Thuy was wanted by the FBI on terrorism and mass-murder charges, and her career and her life had been ruined by sabotage, and she had been forced to leave behind the only man she had ever loved to die a certain death in a zombie-filled building, it was hard for her to fully empathize with someone who hadn't had their full beauty sleep for the night.

"Yes," the woman insisted. Her name was April Lopez and she had seen the miracles Courtney had been able work with only a phone and a will of iron. April, a large woman, twice Thuy's size moved in front of Courtney. "Yes, she has had it rough. Now, how can I help you, *ma'am*?" She knew Thuy's name, but didn't much care for it and nor did April like how bossy Thuy always acted.

"For one, you can tell me what's the situation with the helicopter that Courtney promised me. It's been three hours. Do you understand what that means? Deckard and the others have been out there alone for three hours."

April, who figured that those sad few they'd been forced to leave behind had died two hours and fifty-five minutes before, tried to give Thuy a sympathetic smile as she said: "We are doing everything we can. Unfortunately, the army isn't giving up any of their helicopters just yet."

Despite the hundred-pound difference in their weights, Thuy stepped forward aggressively, saying: "Then we have to make them."

"You can't just make the army do anything, especially with their helicopters. Everyone knows that. There are channels you have to go through."

"Then what are you waiting for? Get going through those channels."

"I can't," April stated baldly.

Thuy stuck her hands on her thin hips and said in a louder voice: "Then wake Courtney up so there will be someone around here who knows more than the words: I can't."

April glared. "Would you like these words, instead? I won't!" She had been loud and behind her, Courtney stirred.

"Looks like you just did," Thuy said and then slid around April as she turned to see that she had indeed woken Courtney. Thuy greeted the dispatcher with a strained smile. "I'm glad you're awake. We need to see about those helicopters you promised me. The line is holding and stable. The rate of attack has slowed. All in all, this is the perfect time to send out a couple of helicopters."

Courtney blinked slowly for a few seconds and then mumbled: "What's the reserve fuel situation look like?"

"That's what I was trying to tell Doctor Know-it-all, the fuel reserves are gone," April said, throwing Thuy a smug look. "And so are the reserves in Albany and the supply net at Newark is off the air. They're not responding. We're basically stuck without fuel until morning."

"I'm not asking for much," Thuy insisted. "With Ms. Glowitz and Mr. Singleton's condition, I have roughly calculated their probable speed at 3.2 miles an hour, that gives us a search area of only two-hundred and ninety miles. I know that seems like a lot of land to cover, but there are five people out there who stayed back so that everyone in this tent could live. We owe it to them."

She stared around as if daring any of the dispatchers to say otherwise. No one would meet her gaze and no one disagreed. "You're right, we do," Courtney said, "however, Colonel O'Brian has shut me down every time I tried, and believe me, I have tried Dr. Lee, maybe too much. He's having some flunky run interference and I can't get him to take my calls."

"Then we go over there, together. There's another reason we need those helicopters, we're running out of ammo."

A sigh broke from Courtney, long and sad. "I know, I know, I know. Damn it, Thuy, I've been trying to get more, but unfortunately the New York National Guard was not prepared to fight a war in the middle of their state. They've gone through at least a million rounds and there just isn't anymore to be had."

Thuy began: "What about the other states? What about…"

"I've tried them all," Courtney said, interrupting. "Mass-achusetts, Vermont, and New Jersey buttoned up their borders yesterday evening. Nothing's going in or out. Pennsylvania closed theirs…" She looked at her watch. "It's been closed for three hours and it's making a complete mess of everything. It's like the entire northeast is one giant traffic jam. And Connecti-cut…Connecticut is as bad off as New York. It's turned into a hodgepodge of fortified cities, each one ready to kill anyone who tries to cross their lines."

"What about Washington?" Thuy asked, with little hope in her voice.

Courtney grimaced. "I've tried. They think the situation has been contained. They're delusional."

Chapter 3

1—3:42 a.m.

Scranton, Pennsylvania

Danielle Salmon stood in line at the A&P like everyone else. This was the first time in her life she had ever stood in a line *outside* the A&P looking to get in. And it was the first time she had ever gone to the grocery store armed. In the purse that she clutched to her chest was her husband's hunting knife, seven inches of razor sharp metal.

She wished he was there with her. The man behind her had been crowding closer and closer and now was practically on top of her. He was thinking of cutting in line—she just knew it. Every time the line moved forward a few feet, he moved in toward her by an inch.

In the three hours she'd been there, he'd inched so close that she could smell his breath. Now they moved again, four feet this time and he moved slightly more than four feet so that he stood just over her right shoulder. Her hand stole into her purse to grip the handle of the knife.

It rattled against her phone as her hand shook. She wasn't going to stab him, but she wasn't going to let him cut in front of her, either. Her family couldn't afford it. Their stock of supplies—only a day into this nightmare and they were already using the word supplies—was low, at least according to her husband, Trent who had pulled every single can, slice of bread, piece of cheese, and cracker out of their pantry, freezer and fridge.

"Nine," he counted after he had stacked all the items in little piles. "Each of these represents a day's worth of food and we only have nine." His eyes kept roving, back and forth, over the piles, unblinkingly.

"That should be enough, don't-cha think?" Danielle replied. "They are saying that it's an isolated event and that it's contained." The day before, they had sat in front of the TV, watching the news, each channel basically reporting the same thing over and over again. They had been mesmerized, from the moment they had gotten up to just after two in the afternoon.

Danielle had allowed herself to be placated by the official government statements. Her husband, Trent had the opposite reaction. He had become a ball of nervous energy running around the house, counting rolls of toilet paper and filling buckets with water.

"He's overreacting," she had said to herself. After all they were over a hundred miles from the quarantine zone. She'd been relieved when he left, saying something about "getting to the bank." He'd been gone for two hours and when he came back, he was white-faced.

"We need to get to the store, before it's too late," he said.

His over-the-top melodrama made her suddenly angry. "Don't be like this in front of the kids! You're going to scare them." He laughed high up in his throat like a turkey gobbling. That made her re-evaluate her husband; he looked as though he might drop a load right there in his pants. "Did something happen at the bank?" she asked.

"They were closed…all of them."

Confused, she glanced at the clock; it had been only 4:30 in the afternoon. "Wait…is this a holiday? Why are the banks closed so early?" Something wasn't clicking. Something wasn't right.

"They ran out of money, I think. So I tried the ATM, but it was out as well. They all were. I went to ten different banks and they were all closed and their ATMs were, like empty. Finally, I saw a bank that was open. The line went around the block. Everyone is pulling their money, babe. And you know what'll be next."

She knew. Instinctively, she knew: money, food, guns. They split up. Danielle took their youngest daughter, three year old Wanda to the store, while Trent went to buy a gun, only there were no guns to be had at any price in the city of Scranton, Pennsylvania, and barely any food.

The local A&P was an utter mad house. People were hauling around two or three carts at a time and every aisle was jammed and the shelves were being picked clean. This frightened Danielle worse than any news story.

It took her three hours to fill half a cart and by that time there was almost nothing left to buy. When she finally paid for her five meager bags, she went to her car and cried until Wanda started crying as well.

After that, she went to another store and bulled her way about, nearly getting into a fight, but managing to get two loaves of bread, three jars of marmalade, a box of granola and two pounds of hamburger; this last item she actually pilfered from an old lady's cart when she wasn't looking.

But that was all she could get. By ten that night, she was worn out, but had managed to increase their supplies to about sixteen days. Although Trent hadn't been able to find a gun, he had managed to fill both cars with gas, a feat that had taken him the better part of four hours.

They were exhausted and yet they both had *what-if* scenarios playing endlessly in their heads. What if the army massacres continued? What if the zombies couldn't be stopped? What if the Quarantine Zone expanded to take over the entire northeast? What if the banks remained closed and the family ran out of money…out of food…out of gas?

What couldn't be imagined the day before was suddenly very real. States were closing their borders, they were shutting down airports and stopping ships from docking in their ports. The government was force-feeding reporters the "news" and internet service had been suddenly and suspiciously discontinued.

People were panicking and now at 3:42 a.m. Danielle was right there with them. Her husband was at a different store waiting in his own line, while their two children were home alone, hopefully asleep. "Oh, please let them be asleep," she whispered, as the line edged forward another three feet.

She had a thousand *what-if* scenarios concerning leaving the kids alone, most having to do with fire. The frightening images in her mind were eating her up, making the nervous thrill inside of her that much worse. She was a live wire and the next time the man behind her moved, actually touching her now, she jumped.

"Get back!" she screamed, the knife from her purse suddenly in her hand and pointed at him. There wasn't much to see of him: faded jeans, a dark coat zipped up to his chin, and a baseball cap with the word: CAT emblazoned on the front. "Get back," she screamed, a second time when he froze at the sight of the knife.

"What's wrong?" another man asked. He was a big, burly sort who puffed out the fabric of his coat with his large biceps and his even larger gut.

"He was trying to cut in line," Danielle accused, pointing her knife at the man in the CAT hat.

"I wasn't, I swear."

He seemed suddenly smaller, less evil and his shaking hands elicited compassion from Danielle. She lowered the knife, but just then a woman three people back hissed: "Yes, he was. I saw him. I saw him cutting. We can't have cutters!"

Another woman took up the cry. "I saw him, too. He was creeping up on that poor woman." In seconds the dull and sullen crowd turned into an angry mob and the man in the CAT hat was punched and kicked out of line. He stood off to the side and tried to plead his case, but someone threw a rock at him and soon he was driven away by a shower of rocks.

The crowd buzzed in ugly happiness when the man had run off—there was one less person who'd be taking food from the rest.

2— Baltimore, Maryland

The same fear-induced shortages were gripping most of the east coast and in a number of cases the mobs weren't content to simply punch and kick and stone a perceived threat from their midst. There were lynchings, shootings, stabbings and, in three cases, people were burned alive in their cars.

Sayid Mochtar thought he was shrewd enough to avoid that fate. He was a proud American, the son of an Iranian dissident who had come to the states thirty-four years before, smuggled aboard a freighter. His father had died young and destitute; however, his son was a self-made millionaire, a fact that he let slip at every party he had ever attended.

True, he was worth only a little over 1.1 million, but it was still a million and quite an achievement.

And now he saw a chance in the bizarre turn of events happening in New York to get far more secure in his millionaire status. He was the majority owner of six gas stations in the greater Baltimore area, and had both a fuel truck and an eighteen wheeler crammed with his normal weekly shipment coming in that night after hours of delay stuck in traffic.

Sayid ordered both trucks to his largest store where he instantly jacked up the price of everything. His regular unleaded gasoline went from four dollars a gallon to forty dollars a gallon and bottled water went from two dollars a bottle to twenty dollars. Chips and candy, and everything in between saw a like increase.

It only made sense to Sayid. Everyone was hoarding, everyone was stockpiling. Supplies were at the lowest he had ever seen them and demand was through the roof. And although Sayid was the son of an immigrant, he understood better than anyone that the law of supply and demand was as basic and as immutable as the law of gravity.

It made sense and it also almost started a riot.

Despite it being four in the morning with a chill rain falling, the majority of the residents of Baltimore were awake, either waiting on the latest news report or standing in long lines outside of supermarkets. For the most part they were tense and nervous, but many of them were also angry—someone had done something to disrupt their easy, first-world lives and they were ready to lash out.

Sayid knew there could be trouble and was openly carrying a pistol, as were his two clerks, and yet it took only a minute for things to get out of hand. When the first customers rushed into his store and saw the prices on the goods, they went nuts, screaming at Sayid and throwing his own goods at him.

Rumor of the exorbitant pricing went through the mile-long line like a burning fuse and quickly the line disintegrated as people rushed the store and began hammering on the windows, while others tried to steal gas.

"If you don't like it get out!" Sayid yelled. "Go find your gas somewhere else." Of course there was nowhere else, and he knew it. A few people tried to pay what was being demanded, but were bullied by the others not to.

In ten short minutes, Sayid was forced to call the police, but to his dismay the ranking officer, a sergeant in riot gear with a face that was so slick with sweat that he looked as if he'd been anointed with oil, actually sided with the rioters until Sayid pointed out that there were no anti-gouging laws in the state of Maryland.

"Besides, this is all about supply and demand," he explained. "I'm performing a valuable service to the community."

"That's not the way I see it," the officer shot back. "I see you taking advantage of a terrible situation in a manner that's practically theft."

The people around them all started shouting, calling for the police officer to arrest Sayid. "It's not theft!" Sayid yelled, trying to be heard over the crowd. They only shouted louder, screaming for blood. He turned to the sweating sergeant and gave him a wide smile, thinking that if he could convince the sergeant of the righteousness of his cause he would do the right thing and break out some tear gas or start whomping heads with his billy club.

"We are having these shortages *because* stores aren't raising their prices. Take the bottles of water for instance. I only have about five hundred bottles and if I don't raise my prices to accommodate the market situation, what's going to happen is that the first person who comes in will buy all my water because they're afraid there won't be any left tomorrow when he comes back. Don't you see what will happen? It'll become a self-fulfilling prophecy."

The sergeant, who had scraped by in high school and was sneeringly anti-intellectual, wasn't impressed with high-sounding words like *self-fulfilling prophecy*. "No, I don't see, because I bet you'll get another shipment in tomorrow so that won't…"

Sayid interrupted him: "No, I won't. My trucks come once a week, which means when that first person buys all my bottles of water, the next person is going to be shit out of luck. Where's he going to get his water from?"

"He'll get it from the tap like we all used to," the sergeant shot back. "There's nothing wrong with tap water."

The smile on Sayid's face turned thin. "Okay, yes, for now the water is still on, but think about when my gas is sold out. At four dollars a gallon, it'll be gone in the next three hours and where is the next person in line going to get his gas? You see, if the prices are high, then each customer has no choice but to only get what they *need* in the short run. That way everyone gets a shot at getting some of the things they need. Ask the people: would they rather have five gallons of gas at forty dollars a gallon or no gas whatsoever at four dollars a gallon?"

With the noise, it was impossible to ask anyone anything and the sergeant didn't bother trying. "Okay, I get it," the sergeant said. He really didn't and just thought that Sayid was a greedy son of a bitch, and yet he wasn't breaking any laws. "I get the law of supply and demand, but what you don't understand is the law of the mob. Look at them. Do you think they're going to listen to you go on and on about what's going to happen in three hours? No. All they see is that you are basically robbing them. Now, I suggest you lower your prices or there will be trouble."

He started to leave and Sayid grabbed him. "Hey, where the hell are you going? You can't leave."

"Actually, I can. The city is a powder keg and idiots like you are lighting matches all over the place. I have two more calls just like this one and a number of shootings to investigate. So do the smart thing and lower your prices and you'll be alright."

He shouldered his way through the crowd, leaving Sayid with two frightened clerks surrounded by a thousand angry people. "What do we do?" one of the clerks asked. He looked as though he wanted to ditch the blue vest that marked him as an employee and blend in with the crowd.

"The prices stay the way we have them," Sayid said, his pistol in hand, swiveling back and forth. "If the people want their gas and food bad enough, they'll pay, if not they'll go somewhere else."

While the crowd inside the store were cowed by Sayid's pistol which he kept out and at the ready, the mob outside grew increasingly vocal. They chanted, screamed threats and threw stones at the window, causing the glass to bloom white stars. It wasn't long before things got out of hand. A small group huddled around the gas intake feed line, trying to figure out how to siphon the gas straight from the tank buried beneath the pumps.

When Sayid saw someone dragging a hose across the parking lot, he charged to the door, knocking people over. He fired twice into the air, sending those around him screaming for cover. "Keep away from there, damn it!"

He figured he had shown them who was boss, but the next time he turned around, the starred glass on that side of the building was shot through with an orange glow. "Oh no," he whispered. The crowd was going in every direction as he ran out to save his precious fuel before the entire place went up like a bomb.

Flame and black smoke shot up almost to the covered roof and the air was already hot enough to make Sayid cringe as he grabbed the heavy steel cover to the intake lines. He couldn't put it back in place by hand without having his eyelashes burnt off, and so he squatted with a leg thrust out to kick the cover over the fire. The orange flame blinked out; however the smoke continued to belch upward like a chimney.

He backed away, hurrying to the "safety" of the store and watched the smoke with a fearful expression on his face, wondering whether the tank would explode. He wasn't the only one. The entire crowd gave the tank a wide birth, but after a while the smoke became only wisps.

"Ok then," Sayid mumbled and looked around the store. It was in shambles with a couple dozen people crammed inside, picking through the goods that were scattered everywhere. As he watched, he saw one woman try to slip a bag of M&Ms into her purse. He screamed her out of the store, looking like a wild man, a thick throbbing vein sticking out on his forehead.

The woman, a thirty-two year old, single mother of two named Jenny Fineman, scampered out of the store, tears on her face. She had all of forty dollars to her name and no credit whatsoever and very little left in her bare fridge. She was scared to death that things were going to get worse, because she had no idea how she was going to feed her kids or herself.

People asked her what had happened and she lied, saying that Sayid was "going crazy in there."

"I'll fix him," someone said. The man held a gin bottle in one hand and a lighter in the other. He poured the gin over one of the fuel pumps, lit it and ran. The gin ignited with a *whoomp!* In no time, cyclones of flame spun into the air growing right before their eyes. A second late another pump went up with a strange crumpling noise.

Sayid stared through the starred window, unable to comprehend what he was seeing. They were burning the gas. That made no sense. He took a step toward the door and then paused, realizing that the fire was too great. He wasn't going to be able to smother a pump fire so easily. The only way to keep the whole place from burning down was to shut off the gas that fed the pumps.

He turned, took four steps through the crowd and then grunted in pain as what felt like a shiver of ice went into him, paralyzing him from the mid back down. The ice was then covered in something warm and wet—it was blood. An amazing amount of blood ran down his shirt. Someone had stabbed him in the right kidney.

The pain in his back stole his breath. He fell, grabbing in vain for the bubblegum rack. He was still there gasping for breath nine seconds later when the first explosion shattered all the windows on the west side of the building.

In the ensuing panic, four people were trampled to death. Another two died of asphyxiation as they tried to run *into* the gas station to steal what they could before the fire engulfed the entire building. Sayid lived long enough to have his face stomped on by Jenny Fineman who was one of the lucky ones who made it back in despite the fire raging thirty feet away.

She had never stolen a thing in her life before she had stuck those M&Ms in her purse. Now, she took Sayid's pistol, wallet and keys. On the way out she stuffed her purse with as much as she dared and then ran, pausing only for a second to click the fob on Sayid's set of keys.

The lights on a Mercedes blinked on and off. She sprinted to it and instead of thinking of herself as a bad person who was adding a charge of grand theft to the petty larceny and assault she had just committed, she grinned, thinking that her luck was finally turning.

3—Washington DC

Marty Aleman, Chief of Staff to the president, waved aside the two secret service agents and thrust himself boldly into the president's private bedroom, but stopped only a few feet inside. It wasn't just dark in the room, it was so black that he couldn't see his hand in front of his face.

A second of groping on the wall found the switch, and when he flipped it up, the president groaned, waving a hand at the light as if he could shoo it away like a bad smell. "Turn it off," he groused. "I have a wakeup call set for five. Go away."

"You ignored the call, sir," Marty explained, going to the window and yanking back on the curtains. A grim, wet, DC morning stared back at him. Opening the curtain hadn't done much to help illuminate the room and nor did it make it anymore cheery.

From where Marty stood, he could see that 15th Street was already clogged with traffic. There were more people out and about than was usual for that time of day, and Marty knew why. The disruption of the normal traffic flow around the city coupled with mounting fears, caused people to think more about the future than they usually did. Lines at stores already stretched several blocks.

"Five already?" The president had turned from snappish to groggy, with a touch of petulance thrown in. He wanted to be babied—he was used to it. He wasn't used to zombies and soldiers thinking they knew more than he did. And he definitely wasn't used to having to deal with an actual crisis.

It was horribly inconvenient. He had missed his normal afternoon round of golf the day before and he'd had to reschedule two different donor meetings in lieu of the much graver military ones, and perhaps worst of all, the crisis had kept him up late the night before. After ten at night, he was basically a zombie himself.

"So what's going on?" he asked, scraping sleep pebbles out of his eyes and then scratching his scalp through his thinning silver hair. "More bad news, no doubt."

Marty shook his head. "Just the opposite, actually. The line held, sir!"

"You act surprised, Marty. Weren't you the one telling me all day that the military would hold. Were you lying then?"

Lying was about thirty percent of Marty's job and lying about lying took up another ten percent. "Of course not," he lied. The truth was that at about ten the night before, the reports from the western border of Connecticut suggested that General Collins' force had been overrun and there wasn't anything standing between the million people in Hartford and an army of zombies. And yet, somehow Collins had held.

"The situation isn't perfect, mind you," Marty added. "The word from Connecticut is that the soldiers are cut off and running out of supplies. They should…"

The president interrupted: "What about FEMA? You said they would be able to start shipping supplies today."

"Later today," Marty allowed, again lying. He had no idea when FEMA would get moving. They had warehouses full of goods: canned food, bottled water, blankets, tents and such, but most of it was located in the deep south where floods occurred, or in the midwest's "Tornado Alley," and along the southeast coast where hurricanes struck two or three times a year.

There were two warehouses in Pennsylvania. Unfortunately, that put them on the "wrong" side of the situation, and the trucks which were mated up with the supplies, were useless since the roads were impassable with traffic and/or zombies. The items would have to be flown in, but of course, they couldn't be flown directly to Bradley Airport ten miles outside of Hartford, because it had gone from a madhouse at three p.m. the day before to a ghost town by ten.

Everything would have to go into Providence first and then be trucked across a closed border into a state consisting of little more than fortified towns. Marty was sure it would work itself out, but first, he had to avert a national crisis of faith.

"FEMA will do its thing and you will do yours. We have to show the nation that you're on top of this, that this is what you're lasered in on. People are getting a little weird and what they need now is to see you in action. I have Mitsy over in communications getting some B-roll footage ready from when you were at Fort Benning last year. Never before seen stuff, the networks will eat it up."

"That was a good trip," the president said, vaguely. "They were all very nice and the weather was good. I was surprised how pleasant it was."

"Yes, yes, it was great, but let's concentrate, sir. We need to stay on message and that message is: *the situation is under control*."

The old man nodded and repeated: "The situation is under control…but is it? I don't want to go around…"

"The situation *is* under control," Marty repeated, with the soothing voice of a hypnotist. "To the south, New York City is no longer threatened. To the east, Boston is fine. In the west is the Hudson and a whole lot of nothing. Our only point of worry is the Connecticut border. It's got some holes, but the situation is under control."

"What about casualties?"

Marty kept his ire in check. The old man wasn't cooperating this morning. "Let me give you the bullet points that you need to repeat over and over today. First and foremost: 'the situation is under control.' That is key to calming down the rest of the country. Second, there are 'heavy' casualties and we're doing everything we can for them. We've got FEMA rolling. We're coordinating with 'disaster relief agencies,' such as the Red Cross, and we are asking for everyone to do their part and donate blood."

He paused and waited until the president repeated the first two points. Marty waited a second too long and the old man got off track. "And…and is it time to federalize the situation, yet?" He hadn't always been so helpless, but after thirty-three years in the public eye, it had become easier and easier to just do what his handlers told him to do and say what they wanted him to say. Gradually, he had also come to let them do his thinking for him.

"Hold on. Staying on message is key. One: the situation is under control. Two: we're doing everything we can for the people affected by this tragedy. Three: we are very proud of the men and women in uniform who stood in the breach to protect this great nation in our hour of need. Four: We are going to bring to justice everyone responsible for this catastrophe. Now you say it."

The president ticked off the four points using his fingers to count along so that he didn't miss any. Marty beamed as if the President of the United States was his star pupil. "Exactly right sir. I can't stress enough that those four points need to be repeated on every channel all day long. Especially the last point. The people are angry and they're going to want to blame someone and it can't be us."

"No, we can't have that. Though I don't see why they would. We did everything we could, right?"

"Yes of course, Mr. President, however people expect perfection. They're going to want to know why we didn't have ten army divisions in New York yesterday morning. And they're going to want to know how we allowed this pharmaceutical company to develop such a horrible disease in the first place."

For the first time, the president looked truly frightened, "And what are we going to say?"

"Oh, don't worry about that. The lapses on the military side will be blamed on the previous administration. We'll make sure the reporters are briefed about how they were *only* concerned with foreign intervention and we'll make sure to play those soundbites where you wanted to remake the military into something closer to the peace corps. And we'll blame our friends on the other side of the aisle about the pharmacy fiasco, too. Remember: they are all about deregulation and this is simply the chickens coming home to roost."

The president didn't ask what regulations, if any, had been relaxed. He only bobbed his head so that his pillow-styled hair waved gently. "The situation is under control. We're doing everything we can. Proud of our servicemen. Justice for the domestic terrorists and chickens coming home to roost. Got it. But what about federalizing the situation? You said Collins was surrounded. Doesn't that mean more of those things will get out?"

"We have a conference call set up with all the governors involved and I can guarantee they'll beg for you to swoop in and save the day."

"And how do we do that? This has been one fiasco after another."

Marty grinned and rubbed his hands. "Easy. Last night you put the 82nd Airborne Division on alert. Well, I did, in your name, actually. You also have elements of the 101st getting ready. So this is how it will go: at 6:30, you will issue a live statement. At 7:00, you will have a conference with the governors after which you'll give another live statement addressing how the situation is perilous, but that you are using your authority as 'Commander in Chief' to save the country. At 8:30, we have the first parachute drops just west of Hartford; I'm getting camera crews in place ready to show it in all its patriotic glory."

"Won't it be dangerous?" the president asked. "I mean, everything else was screwed up with the army. What happens if the wind changes and it blows those chutes right into the quarantine zone?"

"Sir, the men drop from a height of about eight hundred feet and they'll be nine miles from the old quarantine zone. So there's nothing to…" Marty paused as he saw the old man's confusion. "There's going to have to be a new border of the quarantine zone. At least on the Connecticut side."

The president's eyes narrowed. "And what about all those soldiers who are surrounded? What sort of, uh, rescue mission do you have planned?"

Marty squirmed slightly as he answered: "None…at the moment. But we will be keeping them resupplied, once we get the air assault side of things complete. I'm thinking around noon we'll set that off. Picture it, sir: eight hundred helicopters flying in one tremendous formation. We've been getting every helicopter we can scrounge up and sending them to Fort Campbell. At noon you'll do another statement on the White House lawn and, as you finish up, the choppers will swoop by."

"Eight hundred, wow," the president said, envisioning the spectacle and not for a second considering the ramifications of stripping the army of their much needed copters, which were even then making themselves felt in the Zone.

"And that's just the start," his chief of staff said. "They'll parade over Washington, Baltimore, Philadelphia, half of New Jersey and finally New York City. It'll be the kind of thing that will unite this country under your leadership, sir."

The president grinned, his cheeks straining with excitement, while two hundred and six miles to the north east, the zombie that used to be Simon Moyer, Sunday School teacher and all around good guy, stumbled onto a little lane called "Lower Road," six miles from the New Jersey state line. There wasn't much to Lower Road or the land around it. Two lanes of empty asphalt surrounded by now abandoned farms and empty forest.

The road was of such insignificance that no one was manning the crossing from New York to New Jersey, which was marked only by a small sign that read: *Welcome to the Garden State—Keep it Clean!*

The governor of New Jersey had long before ordered his border closed, but since the quarantine lines were "officially" holding, at least on the western and southern sides, he had left it relatively unguarded. In truth, he had little choice. Most of the New Jersey National Guard was already in New York and the rest was spread out over a hundred miles of permanently fused traffic, and the state's remaining police forces were busy everywhere trying to calm a panicked population.

There simply weren't enough men or women left over to guard every single road, street, dirt track, stream, river, forest trail and highway between the two states. Simon Moyer had a straight shot into one of the most densely populated areas of the country.

Chapter 4

1—5:19 a.m.
The Quarantine Zone

An hour before, a bank of fog sitting in a low spot on the road had saved Deckard's group. The zombies had been getting closer and closer, however the sudden swirling grey had thrown them into confusion, allowing the group to hobble away. But the fog hadn't lasted and soon the chase was on again.

The six of them were at the end of their limits when they came across a tiny hamlet that sat all by itself on the lonely road. It was an odd duck of a place that looked as though it belonged in a bygone era. There was a gas station with sixty year old pumps rusting on a concrete island, a twelve-stool diner that had been a little ranch home at some point, a post office of red brick, a knick-knack tourist trap that claimed to sell antiques but looked like a second-hand shop, a church that was just as quaint as could be, and a used car lot that looked as though it sold rust on wheels.

Deckard pointed Max and Sundance into the first building: the diner. With its long front window, it was not a place in which they could make a stand against the hundreds of zombies that were following along in their wake. Even one zombie would have been enough to take down the window. Still, Deckard saw that the sick people on his team were steps away from the point of collapse or, in Stephanie's case, past that point. Chuck was basically carrying her.

Lastly, came Dr. Wilson straggling up out of the dark, looking confused at finding himself all alone. Deckard ran out to him and shoved him towards the building. When they were inside, Deckard hissed: "Find bleach or ammonia or anything to cover your smell."

He then ran back out, waving his arms at the horde that had been on Wilson's heels. "Hey you guys! Come and get me! I'm right here!" The creatures leered with an evil hunger in their eyes—those that had eyes, that is. The zombies following them were the most wretched of their kind. Some looked like they were being held together by cat gut or odd white wire. All of them had been fed off of and mauled horribly so that they dribbled blood or pus and dragged ropes of intestine behind them.

And yet they came on and on, slowly but relentlessly, never tiring in the long chase.

When stronger, fastest zombies joined the horde, Max Fowler or Deckard had taken care of them with well aimed shots. Unfortunately this had only attracted more of them. Now, they were coming from every direction, centering on the tiny hamlet.

"Right here. Look at me," Deckard said, bringing up his weapon. He began plugging them one after another at a range of about twelve feet. The crash of his M4 rolled down the no-name street and echoed up into the hills. As he fired, he slowly backed away, leaving bodies in his wake. After firing off a dozen rounds, he turned to clear his six, where more were coming in long lines.

More shots gave him a hole through which he jogged away into the last of the night, pausing every hundred yards or so to kill a few more. Soon the gun was only a far off crackling sound and the streets were empty.

Fowler took charge the second the zombies disappeared from sight—no one else was capable. Chuck, Stephanie and Dr. Wilson had all collapsed. They had pushed themselves as far as they could and now that they were lying in heaps, they couldn't get their limbs to move again. Even Sundance just lay there, panting, his ears drooping with fatigue.

Max slunk around the diner's stubby bar, his feet crunching through spilt cornflakes. At some point, the place had been the subject of a very thorough looting. Besides the cornflakes lying on the floor like leaves on a forest floor, there wasn't anything left that was edible. There were cleaning products, thankfully.

In seconds, Max had poured the contents of a bottle of bleach all along the doorway and then, as an added precaution, he traced a semicircle around the prone bodies of Chuck, Stephanie and Dr. Wilson.

"That's not good for us to inhale," Dr. Wilson said. He swatted at the air in front of his face, languidly as if he were a southern belle oppressed by a heat wave. It was all the energy he had left to expend.

"It's a might bit better than getting your face eaten off," Max said, pulling his camouflaged shirt up over his nose. The others did the same, coughing into their shirts, or wheezing, or looking like they were on the verge of passing out.

Amorphous black blobs hung in Stephanie's vision, like strange balloons. She reached out for one with a hand that tingled and fingers that were numb, making contact only with air. This was disconcerting, but what was truly frightening were the hundreds of needles that stabbed her lungs every time she took a breath.

It was the cancer blooming like huge death roses in her chest. All during the night it felt as though the tumors had opened wider and wider. She knew that soon they would take over and turn her black from the inside out. Then it would be like trying to breathe through a clogged straw…and then, as they got even bigger, well, she wouldn't be able to breathe at all and she would die.

"It'll be aw-right, darlin'," Chuck Singleton whispered and, as though his country drawl held magic, it suddenly was *aw-right*. She relaxed and gradually the pain in her lungs drifted into the background of her exhaustion as she fell asleep leaning on his phlegm-rumbly chest.

Deckard was gone for an hour and it took that long for Chuck to finally overcome the shakes that had been making him feel old. The crummy cough, which brought up ugly wads of grey tissue and snot, took longer to disappear. He was still dying, but at least he was dying at the pace he had been at the beginning of the week. Instead of his death being an hour away, it was now "only" a month or so off.

Of course that would be only if he were very lucky. There would be no more running for either him or Stephanie, at least not for a while. And their ammo situation, about two hundred rounds split between five people, meant that they were not going to do much in the way of fighting, neither.

And so that left dying as their only option.

"You were gone awhiles," Chuck said when Deckard crept into the diner. "I didn't think you was coming back."

"Just making sure those zombies were far down the road." Deckard leaned his black assault rifle against the door and groaned his way into a sitting position. Wincing, he pulled off his shoes one at a time. They were patent leather and expensively fancy—and not meant to be worn running marathons. Each step of the last hour had been a trial.

When his socks came off, he saw the blisters that had formed during the long night of running for his life. Half of them were open and weeping clear fluids, while the other half were bulging balloons that were on the verge of popping.

"Either of you see any Band-Aids?" Deckard asked. Only Max and Chuck were still awake. Stephanie looked exhausted even in sleep and Dr. Wilson was slumped against a booth, his head on the cushion.

"No, sorry," Max said. "But I wasn't really looking."

With a new grimace, Deckard stood and limped toward the counter, making sure to stay low just in case there were any zombies out front. Movement drew his eye, not out front but to his left. Across the diner's bar was an open area where the cooks used to sweat over the food they were preparing.

Now there was a strange man, dressed all in blue denim, making the black shotgun in his hands look like nothing more than shadow. Deckard knew better, especially when the shadow was pointed right at him. He turned to shout a warning, only just then he saw something moving outside as well.

Two more men, both with weapons drawn. One angled for the door, the other had his gun trained on Max, who was turned away and didn't see what was going on. Deckard had a perfect view of the man. The early morning light was shining across his face at just the right angle to highlight the darkness in the man's eyes—the unnatural darkness.

2— Hartford, Connecticut

The work of two-hundred and fifty thousand men, women and children laboring like ants all through the night had turned Hartford into a fortified city. For the most part, the walls were built of cars and trucks, but in some places felled trees were hoisted one on top of another like giant *Lincoln Logs*, and in others the walls were little more that massive mounds of dirt and debris with a hand-dug moat in front.

The work was a spontaneous event with little help or guidance from the city. For the most part the offered help was rejected. Without asking "permission," the people had already appropriated every school bus, fire truck and Department of Transportation vehicle in the city limits and by dawn the forty mile, meandering and amoeba shaped perimeter was complete. The city was a hundred percent contained.

It wouldn't be able to withstand an assault such as the one that had occurred thirty miles away on the western border of their state, but most people felt that the walls were strong enough to repel an attack by a few hundred or even a few thousand zombies. And it would certainly protect against the strays.

Every avenue of approach was watched over by weary people, some with guns, some with bats and clubs. One fifteen year old boy had constructed his own flamethrower and was eager to test it out on one of the living dead.

The wall was, in fact, too well protected. Every gun in the city was pointed outward while in the interior where the streets were still gloomy with shadow and the buildings were crammed in on themselves, things were beginning to come "alive."

They were, for the most part, sorry excuses for zombies. Jaimee Lynn's pack of zombie children were voracious feeding machines and when they were after hot blood they attacked in a wild frenzy, leaving their victims in tatters. It was hours before the Com-cells could repair these bodies well enough for the dead to rise and it was just as the citizens of Hartford were congratulating themselves on their fine wall, that the first of these new beasts crawled out from the basement of an abandoned building.

It had been a woman once, a mother of three. Now its sex was unrecognizable. It was a horrid thing with flesh hanging off it like raggedy, dripping scarves of grey. Slowly it came up into the morning light. The sun burned into its eyes and so it turned away and headed west where there were more shadows.

The beast could only walk at the speed of a drunken stumble and, Com-cells aside, constituted a threat only to the very, young or the very, very old.

Two blocks away, twenty-four year old Faye Carter had been up since the crack of dawn when her one year old started making chirpy, happy noises in his crib. Normally Faye would have let little Ray-Ray babble for a few minutes so that she could fully wake up, however, on that particular morning, she had been fully awake from the second her eyes popped open.

Her husband's side of the bed was cold. He had gone out the night before to volunteer with building the wall and he hadn't returned. The first thing she did was reach for her cell phone—no service.

"It's all good," she whispered. "Ain't no zombie attacked Hartford." She would have known if they had. Faye had slept with one ear cocked and the windows open, listening for the first sound of gunfire. There had been none.

She'd also kept the TV on all night, the sound turned down so as not to wake little Ray Junior. There was a live feed showing the wall and the people on it. Faye went to the end of her bed so that she was a foot from the screen, searching the faces, looking for her husband.

Fifteen minutes later, when little Ray-Ray began to get upset, beginning to cry, Faye couldn't pull her eyes from the television. She had seen him! Ray Carter was a strutting, big black man who couldn't be missed. She spotted him the instant the cameras panned over him, though they did so for barely a second.

Ray Junior sent up a lusty howl. "I'll get you a bottle in just a moment," she said. "Keep your diapers on." Still, she lingered, hoping for another shot of her man.

Then there was a muffled thud from the nursery that burned through her desire to see her husband—nothing in the nursery could have made that sound except Ray-Ray falling out of his crib.

"Sweetie? You okay?" she asked hurrying for his room. "You ok…" She stopped in his doorway, her mouth hanging slack and her eyes bulging. The sound Faye had heard hadn't been Ray-Ray falling. The screen from his window had been knocked inwards and now there was a monster, half-in and half-out of the nursery.

The thing was grey with black eyes and black gums. Its face had been mostly eaten away and a hunk of flopping scalp hung over the crib dripping black ichor onto little baby Ray-Ray. It was horrible and Faye recoiled momentarily as it reached into the crib with arms that had small teeth marks up and down the open flesh and hands that were missing fingers.

"No!" Faye screamed and jumped forward. She grabbed the near end of the crib and hauled back on it, accidentally dragging the monster…no the *zombie* into the nursery. Snatching Ray-Ray from the crib, she ran out of the room, slamming the door behind her and in seconds, she was out on the street running, her bare feet slapping on the pavement, the chill of the morning sliding up under the long t-shirt of Ray Senior's that she always wore to bed.

She ran with no idea where to go. Everyone knew that the police were off fighting at the border and that most of the remaining emergency services were at the wall, helping out. Faye didn't know if she would have called them anyway. Just as she came to the corner of her street, it dawned on her that if she told anyone about the zombie they would think she was contagious, which she was sure that she wasn't.

The zombie hadn't bitten either her or Ray-Ray, but would that matter? Everyone in Hartford was on edge. They were scared and Faye knew that scared people were apt to do anything. The idea of being kicked out of the city…literally thrown off the wall, had her in a grip of panic.

What she needed to do was find a way to clean up little Ray-Ray before anyone noticed the black speckles all over him. Then she would find her husband, because he would know what to do. He was smart. He would kill the zombie and bury its body in the basement and nobody would know.

The plan was sound except she didn't take into account the fact that both she and Ray-Ray were already infected. As well, she had left her keys back at the house; she would have to walk the four miles to the bridge she had seen in the background of the news cast, which she was pretty sure was the bridge that crossed the Farmington River along route 44.

After using puddle water to clean her child, she set off, trudging on empty streets. It was an hour long walk and another half an hour of asking around in the area of the bridge before she discovered that she had missed her husband. He had left, thirty minutes before, saying that he would be back after checking on his wife and child.

Faye groaned. He was going home expecting to find her, but would end up finding a zombie, if it hadn't figured a way out of the house by then. Suddenly exhausted and feeling ill, she slumped against a forklift that had been pushed aside after its battery had died. Her bare feet were bleeding from the long walk and her head was thumping like mad. What was worse was that little Ray-Ray was crying nonstop in a way that wasn't like him at all.

Thankfully an ambulance sat parked just down the street. She limped over to it and found a very sympathetic woman in blue who was contaminated seconds later as she inspected Ray-Ray, breathing in the spores that Faye hadn't spotted and which had matured with the warmth and damp of the sweaty baby.

The EMT made matters worse by stripping little Ray-Ray, placing his diseased onesie on the bench where the Com-cells spread and replicated. After another thirty minutes when Ray-Ray refused to calm, the EMT driver decided to take mother and baby to the closest emergency room where the staff was harried, running around in a controlled chaos and the wait just to be checked by a triage nurse was over an hour.

By the time Faye was ushered into a curtained off room, her dark brown eyes were substantially darker than they had been, but no one noticed. They were focused on the now listless baby who was stuck with needles and fed drugs through tubes.

When Faye complained about a headache, she was given white pills and when the nurse wasn't looking, Faye stole more, chewing them without water, uncaring that her tongue turned white. The pills helped a little, just enough for her to think through the pain. Unfortunately, all of her thoughts were as black as her nerves which were being eaten up by the Com-cells.

She couldn't get past the idea that the nurses kept taking her baby's blood. "They're vampires," she said under her breath. It wasn't a far-fetched idea, after all, if zombies existed, why not vampires? "But they ain't gonna get my baby." That was a fact in her mind. She would kill any of them motherfuckers to save her baby.

Strangely, Faye felt like killing them even if they weren't vampires…but that wasn't right. She knew it wasn't right and yet the idea persisted. She squeezed her eyes shut, but the thought of killing wouldn't leave her. It was all she could think of. Killing and blood. Lots and lots of blood.

"I gotta git," she whispered, frantically, taking a quick peek through the curtain. None of the hated nurses were near. "It's now or…" Again the vision of blood came to her and threatened to overwhelm her.

She knew it was wrong, just as she knew that a large part of her didn't care. Before she could do anything *evil*, she popped the IV out of Ray-Ray's pudgy little arm. It bled, but it wasn't the right kind of blood to satisfy Faye. It was dark and it smelled awful.

Before she could leave, Ray-Ray started to cry, sending waves of agony through her aching head. Viciously, she slapped a hand down over his mouth and squeezed with appalling strength. It took a half a minute for him to calm down and when he did he just lolled there, his head swinging about as if on a loose cord. She wasn't concerned. He was asleep, that was all—or so she told herself.

Faye ran from the hospital and by the time she got back to the little, ranch-style house, Ray-Ray had awakened and was staring at her with eyes just as black and shiny as a beetle's. She was reeling at that point; reeling and starving for blood, and yet her maternal instinct to get her baby home and safe, kept just ahead of the evil desire to kill and gorge herself on blood.

Her instincts failed her completely when she saw Ray Senior. He had found the zombie and after a tussle that trashed the little house, he had killed it with his bare hands. As his breathing calmed he discovered a new fear. It was a certainty that he had been contaminated by the zombie and that meant he was going to die. The only thing that gave him any solace was that other than the zombie, his house was empty. His wife and child were safe. He felt he could die knowing that—only, out of the blue, as he had been standing there in the midst of an hour long depression, he saw his loved ones coming towards him.

Tears of joy filled his eyes and he wanted to run to them but he knew he shouldn't. He had to stay in the house and die there so that no one else would get sick.

"Stay back, darling," he said, as she headed straight for the door. She ignored him and he backed away. "Stop, please. There was a zom…" His breath caught in his throat as he saw her up closer—there was black gunk in her eyes and more of it drooling from the corners of her mouth.

He had been able to slay a thin, ragged zombie without too much of a problem, but Faye Carter was a different story. She was in her prime and fully formed and altogether evil. Overcome with hunger for her husband's blood, she dropped her child, and charged.

At first, love caused him to pull his punches, but after he hit her with a few stiff jabs and she didn't blink, he was forced to really fight. He swung haymakers, breaking her nose and cracking bones in her face. She didn't seem to feel a thing.

Eventually, she got her hands on him and her nails were like the claws of a wild beast and her strength was appalling.

A misstep on his part and they went down, wrestling on the carpet where she was all teeth and animal fury. No matter what he tried, he could not pry her off. He attempted a stranglehold to knock her out, however her teeth tore into his bicep and before he knew it she was drinking from his brachial artery.

The pain was immense, but the horror of it was mind-boggling and turned him limp. He shrieked, reaching into her mouth to pry her jaws apart. It was a mistake. With a grunt, she took off one of his fingers, sucked the marrow out and spat the bone onto the carpet, all in the course of three seconds.

Now he was down to fighting with one hand and soon she had his wrist in her mouth and latched on, sucking blood through her gritted teeth. The pain was too much. He opened his mouth to scream, but then saw his child.

Little Ray-Ray had crawled into the midst of the battle and now knelt over his father, his mouth open wide, showing off nine little teeth. The baby lashed in with those sharp little teeth, aiming for Ray's right eye, but missing and latching onto his cheek instead. The pain was secondary to the horrible sucking that Ray was subject to. It was sick and was matched by the sound coming from just below his left ear. Faye had forgotten his wrist and was now at his neck and her teeth dug into his flesh with the sound of a crocodile feeding.

With teeth-snapping frenzy, she found the fat carotid artery and drank hot blood right from the source.

3—Hartford, Connecticut

Ray Carter's screams had people for half a mile around locking their doors. With shivers running up their spines, they went back to their TV sets and watched as the president made his statement: *The situation is under control. We're doing everything we can. I'm so very proud of our servicemen. And there will be justice for the domestic terrorists who started this!*

He went on longer than this of course, it would have been unnerving to the nation as a whole if he hadn't. In the manner he was known for, he spent ten minutes basically repeating the four statements in various ways, and the people were reassured, all except those who could hear Ray Carter's screams.

They weren't comforted. They were afraid because those screams and more like them had split the air periodically all night long. They were afraid that there were zombies in their midst and they were more afraid that someone would find out. They figured they'd be trapped in the city forever if anyone from the outside were to find out.

58

For Jaimee Lynn, who was just stirring, blinking at the hated sun, the screams had her tummy making a rumbly sound. The other children, mutilated and disgusting, turned their black eyes to Jaimee and started mewling: "Hungy, hungy, hungy!"

"Alright! Hush up and we'll get some food." She glanced down at the woman they had killed the night before, the same woman she had slept in for warmth. The woman was "alive" sorta. She moved her mouth and stared at Jaimee Lynn with one big, black, spore-filled eye.

"We cain't use you no more," Jaimee Lynn said and then turned away.

The pack followed her, many of them hardly limping at all and Misty actually talking: "Jamy. I uh is hungy. I uh is hungy!"

"Hush up!" Jaimee Lynn said and then pushed Misty down. She felt like kicking Misty and did so with a sneer. "Now hush." Jaimee stared around at the city of Hartford. It was quiet, much quieter than it should be. She knew it on a gut level. There had been screams, really juicy screams and yet no one had come running and there hadn't been any sirens. The city felt hollow. There was fresh blood but most of it was locked away behind doors and windows. On that same gut level, Jaimee Lynn knew that the people had been warned. They suspected that there were monsters in their midst. And that meant it was time to move on to fresher hunting grounds.

Looking back at her pack, she saw some were straying, sniffing the air, letting their hunger overcome their simple minds. "Hey!" Jaimee Lynn snapped. "Get on over here. Iffin you wanna eat, y'all will come with me."

As they straggled back, Jaimee Lynn took a moment to sniff the air like the others had and decided south was best. They were on a slight rise and she could see houses by the thousands. Nice homes where the families would be plump and juicy; their skin soft from lack of "real" work as her daddy would have said.

She started marching along, making sure to keep to the shadows and the smaller streets. These too, were strangely quiet, though from time to time, she caught sight of people hiding behind boarded up doors and windows. They were afraid of her and that was no wonder, she led a gaggle of black-eyed and bloody children that were straight out of a nightmare.

The people hid. Despite that the Colt Corporation manufactured guns right across the river in West Hartford, the capitol had never been much of a "gun" city and after the Sandy Hook massacre it had become even less of one, with strict new laws being rushed into place. The few people who owned guns were now at the wall, brandishing them haughtily as if they alone they had known something like a zombie apocalypse was possible.

This left the interior defenseless and the people could only cower. Jaimee tried a few doors and found that she was too weak to get through them. The grown-ups on the other side of the doors were too big, anyway, she told herself. They might not have guns, but they had bats and knives.

Discouraged, she turned away from these mini-fortresses, leaving behind black mold and spores that lingered on door handles. After an hour of walking, even she was beginning to whine in her throat from hunger. She wanted to give into the urge and simply fling herself at the next house, tearing at the wood and brick with her fingernails.

But she held back, knowing that something better was coming—that something better was just down the next street.

It wasn't long before she came across that something that was indeed better than uselessly clawing at heavy wooden doors: an old woman walking a blind cocker spaniel. Neither of them cared much for what was going on in the world. The old lady and her dog had their routines and stuck to them come hell or high water. The little kid zombies fell on them with such savagery that there wasn't enough left over for the Com-cells to reincarnate.

They ate her right on the sidewalk under the shade of a willow and although her cocker barked its little pea-brain out, the old lady barely squawked.

A Mini-Cooper came by the slaughter, seeming to drive by itself as the man in the front seat, Jerry Byrne, stared at the scene as if hypnotized. Only when the Mini bounced off the bumper of a Lincoln Navigator did Jerry come to his senses.

"Those were zombies," he said, peeling away. "I got to tell someone."

Chapter 5

1—6:23 a.m.
Hartford, Connecticut

General Arnold had been trying to get away for the last three hours, but there was always somebody near asking questions, or demanding answers. But even if there hadn't been, Beatrice had failed him. She'd had one job and that was to pilot the boat fifteen miles down the coast, a trip that shouldn't have taken even an hour and yet here he was still waiting.

In the meantime, he had been practically chained to his phone by generals in Washington and at Fort Bragg and Fort Campbell. They were still operating under the delusion that the situation was salvageable.

They were planning an airborne operation along a wiggly line that went from Torrington down to Bridgeport. Although they had maps and plenty of resources, they plied him with endless questions concerning weather conditions, the topography of the land, the road system, the crops they might find in the fields and whether poison ivy was an "issue."

He answered, sitting at his desk with his chin in one hand, his eyes rolling at the ceiling with every stupid question.

Next he was briefed on the actual operation, which had been named: *Operation Swift Stand.* The name, chosen in order to reinforce the president's dedication and "quick" reaction to the zombie problem, didn't make much sense to Arnold. The two words were almost contradictory, but in truth he didn't care because it wasn't going to work whether it was properly named, or not.

The initial airborne force of four thousand men was to be dropped along a line forty miles long. It worked out to only a hundred men per mile. He had laughed when he heard this and had been barked at by some general with more stars on his collar than brains in his head.

"What's your problem, Arnold? Do you have a better plan? If not, keep your trap shut. You act like we have a hundred C17s just sitting down at Pope, ready to jump off any old time."

General Arnold had swallowed his pride and said: "Of course not. I'm just tired, I guess."

"Pull it together," the four-star general had growled and then went on to finish his briefing. Arnold listened politely, didn't bother asking any useless questions, and at the end, he was properly respectful. He then went to tell the governor of the plan —this really was his entire job. He was a major general with thirty-five years under his belt and he got paid to act as a go-between.

Of course, Governor Warner wanted everything broken down. "It's really a rather simple operation. That first echelon will drop at these LZs. LZs are Landing Zones." He marked them on her map, numbering them one through twelve. "They'll spread out, linking the LZs in a single long, very thin line. The following waves will come every three and a half hours, just enough time to land the C17s, refuel them and send them out again. At first the men will be supplied by air, but once we get Bradley airfield secure and operating, then we'll fly in reinforcements and supplies. Your western border should be secure by about noon."

It all sounded great when General Arnold explained everything in that calm way of his and the governor foolishly relaxed. She thanked him for his service and was going on about all of his good work when the phone rang.

"It's the president," she said and shooed him out.

The first thing General Arnold did when he stepped out of the governor's office was to check his phone—still no call! Turning to the side, he thumbed Beatrice's number only to have it go to voicemail. Had she drowned? Had she managed to sink the boat? Or had she forgotten her phone?

Maybe she had left a message in his office, he thought to himself. It could be disastrous if she had. Hurrying, but trying not to appear as if he were hurrying, Arnold slipped into his office and listened to his messages while huddled in his seat. He had dozens of messages, almost all of them from frightened servicemen's wives asking about their husbands, who they hadn't heard from all day and night.

Arnold erased each after hearing the first sorrowful note, cursing the fact that his number was listed on the capitol website. After twenty minutes of this, he ran out of messages—Beatrice hadn't called.

"Maybe the Army's plan might work," he said, grasping at foolish hope. The map suggested otherwise. Forest and suburbs would be impossible to hold with only a hundred men per mile. Of course the real problem was that so far the undead had proven to be unstoppable no matter what the military had done. Somehow they just kept coming, turning up everywhere they shouldn't.

Almost as if his thoughts had jinxed the plan before it had a chance to get off the ground, his phone rang. Hoping it was Beatrice, he snatched it up.

"General Arnold? We have a situation down at the front desk."

Arnold rolled his eyes. "Call security." He went to hang up but the man practically screamed his name.

"General Arnold! This is security. Please, you have to hear this right now." The man lowered his voice and whispered: "It's about zombies…in Hartford."

The general's eyes shot wide. He glanced around before partially covering the mouthpiece of the phone and whispering: "Don't say a thing to anyone. I'll be right down." He took the stairs three at a time and, breathless he came up to the security desk. The general had passed by the guard every day without ever really noticing him. Now he looked close and saw a septuagenarian, straining to see through coke-bottle glasses. Next to him was a doughy, pallid, middle-aged frump of a man who was in a literal lather, his face dripping with sweat.

"I saw them!" the man said when the general was still twenty feet away.

Arnold grimaced and glared the man into silence, before pulling the guard aside. "I'll take care of this. Make sure you keep your lips sealed, got it?"

"Loose lips sink ships," the guard said and then mimed locking his mouth shut, going so far as to "throw" away the key with a little gesture.

"Loose lips also will get you brought up on charges of treason," Arnold replied in a hard whisper. "You will tell no one, got it? If you do, you'll start a panic."

The guard nodded emphatically. "You can trust me, sir. I was in 'Nam. I know about operational security. I know what it meant to the front line troops when…"

"That's great," the general said, interrupting. "Now, stop talking and listen. When I say no one, I mean even the governor.

That woman is extremely flighty if you know what I mean. Very high-strung. We don't know what she might do, so no matter what, keep this to yourself."

Arnold clapped the guard on his bony shoulder and turned him away before addressing the civilian. "I'm General Arnold, thanks for coming in." He stuck out his hand, but then pulled it back, quickly. There was no telling where the man had been and what he had touched. "So you saw something? Can you tell me about it without raising your voice? You don't want to make matters worse by causing a panic, do you?"

"No, of course not," Jerry Byrne said, keeping his voice pitched at a conspiratorial level. "I saw a bunch of *them*. You know, zombies. There was a whole pack of them right by Quaker Street and Fern. They were all covered in blood and there was black stuff coming out of their eyes. And they were eating someone, this old lady. It was disgusting and—and I knew I had to tell someone, so I came straight here."

Jerry's short narrative struck the general like a kick in the stomach and yet he smiled, though the smile didn't reach his eyes, which were wide and crazy. This was exactly what he had feared would happen. This was exactly why he needed his boat. "Quaker and Fern?" he asked.

"It's a mile and a half west of here. I was going to get some gas, just in case, you know, when I saw…"

Again Arnold interrupted him. "Okay, I got it. Forget the gas, and forget you ever saw those zombies. For now, I need you to go home. Take a different route. Don't go searching for them. I'll have a platoon of soldiers hunt them down and burn their corpses, but to be on the safe side, go home, stay home and lock your doors. It is your patriotic duty not to tell anyone. No one, do you understand? If you do, this city will self-destruct and it'll be on your head."

Jerry swore on his mother's grave that he would keep the secret, and when he left, General Arnold ran back up to his office. He had to call Washington with an important question he hadn't bothered to ask before. "General Heider? Hello, this is General Arnold in Hartford. I have a quick question concerning the remnants of the 42nd that are surrounded west of the city. You hadn't mentioned them specifically and I had assumed that the paratroopers were going to link up with them."

Actually, he had assumed the opposite—he figured that they weren't going to be rescued, but now that there was a zombie sighting in Hartford, he needed to hear it for himself.

Right off the bat, Heider confirmed Arnold's suspicions by sighing. "No, sorry. We have no way of knowing the level of contamination those soldiers might have faced. They are to remain within the boundary of the Zone until such time as it can be scientifically proven that they will not be a threat, biologically speaking, that is. But don't worry about them. We're going to make sure they'll be resupplied."

"By helicopter?" Arnold asked, thinking that if Beatrice was dead or the boat sunk, he might be able to slip out of the city on a helicopter.

"No, too much risk," Heider answered. "Helicopters are no longer allowed to even fly over the Zone. Now, please don't say anything to anyone just yet. It'll hurt moral and…"

Arnold stopped listening. His eyes were on the map, and his mind dwelled on escape. His worst fears had just been confirmed. If it was found out that there were zombies in Hartford, the army would move the parachute drop east to encapsulate the city, trapping a quarter of a million people in a new and ever expanding Zone.

He knew what would happen then: Hartford would become a breeding ground for zombies. A quarter of a million of them.

"Thanks, sir," he said, and hung up on Heider. The proper, noble thing to have done would have been to gather a squad of men to hunt down the zombies. But in Arnold's mind that was only putting off the inevitable. Without another word, he left his office, the building, and the city.

At the wall he used his rank to bully a bolt-action 30-06 and a Jeep Wrangler from a patriotic citizen. Without looking back, he sped south to the ocean, leaving Hartford in the hands of fate and one seven-year-old demon child.

2—The Connecticut Bubble

In complete defeat, Courtney Shaw pushed back from the folding table where she kept her radio and satellite phone hot from use. She shook her head at Dr. Lee, who had just slipped in through the tent door, asking the same question she'd asked every hour: "Where are the helicopters?"

"It's not going to happen. There isn't a single military helicopter available. I just found out that they've all been pulled for some big operation."

"What about civilian helicopters?" Thuy asked. "Or perhaps medical ones? Certainly you can scrounge up one or two of those? I know you…" A smattering of gunfire outside the tent stopped her. The noise of battle grew in intensity and then faded.

Courtney shook her head again. "No civilian ones either. The military has nationalized every airstrip for five hundred miles outside the Zone. I'm sorry, but we can't do anything for them. But…but they have Deckard. He's a tough one, Thuy. I thought some of the state troopers were hard guys, but Deckard is like a rock. He should be fine…they all should be," she added, thinking of Max Fowler.

"We should be worried about ourselves," April Lopez said, earning herself a sharp glare from Thuy. "So sorry about your boyfriend, but we're just as fucked." The other operators began nodding, glumly. Everyone in the tent knew about the impending paradrop and what it meant.

Using her wiles, Courtney had discovered the exact time and location of each of the twelve drop zones—the new boundary of the Quarantine Zone would be five miles to the east of them. It meant that once again they would be trapped. The news had cast a pall over everyone except Thuy, who acted as though only saving Deckard mattered.

"I wish I could help," Courtney said to her. "But I can't. I swear…but…but maybe you can help us. Maybe you can figure a way out of this."

"A way out?" Thuy's eyes were gritty and her brain felt slow. She was mired in feelings that weren't normal for her: depression, guilt, sadness, and fear. Instead of dwelling on the present or a possible future, she had been reliving her mistakes, and there had been quite a few.

"Yes," Courtney said, and then explained what she had learned. "I was thinking that if we hurry, we could get across the new line of the Zone before the jump happens. The only problem is that Colonel O'Brian is sticking to his guns. He won't retreat without orders and General Arnold isn't answering calls anymore."

"Have you spoken to O'Brian in person?" Thuy asked.

Courtney shook her head. "No. He won't see civilians. He says he doesn't have time for us."

Thuy stifled a yawn and said: "I'll talk to him; however if he won't listen to reason, then it only makes sense that we try to leave on our own. Gather all the weapons and food that you can carry. A radio too, would be good."

"We can't," April said. "We aren't allowed out of the perimeter."

"I'll talk to him," Thuy said, again and then stepped out of the tent, letting the early morning sun strike her as she took a deep breath. Even with the possibility of being trapped once more in the Zone, Deckard was still foremost on her mind. He had been out in the wilderness for over five hours now and she could imagine a thousand terrible things that might have occurred.

Still, she had some hope. The sun had only recently risen on the hill, showing the utter destruction that the waves of Apaches and Blackhawks had unleashed on the zombie horde the night before. It was a horrible sight and yet it was also a sight that had filled the entrenched soldiers with relief.

Bodies lay in heaps and mounds and black blood flowed into pools that resembled pools of tar.

Some of the creatures were still alive and there were more straggling up out of the woods, but their numbers were few and the obstacles between them and the top of the hill were many. Now with the sun climbing higher into the sky to light the battlefield, the soldiers could kill the beasts at safe distances.

With giddy smiles that showed how happy they were to be alive, the soldiers relaxed on the lip of the hill and took turns "popping the stiffs." Ammo was dangerously low; however it appeared that it would last.

"It could be the same for Deckard," Thuy whispered. It was all the hope she would allow herself. Pushing him from her mind, she straightened, and went to the command tent, where a soldier stopped her from entering. All of the soldiers were armed and yet this man's M4 seemed more "present." He was tense and his finger was actually within the trigger guard. That seemed strange and unprofessional even to Thuy.

She gave him what she hoped was a disarming smile and said: "Hi there. My name is Doctor Lee. I'd like to see the colonel, please."

"Sorry, military personnel, only."

"I understand, but this is a matter of some urgency of…of a scientific nature, so if you will simply…"

The soldier stepped forward, aggressively, making Thuy feel even smaller and weaker than she was. "I said no. The colonel's orders were very specific: No civilians at all. Period."

"Of course, of course, sorry," she said, backing away with her hands up. She took two steps too many and knocked into another man, making her jump. Even before she turned, she could smell two battling odors: whiskey and sweat.

It was John Burke, looking wary, his blue eyes at squints, his sandy blonde hair sticking up like a rooster's comb. "What's wrong?" he asked. "Why y'all wanna see the *Big Boss*? Somethin' bad comin'?"

Thuy gave a quick glance around and saw that there were too many people nearby. She pulled him away from the tent so that she wouldn't be overheard. "There's going to be an airborne operation designed to establish a new defensive line. Unfortunately, they are dropping five miles east of here. It will put us on the wrong side of the perimeter of the Zone."

"Ah shit," Burke said, rubbing a hand over the stubble of his chin. "When's it happenin?"

"In an hour or two. We have enough time to pick up and move to safety, but only if we hurry. The problem is the colonel who took over after General Collins died is refusing to disobey orders. I need to see him. I need to talk some sense into him, but he won't see civilians."

John blew his whiskey breath over Thuy as he sighed dejectedly. The two of them were quiet for a few moments as they looked around at the hilltop. Suddenly Burke snapped his fingers and said: "You know whatcha could do? Y'all might could get dressed up like one them soldier boys. They ain't got a fuck-all clue who's runnin' about this camp and there is some girl soldiers, you know. That's right. Get yo-self some girl camouflage and then just tell 'em you's a major or sometin'."

She raised an eyebrow. "That is a smart plan, Mr. Burke."

"Y'all don't need to sound so surprised. We gots schools and such in the south, you know."

"Of course, sorry," she said, absently, her eyes scanning the perimeter, looking for one person in particular. "There she is! If you'll excuse me Mr. Burke," she said and then tromped away, not realizing that Burke followed along after. Thuy was entirely focused on PFC Cindy Austin.

She stood with a group of soldiers, one of whom was taking careful aim at a straggling zombie. Ammo was so low that Thuy waited for him to pull the trigger before she approached the group.

"Miss Austin, if I can have a word." Somehow, Thuy had retained her beauty despite a day of hard fighting and scrambling over half the state. Her golden tan was unmarred and her silken black hair still full of shine. Cindy was immediately self-conscious, knowing that she looked bedraggled at best.

"Yes?" she asked, touching her own hair. It felt like a mop and she attempted to smooth it down.

Thuy pulled her aside. "I need your clothes," she said and then explained what was happening. "I won't tell anyone where I got them, you have my word." After the last harrowing twenty-four hours, Cindy was easily persuaded. They changed in the communications tent—at least Thuy changed.

Although Cindy wasn't fat by any measure, she couldn't match Thuy's elegant form and had to settle with wrapping herself in a woolen blanket. "Are you just going to try to march right in there?" she asked, Thuy. "Cuz, I don't think that'll work. He's going to know right off the bat that you aren't real military. For starters, no one looks like you."

"It's not something I can help," Thuy said, and now it was her turn to touch her black hair, self-consciously. "If only I could find a helmet or a hat." In their mad head-long retreat, helmets and backpacks had been some of the first things jettisoned by the soldiers.

Cindy had hers, along with all the rest of her gear, but she didn't think it would help Thuy. Only deception could. "Maybe with the help of these ladies and some of the soldiers on the front line, we can get you in to see the colonel." Cindy quickly outlined her plan and in seconds the dispatchers rushed out to find any officer they could in order to explain that there was a "meeting" in ten minutes with the new commanding officer.

Courtney hurried to where Cindy had last seen Specialist Jerome Evermore and dragged him back to the communications tent, where he stood uncomfortably eyeing Cindy wrapped in her blanket.

"You want me to cause a distraction?"

"It's just one guy," Cindy assured. "And only long enough for Dr. Lee to get in to see the colonel."

Jerome's stomach had begun to ache at the idea of being trapped within the Zone. Things seemed okay at the moment, but there was no way of knowing how long that would last. Experience had taught him that things could change in the blink of an eye. "Ok, sure. Just point me at the guy and tell me what to do."

His part was simple. When the last of the officers went into their "meeting" he would approach the guard from the right, talking to him and focusing his attention long enough for Thuy to scamper around the side of the tent and slip inside.

He almost wasn't needed. Three officers: two lieutenants and a captain were given access by the guard, who had no reason to stop them. Seconds later, someone from inside the tent began yelling at the top of their lungs: "Who the fuck let you in here?"

"Oh shit," the guard whispered. He glanced back, wondering what was happening and what kind of trouble he was about to get into. A second later, a soldier tapped him on the shoulder.

"What's going on?" Jerome asked, trying to look the guard square in the eye. "It sounds like someone is getting reamed out in there. I'd hate to be the person who is on the receiving end of that shit storm, if you know what I…" He paused as the Asian woman he was trying to help calmly walked around the corner of the tent and slipped in as if she ha every right to be there. "Never mind," Jerome said and turned away, heading quickly for the communications tent and ducking inside.

He found the four civilian women and PFC Cindy Austin huddled at the door peeking out. "That was easy enough," he said, trying to sound like a cool customer, although he could feel sweat dripping down his back. He was sure that he had broken all sorts of military laws, and he knew that the army had never been easy going on criminals.

Thuy was feeling the same sweating sensation. The air in the tent was hot and close. She had expected there to be maps spread out on tables, and computers glowing, and phones humming, and perhaps even little figurines representing different units. In reality, the tent was shrouded in gloom, making everyone seem shadowy and a little scary.

One man, balding save for a fringe around the dome of his head, was in mid-scream when she came in. He had been ripping into the three officers who had gone in seconds earlier and now he turned on Thuy. Courtney's description of Thuy as being "unlike" anyone else seemed right on the mark as Colonel O'Brian could only splutter at her sudden appearance.

Finally, he spat out: "Who the fuck are you?"

"My name is Dr. Thuy Lee. I'm a geneticist and former head researcher at R&K Pharmaceuticals. I'm a scientist, sir and

I know what has caused this outbreak. You might consider me an expert and as such I need to warn you…"

"What you need to do is shut your mouth," the colonel hissed. "I know who you are. There's a warrant out for your arrest. You started this. All of this is your fault. All of it. All—of—it! You deserve to be punished, Doctor. You deserve what's coming to you."

A grin crossed his face and he turned to the captain who had just walked in and ordered: "Tie her up. Tie her up tight so she can't get away."

"Tie her, sir?" the captain asked, glancing toward Thuy with a raised eyebrow. "I doubt she's going anywhere and you wouldn't want her lawyers using…"

"Her lawyers!" O'Brian screamed. "there's not going to be any lawyers. Not this time. This time *we* will hand out justice and it will be swift and cruel." He leaned in close and Thuy shied back, not afraid of the man but afraid of what he carried. He had taken one trip too many close to the lines—his eyes were shiny dark.

Chapter 6

1—6: 49 a.m.
The Quarantine Zone, Gamet Corner, New York

Stephanie Glowitz saw Deckard's eyes go wide and not a second later, Sundance let out a low, grumbly growl. The German Shepherd tried to stand, but Chuck pulled him close with one hand while the other reached slowly for the M16A1 he had carted around all night. It sat among the litter of cornflakes two feet away.

Stephanie's first thought was that a zombie had caught wind of them and was heading for the diner—and she wasn't wrong.

A man in blue denim with a shotgun held up to his shoulder suddenly stepped from the kitchen, his work boots making a crunching sound as he came into the room. He had the big bore of the gun pointed at Max Fowler, the only one of them who was currently holding a weapon.

For some reason, the tension in the air was thick and Stephanie was about to give the stranger a wide toothy smile when the door to the diner eased open and in walked two more men, one old and grizzled, with a grey ponytail that hung down the back of the worn leather biker's jacket he wore, and the other, middle-aged and wearing a tired suit that was getting shiny in the seat. They each held a pistol in one hand and an opened bottle of tequila in the other.

"They don't smell right," the older man said, sounding confused. He swung his pistol, a big black hunk of steel, back and forth so that each of them had it pointed at their faces for a few seconds at a time. Stephanie got the shivers when it swung her way, while Chuck only glared.

"They smell good to me, Mitt," said the man in the old suit. He wiped his eyes with the back of his hand, smearing black gunk around so that he ended up looking like a woman who had cried mascara down her face. He then breathed in, enjoying the odor in the room as if he were breathing in an apple pie that had just been pulled from the oven. "They smell real good to me."

Mitt looked ill and nervous…and slightly hungry. He kept licking his wrinkled lips with a tongue that was an ugly color. It was almost a match for his leather jacket. "I don't know, Gil. They ain't right."

The as yet named man in the denim came to stand over PFC Max Fowler who had his M16 sitting across his thighs, pointing at the wall. There was no way he could yank his gun around fast enough. "This one is with the government. He's one of their attack dogs."

"Cliff…Cliff, that's a real dog, Cliff." Mitt used his handgun to point at the animal.

"I'm talking about the soldier, you idiot. He's with the government. He's one of them that did this to us."

"Oh," Mitt said. Cliff began nodding as he took one hand off his gun to reach into his jacket. Stephanie suspected he had a knife stashed there, but he pulled out a bottle of gin and unscrewed it with his thumb, letting the cap roll away. He downed the entire bottle without blinking an eye and then viciously threw it at Max.

Although Cliff was right on top of the soldier, he missed and the bottle shattered against the wall next to Max's head.

Sundance went wild, snapping teeth that were an inch long and fantastically sharp. Chuck had to forget his gun to keep the dog from attacking…and from getting killed. Cliff had turned his shotgun toward the dog and was aiming down the barrel.

"That a government dog?" he asked. "That one of them police dogs that the government sics on poor, innocent people?"

Chuck shook his head, while his hands dug into Sundance's fur. Next to him Fowler said: "It's just a dog we found. He's trapped just like the rest of us."

The gun swung back to point at Fowler. "You ain't trapped like the rest of us. You're with the government. You did this to us. I'm trapped because of you!" Cliff took a step closer, so that the gun was inches away from Fowler's head. Stephanie could imagine she could hear the trigger creaking back as he started to pull on it.

A real sound, the crunch of cornflakes, came from behind Cliff, making him spin. Deckard had shifted position slightly and now he had every gun pointed at him.

Deckard wore an odd grin and his eyes were strangely bright. "You're trapped, too?" he asked, as though excited by the idea. "You must be one of us. We're trapped too, b-by the government. They were doing experiments on us, but—but we escaped. PFC Fowler helped us." He pointed at the soldier.

"Yes," Stephanie said, catching on. "He's on our side and… and he can help you, too."

"Really?" Mitt asked. His eyes were dark, but he was still mostly human. The other two were minutes away from being full-on zombies, with only the alcohol keeping them from turning into blood-thirsty monsters. "You hear that, Gil? He can help us."

Gil scratched his thinning hair with the forward sight on his pistol, looking dubious. "How? How can he help us?"

Mitt looked to Stephanie, who looked to Deckard, who answered: "He knows the way out and…and he knows where to get a cure for your headaches." Deckard lowered his voice slightly and leaned in toward Cliff, saying: "Have you ever heard of R&K Pharmaceuticals? They're the ones that started this and they have the cure."

"That's right," Fowler said. "If you have a car, we can save you."

Gil and Mitt looked as though they had bought the story hook, line and sinker. "We have a truck. Will that do? It's right out back of the post office."

Cliff was unconvinced. "Maybe we should talk to the others before we agree to anything. That's…that's what we'll do. And if they don't like it, then we should kill them. That's what we should do. We should kill them and…and…" A grin twitched his lips and then he swallowed loudly.

He was getting hungry. The feeling had been getting stronger over the last two hours, ever since Mark Jensen had come back to Gamet Corner with a bullet in his leg and a big bite out of his right arm. Mark and two others had tried to find a way out of the Quarantine Zone, but had run into trouble instead.

And now everyone was fighting savage headaches and feeling strangely hungry for something warm and clean and fresh. Cliff couldn't understand this new desire for blood or the sudden avalanche of anger that had taken over his head and wouldn't leave no matter how many pills he swallowed or how much gin he guzzled. He wanted to kill these government people right there, even though it made perfect sense to keep them alive.

He couldn't make up what was left of his mind and so he decided to leave it to the others. They would know what to do.

Ever since Mark Jensen had come back, there had been a sort of "hive" mentality among the few survivors left in Gamet Corners.

Deckard saw the look of confusion. He was counting on it. Under no circumstances could his little group go with the three strangers. Clearly, they were infected, but what wasn't known was if they were contagious yet. He figured that they had to be close which meant it would be certain death to go with them.

Chuck knew it as well and caught Deckard's eye. Just like that, there was an understanding between them: they would fight. PFC Max Fowler was also on board. He bobbed his head and gave Cliff and his gun a significant look. Chuck cut his eye toward Gil and that left Deckard with the task of disarming Mitt.

They just needed the right moment which wasn't slow in coming. Cliff gestured towards the door with his shotgun, saying: "Get up, all of you. And don't touch those guns."

"Of course," Deckard said, raising his hands. "We're all on the same team." The others stood, slowly in Stephanie's case and painfully in Dr. Wilson's. The snap of his aging tendons and the groan he let out when he got to his feet were the only noises he had made since the sudden appearance of Cliff.

He had been quiet this entire time, feeling an impending doom surrounding him. Nothing had gone right in the last two days and he didn't expect this to be any different. Dejectedly, he walked out of the diner with his hands up and didn't see the look Deckard was trying to slip him, and he didn't see how Chuck's muscles were bunched and ready, or how Fowler was half a second away from punching Cliff in the jaw.

Cliff had his eye on Deckard, but his gun was pointed off to the left slightly. Fowler was ready, as was Chuck, who was only a step behind Gil and fully prepared to wrest the pistol out of his hand. The only one of the three who wasn't ready was Deckard, and that was because Dr. Wilson had put himself between Deckard and Mitt.

"Dr. Wilson? Could you…" Deckard jerked his head to the side which he thought was all the hint he could get away with.

Wilson didn't pick up on it. "Could I what?" he asked, faintly. His hips felt as though they had rusted in place in the couple of hours they had spent in the diner and he grimaced with every step.

"Never mind," Deckard answered. The moment had passed. Gil had stepped out into the light and had moved a few feet to the side, the bore of his gun shadowing them. If they fought out in the street it would be a massacre.

Mitt led the group down the street to the post office, a low brick building that stank of old piss and decayed meat. It was cool inside, cool and dark. Deckard squinted through the gloom, looking for anything that could be used as a weapon, however the main floor was basically empty.

A few tables, some plastic bins, a few thousand crisp, white envelopes and stacks of circulars was all he had to work with. There wasn't even a box cutter sitting out. Sundance wanted to come in with them, but Fowler shut the door in his face. He thought it would be better if the dog wasn't trapped along with them.

"There are people here?" Stephanie asked, grimacing over the smell and wishing she was outside with Sundance.

"Downstairs," Gil said, swigging from his bottle and then running his sleeve across his mouth. Again, Mitt went first, heading through a doorway and then down a set of stairs that led to a murky basement where the only light was what filtered through dirty little rectangles of glass set high up on the wall.

He disappeared down the stairs and Stephanie was slow to follow. The smell here was worse, enough to make her gag.

"What's your problem?" Gil asked, glaring down at her. "You don't like our little home? Because that's too bad if you don't. *You* made us live here and you made us like this. You and all of your government buddies."

"That wasn't us, remember?" she said, speaking quickly. "Remember, we're on your side. And remember we can fix you, too."

"Oh yeah," he said, taking another swig. "That's right. And we have to tell the others." He pointed down the stairs with the bottle.

Stephanie went down slowly, each step letting out a desolate creak. At the bottom, there was a jumble of dusty bins and boxes and there were empty liquor bottles by the dozens and there was blood in a pool of red and a body on the floor just a few feet away. It had been a man. His face had been torn off, his fingers were all chewed down to nubs, his belly was laid out and open.

The blood was so fresh that Mitt laid tracks in it as he went to stand over the body. "What did you do?" He looked ghostly pale in the dim light. "Why did you kill Frank?"

Someone hidden by the dark, answered: "He was wrong, Mitt. You know that. He was one of *them*."

"Just like these, I bet," someone to their left, hissed. "They smell clean. They smell like him!" A bottle whistled through the air, missing Stephanie by a hair. It smashed into a thousand shards and drenched her in gin. A second one was thrown, only this one dinged off of Mitt's head, clipped the rail of the staircase and bounced, unbroken at her feet.

Stephanie had thrown a defensive arm over her face and now she could just make out three creatures hiding amongst the boxes. They were black-eyed, their mouths were red gashes, and blood dripped from their chins. They were zombies, keeping it together by the barest of margins.

They started forward, the red gashes smiling wide.

2—The Connecticut Bubble

The president had given his remarks, stressing his four main points, and he had called all the governors involved and smiled benignly as each of them begged him to federalize the situation, and now he watched the live news feeds of Operation Swift Stand.

Practically every television channel replayed the same footage of roaring planes and formations of men geared up and ready to board the waiting C17 Globemasters at Pope Field.

The men were so loaded down with gear they could only move at an awkward shuffle. Along with their bulky parachutes, they carried M4 assault rifles, six thirty-round magazines, MOPP gear, protective masks, 5 MREs, a gallon of water, radios, maps, bibles and all sorts of other minutia that soldiers used.

Once they boarded the planes, they plopped wearily down in the cargo netting and waited as all ninety planes were loaded.

In order to increase the "wow" factor, more planes and more battalions had been added to the initial stage of the operation as the morning progressed, until almost the entire 82nd Airborne Division was scheduled to jump in one mass event.

Optics was the reason given by the White House. It was all the politicians seemed to care about. How would the operation look on television? They made constant unrealistic demands: could the men stand straighter under their immense burdens?

Could we get them to stop sweating? Can they be made to look stoic? Can we get five planes to take off at once?

In spite of the Washington officials trying to turn the operation into something out of Hollywood, it began on time as the first of the huge planes took off at seven sharp, roaring into the bright blue North Carolina sky. People across the country watched with tears in their eyes.

Five hundred miles north of Pope Field, Dr. Thuy Lee had tears threatening to spill from her eyes as well. She found herself trapped in a dark tent with a number of people who were quickly turning into zombies. They were all soldiers who had fought the beasts throughout the night and at some point one or more of them had brought the disease into the command tent.

If it weren't for the pills they were endlessly popping, they would have been eating people by then. As it was, they had turned paranoid and murderous, and Thuy was the object of their hate.

"I told you to tie her up!" Colonel O'Brian hissed at a tall engineering captain who had walked into the tent just before Thuy. Needless to say, the captain was utterly shocked at the order.

"I don't think I can. I-I mean that's not a lawful order, is it?" He looked at the other two men who had just entered. The pair of lieutenants glanced at each other, neither understanding the situation or wanting any part of it, and yet they had been asked a question by a ranking officer.

"Maybe it is," one said. "Martial law has been declared. I-I don't know about punishing anyone, but we can detain civilians, especially if it's been thought that she has broken the law."

"Yes! Yes!" shouted O'Brian, jabbing a finger in Thuy's face. "That's right. Now tie her up and be quick about it."

"Yes, sir, but maybe we should listen to her," one of the lieutenants suggested. "If she knows anything about the virus…"

"She's a traitor!" O'Brian yelled and then put a hand to his head as if the volume of his voice had cracked his brain like an egg. His head thudded so badly that he sometimes saw double.

Thuy didn't know what she would say even if she had been allowed to speak. She had come into the tent with the idea of trying to talk the ranking officer into moving the entire force outside the proposed expanded limits of the Zone. Now, after seeing the advanced stage of the disease that Colonel O'Brian was in, she wouldn't even make the attempt.

She had enough guilt on her shoulders without being the cause of another outbreak of the disease.

Blinking back the tears that threatened to come, she held out her wrists; they were tiny, bird-like. "I will consent to being tied up if you will listen to me. The danger has not passed. The Comcells are extremely hardy and not easily eradicated and, in case you haven't noticed, we are surrounded by thousands of diseased bodies. Soon the flies will come and I have no way of knowing if they will be able to transmit the disease."

"But you have a guess that they will?" the captain asked.

Thuy shrugged. "I am uncomfortable making guesses, but in this case we should assume the worst. This entire camp needs to pick up and move…"

"Hold on!" O'Brian suddenly shouted and again put a hand to his head. "Do not listen to her. She-she started all of this. We can't listen to her. We-we have to punish her. She has to be made an example of."

"I have a knife," one of the men in the shadows said, his voice just as hard and emotionless as the long steel that glinted in his hands.

"Yes," O'Brian said, quieter now. His own yelling seemed to have made him woozy. "We can use a knife. I think that would be allowed under the circumstances." He went for the knife, while the healthy officers shared looks of incredulity.

"Sick," Thuy whispered to the captain, and then jerked her head to indicate the colonel.

"Huh?"

"Sick!" she whispered louder.

Before the captain could blink, O'Brian came hurrying back, the black gleam in his eyes matching the shine on the blade. "I was thinking of waterboarding her, but I like the idea of a knife. It's perfect. We'll use it to get the information out of her. We'll cut it out."

"I-I thought you were looking to p-punish me," Thuy said, her eyes so focused on the knife that everything around it seemed to fall away. To her, the steel floated in the air, getting closer and closer, and her stomach began to flutter and her throat grew tight.

"Right, punish," the colonel said, nodding in agreement. "To hurt her. I mean, I-I …we have to punish her to set an example. That's right."

Thuy knew enough never to contradict anyone afflicted with the disease. It would only spark opposition. Her only option was to lead the colonel in the direction she wanted him to go and for her that direction was out of the tent.

"If you wish to set an example, then it should be done in public so everyone can see."

The colonel jumped at the idea. "Yes, public."

"This is going too far," the captain said, stepping between Thuy and the colonel. His heart was in the right place, but he wasn't thinking. The colonel was on the edge of sanity where life and death were matters of whim. The knife was supposed to be for the hated woman, but the colonel couldn't have people talking back to him. Anyone who did deserved punishment, and the knife was just begging to be used. He ripped the blade into the captain with such force that the tip projected half an inch out of the man's back.

The captain made a noise that was part gasp, part confused bleat—then he simply choked on the blood filling his lungs. There was a moment when everyone stood completely still and watched him drop to his knees, and then slowly collapse forward onto his face. The second he did, Colonel O'Brian tried to grab Thuy.

She screamed and jumped away, but was far too slow, and O'Brian was able to snag the borrowed camouflage shirt that billowed around her. He pulled her in close, dragging her toward his other hand where the bloody piece of metal awaited to stake her just as it had the captain.

3—Northern New Jersey

The zombie that had been Simon Moyer tromped mindlessly along, searching for his next meal. Like all zombies, he was desperately hungry, endlessly so. The hunger drove him, it kept him moving even though he hadn't had the slightest whiff of a human in hours.

By the time the gaggle of C17s coalesced into one mighty formation and began its great sweep over every major city between Raleigh and Boston, Simon was deep into Northern New Jersey where the greenery was lush and the land dotted with lakes and ponds. It was a land of second homes, cabins, and little getaway properties, and with the Quarantine Zone so close, just across the border, it was *almost* completely empty.

Other than the squirrels and birds and the occasional fox, the only things that moved in the placid countryside were Simon, a man named Donald Biggs, and a gentle, but thick fog that had blanketed the area all night. With the sun rising, the fog was gradually dissipating where it had settled in the hollers and stream beds and the folds in the land.

The three: Simon, Donald and the fog happened to meet in one of these low areas where visibility suddenly dropped from sixty yards to five feet.

Donald, who lived in Newark, two hours away, had been glued to his television for half of the previous day and, as things deteriorated, he had begun to worry about food, just like everyone else. He was not well provisioned because, after all, the Food Lion was just down the street and wasn't it always simply stacked from floor to ceiling with food?

The worry over food had him hurrying down the street and what he saw there made his stomach turn a flip: the store had become a mob scene. People were yelling and pushing each other and throwing punches. Even as he stood, watching with his mouth hanging slack, he saw one person stab another over the last can of tomato paste.

That had sent him scurrying back home…back to his television and his mounting fear, which peaked when the talking heads on the 24-hour news channels reported on a number of delivery trucks that had been hijacked.

A lack of food was a problem and his dad's little fishing cabin up in the green part of Jersey was the solution. The place: rustic, dusty, and mouse infested was as stocked as a fallout shelter. Sure, some of the cans of beans were stamped with dates that suggested they had expired last century, but Donald was more of a beggar at this point.

He knew he had no choice: he had to get that food, and so he set out for the cabin, thinking that it would take him a couple of hours. He hadn't counted on the endless traffic. Luckily, he was going against the grain and after five hours he got what he needed and turned back, his Tercel crammed with six week's worth of Spaghetti O's, beef ravioli, baked beans and tuna.

More luck seemed to be with him as he found a practically deserted back road and was able to pick up speed. He drove with a heavy foot and white knuckles. Just then, it wasn't zombies that he feared. As far as he knew, they were all still a hundred miles away and safely holed up in the Quarantine Zone. What he feared was the desperation of his fellow man. He feared highway robbers. He feared a ruse and an ambush, and so he raced along at speeds that were about twenty miles an hour beyond reckless.

He wasn't going to stop for anything on the twisted little snake of a road—not even if he ran someone over.

The Tercel, a blue streak in the green forest, was doing sixty when the road dipped and the fog was suddenly a cloud, dense as dragon breath. His foot came off the gas to hover over the brake, but he didn't slow down because if there was ever going to be an ambush, it would be here and he wanted to be prepared.

Still, he was caught off guard as Simon stepped directly into the path of the Tercel. Donald screeched and his brakes screeched; there was a thud and a thump, thump, thump sound as Simon smacked the grill, the windshield and bounced off the trunk. The car slewed to the right from the impact, but Donald somehow kept it on the road...and kept it going.

"It was a trap," he hissed, staring into the rear view mirror and seeing Simon climb to his feet; he blamed the fog for seeing the man as grey, and his shredded clothes he figured had been caused by being hit and thrown over the car. "Or he had ripped them up before jumping out at me."

Donald pictured the man as part thief and part stuntman. He'd heard of scams like that before. Someone "pretends" to get hit by a car and when the motorist pulls over, they get robbed and then stuffed in the trunk where they die a slow, suffocating death.

"That's not going to be me," he said and then pegged the gas. His driving became even more reckless and he ended up skinning blue paint off the side of the Tercel more than once. He didn't care. Survival was all that counted.

An hour and half later, he slipped the Tercel into his garage to inspect the damage and, more importantly, to clean off any blood and incriminating evidence.

Strangely, all he found were smears of black gunk on the hood. He gave them a quick sniff, and then made a face; the gunk smelled of death. "What the fuck?" he asked in quavering voice. The sight and smell of the gunk, as well as the subconscious idea that what he had hit hadn't been a robber, had his stomach making nervous turns and so he cleaned the car meticulously and then cleaned himself even more so.

But it was too late for Donald Biggs. He had snorted in the deadly spores with that one sniff, and an hour later, he lay in his basement screaming into an old blanket that he was using to try to keep the light from burning out his mind.

Soon his pain would give way to anger and that would be forgotten, drowned out by an all-consuming hunger.

Chapter 7

1—Shanghai, China

General Hir Okini's helicopter skimmed north, three hundred meters over the burned out remnants of what had been, not only the most populous city in China, but also in the entire world. Shanghai, once touted as the Pearl of the Orient, a beacon for all of Asia, had teemed with twenty-four million people, a number that could hardly be comprehended.

They lived, crammed one on top of the other with almost no room to stretch, eking out their dull, slow lives. They ate, they slept, they worked like faceless drones, in the sprawling city that had all the personality of an anthill.

Where once change had been slow and forced, now it was dynamic. Below Okini, all of Shanghai was on the move. It was a city of the dead and a city on the move.

Even with the blue plastic hood of his bio-suit constantly slipping down to cover his eyes, General Okini had no problem seeing the corpses. They weren't laid out and bleeding like proper corpses. No, they walked or stumbled or, if they didn't have legs, they dragged themselves. They moved west, always west.

They really couldn't go in any other direction. Shanghai sat on a peninsula, jutting out into the East China Sea, and the infected, walking corpses didn't seem to care for the water. This little thing had kept them from spreading out in a hundred directions.

They went west and behind them were a thousand fires belching smoke into the sky as entire city blocks burned unchecked. If Okini had his way, he would have purposely turned the entire city into one big ash heap, but he was not the General Secretary and could not snap his fingers and have everything be as he commanded.

Still, as a ranking member of the Party and the Vice Chairman of the Central Military Commission, he was able to read the "Most Secret" reports concerning the creatures. What had amazed him wasn't their virility, it was just how quickly the disease spread. Unlike the rest of the twenty-five person Politburo, he had actually seen the infected creatures up close.

One of his first acts, after he had been tasked with his new orders: *Protect the City of Suzhou and Lands West*, was to send commandos into Shanghai to snatch up infected individuals for study. Half the commando teams failed to return, but those that did brought back creatures that were more monster than man. Even chained to gurneys, they would hiss and gnash their teeth. One even tried to bite off its own hand to get at Okini.

They were vile things, fit only to die in flames.

He was only one of a few in the Politburo who held this opinion. Most of the others urged restraint and cried that more time was needed before Okini's more drastic solutions were put in place. *It has only been two days,* they said. *Let's at least get a scientific point of view,* they whined. Hundreds of scientists from every imaginable field had been flown in the night before to study the problem that the horrible creatures represented. The scientists talked about cures and vaccines, and one fool talked about rehabilitation for the infected.

Okini knew better. Cures were a long-term solution to the disease; fire was the short-term solution and he was pretty sure that there was only time for the short term solution.

Nothing was more obvious to him, especially from his current vantage point. He motioned the helicopter west and in minutes it was flying over the easternmost suburbs of Suzhou which had once been a suburb of Shanghai but had grown into a massive city in its own right.

The leading edge of the zombie army had just crossed the S5, the main north-south highway. The streets crawled with the dead going here and there, hunting down anything remotely human to satisfy their lust for fresh blood.

Unfortunately, Okini didn't have the authority to call in airstrikes on his own cities. He had been given an order for containment only, not eradication. In his ice-cold heart, he knew that was a mistake. The westward march of the disease would sweep over Suzhou which had a population of over ten million people—ten million doomed people.

At least here the Politburo had listened to reason.

Once Okini had explained that he didn't have the resources to move the necessary military assets into place to stop the zombies *and* to save the local population from the coming threat, it was decided that the people would remain in place. It was only logical. The roads west of Suzhou were narrow, sometimes only muddy tracks, and already the military traffic crept along making Okini's logistical issues a nightmare. If ten million refugees were added to the mix, the roads would become fused with no one being able to go one way or the other.

"Are the people of Suzhou just going to sit there and wait to be killed?" a party chief from the Jiangsu Province had leapt up to demand.

"Of course not," Okini had answered. "The people will work and they will fight and they will die." He was solemn for a moment before he looked up with a fierce expression in his brown eyes. "Or would you rather that they run to Nanjing? And then when the demon-army comes to Nanjing, they can all run to Beijing. Where would you have them run to then? Would you like them to come here?" This had ended all discussion.

Twenty hours earlier, the entire population of Suzhou had been forcibly pressed into labor gangs and set to work digging a ditch the length of the Suez canal, which they were told would stop the zombies. Okini had given them a day to complete the project. It was, of course, impossible. There was no way it could be done, but that was okay with Okini.

He knew that the work would keep their minds focused and their feet from running. Soon, they were too tired to run and yes, it was true they would also be too tired to fight properly, but he had no expectations that they would prove to be anything but a speed bump to the steamrolling zombies.

In his opinion, this was the beauty of China, the peasants knew their place. They knew that they were not special little snowflakes. They were only cogs in the machines. They were worker ants who lived to toil. They would sweat and break their backs and then they would die, doing their part in defense of the country.

All that night and most of the next day, the peasants labored without pause. They cleared the land in a wide lane that ran from the Yangtze River in the north to Taihu Lake in the south. Those who had shovels, pick-axes or hoes dug until their hands blistered and bled, while those without watched until whipped to their hands and knees to scrape at the soil with rocks or sticks or anything they could find. They dug until the zombie army could be seen.

The sight of the beasts was so horrid that some of the peasants tried to run away. Okini ordered his army to gun them down. They had been warned not to run.

Even if they had been able to break out, they wouldn't have gone far. In their wisdom, the Party had not put all their trust in the one giant ditch. Rightly fearing a break through by the zombies, they conscripted the entire population of the Jiangsu Province in order to build a second ditch forty miles to the west.

This one was a proper ditch. When it was finished, it would be impressively deep and wide. On the eastern side, it would be strung with barbed wire and on the west, the earth would be built to heights of up to seventy feet in places.

Every backhoe and bulldozer, shovel and pick within a hundred miles had been confiscated, and now the peasants of Jiangsu were tearing down everything in their path. When complete, in two day's time, the ditch would be a modern marvel and yet Okini didn't think that even it would stop the army of undead.

Their numbers were unthinkable and the dreadful army would only grow after they consumed the citizens of Suzhou, who trembled behind their tiny ditch, clutching their sticks and shovels.

That their pathetic line would fail was a foregone conclusion in Okini's mind. What he needed was for the Politburo to see it fail. When they saw it crumble and when they saw how quickly the dead came back to life, he would demand proper airstrikes and he felt sure he would get them. He would create an inferno, a storm of fire that would scorch the land and incinerate everything, living and dead within twenty miles. Only then would China be safe.

"How is the shot?" Okini asked into his microphone. "Do we need to get closer?" With him on the helicopter was a cameraman, also garbed in a head-to-toe blue bio suit. The man leaned out over the horde as it closed in on Suzhou.

"No, sir," he said, shaking his head frantically, which made an annoying plastic swishing sound in Okini's receiver. "We are plenty close. Please. I have the ability to zoom in. I am getting everything from here."

Okini studied the man with a flat expression. "You had better," was all Okini said, looking down at the incipient battle. On one side, the zombies, a great wiggling mass that covered the earth like a plague of locusts, swept forward in an unstoppable wave. They went on like that, stretching over the eastern horizon.

On the other side were the peasants, ten million strong, lined up shoulder to shoulder in a great phalanx a hundred miles in length and a hundred feet in depth. The hardiest men stood in front, holding what weapons they had been able to scrounge, usually the same tools that they had used to hack out the shallow ditch. Behind them were slim teenage youths and middle-aged men with pot bellies and skinny arms. Behind these stood the women trying to shield their children and finally, in the last line, were the oldest among them: little toothless grannies and men bent over walking sticks.

Behind all of this was the army, or at least that part of the army Okini had been able to hustle into position on such short notice. It was a force made up of elements of four different divisions making communications and the command structure a headache. On the plus side, Okini had two hundred tanks and armored personnel carriers available as well as three hundred artillery pieces already in position.

When the leading edge of the horde came within a thousand meters, Okini calmly ordered his artillery chief to commence firing. Even over the thrum of the helicopter's engine, the thunder of artillery could be heard, as all three hundred pieces fired at once. Seconds later, clouds of black smoke and brown dirt shot into the sky and the air roiled, buffeting the helicopter.

Although the cameraman let out a muffled cry, all Okini said was: "Excellent. Fire for effect." There was really no reason to direct their fire since there was no way they could miss.

Every shell hit home. Every shell sent body parts flying and filled the air with spores and vaporized blood and shards of bone. Twenty or thirty of the beasts were destroyed with every strike, which seemed great up until Okini did the math.

His three hundred artillery pieces had been drawn by three hundred trucks. And each of those had been able to carry only a crew of five plus thirty of the hundred-pound shells of high-explosives. Quick math showed that three hundred pieces of artillery, multiplied by thirty shells, multiplied by thirty deaths per explosion meant that *optimally* his artillery would destroy a little over a quarter of a million of the creatures.

It was a drop in an immense bucket. The drop was enlarged in the slightest when Okini ordered the tanks and personnel carriers to add their destructive powers to the carnage. The leading waves of zombies were ripped to shreds as the Type-96 tanks fired their 120mm semi-automatic-loading cannons into them. Again, it was like shooting at the ocean from the beach—they couldn't miss.

For thirty minutes, firepower alone held the undead back. The carnage was so fantastic that the peasants began cheering and jumping about in wild celebration. From ground level, it looked as though the undead horde was being utterly destroyed.

From Okini's vantage, the truth was sadly obvious: despite the prolific expenditure of ordinance, not even two percent of the horde had been killed. When the pall of diseased smoke that hung over the entire length of the ditch finally lifted, the peasants were dismayed to see the undead marching forward still.

Within the phalanx, local Party officials who had been lied to repeatedly about the lack of real danger, yelled patriotic slogans in order to stiffen the resistance: *We fight for home and homeland! We fight for the Party! We fight for China!*

In spite of the cheerleading, a number of people tried to flee and again the army shot them down—they were the lucky ones.

The zombies, nearly twenty-four million strong, poured over the ditch as if it wasn't there, and struck the front line of the peasants with a savage roar. In seconds, the two titanic armies were locked together so tightly and so fiercely that it was impossible to swing a weapon let alone a fist.

The fight became man against beast, fought tooth and nail. There was no winning such a fight. The battle surged back and forth along the lip of the ditch as the two masses of humanity locked horns. It was a wonder that the line lasted as long as it did, but after an hour, it finally broke in fifty places and was simply overrun in fifty more.

Only then did Okini act the part of a general. Wherever there was a hole in the line, he rushed in army units to plug it up and soon the sound of automatic rifle fire was nearly as loud as the sound of the screaming.

Another hour into the battle, the men of the front line had been killed and now the teenage boys flinched back into the middle-aged men. Frequently, these would fall back into the lines of women and before Okini knew it, entire sections of the line were running, heedless of the screaming party officials or the bullets of the army trying to stop them.

Tens of thousands of zombies poured into these gaps and it wasn't long before there wasn't a real line at all. There were only islands of humanity being attacked from every side. Okini had to decide whether to send in the tanks and the personnel carriers. Their machine guns were already out of bullets, but they could still rend the zombies beneath their treads.

It was horrible to watch as the metal monsters roared into battle, crushing the zombies and spitting out dripping flags of flesh behind them. In minutes, the tanks went from camouflaged green to glistening black. They circled the islands of humanity, doing their best to keep the zombies away, but all in vain.

Most of the remaining adult peasants had been contaminated by the Com-cells long before and now they began to turn into the very beasts they had been fighting. The islands began to devour themselves as the tanks drove around them, their crews gradually growing sicker and sicker.

It wasn't long before General Okini saw that the battle had ended and that the zombie horde, instead of being crippled, had been augmented. He guessed that China now faced thirty million zombies, instead of twenty-four million.

"Did you get all of that?" he asked the cameraman. The younger man, who was green behind his mask, nodded. "Good. I'll need it edited down to thirty minutes. Keep five minutes of the artillery bombardment, ten minutes of the infantry attacks, ten minutes of the tanks running about and the last five minutes will be the peasants turning on each other. I want twenty-five copies total. Don't even think about making a copy for yourself."

Of course, the cameraman made a copy and it wasn't long before he was making a load of cash under an assumed name by posting the video on the internet and selling advertising on the home page. He needed money, badly. The only way out of China now was through fantastic bribes.

2—Montrose, New York

By the time the Politburo saw the video it had circulated halfway around the world and was being shown on American television. Lieutenant Eng of the People's Liberation Army sat in front of a TV screen, staring in utter disbelief. He knew people in Suzhou. He had lived in Shanghai! That was his country and his people. Seeing the endless lines of zombies made him weak.

Next to him, Anna Holloway, who had been massaging the broken fingers on her left hand, chuckled and said in a whisper: "Well, that changes things a little."

Eng, who had access to a fake passport and Visa, had planned on slipping down to Mexico and from there catching the next flight out to China, only there weren't any flights back to China. They had all been canceled and now he knew why.

China was convulsing under a major outbreak of zombies. By the looks of it, one that was much worse than what was happening in the states. Eng had been planning on ditching Anna and the others as soon as he had the chance, but now he didn't know what to do or where to go.

It wouldn't be long before it was discovered what he had done and then he would be wanted on terrorism and mass-murder charges in two countries. He put his hands over his face and groaned.

"You need me," Anna said to him, keeping her voice low so the others wouldn't hear. There were ten of them stuck in a little motel off of Route 9 in the town of Montrose, New York. It was an empty place, a mile from the Hudson, and eleven miles from the southernmost point of the Quarantine Zone. Anyone with any sense was long gone.

The night before, five of them had escaped the Zone by taking a like number of hostages and forcing an army helicopter to fly them to safety. Now it was hard to tell who were the good guys and who were the bad guys—except that is, for Eng and Anna. They were the only ones armed and both were desperate enough to kill. Yet all the hostages were alive and, ironically, the only one tied up was one of the hostage takers, a man named Meeks—Special Agent Chaz Meeks, FBI.

The moment the helicopter had landed in the parking lot of a grocery store, the guns had shifted away from the innocent as the hostage takers had aimed them at each other, no one trusting anyone else. Lieutenant Eng had a Glock pointed at Meeks who had just aimed his Beretta at Anna. She had her gun pointed at Bob, but only because she had seen his gun jerk up; however, he was aiming at Eng, while the last man, a nobody named Alan kept his gun moving all around. He had no idea what was going on; he just didn't want to die.

"Put the gun down or I'll shoot her," Meeks yelled over the noise of the helicopter.

"Go right ahead," Eng yelled back. "You'd be doing me a favor." Anna detested Eng and knew the feeling was mutual. If there hadn't been a gun pointed Eng's way, he would have let Meeks kill her without a qualm.

"I just want to get out of this alive!" Bob cried, "So maybe we should all put our guns down."

Eng dared a glance toward him, saw the gun pointed his way, and said: "You first." Bob lacked the courage to lower his weapon and so, with the helicopter blades whipping above them, the five-way Mexican standoff continued until the pilot unbuckled and climbed out of the cockpit.

"Get the fuck off my bird!" he screamed. "Or so help me God, I'll take you right back over the Zone and turn her sideways and drop you at a thousand feet."

Alan was the first to point his pistol up and then Bob. Meeks was next, but only because Eng, who no longer had anyone aiming a gun his way, stuck the barrel of his Glock in Meeks' ear.

Anna was last, and the second she lowered her gun, the pilot pointed to the parking lot he had landed in and said: "There's your freedom. Go!"

The ten of them jumped out. When they were all out, two things happened: the standoff recommenced and the chopper lifted straight up. Anna had the upper hand in the standoff this time. In her right hand was the pistol and in her left was the vial of deadly Com-cells she had stolen from R&K Pharmaceuticals. Bob and Alan were quick to give up their guns and now with two guns pointed at him, Meeks dropped his Beretta so that it clattered onto the pavement.

Then it was just Eng and Anna. "You need me," she said, "and I need you. There's no reason for either of us to die." There was no question she hated the Chinese bastard, but she was screwed six ways from Sunday. When the blame came down, she would get her share and when prison sentences were handed out, she could expect to get more than her fair share. It would be twenty-five to life for her—if they didn't tie her into Ol' Sparky and light her ass up.

It would be worse for Eng and he knew it. Right there, a shaky alliance was formed. Their mutual enemy, FBI Agent Meeks was disarmed and bound. Bob and Alan gave up their guns, voluntarily. The two men had been wine-reps and although they both could wield a corkscrew with the dexterity of a ninja and could decant a merlot in ten seconds, they were weak. Both were, essentially, pacifists in a time of war.

With the leadership hierarchy settled, they stared around at the town of Montrose, where the only things that moved in the dark were mosquitos and packs of stray dogs sniffing at lamp posts. The place was utterly deserted. Being so close to the

Zone, the town's inhabitants had fled early the day before, a good number of them looting the local grocery store on their way out of town.

The store's long front window had been smashed in and Anna's feet crunched glass as she led the way into the dim building. There was little in the way of merchandise left. All the food was gone. There wasn't so much as a can of beans or a carrot stick left on the shelves.

Along with food, any item that was considered to be immediately useful, such as toilet paper and batteries, had also been stolen. This left an entire aisle of greeting cards, a few spices and, thankfully a hundred different cleaning products. There were a good thirty gallons of bleach sitting right where anyone could have grabbed them.

The ten of them used toilet brushes and diluted bleach to scour themselves. At first they concentrated on their feet and then it was noticed that one of the hostages had black specs high up on her calf. Everyone immediately stripped off their pants and socks and took to scrubbing their legs and feet. Hands, arms and faces were next.

The fumes from the bleach were noxious, but no one complained too loudly. Their choice between a bad smell or death was an easy one to make.

Next, the little group, half-naked and freezing, wandered down the empty streets looking for clean clothing. Eventually, they found a boutique that sold high-end women's apparel. This store hadn't been broken into and was locked up tight. Alan, who was the largest of them, shouldered in the door. Everyone found something that fit, even the men, although they didn't look happy wrapping themselves in bright colors and sassy patterns.

They were warm at least.

At that point, it was after one in the morning and everyone was too tired to go on. The motel was the best solution. Mattresses were dragged into the largest room and everyone fell asleep in seconds.

Now, with the sun up, the group was awake and watching TV as if they were a bunch of teens at a sleepover. The news, at least in America, seemed to be good. The army was coming—the real army—not these backwood National Guard hicks who were being blamed for screwing up the containment.

The army meant rescue and a return to normalcy and the group chatted excitedly until Anna said: "I wouldn't believe it if

I were you. The disease is going to spread over half the country before it's checked, mark my words."

That killed the excitement as if a switch had been thrown. Everyone in the room had been to the edge of death. Whether by luck or their wits, they had lived when a hundred thousand hadn't. They were survivors and each had been changed by the experience.

Trust was gone. They listened to the promises of the president and heard his grandiose plans for the paratroopers and air assault soldiers, and doubt crept in.

"We need to get moving south," Anna said to them. "We need to get as far away from the disease as possible."

"How?" Alivia asked. She and her little brother had been the only hostages who hadn't begged for the chance to leave a building surrounded by a thousand zombies—she hadn't fought it either, which suggested to Anna that despite being in high school, she had brains and guts.

Anna shrugged. "By car, I guess. It's the easiest way. But first we all have to get some shoes." The boutique had sold a few stylish stilettos none of which were less than four inches in height and thus were useless for any sort of journey. Anna went on: "We'll split up in teams of twos. Alivia and Jack." she said pointing to the pair of teenage siblings. "Alan and Renee. Bob and Meg. Eng and Meeks. And lastly, I'll go with Jenny. Remember, if you find any Nikes in white, size six, grab them for me. Ha-ha."

The ten of them got to their feet and went out into the morning sunlight where they blinked like owls and shielded their eyes with their hands. Everything seemed still, but strangely normal. There was even the smell of burning leaves on the cool wind.

Eng caught Anna by the arm before she could join the others. "What are you doing?" he demanded. "Shoes? If they have shoes they'll run away."

"Let them," she answered. "What do we need them for? If you ask me, they're all dead weight. If they run, then it'll be for the better, all except for Meeks. He's FBI. We can't risk keeping him alive. He can't be here when we meet back up." She lowered her voice to a whisper. "Make sure it's quiet. We'll say he took off when you weren't looking." Eng only grunted, but his sly eyes shifted to the FBI Agent and Anna knew that one problem would be taken care of.

The group broke into their five teams, going down different streets. Anna made sure to keep Jenny close. And she made sure to chat about shoes and other inconsequential things in the friendliest manner. As always, she played a dangerous game and she played to win. She had to over-awe Jenny with her vivaciousness just in case there was ever a trial and a jury, and there was a need for a friendly witness who would remember how relaxed and easy going Anna had been.

Eng wasn't nearly so friendly. Taking hold of the electrical cord that bound Meeks' wrists, Eng hauled him away from the rest of the group, heading down a side street. Rocks and twigs bit into their feet as they bypassed the front door of the nearest house and headed into the backyard where the grass was neatly trimmed and bordered by a chain-link fence. The fence had a gate that led to a neighbor's yard. Eng went right for it, hustling Meeks along.

"Hey? What's wrong with that house?" Meeks asked, jerking his chin around at the house they had just passed. "You don't think they have any shoes in there." He tried to smile, but his nervous lips wouldn't hold still. He didn't know whether to smile or grimace and he didn't know if he should laugh crazily or scream. There was only one reason to ignore a perfectly good house.

"It was a woman's house," Eng answered. For some sick reason, Meeks' fear egged on the brutal killer within Eng. Unlike Meeks, Eng was able to smile convincingly. "I'm not going to pick out shoes for a woman. Only you American 'men' would do something so pathetic. You act like eunuchs half the time. It's embarrassing."

Meeks, who had thought the same thing about his fellow Americans on occasion, relaxed and managed to smile, despite the insulting look he was being given.

The two went through the gate and Eng pointed at the back of the next house where a pile of wood had been hand-split. "A real man cut those logs. This is a man house." They went to the back door. Eng knocked and paused, listening, not just for movement in the house, but also for the others in the group.

He heard nothing.

"The coast is clear," Meeks said. "Say, could you untie me, my hands are starting to go numb. I'm not going to run away or anything and I'm not a threat. I'm ruined at the FBI. I took a hostage in order to save myself. You don't get to come back from that sort of thing. So, you don't have to worry about me, ok?"

Eng regarded him with his flat, black eyes. A dead bass had warmer eyes than he did. When he smiled, the eyes stayed just as cold. "Sure. Turn around."

When Meeks complied, Eng crushed his skull with one of the hunks of wood.

Chapter 8

1—8:08 a.m.
The Quarantine Zone—Gamet Corner, New York

Deckard's group was trapped in the closest of spaces with no way to turn. The dark staircase leading into the basement of the post office was not terribly wide or all that long. It was a single flight with enemies in front and behind.

Three "almost" zombies began to push through the cluttered basement, heading for Stephanie at the bottom of the stairs, while behind them at the top stood Gil and Cliff, both black-eyed and foul-smelling.

Gil loomed above Deckard, the pistol in his hand aimed at the back of Deckard's head. Above Gil, at the very top of the stairs stood Cliff, his long Mossberg 590 shotgun held loosely and somewhat forgotten in his hands. The dead body that Mitt stood over drew most of Cliff's attention. The clean coppery smelling blood rising up from it was a heady perfume that had him drunk with a sudden nasty hunger. That sensation vied with a piercing jealousy—the others had begun to feed!

The urge for clean blood was so great that he wanted to cast aside the gun and launch himself down the stairs at one of these new people. They smelled good and clean and their promises of helping with the terrible ache in his head were all but forgotten.

Stuck in the middle of everything, Chuck found himself in, what his grandma on his mama's side, would have called a "gen-u-wine pickle." He could go neither up nor down. He couldn't fight or run away. He had no gun, no knife, no nothing.

All he had on him was a twenty-five-year old Zippo lighter, the very thing that had got him into the mess in the first place. The first time he had seen a Zippo was ages ago, or so it seemed. He had been a skinny seventh grader standing in line at the Norman Multiplex waiting to see *The Silence of the Lambs* when up walked Randle Bush, smacking a Zippo open and closed, producing flame with a practiced hand and making a show of lighting up a Lucky Strike. Randall wore a denim jacket and leather gloves with the fingers cut off. In Norman, Oklahoma he was the height of cool, and at that moment, seventh grade Chuck knew he had to have a Zippo and a cigarette.

The cigarettes had been a death sentence. Now, he just had the lighter, a chest full of tumors and a sudden desire for more life. Stephanie was the reason for that desire. She smelled of gin and fear as she backed into Max Fowler.

"Steph, get back!" Chuck yelled, pushing past Dr. Wilson, who was retreating up the stairs despite Chuck's mad scramble to get to Stephanie and despite the fact that what was up the stairs was as dangerous as what was down them.

Only Max Fowler was really in a position to do anything productive and he didn't hesitate. He pushed Stephanie behind him and reached down to snatch the bottle of 151 rum that had been thrown. Then, in an oddly childish move, he stepped quickly back up on the last stair as if the basement floor was lava and he didn't want to burn his boots.

The bottle was basically the only weapon in reach and Max brandished it above his head, threatening the three "almost" zombies, who still had enough working brain cells to see the bottle as a threat. They stopped, but Chuck knew that it wouldn't be for long.

Their hunger would overcome their fear of being bashed with the bottle, and although Max was young and strong, they would eventually drag him down and eat him—if they weren't all shot before that.

"We can help you!" bellowed Dr. Wilson to the sick men. "We can help you!"

One of the three "almost" zombies could be seen attempting to think through what that meant, while the other two ignored it altogether. Their eyes were on the man holding the bottle and their black, dank mouths were open and dripping dark saliva. It would be seconds before they attacked.

Chuck knew they needed to do something. They needed a weapon, but all they had was the bottle of rum and a lighter. "Well, shit," he drawled and dug out the lighter and, just like 'Ol Randal Bush from twenty-five years ago, he made a show of snapping it open.

"Max!" Chuck hissed, holding up the lighter. "Molotov!"

The soldier blinked before understanding widened his eyes. He now lifted the bottle high and sent it crashing down at the foot of the stairs, where the rum mingled with the gin in a highly flammable pool.

Chuck tossed the lighter and in an instant, flames leapt up enveloping the floor in front of the stairs. Max, Stephanie, and Chuck stepped back. Deckard did not. With the gun at his head, Deckard had nowhere to go and no time to get there. Besides, he knew people. He knew their reactions in pressure situations.

Most normal people would back up and continue to make threats. They would be averse to killing, they would be slow to pull the triggers on their guns. But these weren't "most" people. They were on the verge of becoming monsters and it wouldn't take much to push them over the edge. The fire was that little push.

Gil cursed and thumbed back the hammer on his black pistol, while Cliff cried out, yelling gibberish and hauling his shotgun up. Deckard leaned back into the barrel of Gil's gun. He had to keep contact with it long enough to make his move. In fact, it helped that Gil had it pushed into his head as hard as he did. It made things easier when Deckard suddenly jerked to the side and grabbed the gun. Gil did the expected and pulled the trigger, sending a slug into the wall.

Now Deckard made a fatal mistake. Against two opponents like this the thing to do was to use Gil as a shield against Cliff by holding him close. Next, Deckard would twist the gun out of Gil's hands and then, still with Gil draped over him, he would put five holes into Cliff and that would be that.

Except, these weren't normal men.

Gil was no longer able to process a fight in terms of attack and defend. All he cared about was getting his teeth into Deckard's skin. Gil abandoned the gun and tried to take a chomp out of Deckard's shoulder, but only got a mouthful of shirt.

Cliff did the unexpected as well. He fired the Mossberg without regard for the fact that he had friends below him. In fact, he fired simply as a reaction to Gil firing. There was an explosion of light and sound just above Deckard followed by a hot blast of air and a thudding sound.

Deckard had never *heard* someone get shot before, but he was close enough to Dr. Wilson that the odd noise, similar to someone smacking a punching bag with a baseball bat, cut through the rush of the flames and the sound of people struggling on the stairs.

And he couldn't miss it when Wilson let out a cry: "Oh, God, no!"

In desperation, Deckard twisted his body, spilling Gil off his shoulder so that he fell into Dr. Wilson's legs, knocking him back into Chuck.

At that moment, Cliff could have shot them all down, one at a time. There was nowhere to hide and nowhere to run. Cliff had been rocked by the force of the twelve gauge, the gun almost leaping right out of his hands, and now, like a drunk who couldn't quite catch up with what was going on around him, he was just bringing the weapon to bear on Deckard who was equally unprepared.

Gil had given up his pistol so easily that Deckard had fumbled it and was just picking it up when Cliff pulled the trigger on the Mossberg…on the pump action Mossberg. The trigger was stiff beneath his finger because, with the Com-cells covering his brain in black hate, he had forgotten to chamber another round.

Just as he started to pump the gun, Deckard shot him, the bullet blasting up into his right cheekbone, through the rear of his right eye socket and then up through the lower floor of the cranium and into the brain—a perfect shot for someone who didn't want to spray blood everywhere.

Cliff's left arm shot straight out as if giving a Nazi salute and then he fell back. Deckard didn't watch. He spun and took careful aim at Gil, who was lower down and turned away as he struggled to get to his feet. Deckard aimed for the back of the head and could only hope that the bullet didn't fly out and spray everyone below with diseased blood. The 9mm bullet went in through the brain stem, killing Gil in an instant. Where the bullet went from there is anyone's guess, but it didn't come blasting out and that was all that mattered.

"There's one more," Fowler cried, pointing over the flames and deeper in the basement.

Deckard hadn't forgotten Cliff and if he had, the two bullets that came flying from the basement a half-second later would have clued him in. Both were misses. One bullet grazed the wall next to Stephanie's head and the other went nowhere near the stairwell.

Mitt still had a chunk of working grey matter left between his ears, meaning he was still human enough to fear for his own safety. He had fired as he ran for cover and his shots weren't aimed. Worse than his lack of aiming was his selection of cover. The cardboard box that he hid behind contained only a few old mailbags and when Deckard fired three times into it, all three slugs went right through the box to punch holes into Mitt.

"Up! Everyone Up!" Deckard cried the moment Mitt flopped over. He didn't bother wasting any bullets on the three "almost" zombies. They were staring at the flames and probably would continue to stare until the place burned down around them or they died of smoke inhalation.

Getting up was not so easy. Dr. Wilson, the heaviest of the five of them had been shot high up on the right side of his chest. His clavicle and three ribs had been shot through so that he couldn't use his right arm. Worse, his lung had been punctured by a single ricocheting pellet, and now blood leaked down into his lung, making him wheeze and cough.

Every move was a misery and with each breath, he sucked in more blood. It was a struggle to get the doctor out into the daylight.

"I'm going to need you to get any sort of medkit you can find," Deckard told Fowler, after they had lain Wilson on the sidewalk just down from the post office. "And some more bleach. We need to clean ourselves up if we are to stand any chance."

"Don't bother…with me," Wilson choked out. "How…can I…get away…like this?" His right arm hung limply, blood drained from his wound in rivers, and he couldn't stop coughing. He would be a magnet for the undead.

Deckard gave him his warmest smile. "I've got some ideas how we'll escape the zone. Don't you worry about a thing." Deckard worried enough for both of them. Stray beasts, only shadows at the moment, were already headed their way.

2—The Connecticut Bubble

"In public!" Thuy pleaded, her eyes on the long bloody blade of the knife. "You wanted it public. M-my punishment. You wanted it in public so no one could blame you, remember?" She had gone from a confident, take charge woman to a weeping, begging child in the span of seconds.

Colonel O'Brian had his fingers entwined in her hair and the knife inched ever closer as he tried to recall exactly what he had said only a minute before. "Yes, right, now I remember. A real punishment, one that everyone can see and maybe even partake in."

He blinked the black from his eyes and then stared around, ignoring the body of the dead captain and the hot blood, but only with difficulty. O'Brian was disgusted with this new lust for blood. He didn't understand it and was embarrassed by it, so he pretended not to see the body or hear the blood calling to him. He pulled his gaze from it and centered it on the two lieutenants who had accompanied the captain into the tent.

"You," he said, pointing at the closer of the two. "Get me rope or chains or better yet, handcuffs. There were MPs around, go get them and…and a truck we can tie her to it. We can't let her get away. She did this to us."

"I won't run, I promise," Thuy said.

O'Brian threw her down and pointed a finger at her. "Shut up! Don't say another word." He turned back to the lieutenant. "And you? What are you still doing here? Go get the damn MPs like I said. Do I have to explain what a fucking order is?"

"No sir," the lieutenant answered and then backed to the door with Thuy pleading silently with her eyes for him not to leave.

The colonel's mental state was unraveling quickly. He stomped around Thuy and she followed him with just her eyes. Really, it was the knife she watched as it circled her, a single bloody horse on a deadly carousel. She huddled in a ball, doing her best to appear tiny and weak, something too unimportant to be bothered over.

One of the shadowy figures in the corner of the tent groused, "We need more pills. They are gone, the bottle's fucking empty."

"Maybe she took them," another said, bringing his gun up and pointing it at her. She began to tremble and it wasn't just a little tremor, either. Her muscles shook with such violence that it felt like she could shake apart.

"Th-they have s-some m-more in the m-med tent," Thuy stuttered. "I c-could g-go get them for you."

Suddenly, O'Brian stopped his pacing and the bloody knife was right up next to her eye, its point so close that it was a red blur. He laughed, a strange connection of running letters: "Ah-ah-ah-ah-ah! You would like that. You say that you'll get some more morphine but then you'll run. I know it."

"I could go get some for you, sir," the other lieutenant said. "I can zip over to the med tent and I'll be back in a jiffy."

"A jiffy? I hate that word." O'Brian stood, looking at the lieutenant closely, his dark eyes narrowed, a gleam of light shining off his bald head. "I don't think so. I don't think so at all. Who are you?"

"Lieutenant David Schmidt. I'm with the…" Schmidt's tongue froze as the colonel brought the knife right up to his belly and poked him with it.

There was a queer light in O'Brian's eyes as he said: "I don't know any Lieutenant Schmidt. What about you guys? Do you know any Schmidts?" The others in the tent shook their heads. "That's what I thought. You came with her didn't you? You all came together. You're all in league…and that other lieutenant, he is as well."

O'Brian pressed the knife deeper, almost cutting through the young man's shirt. Schmidt sucked in a breath. "You need to be punished as well," O'Brian said and now the point dimpled the man's flesh. "But not yet. We'll do it all at once. We'll *cleanse* the camp of you and your type. Watch him," O'Brian barked and then stormed out of the tent, pausing only long enough to pick up a discarded M4.

The other infected soldiers came forward with their guns pointed, all save one who came up behind the lieutenant and thudded the butt of his weapon square into the back of Schmidt's head. He crumpled to the dirt floor of the tent, moaning loudly enough to be heard through the thin canvas.

"Shut up," hissed one of the men. "Shut up right now or else." He followed up the threat by demonstrating the "or else" with a swift kick to the face. This unnecessary violence sparked more and soon all five of them were stomping the lieutenant into a bloody mess.

Her guts churning in fear, Thuy retreated to the corner of the tent and huddled there in a ball, desperate not to appear threatening in any manner. In fact, she tried to appear like nothing more than a bundle of clothes. Her green-on-green camouflage worked so well that the infected, with their limited vision, didn't see her at first glance.

Still, it took all of two seconds to find her and then they advanced with murder in their blackened eyes and that was when a gunshot rang out, cutting through the air. Lieutenant Colonel O'Brian had just caught up with the lieutenant.

"He's nothing but a traitor, and a deserter, and a spy," O'Brian mumbled.

The lieutenant stood in front of a group of soldiers and was pointing back when he saw O'Brian, with his rifle up and pointed. "Wait," the lieutenant said. "I was just…" The colonel did not wait; he shot the lieutenant without so much as blinking.

"That man was a deserter and a traitor!" he cried, marching up to the body which now pumped out fine blood into the dirt, wasting it. The colonel shook his bald head to clear the sudden need that had come over him. Some of the soldiers backed away from him—they were going to run!

"No one can leave this camp! Our orders are to stay put and hold the line. Anyone who tries to leave will be considered to have broken the quarantine and will be shot. Is that clear?"

The exhausted and stressed-out soldiers who had witnessed the scene began nodding and mumbling: "Yes, sir." Quite a few of them had been involved in firefights the day before with civilians and all of them knew that the rules of society had changed for the worse. People…and soldiers could be killed almost out of hand.

"Good, now get back to your posts and if you don't know where that is, get out to the line and find a spot." O'Brian watched the men leave, each casting only one glance back.

Normally, the men might have confided in a supervisor or a friend about what they had just seen; however, the group of soldiers were from a mish-mash of different units and they rarely knew anyone around them. What also kept them from saying anything was the fact that they believed the colonel was right, not just within the bounds of military justice, but also morally. They had seen the zombies up close and they knew that drastic measures were the only way to keep the situation in hand.

O'Brian's head was beginning to pound and all he could think about was cleansing the camp—and clean blood. "No, the camp first. We get rid of all the traitors and then we can have something to…" He swallowed loudly, unable to bring himself to say what he truly wanted.

Cleansing the camp wouldn't be easy. All around him in a great circle were men and women, most of whom were likely traitors and spies. Luckily, he could *smell* those loyal to him. The fight the night before had been very close in certain sectors and black blood had pooled, and in some instances, it had run into the camp. Soldiers had tracked the blood here and there and gradually some were becoming infected.

The ones with the spores eating into their brains had a dank, earthy, pungent smell that would have repelled the colonel the day before.

He went around collecting these men—they were the ones hiding from the sun, popping pills, chugging quarts of alcohol or shooting up morphine stolen from the med kits that had been stacked behind the med tent. They were the ones who tried to hide the fact that they were in severe pain. They were the ones who had become paranoid of their fellow soldiers and they were the ones who were quite ready to kill.

The colonel found nearly a hundred. He pulled them off the line and sent them to loiter in what shade they could find outside of the command post. By the time he made it back himself, his head was thumping hard and the world had begun to swim. The dark in the tent helped a great deal although he was confused by the two bodies lying in pools of blood. For some minutes he stared until he recalled he had killed the captain with a knife… and hadn't there been a girl with him?

Suddenly remembering the traitorous girl, he pulled his gun up and stared about him, unable to find her. "Where is the traitress?" he asked the men he had left behind, just then noticing that they were a bloody lot and the blood was very fresh.

3—Newark, New Jersey

Donald Biggs had long before closed the blinds and pulled the curtains closed. When that still let in too much light, he pinned blankets over his windows and placed towels at the cracks of the doors. An hour later, after downing an entire bottle of aspirin, he retreated to his basement and screamed into a pillow until his liver shut down and he slipped into a coma.

For anyone not under the effects of the Com-cells, the coma would have lasted a few days before an inevitable death. For Donald, the coma lasted long enough to turn his brain utterly black and to repair his liver just enough for it to function—not that he would need it much anymore. The Com-cells would take care of everything. They would keep him alive just so long as most of his brain remained intact.

The moment he woke he found himself voraciously hungry.

Due to some dormant memory, one of very few left to him, Donald stomped upstairs to his kitchen and pulled open the refrigerator door. "Fuh!" he cried as the light burned into his retinas. He wanted to puke and slam the door shut; however the hunger couldn't be denied and so he squinted in where the "food" had always been kept. The only thing that appealed to him was the raw hamburger and even that tasted like plastic in his mouth. He spat it out onto his kitchen floor.

He didn't know exactly what he wanted, but he knew he *needed* something warm, something juicy. His endless hunger drove him, cringing out into the sunlight, where his eyes burned and his brain thumped in such a manner that he felt mad and he pulled at his thinning hair until it came out in quickly forgotten clumps.

The hunger was too great to worry about hair. Donald stumbled to his neighbor's house, a person, whose name he could not remember although he had talked to her every day for the last three years. All he knew was that the shade next to her house was good. Without the sun beating into him, he could see better but what he saw wasn't right.

The street in front of his house was empty. There were the usual number of cars parked, bumper to bumper and a couple of bikes fallen on their sides like dead horses, but there wasn't anything to eat. Nothing moved, not even a stray cat.

His mind was almost ninety-five percent zombiefied by then and that meant there was practically nothing going on between his ears. He craved hot, human blood but didn't know it…not until the first wave of twelve C17s cruised overhead.

They had been ordered to fly far lower than usual in order to awe the public and at two thousand feet, their four Pratt & Whitney F117-PW-100 turbofan engines were loud enough to shake windows in their frames and to set off a few of the more sensitive car alarms.

Just as the president had hoped, people began peering through windows, and many stepped out of their homes to get a better look. Most cheered at the planes in their long lines soaring overhead; some even cried.

Mary Gainor didn't cheer, but she did scream. At the first rumble, she went to her living room window, contorting her body to see the planes. When all she could catch was a quick glimpse of grey fleeting by, she hurried out onto her front lawn and stared up, completely unaware that Donald Biggs, her next door neighbor had suddenly realized what he was hungry for.

The desire flared up in him, over-powering the hate and the pain. He even moaned with greedy lust, causing Mary to jump.

"Donald? Is that…what's with your eyes?"

Of course he couldn't answer and Mary really didn't need an answer. She knew in an instant. She spun around and raced for her open door, screaming: "Run Caleb!"

Her six-year old son ran, but not knowing which way to run or even why he was running, he ran to his mother, colliding with her right at the threshold of the front door. They both went down in a jumble of arms and legs and panicked shrieks. Donald was on them in a flash and for a second his fouled brain and dimmed eyes couldn't understand what exactly he was seeing in the frantically squirming mass of limbs.

That confusion only lasted for a second, and then he bit into a soft leg, Caleb's. The boy screamed, a high note that could be heard up and down the block even over the sound of planes flying by.

The sound energized Mary, all hundred and twenty-eight pounds of her. She went nuts on Donald, kicking and punching and scratching with the adrenaline-fueled strength of a man twice her size. She was able to yank her bleeding son out of his grip and race for the back door, slamming it in his face.

Donald was truly gone by this point. The zombie that had taken over his somewhat soft body had berserker strength and he tore through the cheap door in seconds and, still mad for blood, chased after Mary.

She ran around to the front, carrying her six-year old, a boy half her size. He was awkward in her arms and grew quickly heavy. She couldn't run fast, but she didn't need to. Neighbors had heard the screams and the commotion. Like villagers out of olden days they came in a swarm, carrying any weapon they could get their hands on. The first three men had clubbing instruments: two had bats and the third had his favorite golf club: an eight-iron.

They saw what Donald had become and didn't hesitate to attack. Donald came on, dumb as a bag of nails, thinking only of all the blood, and was knocked back and forth like a human piñata. Unlike a piñata it wasn't candy that came out of him, but Com-cells. Along with the blood that poured from his wounds, the disease was sprayed liberally around.

It took a dozen hearty whacks before he went down and it took another dozen before he ceased to be an overt threat. By that time the entire block had come out to either help or to watch. Many of them were infected as they shook hands with the men who were flush with victory, or who tried to soothe Caleb, whose chest was still hitching, or who helped Mary who had a lump on the side of the head and felt weak in the knees.

"We should call the authorities," someone said.

"We should get away from that body," another added. "It's infected." The crowd moved away, many of them suddenly looking at their hands and arms. They dispersed seconds later, each person hurrying home to wash. A few saved themselves by stripping completely and scrubbing themselves head to toe with bleach.

However, most of them worried only about their hands and face. Not including Mary and Caleb, sixteen people were directly infected by Donald's blood. Another eight were infected by loved ones who tracked blood and spores into their homes on their shoes.

No one knew what to do about Donald. The police were called but the response time was quoted at nine hours and so his corpse just lay in Mary's yard. Dogs came to sniff it over and when they trotted away, they too carried the diseased blood on their paws or snouts so that at least four more people were infected when these dogs eventually went back to their homes.

Mary and Caleb rushed to the nearest hospital and within eight seconds they had infected a friendly paramedic who hurried up with a wheelchair as he saw Mary struggling with her son. One little touch of an elbow was all it took for the Comcells to transfer from one victim to another.

The paramedic dutifully washed his hands but not his elbow. Donald Biggs had infected thirty-one people and within three hours, those thirty-one people would infect two thousand, and, just that simply, that is how Newark became the second American city to fall.

Chapter 9

1—8:29 a.m.
The Capitol Building, Hartford, Connecticut

An hour before, a harried and nervous Governor Warner had turned to her assistant Carla and whispered: "Where the hell is General Arnold?" When Carla only shrugged, the governor said through gritted teeth, "Well, go find him."

As always, Carla had turned to her own assistant. "Find the general and maybe put a leash on him. That guy disappears every five seconds."

The assistant to the assistant to the governor, Charlotte Abato scurried from the room, paused just outside the door to take off the high-heeled shoes, which had been blistering her feet since three-thirty in the morning, and jogged away to scour the building, looking for a man who was already miles away.

At the same time, Jaimee Lynn Burke was just getting hungry once more. It had been an hour since her pack of fanged children had waylaid a very tired Mindy Copeland as she walked slowly home, stooped with exhaustion, after a very long night of hauling downed trees around.

Mindy could honestly say she had done her part in helping to fortify the wall that ringed Hartford, and she had never felt so tired in her life. Her hands were raw and her muscles were numb and weak. She was so weary that it felt as though she were sleepwalking home. In fact, she had her eyes closed for good stretches of sidewalk. She was easy pickings for the pack that closed in from all sides.

Jaimee Lynn let Mindy get close before she leapt out from behind a juniper bush and rushed at her. Then the other children raced forward, like jackals. They brought Mindy down and feasted.

Mindy was still bleating and struggling weakly under the mass of children when an old man named Herman Green came rushing out of the house they were fighting in front of, waving a broom and yelling: "Shoo! Shoo! Leave her alone!"

Three of the zombie children went for him. He squawked very much like a chicken, turned on his heel and made for his front door. The children dragged him down right on his own stoop. He was bitten a half-dozen times before his ancient wife took up the broom in her knobby, blue-veined hands and began screaming and jabbing it at the three children with the business end of the it.

Seeing this wrinkled and grey being who smelled of urine and Ben-gay brought them up short, giving the old man and his wife enough time to scramble inside and slam the door. Mindy convulsed and died just as the old couple escaped out the back door and ran down the alley behind their house.

Gasping for breath, their sprint turned into a shambling walk as they leaned on each other. They made it three blocks before each asked the other where they were going. "I dunno where we should go," Mr. Green said. "To the police?"

"I think we should get you to a hospital," Mrs. Green answered, eyeing his bleeding back. She even touched the black smears around the wounds, not understanding their significance.

"For these scratches? Bah! I've had worse. I was in Korea for seventeen months and that was before we ever heard of post-traumatic stress dis…"

She had heard this a thousand times before and waved him to hush. "The police all lit out of town yesterday. You know that just the same as I do. Maybe we should go talk to Ruth over at the Sun-Rise. Her son works for the state and it's not all that far." For years, Ruth Lundy had gone on about her son even more than Mrs. Green's husband talked about the war and that was saying something.

It wasn't far at all, one block east and two more blocks "up," as Mrs. Green thought of north. At the assisted living facility they were among friends, who were all quite astounded by news of the attack and who fretted over the pair. In their devoted attention they managed to spread the Com-cells throughout the population of the facility.

As none of the staff had shown up for work, Ruth Lundy took charge. The police were called, but that was a bust. Then the fire department and even the ambulance—no one would even pick up their phones.

"Then I will do what has to be done," Ruth said. "My son works for the *state*, you know." She went to fetch her coat and hat. Even with the help of her walker, she moved at a glacial pace and her driving was a frightening thing since her reaction time equaled that of a sloth.

An hour slipped past by the time Ruth arrived at the capitol building and it was another ten minutes before she could make it up the stairs and then came a thirty minute wait while her son was found and produced. In that time, she developed a headache that would not quit. It felt like her head was about to crack wide open and at the same time her eyesight grew dimmer and dimmer.

She thought she was dying of a stroke. Finally, when she couldn't see or even stand, her son Willard Lundy, assistant state comptroller, came hurrying through the near-empty lobby.

"Oh, Ma, what are you doing out of the home?" As always, he felt a touch of embarrassment. She escaped the home at least once a month to inform him of one "disaster" after another: a stopped toilet, squirrels on the power lines, loose girls in halter tops.

"There are zombies in Hartford," she said clear as day. "Abigail Green's husband was attacked about two, um…" she tried to make out her watch, but it was only a glint of metal peeking out of a dark background. "It's been about two hours now." It was actually two and a half at that point and Mr. Green was just lurching out the front door of the Sun-Rise facility with a great hunger working in him for some blood, fresh and hot.

Unaware of this, Willard guessed that his mother had finally gone off the deep end of senility and was just about to humor her, when the guard—Barry something, Willard could never remember his name—suddenly rushed over. "You say there was an attack? Where?"

"Do you mind?" Willard asked, giving him a haughty look. "Don't give in to her. She'll just draw it out. Ma, seriously, you need to go back to the home. I'll visit this weekend. I promise."

"They were attacked right smack dab on their front stoop," Ruth said. "They live off of George Street, just before you get to Cromwell. There used to be a drive-in just down the street from them."

The guard stepped back, perplexed, his eyes shifting to the floor as he pictured how close George Street was. It was far too close in his book and it didn't jibe with what he'd been told by General Arnold a few hours before. "Wait here," he said, before hurrying back to his desk. He was in the process of ringing the general when the assistant to the assistant to the governor, Charlotte Abato, came up barefoot, breathless and looking nervous.

"Hey, excuse me have you seen General Arnold? The governor is looking for him and I can't find him anywhere. I've checked his office twice and the kitchen and all of the offices and everywhere. And he's not answering any number we have listed for him."

"Well, I'm not supposed to say, but…" The guard shot his eyes left and right and leaned in close. "He is supposed to be taking care of the zombie issue here in the city, but I just heard from that lady, there was one spotted at George and Cromwell."

Charlotte looked over at Ruth Lundy and then back at the guard and said: "Huh? What zombie problem? Are you saying there are zombies *in* the city?"

"Yes, there are, but the general said that it was being taken care of and…you didn't know? Really? But you're with the governor's staff, right? He made it seem like you guys all knew."

A sudden numbness began to spread to her limbs; she felt as though she were bodiless and floating. So far the zombies had been a distant threat and there were soldiers and cops between her and them. That was how she'd been able to deal with the insanity of it all. But now…

"The governor doesn't know. No one knows. H-how many zombies are we talking about?"

"I dunno. The general acted as though there were only a few and that it was a manageable number, but now we have this lady. My guess is that it's not many or we would have seen them or people would have called."

People had been calling by the hundreds and not just about zombie sightings. They called about power outages, food supplies, a fire at the hospital, criminals looting empty shops and all sorts of things. The problem: there was only one person answering phones in the capitol building. The normal operators had left the night before and hadn't come back, and probably wouldn't, either.

"Let's ask her what she saw," Charlotte suggested. "Maybe it was nothing." Although Willard Lundy tried to stop them, Charlotte and the front desk guard questioned Ruth. It took five minutes of shifting blather for her to get to the nub: a "pack" of children with black eyes had killed and eaten an unknown woman and then had gone after a man named Mr. Green who had just managed to escape.

"There was another pack of them at Quaker and Fern a few hours ago," the guard said. "Do you think they're the same zombies?"

Charlotte shrugged. "Maybe, I guess, but does it matter? There are zombies here, in Hartford! That...that shouldn't be possible. And, and what's it mean? How are they getting past the wall?"

The guard could only shake his head, while next to them, a dawning look of understanding finally stole over Willard's face. "There really are zombies, here? In Hartford?" The guard bobbed his head and Charlotte said that chances are there were. "Then we have to get out of here," Willard cried, all in a panic. He reached for his mother's hand.

"Don't touch!" Ruth snarled, raking him with her brittle claws and drawing blood. "You didn't believe me. You thought I was lying. You thought I was just someone you could stick in a home and forget about. So fuck you! Fuck you, Willy, you little shit-stain!"

Willard stepped back quickly as if his mother were a rabid terrier. The thought of zombies in Hartford had him terrified, but now his heart felt as though it had turned to cold brass. His mother had never spoken to him like that before and her eyes had never looked so dark. "D-did you get bit by one of them, Mother?"

"Did you get bit by one of them?" she mimicked, a nasty glare to her darkening eyes. "No, of course not, you putz. Do I look like I've been bit?"

"No, of course not." Willard stepped further back, planting a greasy smile on his politician's face. He shifted his eyes to Charlotte and said out of the corner of his mouth, "She's not normally like this. She's different."

Now, both the guard and Charlotte stepped back from the old woman whose face had begun to pucker. Charlotte nudged the guard. "You need to get her out of the building right now."

"Me? It's his mother."

"I don't care which one of you does it. Get her out of this building right this minute. I-I have to go talk to the governor." She turned and sped for the elevators, her bare feet slapping. Once she stepped inside the elevator car, she had second thoughts. The walls were so close and the air was still and heavy and very much suspect.

What if one of them had been in here? she wondered. The scuttlebutt had it that the disease was airborne. If a "near" zombie had been in the elevator, it might have coughed and contaminated it, or it might have touched one of the buttons. She pulled her hand in to her chest and slipped out of the confining space before the doors could trap her. The stairs would do. She ran up four flights without touching anything with her hands, used the crook of her arm to open the stairwell door and started at a full-on sprint for the governor's office.

The first thing she saw was Carla's glare— Charlotte had been gone for ages in her search for the general. The first thing she heard was: "The planes are inbound with an ETA of thirty-two minutes." This from the Secretary of State, who fancied himself some sort of military expert even though he regularly disparaged the military as a bunch of clumsy, uneducated brutes.

The first thing she said was: "There are zombies in the city!" She practically screamed this and it silenced a room full of officials in a blink.

"What?" Governor Warner asked. She'd been in the process of writing down a list of questions she had for General Arnold, the president and the state's attorney general and now her pen was poised just above a yellow tablet.

Everyone seemed to have frozen. The most comical of all of them was the Commissioner of the Department of Economic and Community Development, who had been about to go to the bathroom. He was caught by the sudden declaration with his wide ass in mid-rise sticking out a foot above his chair.

"There are zombies in the city!" Charlotte repeated in the same strident tone. "We have witnesses. An old folks' home was attacked down on Cromwell. And...and one of *them* might be downstairs in the lobby."

The commissioner plopped his fat ass back down in his chair with a thud, which seemed to trigger everyone to ask questions at exactly the same time. Charlotte was inundated and did her best to answer with her limited understanding of the situation.

Warner didn't trust the "new girl" as she thought of Charlotte, and so she sent Carla to interview Ruth Lundy. Next, she had the Commissioner of the Department of Economic and Community Development call the Sun-Rise Assisted Living Center, the number of which was found readily enough; however no one picked up.

"We can send someone over there," the commissioner suggested. By someone, he meant someone other than himself, of course. The problem was that there were very few "someones" hanging around the capitol building. Normally the place was packed with people, however, on that morning, the halls echoed vacantly and somewhat sinisterly, whenever anyone ventured outside the stuffy office.

"Get over there as fast as you can," Warner ordered the commissioner. At the moment, 99% of all businesses in Connecticut had ceased operations and communities were now fortified cities, making the Commissioner of the Department of Economic and Community Development one of the most useless men in the room.

He began stuttering: "Buh-buh-buh," however the governor waved him quiet with an irritable hand.

"Get down there, now! It's imperative we find out ASAP if there are zombies in the city and if there are, we have to know how many." When he just sat there, his jaw hanging open and his jowls quivering, Warner leapt to her feet and pointed at the door: "Go, damn it!"

He left, his eyes wide and fearful. In his wake the remaining officials were too stunned for their usual self-important blather. Only the governor kept her wits. "We should proceed as if the zombie threat has penetrated the city. What are our options?"

Eyes darted around the expanse of polished cherry wood. Like school children who hadn't studied for a test, no one dared to catch the governor's stern gaze. Eventually the Secretary of State worked up the nerve to say, "If it gets out it might cause a riot, and it'll certainly cause a panic. Maybe we should keep this quiet until we know for certain."

"But we do know," Charlotte declared, coming to stand at the edge of the table. "I saw that old woman. Her eyes weren't rheumy and they were filmy with cataracts. They were dark. Even the whites were dark. And her state of mind was…I don't know, chaotic."

The Secretary of State rolled his eyes. "As dramatic as that sounds, it isn't proof. The old lady might be suffering from Alzheimers. If so, she might have imagined the entire attack. Did you ever think of that? And besides, how does a bunch of brain-dead zombie children get past the wall around the city? I've seen it and I've seen the people on the wall. They're dedicated to protecting their city and what's more, they're fierce about it. I guarantee they haven't let a bunch of stray kids in."

Although Charlotte was cowed by the authoritarian bearing of the secretary, Governor Warner wasn't. "The walls have not been thoroughly inspected. We don't know if there is a hole somewhere along it. Perhaps a drainage pipe that was over-looked or a culvert or something. What we do know is that we have a report of zombies in the city. We can't assume that it's false. And nor can we fly off the handle. So what should our first step be?"

Again silence crept over the room until Linda Plano, the Commissioner of the Department of Health, raised her hand. "I think…I think maybe we should move the seat of government out of Hartford."

Governor Warner looked at her in shock. Linda had always been fearless as a politician and public servant. "You want us to run away? That's your first idea?"

Linda nodded, saying: "We need to preserve some sem-blance of government. You are the governor of the entire state, not the governor of Hartford. If there are zombies in the city, then a new quarantine zone will have to be built around it and everyone will be stuck here. You can't be stuck. Your role is too important."

Heads nodded all around the table. Everyone there expected to be able to leave with the governor, abandoning a city of a quarter of a million people to a horrible fate. Warner's first incli-nation was to run far away and not look back, however she hadn't been elected to run at the first sign of trouble.

But to stay meant what? Would they barricade themselves inside the capitol building and try to coordinate things while the city went to crap around them? That was no kind of plan.

She didn't know what to do and was saved from making a decision by the sudden appearance of her assistant Carla who rushed in breathless, pale and shaking.

"That lady downstairs is one of them. She is getting meaner and meaner and her eyes…they're dark and all gunked up."

The governor felt her heart skip a beat at the news. "And what about General Arnold? Has anyone heard anything from him?"

Carla nodded briefly. "The guard told me he left hours ago, supposedly to deal with the zombies. He told the guard that we already knew about them, but he never said anything to me or Charlotte, I swear."

"He's run away," the governor said, breathlessly. She suddenly felt the need to run screaming from the building, herself. She bit down on the feeling and forced herself to do her job. "And the lady? Is she dangerous? I mean…is she contagious? Should she be killed?" Carla nodded without looking up.

The room grew dead quiet as everyone stared at the governor. It was all on her. "That's…that's, I don't know. I guess we kill the woman, I think."

The Secretary of State's lip curled. "You think? I'm sorry Christine but you don't get to make wishy-washy statements. You have to act and you have to act decisively. That's what real leadership is."

"You don't need to remind me, Harry. I know what it means to be a leader." She took a breath, steeling herself. "The lady should be…has to be killed and her body burned. And…and we will move the seat of government to New London. We'll have the mayor run things here. He's to have full leeway in dealing with the infected people. Carla, go and let him know."

"And what about the paratroopers?" the Secretary of State asked. "They can't land where they're supposed to or they'll be behind the lines the moment they touch down, which is supposed to be in twenty-two minutes."

"We'll warn them off. Charlotte, get the president on the phone."

2—The White House Washington D.C.

Charlotte, the assistant to the assistant, was slow in finding the number and four minutes were wasted right there. It took another three minutes to get connected to the president and five more to instill in the man the urgency of the situation, leaving him more than enough time to make a command decision and call off the jump or at least postpone it—the C17s had plenty of fuel and could have flown immense circles around Connecticut for another hour if needed.

The first problem: the president was not command decision material. He liked making decisions only after intensive polling and after focus groups had given their reactions. In his mind, difficult decisions were best put off for another day and another administration.

The second problem: no one seemed to know where Marty Aleman was. The president had never made a decision without Marty's help.

"Let me call you back, Christine. We, uh I mean, I will figure things out and, uh, we'll get back to you."

"Get back? Sir, you don't understand…"

He hung up on her and stared frantically around the Situation Room at the twenty-four men and women seated in high-back leather chairs. The more important of them, his cabinet secretaries as well as the Joint Chiefs of Staff in their finery sat at the long table. The less important of them, such as the vice president, who was texting one of his six mistresses, sat in the smaller chairs that lined the walls.

None of them could be trusted.

Marty had instilled that into the president from day one. They were all politicians, which meant that they were all practiced liars. "Where's Marty? I need him." No one knew. His phone was called and his office checked. As the minutes ticked away, the president had aides running around screaming his name, while at the table sat military officers who would have unanimously told him to postpone the drop.

The first planes were flying over Connecticut by the time Marty was found talking to a New York Times reporter who was being given an exclusive, "inside scoop" on the planned paratroop landings.

Right away, Marty knew that trouble was brewing when he bustled into the Situation Room. He saw it in the president's fearful eyes. "What is it?"

"There are zombies in Hartford!" the president cried, sounding like a child declaring to his parents that there was a monster in the closet. "What do we do?"

Marty's eyes went directly to the news feed playing on the seventy-two inch flatscreen. CNN, with Marty's urging, had managed to convince a dozen local Hartford camera crew to brave leaving the city in order to capture the historic landings live. The crews were just picking up the first of the planes, mere grey dots, looking like distant birds.

Then, in disbelief, he looked at the large screen which sat on the wall opposite the president which showed a large map of Connecticut with the drop zones marked in red and the new perimeter of the Quarantine Zone marked in a friendly blue. It was the same map that had been released to every news outlet in the country. Hartford, with its quarter of a million inhabitants, was clearly visible fifteen or so miles on the wrong side of that friendly blue line. Marty had chosen the blue personally for its calming effect

In his heart, he knew they had to abort the jump; however he saw that they would never be able to stop the lead planes. They would end up with a few planes dropping their loads on camera and then the country would watch live as the rest of the planes peeled away. It would be a fiasco and instead of instilling awe, it would demonstrate that the federal government was as incompetent as the state governments.

Public confidence in the president's ability to stop the zombies would utterly tank, which would lead to his poll numbers tanking as well. This would lead to an increase in looting and murder throughout the country, which would mean more instability…

General Heider held up a phone. "I have General Phillips, the Eighteenth Airborne Corps commander on the line. I'm giving him orders to abort the mission."

"No!" Marty snapped. "Don't. The mission is still a go. We'll just have to reshape it. Tell him to carry on."

Heider's mouth fell open and he pointed at the map with the phone. "They're going to drop west of Hartford. That's what those red circles mean. You understand that they'll be dropping into an area that is already infected?" He asked this of the president, who dutifully turned to Marty.

"Of course the president knows this, but it's too late to stop the lead elements anyway, and we don't know the extent of the issue in Hartford. It might not be that bad."

"You'll be trapping an entire division behind the lines," Heider growled.

Marty steepled his fingers beneath his chin in a show of complete calm. He had never been one for the military because they were so terribly inflexible. "It's not that difficult to understand. The *entire* country is depending on this one operation. If it fails, people will lose faith in their government. There will be mass riots, mass looting and mass death. And do you think we'll be able to stop it once it starts?"

Heider's only answer was a twitch of his shoulder. Marty answered his own question: "No, we won't, because each state will be too busy protecting their borders against zombies and refugees. Mass transit will shut down, highways will shut down, and basic services will shut down. All that corn in Iowa will just rot, because the oil wells in Texas won't be running, because the needed parts to keep them running will be sitting in a boat at a peer in Long Beach, because some schmo is at home taking care of granny, because the services for her are no longer being provided. Do you see how all of this intertwines?"

Sufficiently cowed, Heider nodded, making Marty smile his cold politician's smile. "I want you to trust me, General. We won't forget about your boys. We'll extract them when we have a handle on things and in the meantime, we'll keep them supplied, warm, happy and fed."

Marty had no idea how that would happen, exactly. He figured that the details would fill themselves in, not realizing that things were already at the breaking point in logistical terms.

"Now that we're all in agreement, General, we'll need another division to take the place of the 82nd. If you could scare one up, that would be great."

Chapter 10

1—8:45 a.m.
The Connecticut Bubble

"Find her!" Colonel O'Brian ordered, his eyes like two blazing hunks of coal in his pale face. "Find her and kill her." Thuy had straight up vanished from the tent almost sending him over the edge—and there was definitely a looming edge. It sat like a cliff in his mind. Down in the gorge was black madness and blood feasts. He could feel that edge coming closer and closer.

Two men braved the pain of the sun to search for Thuy, while the rest grew edgy and restless. Nearby, a hundred others with eyes growing darker by the minute, lolled around the command tent, glaring at everyone who came by.

Thuy had managed to escape the tent easily enough. When the gunshots had rung out and the men in the tent had rushed to the door, she had pulled up a steel peg and slithered out from beneath the canvas. Without hesitation, she had rushed to the comm tent where she found Courtney Shaw, two of her police dispatchers, PFC Cindy Austin, and Jerome Evermore, nervously waiting.

"What the hell happened?" Jerome demanded. "The colonel just shot somebody for deserting or trying to leave the lines."

"He also k-killed a captain in cold blood, right in front of me," Thuy answered, her voice breaking. She was shaking all over and couldn't seem to catch her breath properly though she had barely run forty yards. "They're infected. Everyone in that tent was infected. And if they're infected there has to be others who are as well."

Courtney took a step back. "How do we know you aren't?" Now everyone stepped back.

"You don't know, and neither do I. For all we know everyone in this camp is infected. That being said, I do not have any of the symptoms: no headache, no vision loss, no impaired faculties and no alteration in mood or personality. We should keep an eye on each other, careful to watch for those signs."

"What we really have to do is get out of here," Jerome said, going to the door and peeking out. "We have to find an officer who isn't infected and warn them. Hopefully they'll be..." Just then the first of the C17s could be heard approaching in a dull thrum that grew to become maddening in its intensity. It meant that they were minutes away from being trapped once more within the Quarantine Zone.

Thuy went to the door and gaped as the first plane grew from a tiny grey spec into something far more impressive in size. She had to tear her eyes away and focus on a more immediate problem: the leering, ill-tempered soldiers who were far too close to the comm tent.

"O'Brian's going to start a war," she said under her breath. She turned from the door to address the others. "If we have any chance to escape, it has to be very soon. It'll take the paratroopers some time to organize a line and we have to be through it with as many clean individuals as possible. I can't go out there to round them up. I'm too recognizable. Since you two, Mr. Evermore and you, Ms. Austin, are soldiers, you will be able to blend in. Find people who are clear-headed, explain the situation, and move on. They'll either join or they won't and we don't have time to beg. Send them to the west side of the perimeter. There's a little dell where you can't be seen from the rest of the camp. Any questions?"

There weren't any and after PFC Austin took her clothes back from Thuy, the two slipped through the door of the tent and walked directly away from where gangs of angry and infected soldiers sneered up at the planes flying by. With their attention diverted, it was a perfect time for Thuy and the others to leave the tent and hurry to the meeting place, but just as she stepped out, she saw two men leave the command tent, they cringed at the sun, lifting bloody hands to shield their dark eyes.

Thuy knew them in an instant. They had been part of the pack that had beaten the innocent lieutenant to death.

Immediately, she ducked back through the door, only to run straight into Courtney who was trying to struggle a PRC-155 Manpack radio onto her back. For two agonizing seconds the two were framed in the doorway and Thuy's long, silken black hair couldn't be missed. The two men strode across the intervening forty yards with murder in their hearts. Pulling back the door, they charged in, only to come up short. Save for some radio equipment, the tent was empty.

"What the fuck?" one cursed, as he squinted into the corners of the tent. "I saw her. I swear I did."

"She's like a Chinese witch," the other replied.

Thuy, Courtney and the two dispatchers had crawled out from beneath the back edge of the tent and were now hiding behind a Humvee—there was almost nowhere else to hide. The top of the hill was virtually bald. Save for the tents and the few Humvees, there were only six trees and a few low shrubs and it was too far to the western portion of the perimeter to run without being seen.

All they could do was hide behind the Humvee and hope that the two men would turn and look away for a minute. It didn't happen. They went in circles, growing ever angrier as the sun beat down and the planes roared above. Five precious minutes went by before one of them thought to ask the people around the command tent if they had seen the "Chinese" girl.

Fingers pointed right at the Humvee. One of the dispatchers began cursing in a high, whiny voice. The other, April Lopez, shoved Thuy and hissed: "Don't hide with us. They're only after you."

It was harsh but true, and Thuy might have stepped out from behind the Humvee were it not for a blue-tinted knife the size of Thuy's forearm that one of the men held. The look in his eyes suggested he was dying to stick it in someone.

Thuy was *almost* paralyzed with fright. With tiny steps, she edged to the side of the Humvee and slowly put her hands in the air.

Courtney grabbed her and hissed: "Dr. Lee, no. Don't do this."

"I have to. April's right." She wished there was another way, but they were moments from all of them being discovered. They had no weapons or any way to fight, and Thuy knew that she was too slow to outrun soldiers as fit as these. After taking a deep, shaky breath, she stepped out from behind the Humvee. "I'm right here. I surrender."

The man with the knife wore a wolf's grin as he started forward. He had only taken three steps when suddenly there was a scream from across the camp. It was a woman's scream of pure terror that caused everyone to turn. It would have been a perfect time to run, but Thuy was too stunned.

PFC Cindy Austin was being dragged into the center of the camp by her mop of brown hair. She could barely keep upright as a beefy soldier whose eyes were scarily dark hauled her right up to the command tent. "Colonel! Colonel!" he bellowed. "You were fucking right. There are traitors among us and they are planning to take over. This bitch tried to recruit me. She tried to get me to turn against us."

Colonel O'Brian stepped out of his tent; there were smears of black gunk mixed with blood on his bald head. It looked as though he'd been trying to claw his own head open. "A traitor? Why is she still alive?" He had a Beretta stuffed into the waist of his pants. He took it out and shot Cindy in the stomach.

Thuy felt like the bullet had hit her instead of Cindy. "Oh, God!" she said, as Cindy grunted and staggered.

Cindy stood for only a moment before dropping to her knees, clutching herself, her face molded in a rictus of fear and pain, her blood, red and rich, bubbling up between her fingers. The sight of it caused many of the black-eyed soldiers to leer at her hungrily. She began to blubber in fear and agony.

The strength in Thuy's legs gave out and she had to hold onto the hood of the Humvee to keep from falling over. She knew she'd be next. They would drag her out in front of everyone and shoot a huge hole in her guts. It would hurt in a way she had never been hurt before and yet, she knew she wouldn't die, not right away. Gut-shots were a slow death. In fact, she'd still be in the process of dying when the Com-cells finally took over the hateful soldiers completely, and then she'd be eaten alive with no way to run or fight.

Picturing herself lying in the bloody dirt like that, helpless and praying to die, crushed her spirit and sapped the remains of her courage right out of her. Just like Cindy, she cried. Her fear was an avalanche inside of her and she quivered uncontrollably.

The colonel turned and saw her standing there. His look was pure evil. "Oh, please, no," she whispered, as her bladder let go in a hot rush.

2—New York City

Lieutenant General Phillips, commander of the Eighteenth Airborne Corps stepped off the Gulf Stream G650, pausing to squint through the morning glare at the empty airport. Nothing moved. No planes spinning up their engines preparing for take-off, no baggage handlers zipping their carts here and there, no self-important TSA security guards lazing about looking no more effective than a like number of mall cops.

The only plane in sight was the Gulf Stream, and the only people were the general's staff, who looked about equally unnerved.

The quiet in the air was honestly haunting.

Every flight in and out of the northeast had been cancelled. Although New York City was officially free of the "Black-eyed Plague" as some people had begun calling it, no one put a whole lot of trust in what was "official" and what wasn't. And it wasn't just the northeast. Flights as far away as Dallas were taking off at fifteen percent capacity, and even in California most were only half-booked.

Phillips hadn't seen the sky so empty since 9/11 and that had been a walk in the park compared to what was happening now.

The sky was actually too empty. "Where the hell's my chopper?" he groused.

His adjunct, a lieutenant colonel, immediately made a call and a minute later said: "They're going to be a little late, sir. Sorry, but they're civilian contractors."

The general grunted and squinted up at the sky again. It wasn't surprising that they were going to be using civilian helicopters since he had spent half the night setting up the single largest air assault operation in history.

Without regard to any other factor, the president had demanded that the entire 101st Airborne Division be air-lifted in one tremendous move of a thousand miles. To make their refueling problems even greater, the helicopters were to fly in formation, making sure that all eight hundred helicopters passed over the largest of the east coast cities on the way. The president seemed either unaware, or maybe he just didn't care that Phillips' fuel situation was already, for want of a better word: broken.

Finding, allocating, and positioning the fuel took seven men, ten hour's worth of work. As well, it had taken eleven men and thirteen hours to gather the prerequisite number of Blackhawk helicopters necessary for such a massive and ridiculous operation. Basically, there wasn't a green helicopter east of the Rockies that wasn't being used.

And this was on top of the 82nd's parachute drop. Again, the logistics of dropping ten-thousand men on a dozen different

LZs in the space of half an hour was mind-boggling. To start with, there weren't enough parachutes packed and ready to go. All through the night, the chute riggers worked until their fingers bled and their eyes burned. On top of that, Phillips had to make sure there were enough C17s, and enough fuel, and enough ammo, and enough food, and enough of everything—all gathered, all at once.

Phillips hadn't slept in two days. He dug both fists into the small of his back, grimacing as his vertebrae cracked in a long string of snaps. Then, as he had for the tenth time that morning, he checked a secured online app for the status of his fuel reserves.

The projections were way off and not in a good way. He was fourteen percent over the worst estimates, which wasn't a surprise. There was absolutely zero efficiency in either of the two mega operations. As an example, the C17s had circled Pope Field for an hour in order to perfect formations that no one had practiced since World War 2, and the Blackhawks frequently came in to Fort Campbell with zip in their tanks.

For the president, it was all about optics. For General Phillips his job had become all about logistics, which to him was the very height of depressing.

Gone were the days when a general was a tactician first, a strategist second and a worrier over bread and bullets a distant third. General MacArthur's landing at Inchon had been the last time a general had really influenced the outcome of an American war with tactical brilliance.

As overall commander, Phillips' job was actually quite dull. It consisted of hours of paperwork, hours of tracking down snags in the planned logistics, and hours of finding the right people to yell at in order to get things moving again.

Phillips had never before complained about how monotonous and boring it all was, but he complained now. In his view, "this zombie business" was bad news. It was a guaranteed career killer. Secretly, he thought that General Collins had lucked out by dying on the field of battle with a gun in his hands. Had he lived, his life would have been hell.

The same hell that Phillips could look forward to.

There would be no glory in a victory, there'd be no parades and there sure as shit was not going to be any seven-figure book deals to make retiring easier. There would be congressional hearings and lawsuits and endless Monday morning quarterbacking by everyone and their mother about how they could have fought a vast and sprawling zombie horde better than a professional.

To make matters worse, Phillips had to deal with the politicians. He hated this facet of the job more than anything. Despite being the Commander in Chief, the president was the worst of a bad lot. He had no idea how the military operated. On paper there existed some eleven hundred military Blackhawks and the president figured that it wouldn't be too difficult to get a bunch of pilots to fly the helicopters to Fort Campbell, pick up eleven men and go.

He had no idea that what he described would normally take weeks of planning.

"Here they come," his adjunct said, pointing skyward. Five helicopters whup-whup-whupped into sight. They were an embarrassing hodgepodge of traffic copters. The general sighed; he would be traveling in Channel 7's *Eye In The Sky!*

The five landed and Phillips had just started forward when his adjunct grabbed his shoulder and handed over a phone. "Excuse me, sir? It's General Heider of the Joint Chiefs."

"What the…" Phillips growled under his breath as he took the phone. He tried, and failed, to put a smile into his voice as he said, louder: "What can I do for you, sir."

"Sorry to do this to you, Steve, but I'm going to need you to come back to Washington as soon as possible."

Back to Washington? Phillips thought, *What the fuck?*

Hoping that he had heard Heider wrong, he trotted away from the copters and yelled into the phone: "Say again? Did you say come back? Sir, I have a parachute jump that's happening any minute and an air assault operation that is already twenty-five minutes behind schedule."

"Sorry, Steve. I really need to talk to you in person. There's going to be a slight change in plans."

That was a lie that Phillips saw right through. A slight change of plans could be discussed over the phone. A ridiculous change of plans, one that was likely going to be stupid as well as dangerous, was the type that had to be done in person.

Of course, I could be getting replaced, Phillips thought to himself. The idea had a lot of appeal. "I'll get my team back on the jet in no time."

"All I need is you. Leave them in place and have them execute the operations as planned. Nothing should be changed, at least officially."

"And unofficially?" Phillips asked, digging for any hint of what could be coming. The flight back to Washington would take an hour and the briefing probably another hour. He had far too much to do to allow these hours to flit by uselessly. Heider hesitated before answering and Phillips added: "Sir, if there is to be a change of plans it would be a waste of time and resources for me to…"

Heider spat into the phone: "Just get your ass back here!"

3—Hartford, Connecticut

Christine Warner drummed her pink lacquered nails on the table, while her eyes never left the clock spinning its hands in useless circles. The minutes ticking by were irreplaceable.

A total of thirteen people sat around the table, each one with their heads cocked to the side, as if listening for a whisper, but only the steady tapping of Christine's nails marred the tense silence that gripped the room

They waited on two things: the first was the president's return call. It had been ten minutes since he had abruptly hung up on them.

The second thing they waited for was the sound of a gunshot. Nine minutes before, the governor had ordered the summary execution of Ruth Lundy. Speaking the words had been an awful thing for Christine, but then the Secretary of State had slid over a piece of paper. It had been blank.

"Write it down," he had urged in a gentle voice. He had been a prosecuting attorney early in his career, and he had coerced more confessions using that soft voice than he ever had by screaming. He knew that one of humanity's little quirks was that the guilty *wanted* to confess. Whether they whispered it to a fellow criminal when the lights were out for the night and the cell cold or they screamed it with a hundred-watt bulb beating into their faces, they always told someone.

And the truly guilty ones always relaxed once the words were out of their mouths and couldn't be sucked back in. The Secretary of State had seen the signs a hundred times: the sighing, the dropping of the tensed-up shoulders, a gentle bobbing of the head and the little smile that played at the corner of their guilty mouths.

128

The governor wasn't showing these signs. Her crime had not yet been committed. She pushed the paper away, and waited and waited, without looking anyone in the eye. Finally, there came a muffled bang. Only then did her shoulders drop, and she sighed the sigh of the guilty, and her head bobbed as if she were trying to convince herself that she had done the right thing in ordering the death of an old lady who hadn't committed any crime.

The small smile was the one aspect that never showed itself. The likely reason was that, at the sound of the gunshot, she picked up the phone and dialed the White House, making the Secretary of State wonder if she had been afraid that the president would ask what the sound had been, forcing her to lie or confess a second time.

"The president understands your concerns and will call you back, Governor," a snappish male voice intoned as soon as Christine explained who she was.

"He'll have to call my cell, then, because I'm leaving Hartford." She expected this to cause some sort of reaction, but it did not.

The man only said: "Let's have that number."

Christine wanted to go full-on prima donna on this unknown phone answering flunky and scream: *Do you know who I am?* Instead, with everyone watching, she bit the words back, despite their bitterness, and monotoned her number as a robot might.

"It seems the president is a busy man," she told the room, setting the phone in its cradle. "Then again, so are we. If we are to move the seat of government, it has to be done with all possible secrecy or there will be rioting followed by a mass exodus. It has to be avoided at all costs."

A sudden, mass exodus was a nightmare scenario. With the borders closed and every city in the state throwing up walls, where would a quarter of a million people go and who would take them in? How many of them were infected? And how quickly would the infection spread?

If it spread to even ten percent of them it would cause the rest to panic and there would be war. At first it would be city against city as the people of Hartford would flee to nearby Mansfield and demand to be allowed to pass through their hastily constructed walls. When that was denied, what would the people of Hartford do with tens of thousands of zombies bearing down on them?

Christine knew that they would fight to get into Mansfield and she knew the fighting would spread as the infection spread and soon, fleeing to another city wouldn't keep anyone safe and then the three million people of Connecticut would need to go somewhere else, such as Rhode Island, and then when that tiny state was overrun, they would go to Massachusetts because there was nowhere else to go. And they would go, not as beggars asking to be let in, they'd go as little more than a savage, barbarian horde.

It was why the president had to act. He had to change the location of the drop before it was too late.

"To keep the people from suspecting what's happening, we will not be able to take everyone we wish with us. Each of you can bring your immediate family and one or two staff members," Christine stated, bluntly.

Even blunter, the Secretary of State said, "I'm sorry, Governor, but that's too many. We shouldn't even take everyone at this very table." He cast a dark eye at the commissioners of Consumer Protection, Corrections, and Higher Education.

"They're coming with us," Warner replied, coldly. "Not to disparage anyone, but I feel if someone were left behind, they'd talk and the talk would spread. We can't have that."

The Commissioner of Emergency Management raised a hand before she said, "We also have to take into account what we're taking. No one should be allowed to take more than one suitcase. It can't appear as though we are fleeing for good. And we will also need a plausible sounding reason for leaving. I think we should say that we are going to 'inspect' the other cities; their fortifications, and their stores of ammo and food."

Warner nodded to the commissioner. "Those are good ideas, thanks Felicity. I want to leave within the hour so get your family and get back here ASAP." The room emptied in seconds. Carla was about to leave when the governor grabbed her. "Get the mayor over here as quickly and as quietly as you can."

Although the mayor's office was only two blocks away it took twenty minutes for the man to show up, his eyes bleary and red, with his tie hanging loose around his neck looking more like a noose than anything else. When Warner explained what was happening, the man plopped down in one of the chairs, too stunned for words.

"You'll need to keep everyone off the streets and you'll need to set up armed groups within the city limits to hunt down anyone suspected of being a zombie. They should have proper passwords so they can tell each other apart and they should march in formation. It sounds strange, but the infected would never do that."

The mayor had nodded the entire time she spoke, but when she finished, he simply said: "I'm going with you."

Christine was taken aback by the matter of fact way in which he spoke. It was almost as if he didn't think she could do anything to stop him. The Christine Warner of three days before might have been at a loss. This version of her was now a leader more than she was a governor. She had discovered that she wasn't just a pretty face and a fine public speaker. She had found that her soul wasn't a flimsy bit of gossamer. It was a dry strip of leather.

She hadn't blinked as she ordered men into battle, knowing that her forces were soft reservists and beer-bellied guardsman. She had known that many of them were going to their deaths, but she hadn't blinked. And now she had ordered a security guard to put a bullet into an old woman.

"You will stay here," she said, her voice soft and yet full of steel, "and you will defend the city that you were elected to watch over. And if you try to desert your post, I will have you shot. Is that clear?"

Chapter 11

1—9:06 a.m.
The Connecticut Bubble

The echo of the gun was still ringing in the camp when Colonel O'Brian's eyes fell on Thuy. "That's her!" he cried. He was minutes away from going full zombie and the sound of his own voice was like an ice pick in his head. He shuddered and groaned, but did not lose sight of the traitor.

However, he did lose sight of Cindy Austin whimpering and bleeding a puddle of beautiful blood at his feet. The Com-cells caused a narrowing and blurring of vision and he tripped right over her, falling on her without caring in the slightest about her pain.

The Com-cells also caused him to be nearly single-minded in his hate. Cindy didn't even register as a person. Getting to his feet, he trampled her, charging across the open hill, looking to kill. The idea made him giddy…and hungry, and the only thing that would have made the moment better was if she ran. He had a strong desire to chase his prey before devouring her, but Thuy was paralyzed in fear.

Even her trembling was now limited to a vibration that shook her like an old time alarm clock.

O'Brian forgot his gun in his hunger and he rushed up with his mouth stretched wide, but he was brought up short by the stink of her. She smelled of piss. It was bitter and piercing, adding to the pain in his head.

"What is that? What the fuck? Did you piss yourself?" He stopped short, cringing at her in disgust. She had been only dimly aware that she had indeed wet herself. It had been a reaction to intense fear. As a scientist, Thuy understood reactions and she was seeing a strong one in Colonel O'Brian, one that could be exploited.

Her hands went to her wet crotch, felt the damp, coated themselves in it, and then ran themselves across her chest and arms, causing O'Brian to step back with a grimace. "Are you fucking crazy?" he demanded.

She was not crazy. She was thorough and systematic. Her hands went back for a second helping and more smearing— Thuy would rather stink of urine than get eaten alive. Her courage inched up along with the smell and she found her voice. "I-I am not insane, Colonel, I was just hoping to get your attention so that we might speak to each other, perhaps not as equals, since you are an officer and I am not, but as friends maybe. Wouldn't you like that?"

O'Brian seemed almost mesmerized by the soft, slow way in which she spoke. His dark eyes held confusion and he swayed in place. "Huh?" was all he had the wit to say.

"I am talking about a discourse in which we both explain our positions concerning the-the new circumstances in which we find ourselves in. In that way we can internalize and understand those areas in which we disagree." She was blathering, hoping to buy time. Not that she had a real plan in mind, she simply feared the gun in the colonel's hands and was desperate to purchase a few extra seconds of life.

And a few seconds was all she got. The colonel's look of confusion dissipated in a new grimace of pain and up came the gun. He began to pull the trigger, only just then there came a shout from all around them.

Soldiers were pointing into the air toward the east where thousands of paratroopers were jumping out of the C17s into the bright light of morning.

Marty Aleman had been correct in his understanding of the human condition. The green chutes filling the sky made for an awesome spectacle, Captured live on television, it was fast becoming the most watched event in history. Two-hundred and sixty million Americans sat glued to their screens as the paratroopers fell with all the gentleness of autumn leaves and when they began landing, most of America cried and cheered, thinking the worst of the horrible situation was over.

That wasn't true for the men and women trapped in the "Connecticut Bubble." The ones without the gunk in their eyes could see the chutes quite clearly and with even greater clarity they understood what the chutes meant in terms of the Quarantine Zone—they would no longer be protecting it, they would be within it and wouldn't be allowed out.

Soldiers began leaving their posts in droves. Many of the ones who were near the south and east edges of the camp where the forest was close, stole away thinking they could run the five miles between them and the drop zones before the new line was complete. Others ran to the interior of the camp, looking for guidance or permission to start marching east before the trap closed in on them.

Colonel O'Brian was still trying to puzzle out the meaning of the chutes when Thuy took off running. She wasn't particularly fast nor did she attempt to zigzag or otherwise make herself a more difficult target.

The colonel jerked around at her first step and, due to muscle memory, ingrained training, and a new savage instinct to hunt and slay, his Beretta came up even before he knew exactly what was happening.

Then he saw the long black hair like a shadow made of silk and he knew that the traitor was attempting to escape. Even with his dimmed eyesight, it didn't seem possible that the colonel, who was all of twenty-five feet away from Thuy, could miss his target.

Neither could Jerome Evermore. He had come running at the sound of the first gunshot and was just in time to see O'Brian treading over Cindy Austin. He was too far away to see the blood gushing out of the woman and it was a few seconds before he understood what was happening—and that was when the paratroopers began their jump, but unlike everyone else, he hadn't turned to watch. Without thinking about the odds against him, he threw himself down in the dirt and drew a bead on the colonel and although he had never been the best marksman in his unit, at seventy yards with an M68 close combat optics scope, he might as well have been standing right next to the colonel when he pulled the trigger.

Thuy flinched at the sound of the gunshot, her muscles jerking and her skin flaring with an electric current as adrenaline shot into her system. She expected to feel a searing pain, but when it didn't come she figured that the colonel had missed. Hoping to throw off a second shot, she lunged to her right, tripped, and fell into the dirt as suddenly a hundred guns opened up in a hellacious fury of gunfire.

Jerome's shot had blasted out Colonel O'Brian's throat, blasting away a chunk of vertebra and severing the spinal column. He dropped like a rock, paralyzed but still alive. The other infected soldiers who'd been gaping up at the parachutes heard the gunshot and saw the blood shoot out of their leader. They knew right away they were being attacked and they fought back without hesitation.

They turned their guns on everything that moved, anything in uniform and anything with a gun. In seconds, they had mowed down the soldiers who had come from the line looking for orders. Next, they began to riddled the tents and the Humvees.

Thuy dashed back to the Humvee and threw herself on the ground next to one of the dispatchers, who was strangely quiet and unmoving. When Thuy dared to lift her head a little, she saw that the woman was stretched out, staring with glassy eyes up at the blue sky. She had a small hole in her forehead and another bigger one over her right ear. Next to her, huddled in a ball, was April Lopez. She had caught a bullet below her navel and was too fat to see where it had entered. She only knew that the pain was immense and that her blood felt as slippery as oil.

"They shot me!" she wailed. "They shot me!"

Courtney turned her head and saw the dead dispatcher: Tamara Faustin, a woman who'd been her friend for three and half years. She also saw April and her bloody hands. For some reason, Courtney had more sympathy for poor dead Tamara—in life she had been sweet, and in death she had the good sense to keep quiet.

"Will you shut up!" Courtney hissed at April. From where Courtney lay, she could see beneath the Humvee. A soldier was heading for them. She could see grime covered boots and the black tip of a low carried M16. The feet had paused for a moment but at April's cry they hurried for the Humvee.

"We got to run," Courtney whispered to Thuy before jumping to her feet. She made it four steps before the soldier, a black eyed creature with a black-toothed sneer, shot her in the back. Thuy was utterly shocked as Courtney flung out her arms and fell face down in the dirt.

"Oh god!" April screamed, bringing her hands up to her face and peering at the man through bloody fingers. He shot her as well. Bam, bam, bam! It took three shots to stop her from squealing and three more before she lay still.

During this dreadful execution, Thuy did not stir or blink. She was so petrified that she could do nothing but lie perfectly still and play dead. Her heart pounded in her chest so loudly she was sure the soldier would hear it, only he was too busy smacking his lips and making ugly swallowing noises to hear.

For a long, dreadful second, he stood over Thuy and then she felt something hard jab into her back. With sheer force of will, she did not so much as twitch.

Out of the corner of her eye, she saw the man go to Courtney and jab her with the end of his rifle, as well. It made a strange metallic "clunk" sound. He jabbed her a second time, harder and the sound was louder. "What the fuck?" he said, slowly coming to realize that she had on a back-mounted radio.

Courtney had also been playing dead, but she couldn't a second longer. She spun and grabbed the barrel of the rifle just as the soldier pulled the trigger. A hole in the earth appeared next to her head. "Thuy! Help me!"

Thuy was unarmed and had the strength of a twelve year old boy. Nature had not provided her with the direct means to combat a man of the soldier's size and strength and thus, the cold calculations of battle suggested that it made more sense to just lie there and let Courtney die.

And yet, Thuy was not the coldly calculating woman people thought she was. In the middle of a chaotic battle where friend fought friend and blood, both red and black, ran like water, she didn't think about herself, but leapt up and cast about for a weapon.

The closest thing to her was a stone the size of her head which had been unearthed by the passage of Humvees. It sat with its damp side up not three feet away and she had it in a second and thumped the soldier a good one with it a second after that. His skull cracked like an egg and he fell twitching and drooling as his brain went haywire.

With the weight of the heavy radio on her back, Courtney got up with little more grace than a turtle might. Her face was pasty and her mouth was twisted as if it had frozen in mid-scream. She didn't seem to notice the battle going on around them.

Thuy grabbed her arm and dragged her away, heading for the western perimeter. A bullet whizzed through the air near Thuy's neck and in response, she flinched, squinching her shoulders in an attempt to make herself a smaller target. She could do nothing else to protect herself.

The two women were caught out in the open where the grass had been beaten down and the land was flat. They had to keep moving or die. A second bullet passed right between them.

They both cried out and let go of each other just as more bullets zinged between them.

"I give up!" Courtney cried, running with her hands over her head. "We surrender!" Although it slowed them down somewhat, Thuy followed suit and put her hands up as she ran. No one seemed to care where their hands were or what they were saying and more bullets continued to whiz all around them.

"Over here!" Jerome Evermore called from the tree line. He waved to them frantically for a few seconds until they turned and ran at a diagonal straight across the battlefield. The black-eyed soldiers aimed for them, but now their course wasn't so simple for their diseased brains to follow and their bullets zipped behind Courtney who was the slower of the two. It seemed to her as if the bullets were chasing her and she ran harder than she had ever run in her life.

The two ran straight into the forest and dove behind trees, both in tears—at first, but then they caught each other's eye and they began laughing and crying at the same time.

Their hysteria went on until Thuy saw the great grey cargo planes that had just disgorged the paratroopers, heading back south. It was a stately sight, however it also had an air of finality to it. It seemed as if they were going and would never come back.

2— The Quarantine Zone

Gamet Corners was too far away with too many intervening hills for anyone in the little village to actually see any parachutes. Ryan Deckard gave PFC Max Fowler a look. "It's a jump, isn't it?" Deckard asked.

"I don't know. I was never a paratrooper, but if I had to guess, I'd say: probably. I've never seen so many planes like that before. I bet they are jumping in half the 82nd."

Deckard kept his dark eyes sharp on the C17s. "That's a bet you'd lose. Each one of those planes can hold a hundred paratroopers *and* cargo. I'd bet that's the entire division, which means we don't have a lot of time."

"Time for what?" Stephanie Glowitz asked. Just then, time felt like an exceptionally funny bit of business. Time for Dr. Wilson, with his gaping shoulder wound, was being measured in hours. Chuck Singleton had weeks before the cancer shriveled him up and spat him out. Twelve or thirteen, sure, but they were only weeks. Stephanie figured she had at least three months to live and that was if she wasn't eaten alive, first.

"We only have so much time to get out of the Zone," Deckard answered. "A jump of that size means the perimeter in the east didn't hold, or it's in tatters. Either way, we have to hurry if we want find a way to get through before all the holes in the line are filled."

Dr. Wilson waved a soft hand, beckoning for Deckard to come close. "Maybe we should stay here. You know that it's possible we're all covered in the disease and I don't want to be the guy responsible for destroying the world."

Deckard grimaced. There was no time for a lively debate. "We've been around this from the start and so far, those half-diseased guys haven't been all that contagious. And besides, we've taken every precaution we could. We've washed ourselves down with bleach and we've changed our clothes. And if…"

Wilson interrupted: "You're being foolish and wrong. If you go, you'll risk the lives of everyone in the world."

"I wasn't done!" Deckard barked. Wilson flinched back and then grimaced in pain. "Sorry about that, but I need to finish. We are going to get through. One way or another I will get us through, however…" He paused, looking into each of their faces. "However, if one of us shows the first sign of the disease, we will stop immediately. We will disarm him or her and monitor their status. If it progresses, that person will be shot in the head and no amount of pleading will keep me from doing my duty."

A heavy silence hung over the Gamet Corners' diner until Wilson raised a weak hand. "I've had a headache for a while. I didn't want to alarm anyone, but it hasn't gone away."

"And you've had it since when?" Deckard asked.

Wilson tried to shrug, which brought out a moan. "Since sunrise I guess. But it has been persistent."

"You're not infected. You would have turned into one of them by now if you had the disease. You're probably just dehydrated which we will take care of as soon as we can. Okay, we got to roll. Chuck grab the doctor's belt and I'll get his good arm." Together they heaved the man up and leaned him against the wall before shuffling him out the back door where a hunk of rust sat on four bald tires.

It was a venerable Ford Bronco that had been new when Reagan was president. For the last five years, it had been nursed along, held together by duct tape and prayers. Steep hills gave it fits, making it chug and lurch. During afternoons in July and August, it was apt to stop at a red light and not start again until the sun went down. And whenever the temperatures dipped below twenty, it simply refused to come out of the barn.

It did have three things going for it: the keys had been sitting right in the ignition, it had started on the fourth try, and there were no other options left in town.

Sundance was the only one of the group who wasn't skeptical when Deckard pulled it around. With his tail thumping mightily, he jumped up into the front seat and sat there with his dog grin stretched wide.

When they were all in, Deckard eased the Bronco forward, secretly afraid that it would go a mile and then die for good.

It was not a nimble machine; its turns were wide, more like gentle arcs, that left them a few times dangerously close to sliding off the dirt shoulder of the road and down into the ditch.

The Bronco was also a loud car that had zombies flocking in from all sides. Speed was the answer to this issue, and yet too much speed was a dangerous thing. At fifty miles an hour the vehicle developed a shimmy that was downright scary. It felt as if both front wheels were being held on by a single lug-nut each —a single loose lug-nut.

Feeling the sweat trickle down his back, Deckard bled off speed to keep a steady forty miles per hour, but even that was too fast for the circumstances. Chuck Singleton drawled in that seemingly unconcerned way of his. "You know, iffin you hit one of them bad boys at this speed, things will get a might bit messy."

Deckard pictured running over a zombie: half-rotted parts flying, black blood coating the front of the Bronco, Com-cells saturating the air, and maybe a tire or two bouncing away down the road.

Cursing, he slowed down to an agonizing twenty-five miles an hour and putt-putted eastward.

With the number of zombies ticking up, he had to slalom all over the road to avoid hitting them, however it was impossible to miss every one. After a particularly portly zombie took out the side mirror, the last of the blue surgical masks were donned, windows were rolled up and, as no one knew how effective the air filters were in the ancient vehicle, the air-conditioning was switched off.

They sweated and grew increasingly carsick with all the jerking back and forth and the occasional *ka-thump, ka-thump* as they ran over zombies that couldn't be dodged. Their misery lasted for a few miles and then, just as Deckard feared, one of the tires blew. The tires had been showing their steel belts through the rubber when he had first spotted the car and all it took to doom them was a little too much swerving and a single You-hoo bottle that exploded as they ran over it, sending a shard of glass up into the core of the tire.

A jolt struck the Bronco, which suddenly started to shake violently as its rear axle tried to haul around and overtake the front. Deckard fought the vehicle straight, but didn't try to pull over. They were on a lonely two-lane stretch of blacktop with forest and black-eyed monsters ranging along either side. If they stopped, they'd die.

The tire began to disintegrate, first in little crumbles of rubber and then in long strips that looked like alligator hide. Soon there was nothing left of the actual tire and they ground along at ten miles an hour on nothing but a rim. The sound emanating from it was a hell-spawned scream that could be heard for miles in the quiet morning.

Sparks flew up from it continually in an endless 4th of July fountain. The white hot shower was brighter than the early morning sun and it kindled a new fear in Deckard: what if the gas tank caught on fire? He was sure the engine leaked six ways from Sunday, so why not the gas tank as well.

"I guess we'll find out soon enough," he said to himself. No one heard. The screech from the rim had the rest of them covering their ears with both hands.

The Bronco gave out after another mile and a half. To keep its forward momentum as they lumbered into a string of zombies, Deckard downshifted and kept the gas pedal floored. The RPM needled swung far into the red and gradually the oil temperature indicator crept higher and higher. It wasn't long before the engine let out a bang, a thump and a squeal as a belt gave way. The Bronco died right there, smoke creeping from beneath the hood.

"Everyone out," Deckard ordered and then pointed at Chuck. "You take the rear. Keep them off of us without wasting ammo. We don't have a lot. Fowler, help the doctor. Stephanie carry their weapons."

In spite of the now dead truck, luck seemed to be on their side. A hundred yards to the north, a string of slow moving zombies cut toward them. A half mile to the south echoed the last dregs of battle that Thuy had inadvertently caused. Behind them, to the west, came a few hundred zombies lurching along the road. In front of them, to the east, exactly where they needed to go, the forest was empty and quiet.

Deckard took point and led them along the road, pushing on as fast as they could go, which wasn't fast enough. They were a slow, plodding group. Dr. Wilson was game but even with Fowler's help, his injury, age and exhaustion had him moving at the speed of a Sunday stroll. Stephanie wasn't any quicker. She coughed constantly and carried the three rifles as if she had a millstone across her shoulders. Chuck labored to keep up as well. He had to stop every thirty seconds to keep the ever-growing horde off of them.

When they crested a rise that was clear of the forest, Deckard looked back and saw that they weren't going to make it. What looked like a thousand zombies were closing in on them from the rear. They didn't have enough ammo to fight them, they were too slow to run away from them and there was nowhere to hide that the overly sensitive noses of the zombies wouldn't be able to sniff them out.

The obvious course of action was to kill Dr. Wilson, strip Chuck and Stephanie of their guns and ammo and then press forward with all possible speed until they couldn't go any further at which time, Deckard would be forced to kill more of his friends.

"Or I think of something else to save us. But what?" When nothing came to him, he asked a different question: "What would Thuy do?" That was far easier to answer. "She would analyze our strengths and their weaknesses, and pit one against the other using the materials on hand to…"

A grin broke out on his face and he began patting his pockets until he found his lighter. It no longer had that silvery shine. It was a blue-black as though it had been in a fire recently. Twice in the last few days fire had saved them. "Third times the charm," he said and then sprinted down the hill, leaving the others struggling to catch up.

After two hundred yards he jogged off the road and into the forest, looking for the right sort of downed tree branch. In order to make a big fire in a short amount of time, he needed a branch that was six or seven feet long with a halo of dried leaves still attached. He found one in a matter of seconds, and when he lit the leaves, the branch blazed with the light of a dozen torches.

Quickly, he lit the underbrush along the side of the road, concentrating on the long grass and the floor of leaves underfoot. Fire fed fire and soon the smoke was everywhere. For a fleeting moment he wondered: *What if I start a forest fire?*

There were worse things, he concluded as a downed cottonwood suddenly caught fire, filling the forest with a brown haze.

"Get in here," he said, in a carrying whisper when he saw his little group pausing on the side of the road, trying to peer through the smoke. Following his voice, they plunged into the smoke and came out of it a hundred yards later, hacking and coughing, but grinning as well. The zombies had given up the chase and were milling around in confusion on the other side of the blaze Deckard had created.

"Now for the hard part," Deckard said to himself. Fooling zombies with a bit of smoke was one thing, getting past thousands of trained soldiers, who were likely to shoot first and ask questions later, was a different thing altogether.

Again, Deckard took the lead and again, he pushed them as hard as he could. Still, it was a half hour hike before they came up on the new perimeter of the Quarantine Zone. There wasn't a black line in the forest marking the boundary, there were only soldiers in a long line, hidden in the woods. Sudden gunfire, two hundred yards up and to their right, gave away the position of a squad of paratroopers.

Deckard dropped into a crouch and pointed for the others to slip into the brush on the side of the road. "Fowler, you're with me. The rest of you stay here and keep out of sight. Fire your weapons only if a zombie is heading right for you. Chances are they'll be drawn to what's going on up ahead and ignore you if you keep out of sight."

When Chuck gave him a tired nod, Deckard slipped away with Fowler, and Sundance who wouldn't leave his side. They cut through the forest, angling away from a few zombies that were fixated on the sound of the short but furious battle. Men screamed back and forth at each other. One sided claiming to be soldiers and pleading to be let through the new lines, and the other obstinately repeating their orders that no one was allowed to pass.

Deckard wanted no part of that. Begging wasn't going to change anyone's mind and, not only that, it sounded sad and weak. With Fowler twenty steps behind, Deckard crept through the forest, making little more noise than the wind in the trees. At one point he heard murmuring from ahead of him and he detoured to his right, staying low and moving slowly and purposefully.

He was so quiet and sly that Fowler lost track of him a number of times. Fowler wasn't nearly as slick and so he kept further west of Deckard until the older man apparently found the hole in the line he was looking for and tried to slide through it.

But Deckard was not the only one who was slick. On the other side of the invisible line sat a boy with blue eyes and a little smirk. This boy wore a private's uniform, but he wasn't new to guns. He'd been hunting since his father had bought him his first BB gun at the age of five.

Back then it had been rock doves sitting on telephone wires and squirrels nattering in trees. Now, he hunted humans. Minutes before, he had caught sight of Deckard and watched him for some time from within the heart of an illusion. The hunter had long before mastered the art of camouflage and he blended in so well with his surroundings that he was invisible at sixty yards.

Slowly, cautiously, Deckard came on and, had he been going up against a lesser man, he might have slipped on by, but the hunter had him dead to rights. Deckard filled the man's scope, giving him a choice of targets: Right eye, left eye, middle of the forehead—when he pulled the trigger, the hunter knew that he couldn't miss.

Chapter 12

1—10:43 a.m.
Washington D.C.

Lieutenant General Phillips, commander of the Eighteenth Airborne Corp spent the entire flight back to New York fighting a growing headache. It didn't help that his phone rang nonstop as his various commanders called looking for orders, or wanting to be reassured or simply to impart news, most of which was bad.

Due to a mix up on the aviation side of things, General Frank Frazer of the 82nd Airborne Division had three battalions drop onto the same drop zone, meaning there were two gaping holes in his line. One was four miles wide and the other eight.

"Son of a bitch," Phillips cursed. He balled a fist wishing he could punch someone. "How the hell did you let that happen, Frank?"

Frazer actually laughed at the question. "How did I let it happen? I don't fly the planes, sir. I just tell them where to drop my men. The foul up is all on them damned, strutting pilots. Suffice it to say I have the men double-timing it to get the holes filled. It's putting us about thirty minutes behind schedule."

"And the rest of the jump?"

"It was a thrown together mission, sir," Frazer began, already deflecting blame. "Six deaths and seventy-one injuries; that's from the drops alone. I did try to warn you about two of the DZs."

He had been warned. Two of the twelve DZs were "six second" drop zones, meaning all one hundred paratroopers had six seconds to get out of the plane or they would be jumping out over the trees—a nightmare for any paratrooper.

Phillips, who sported a black and gold Airborne tab himself, had gone into the trees three different times and knew what a horrible feeling it was to be heading right for a forest of spears without any way to stop. Military paratroopers fell at a speed that could break a leg upon landing which meant that a tree branch in the eye, throat or even the chest could be fatal—and it had been that day.

To make matters worse, some of Frazer's units had barely gotten into position before they were assaulted by a strange mixture of zombies, civilians, and military personnel, the latter causing many casualties.

"I did what I could about those DZs, Frank, but the pols wouldn't budge," Phillips said. "Let me know when the line is linked, thanks."

He hung up and sat for all of one minute, pinching the bridge of his nose, before General Ed Stolberg, the new commander of the 42nd Infantry Division called. Ed wasn't exactly happy with his new command. The 42nd was no longer a division except on paper. It was now a loose hodgepodge of local police, national guardsmen and straggling groups of civilians who fought with such a wide array of weapons that keeping them supplied with the right ammunition had caused one quartermaster to suffer a heart attack. Their communications were almost nonexistent and their command structure had dissolved so that in some places it was every man for himself. To make matters worse, the 42nd was spread out over three hundred miles of forest perimeter.

Stolberg began his call in his usual asinine manner: "This is the biggest pile of crap I've ever been handed in my life! I got men scattered everywhere. I don't know what Collins was thinking…"

"Shut your fat mouth!" Phillips stormed into the phone. "I'm sure Collins did what he had to do and he died trying save this country. You will not speak ill of him." There was a long silence between the two men that was broken only by Stolberg's heavy breathing. He sounded like a bull that was considering whether or not to charge.

The two generals were both cut from the same cloth and had nearly come to blows on a few occasions. Still, Phillips knew that Ed Stolberg was the right man for the thankless job of reconstructing a division that was not only still in the field but also under constant attack.

"Sorry, sir," Ed eventually growled. After a shorter pause, he went on to report that his lines were suffering from an uptick in zombie attacks. The early morning's calm had given way to a renewed fury which had been shocking for him to witness in person.

"And your lines?" Phillips asked.

"Holding for now, but unless someone has the guts to tell the president to sit down and shut the fuck up, they won't for long." Stolberg was becoming desperate for fuel and ammunition. Because of the horrendous traffic jams, a good portion of the 42nd had been choppered into position by seemingly endless relays of Blackhawk helicopters. Here it was, twenty-four hours later, and the highways were still rivers of steel and that wasn't going to change anytime soon as tens of thousands of cars were completely out of gas and tens of thousands more had been abandoned before they could run out.

This meant that Solberg's supplies would have to be choppered in, only there weren't any helicopters available save for a dozen borrowed from the Coast Guard and even these were parked uselessly on the football field at West Point waiting on fuel. They'd be waiting a long time. The president, with his over the top demand for a show of force, had drained fuel reserves in three states.

"How long before things become critical?" Phillips asked, after listening to Ed bitch for ten straight minutes.

Stolberg grunted out a laugh. "Things became critical about an hour ago. These guard units are on the edge, sir. They shoot at shadows. They'll empty a magazine at anything that moves—squirrels, rabbits, birds…sometimes even each other. Hell, there was a bit of a wind right at sunrise and those guys acted as though the trees were attacking them. I saw one guy go…"

Phillips knew that Stolberg would go on bitching for half the morning if he wasn't cut off. "Well, do your best, Ed. Reinforcements are on their way. The 101st should be arriving in about seventy minutes, unless, of course the president wants to show off for the Canadians as well."

He had meant this to be a joke, but it fell flat, mainly because with this president it seemed like an actual possibility. Phillips wished his subordinate "Good luck" as way of saying goodbye and then brooded as the Gulf Stream dropped out of the low ceiling of grey clouds to land at Reagan National. The runways sat just as silent and empty as JFK had been.

The quiet was oppressive and his brooding kicked up a notch. He had a thousand things to do and it didn't bode well that the president had the balls to pull a theater commander back to Washington in the middle of the largest combat jump in seventy years.

146

More presidential meddling, he assumed. *More photo-ops.* If this was the case, Phillips would be forced to take Ed's advice and tell the president that it was time to let the adults get back to work.

Any more of these political games would leave the 42nd in a dangerous position. Although Stolberg had used the word "critical," Phillips guessed that Ed could hold for another few hours. Using such hyperbole was the game all commanders played. They so feared the very possibility of running out of supplies that they always bitched and moaned and made it seem as if the end of the world was at hand.

And yet, in war, a few hours could be the difference between victory and defeat.

As the plane taxied towards a waiting limousine, Phillips checked Ed's initial supply report. To say that it wasn't "good" was a vast understatement. Still, at their rate of ammo consumption, Phillips figured they had at least two more hours before things became truly critical and that was plenty long enough for the 101st to arrive to save the day. Of course, interspersing twelve thousand air assault soldiers in among the crazy hodge-podge of the 42nd would be another logistical and communications catastrophe which Phillips was sure would age him thirty years.

In the end, he knew it would work itself out. Of course, in the meant time, he also knew that the staff work would have his eyes dry as dirt and red as…

The phone in his pocket rang; it was Ed Stolberg again. *He's found something new to bitch about*, Phillips thought. He almost didn't take the call, but after the fifth ring, he punched the button. "Ed, you know I have other divisions to deal with besides yours."

"Do you have any other divisions that just lost all communications with two thousand men?" Ed shot back. The 42nd's new commander let that sink in before he went on: "I was just informed that we haven't been able to get hold of O'Brian or anyone in the Connecticut Bubble for some time. It's just dead air over the radio."

"Have the Air Force send another recon plane over…"

"I already did and I have the photos. They were just uploaded and…and it's not pretty. You should be getting them any second."

Phillips pulled out a second phone, this one twice the size of his Smart Phone and twice as smart as well. He checked the secure feed and saw that something was being downloaded and decrypted. The phone buzzed seconds later and displayed the first of a dozen photos. With his eyes not as sharp as they used to be he couldn't tell exactly what he was seeing. "Were they overrun? I don't see a sizable IP force in these pictures."

"The first few frames are shots taken an hour ago," Ed answered, the normal belligerence in his voice gone, replaced by something akin to sadness. "The Air Force has had planes over the Quarantine Zone since dawn, trying to pinpoint the larger concentrations of the IPs. They fly over the 'Bubble' every thirty minutes or so. As you can see from those first shots, the IPs are coming in dribs and drabs. So the next few frames don't make much sense to me."

The next frames showed the same hilltop, only now, there were bodies in uniform scattered everywhere on top of it.

Ed waited a minute before saying: "The only thing we can think of is that a group of IPs came up through the forest on the eastern side of the perimeter. That's where the brush is thickest. But how they managed to come all the way around without being seen is still a mystery."

Phillips didn't believe this for a second. "And where are they now? To overrun the perimeter in broad daylight would take five thousand of them, and I'm pretty sure, they would still be lingering over the feast." Just saying those words turned his stomach and he had to pull his eyes from the picture. "Sorry, Ed, but these weren't zombies who did this and they weren't civilians, either. Those soldiers killed each other. The question is: why?"

They both knew there were only two answers: either the men had turned on their officers; a mutiny in effect, or the Comcells had been introduced into the camp. With all the horrible repercussions of the latter, they both hoped for a mutiny.

"Thanks for the heads up, Ed. If you can stay on point with the Air Force Recon guys, that would be great. I'm going to need a count of the bodies within the perimeter. If I had to guess, we're missing at least half of the men who had been on that hill top."

Ed hung up with a murmured goodbye. For close to a minute, Phillips stared out as the capitol whizzed past the window. With his mind caught up on the pictures, the beauty of the city was completely lost on him.

He was still staring when he spied the dome of the capitol building rising up over the trees. A minute later, he was on the grounds of the White House, and five minutes after that, he was in a storage room in the basement sitting on a folding chair that creaked under his weight whenever he shifted position. The room made no sense unless they were down there with the sole purpose of hiding from someone.

Surrounding him on their own little chairs were the seven members of the Joint Chiefs of Staff, the Secretary of Defense, and Marty Aleman who was standing, uncomfortably smiling down on General Phillips as though he were a principal about to discuss truancy with a naughty boy.

"It seems that an issue has come up that may have an effect on your dispositions," Marty said, speaking to Phillips and ignoring the others in the room.

"If this is concerning the 'Connecticut Bubble' having been overrun, let me assure you that I know already. As much as I…"

Jumping up, with a scrape of metal, the Secretary of Defense interrupted: "When the hell did that happen? Why the hell wasn't I kept in the goddamned loop?"

Before Phillips could answer, Marty stepped between the two men with his hands out. "This is, uh, bigger than that I'm afraid." That had everyone's attention. "There have been reports of attacks in Hartford."

"Hartford, Connecticut?" the Secretary of Defense asked. Instead of answering, Marty lifted his eyebrows as if to say: *Is there another Hartford?* "Right, sorry," the secretary mumbled. "Has this been confirmed?"

Marty nodded, solemnly. "Since the initial call, there have been six more sightings of zombies within the newly walled city. Three of them with still pictures and one with video."

"Since the initial call?" Phillips asked. "When the hell did that call come in and why didn't you tell me? Wait! You knew before the jump! What the hell? You knew before the jump and yet you let them jump anyway. Why?"

Phillips' seething anger couldn't be ignored and nor could it be brushed away with the usual sort of vagaries that Marty had perfected in order to keep his secrets. This was the Theater Commander and, as such, he should have been informed. But he hadn't been for a reason.

The Chief of Staff for the Army, General Heider had been the one to suggest bringing him back to Washington in order to break the news. "He'll talk to the press if you don't bring him in," Heider had explained. "I know him, he'll raise a big stink. The man is a Boy Scout."

Marty was seeing that *Holier-than-thou* attitude in person. "Look, General Phillips, I know your reputation. You're one of the good guys…maybe one of the last of them. You see things in stark black and white when there are, actually, shades of grey for everything. I know that it's hard for you to imagine but this is a shade of grey."

"Condemning my men is a shade of grey? Leaving the entire eastern perimeter wide open is a shade of grey? How on earth is that a shade of grey?"

Finally, Marty took a seat in one of the folding chairs and then gestured for Phillips to sit as well. When he did, losing a portion of his anger in the process, Marty explained the delicate nature of society and how it was wholly built on trust.

"Money being a fine example," he said. "A dollar is only worth a dollar if everyone believes it to be worth a dollar. Laws only work if everyone believes in the government's right to pass them and enforce them. Civil society works right up until you can no longer trust your neighbors…or your government."

"Dropping my men into a known infected area is a prime example of losing trust," Phillips said and was surprised when Marty began nodding in agreement.

"Yes, exactly, but by the time we found out and were able to alert the planes, the jump would have already commenced…on live television. If we had stopped it, the American people would have seen a few thousand measly parachutes. They would have then found out how their government had messed up, yet again, and dropped soldiers into an infected zone. How much trust would they have in their government then?"

Phillips shrugged. "Probably the exact right amount of trust."

"Yes, they'd have very little," Marty agreed. "Do you know, right now there are people killing each other in Pittsburg over cans of tuna? Do you know that Baltimore is practically a police state? Did you know that about a third of Newark, New Jersey is on fire? Those people looting and murdering don't trust their government. Those people don't trust that their society will make it another week. What would have happened if we had aborted the jump and explained that we fouled up, yet again?"

The general dropped his eyes instead of answering. His mind painted a picture of runaway panic filling the streets of every major city. The death toll would certainly be higher than the twelve thousand men he had dropped into Connecticut.

But Marty wasn't done. "What would have happened in Hartford? A quarter of a million people suddenly finding out that they've built a wall to keep the zombies out and now they're trapped inside with them instead. The bloodshed would've been atrocious."

"They know now, don't they?" Phillips asked.

"No, and it's not surprising since the good citizens of Hartford saw the jump on television just like everyone else in the country. They still have trust in their government and they want to have trust in their government. For the most part, they are on the wall or holed up in their homes, praying. But when they do find out there's going to be trouble. It's why we have a new mission for the Eighteenth Airborne Corp...and no, you're not going to like it."

2—The Quarantine Zone

Thuy was down to a plodding jog, her breath ragged and her head dizzy, but she was fresh as a daisy compared to Courtney Shaw. With the heavy radio strapped to her back, Courtney was in agony with every step.

She had asked Specialist Jerome Evermore to take it for her, but he had said: "Fuck that. What good is a radio?"

The question that Courtney had to ask herself was: what good was she without a radio? She couldn't shoot a gun all that well and she wasn't in the best shape, and no one would ever look to her for leadership. Her natural skill was with the radio.

But, oh boy did it hurt. With every step, it dug into the small of her back, and the strain on her shoulders was beginning to wear her down. Still, she ran on.

There were others in the forest, running. Sometimes they were mere shadows among the trees, while at other times they strayed close. But never too close. Trust had been murdered on that hilltop. Soldiers now looked at each other, not as brothers but as possible enemies, because no one knew who was infected and who wasn't.

A man to their right went down, screaming about his ankle. "It's broken! Son of a bitch. Hey, stop, please. I hurt my ankle." No one stopped. What if he was only faking? What if he had been secretly turning into a zombie this entire time? What if he waited until you got close and then tried to take a bite out of you?

Those who fell out were left behind and quickly forgotten.

Everyone went east with the same purpose. They had to get past the new perimeter before it was fully formed or they would be trapped once again. Some soldiers got lucky and managed to slip through where the holes were miles wide. Other soldiers were in great shape and ran for all they were worth. Some of these were able to steal through the smaller gaps in the line before it solidified.

Most of the soldiers were neither lucky nor fast. When they came up on the men of the 82nd they were given the choice between going back the way they came or being shot. Fear of the zombies drove men beyond devotion to duty and even patriotism.

They were desperate to escape and dozens of firefights broke out all along the line.

Thuy's little group halted a few hundred yards back from one battle that raged along a quarter mile of forest. "Who is going to win?" she asked Jerome.

"How the hell should I know?"

"Because you're a soldier. Which side has the bigger guns?"

He rolled his eyes and answered: "It's not about who's got the bigger guns, well at least not in this battle. I don't hear any 240s or fifty-cals and, thank God, they aren't bringing in artillery. They're all using the same basic gun type, which is good."

"Good for whom?" Thuy insisted. "Who's going to win? If it's the men on our side of the line, then all we have to do is follow them when they move up. But if it's the other men then we need a new strategy."

Jerome sat still for a minute, listening to the ebb and flow of battle as two highly trained groups of soldiers fought, using tactics well known to each. "We're going to lose," he answered, picking up a rock and flinging it in anger. "They have much more ammunition. You can hear our guys conserving their ammo. It'll be over in a minute or two."

"They also aren't acting as a coordinated force," Courtney said. She had turned on the radio and was listening to the terse commands and the *sitreps* through a headset. "Those paratroopers are doing it right. They're bringing up troops from other units."

"What units?" Thuy asked.

Courtney shrugged. "I don't know. Charlie company or something like that. Two platoons are moving west…wait, they're asking for smoke. What's that mean? And what's *a soup sandwich?* And what's *a butter bar?*"

Jerome had been in a squat and now he eased upward trying to see through the trees. "A *soup sandwich* is just like it sounds —you know, everything is all messed up, and a *butter bar* means a second lieutenant. It usually means they don't have much experience. And the smoke…there it is! The smoke is used to mark a position so you don't accidentally shoot the wrong people."

Thuy saw the blue smoke rising above the trees. It was strange to her that the most technologically advanced army in the history of warfare used such a simple signaling device. It seemed like something a cavemen would use. "Maybe we can use this to our advantage. Do you have any thing that turns smoke blue?"

He pointed at his web gear, where two canisters were hooked. One had a green mark on top and the other, red. "This is all I have."

"Do the colors have meaning?" she asked. "Is red danger and blue equal to friends."

"No, the colors are interchangeable," Jerome said. "They can mean whatever you want them to mean, but friendly units have to know their meanings, too or they're, you know, meaningless."

"It's the nature of all forms of communications, Mr. Evermore," Thuy said. She turned to Courtney. "Find that *butter bar*. Find out where his men are situated; I need to know his boundaries, if that's what they are called. Maybe we can play on his inexperience and slip through the lines. Mr. Evermore, everyone on that radio seems to have a bit of a twang to their voice. Can you impersonate someone from their state."

He cleared his throat and drawled out: "That's a 'firmative, ma'am. That's how they talk, y'know. Everythin' is: y'all this and y'all that. We gots us some op-four north of our po-sition. Let's po-lice up this here area."

"I'll have to trust you on this," Thuy said, basically dismissing him as an officer might. She didn't know Jerome Evermore very well, but what she did know hadn't impressed her. Sure, he was brave and could fight, but he also talked too much and in her experience, people who talked too much had a tendency to think too little.

She needed quiet in order to formulate her plan. She also needed information. Where were the boundaries between units? Who sounded tough and confident and who sound uncertain? Who was moving and from what direction? She needed information in order to exploit it.

This was one of the few times in her life, Thuy found herself without something to write with and so she cleared away the leaves and brush from the forest floor and found a sharp stick.

Courtney began reading her a list of call signs: Black Finger 1, Black Bear 1 and 2, Black Knight 1 through 4. Then, from slightly further away, were Apple 2 and 3, Banana 1 and 3 and Apricot 3.

There were others on the net, men using names instead of call signs, men cursing each other, and men in obvious fear. These were usually hushed and snapped at by the more officious sounding soldiers.

Thuy listened intently, looking for a pattern, looking for weakness in the sound of people's voices and how quickly they answered. "Tell me, Ms. Shaw, where do you think Black Finger 1 is?"

Courtney had been scratching in the dirt as well. Now she looked down at her notes for a moment before standing in order to compare what she was hearing with the actual lay of the land.

"See that smoke?" There was a brush fire going, ignited by tracer rounds. It wasn't a life threatening blaze just a smoldering haze that drifted up two hundred yards to the right of their position. "Black Finger mentioned that there were friendlies in it and not to shoot there."

"Perfect," Thuy said, grinning. "We need to angle in that direction. And Mr. Evermore, I'm going to need that 'twangy' voice of yours ready."

Jerome stood and cracked his back, saying, "That's an 'firmative, Black Knight 1." Black Knight 1 was clearly the officer

154

in charge of the area; the *butter bar* that had been referenced earlier. "How's that?"

Thuy gave him a thumbs up, a gesture she incorrectly associated with soldiers, and then moved out, creeping through the underbrush. The firefight was no longer the battle that it had been. It had tapered away to a few men trading shots with the majority of the firing having drifted south.

To Thuy, it sounded like snipers on both sides going at it in a dangerous battle of expert shots and as they got closer and closer, she was sure that even then she was being targeted. Soon, her fear got the best of her and she froze behind a tree.

To Jerome, it sounded like a bunch of scared kids shooting at shadows. When Thuy faltered, he took the lead, angling across the front of the formation to where the smoke was thickest.

At the rear of the group was Courtney, walking in a hunch, still with the headset on her head, listening to the different conversations going on. The soldiers were excited. They had repulsed the enemy and now they were bragging, boasting of their kills, or just jabbering, happy to be alive. In the middle of this was Black Knight 1, trying to rearrange his lines as units were repositioned to deal with new threats. His voice had risen as he moved men here and there so that a radio wasn't needed to hear him a hundred yards to the south.

"Maybe we should hold up a sec," Courtney whispered. "They seem a little confused about what's going on. If we're not careful, we might blunder into them and get shot."

"Let me listen," Thuy demanded. She was so focused that she didn't see it as rude at all that she snatched the headset off of Courtney's head.

"Move back to your left Black Knight 2," a voice said. "Black Knight 2? Move to your left…Come in Black Knight 2!"

Thuy's dark eyes flew open wide. This was it. This was their chance to slide through the lines, but only if they were quick. "Mr. Evermore! Black Knight 2 hasn't responded. Ask them: *to the left of what?* Hurry, quick!"

Jerome crawled back to the two women and grabbed the mike. "To the left?" he asked in a country mumble, hoping that his voice could pass as anyone's. "To the left of what? I got me some smoke all around us."

"You got what, Black Knight 2? Say again?"

"I got grey smoke all around me and I swear I had fellas shootin' from front and from behind. Where the hell did you send us, LT?"

"Grey smoke? You stupid son of a bitch, you went too far to your right and you shifted too far forward. The orders were to shift your squad one hundred yards to the right and spread out! You're almost two hundred yards out of position!"

"Sorry Black Knight 1, we had a whole mess of hostiles and it was hard to keep track. I'm gonna shift back. Just make sure I have no one in front of me. The boys are jumpy as hell." Jerome looked back at Thuy and Courtney. They were more "twitchy" than jumpy.

"Copy that. Give me a minute and then move directly east. It'll be clear. Out." The LT began barking into the radio, shifting men about once more.

The ruse seemed to have worked and Courtney almost wilted in relief, sagging back against a tree. "Thank God. We're finally free," she said, too tired to even grin.

"What are you talking about?" Jerome hissed at her. "Get up! Get up! It's going to take them all of two minutes to realize that we ain't who we said we were, so come on."

He pulled Courtney to her feet and dragged her through the smoke in a rush, letting Thuy shuffle along in their wake. After two days of fighting for their lives, both women were dog-tired and had to will themselves onward. Jerome, on the other hand, never felt better. Adrenaline pumped through his veins giving him a heady rush. He was going to live. He was going to make it when so many had died. In his mind, that had to mean something.

"Destiny," he whispered as he saw something glinting on the ground. There were brass shell casings in the leaves around the base of an elm tree. They were warm to the touch. A soldier of the 82nd had been tucked up under the elm not a minute before. "Now we're free," he said, grinning.

Chapter 13

1—11:24 a.m.
The Eastern Border of the New Quarantine Zone

The bullet left the hunter's gun and struck exactly where he wished it to strike: a pine tree with a trunk a foot in diameter, seven inches from Deckard's right eye.

Bark flew and the smack of the bullet was loud in Deckard's ear. He dropped so suddenly that for a moment, the hunter thought he had hit the man instead of the tree. A second look down the scope on his M4 showed Deckard scrambling around the base of the tree, bringing his weapon to bear.

A grin turned up the corners of the hunter's mouth—the man was fast, the man was good, the man could've been a worthy opponent under different circumstances.

"I could've put that in your eye," the hunter called out. "I'm looking at you through a *Su16 Tactical Scope*, so do yourself a favor, turn around and start walking."

A cold wave of goosebumps broke out on Deckard's arms. A man who used a *Su 16 Tactical Scope* wasn't someone to mess with, especially when you came into *his* territory.

And Deckard was certainly in someone's well prepared trap. The brush had been cleared in a wide belt so that there wasn't any cover beyond the trunks of young trees. These were barely wide enough to hide a man and that was only when he was being seen from straight on, and there was no telling where the shooter had hidden himself.

To Deckard's front, the land sloped gently upward and the forest there was so thick a marching band could be hiding within it and he would never have known. Still, he eased upwards, searching for the shooter. He could almost feel the crosshairs that he was sure were centered right on his forehead. It gave him a maddening itch right between the eyes, that he refused to scratch. It would have been seen as a sign of weakness.

The man with the rifle had chosen his position like a pro. For all intents and purposes, he was invisible.

"If you have a scope, then you can see we aren't infected," Deckard called out. Slowly, he stood, with his empty hands held out from his sides. "See? My eyes are clear. I'm not suffering from any delusions and I really, really don't want to eat you. I could go for a steak, right now, but just as long as it comes from a cow and not a person. Ha-ha."

The poor joke made the still air feel dead. Deckard turned toward Fowler and gestured for him to stand. "We even have soldiers with us. This is PFC Max Fowler. He's a proven zombie fighter. Our knowledge of the beasts would be very valuable to you. Turn around Fowler, nice and slow."

It was obvious that Fowler was barely keeping it together. His eyes were big circles that went back and forth, searching for the gun that he knew was aimed at him. Looking like an owl-human hybrid, Fowler's body slowly turned, but his head remained fixed forward, twisting around on his neck so much that Deckard thought it just might pop off. Eventually the strain became too great and Fowler spun, his head whipping around to sit straight on his neck once again.

"You see?" Deckard said. "We're just normal guys like you."

"What about him?" the voice called out.

What about who? Deckard was about to ask, only at that moment he heard a sound behind him. It was Dr. Wilson coming forward, looking like the walking dead. His eyes might have been clear of the disease, but they were heavy with misery.

"Oh him," Deckard said and tried to grin. "That's only Dr. Wilson. We had a run in with some trigger-happy locals. Yes, he was shot, but he is not sick. Just look at his eyes." Quieter, Deckard spoke to Wilson out of the corner of his mouth: "Stop, right there, Wilson. Don't go any further."

Dr. Wilson didn't stop, he shuffled on. Now, Fowler hissed: "Please, Wilson, stop. He'll kill you if you keep going."

"That's ok," Wilson said, speaking in a dry monotone. "I can't go on. I'm too tired and I've lost too much blood."

"Wilson!" Deckard growled. "Stop right there. That's an order. You're one of us and we won't let you die. Do you hear me?"

Wilson nodded, but kept going. He stared straight ahead, his eyes wide and blank. "This is the only way. I'd slow you down. We both know that. We both know that this is for the best." He kept coming and now he came parallel with Deckard, about fifteen feet to his left.

He carried a gun. It had been Fowler's. The soldier had set it aside when he had stood to display himself and now Wilson held it pointed out in front of himself.

The voice hidden in the woods called out: "Stop that man or I will."

Deckard took a step forward, but stopped when the barrel of the gun swung his way. He held his hands up and pleaded for the doctor to give up the weapon and to "listen to reason."

Dr. Wilson was beyond reason. He wanted to live and actively feared dying, and yet he couldn't force himself to go on. What was the use? They had gone from one end of the Zone to the other and all of their roads had ended in death and misery. If he turned from this path, his death would only be put off for a short while longer. An open wound would soon fester with Comcells and then he would be worse than a hindrance.

He kept going until the hidden voice of the hunter yelled out: "Take care of your own."

"We don't have the supplies," Deckard said. "I did the best I could with what medical supplies we had, but it wasn't…"

"That's not what I meant," the hunter replied.

Deckard was slow to catch on. It took him a number of blinks before he realized that the hunter wanted him to kill Wilson. It would be a mercy, there was no doubt about that. Wilson was a bloody mess and was fading fast. His pain had to be atrocious.

But he was also Deckard's friend. That wasn't something he took lightly. He didn't kill his friends simply because they became a burden. At the same time Wilson had the right to die with some dignity, instead of mewling out his last moments as he became one of *them*.

Making no sudden moves, Deckard picked up his M4. When the strap rattled against the stock, Wilson stopped and glanced back. Now, the dull orbs held fear and his ragged breath picked up tempo. Deckard aimed, but when Wilson sniveled he lowered his gun. "I can't," he said.

"Don't draw it out," the hunter called. "Don't be cruel or I'll put a slug in his head with him looking right at me."

There was a reason why people got shot in the back of the head; no one wanted to see their death coming. Wilson was no exception. He tucked his chin down, and looked at the ground, his body shaking.

Deckard could see tears catch the light as they fell from his jaw. "Or you can let him go," he yelled. "Just let us walk on by. We know the danger and we know the symptoms of the virus, and we aren't afraid to die if that's what needs to happen…but it doesn't need to happen just yet."

"Take care of your man," the hunter said again. Although he had hunted and eaten many animals, he had never killed a man before and now that he was down to it the idea set his teeth on edge.

"No," Deckard stated. "I know he's an innocent man who is weak and harmless. I won't kill someone like that. It would be murder and if you shot him that would make you a murderer. Is that what you want to be? If so, go ahead and do it. Get it over with. If not, let us walk on by and no one will know."

The hunter wasn't one for deep moral quandaries, they tended to make him grouchy. Purposefully, he kept to the simple road. Murder was wrong, but so was disobeying a direct order. For the sake of the country, he couldn't let anyone pass. Given the lives of millions on one hand and only one life on the other, he had to go with saving the greater number.

He pulled his trigger in answer to Deckard and a 5.56mm bullet blasted a hole in Dr. Wilson's head before he even heard the sound of the gunshot. His body collapsed onto itself and as it did, Deckard jerked his weapon up—almost to his shoulder.

"I wouldn't if I was you," the hunter drawled. He had Deckard's torso in his sights and there was no way he could miss. "If you put that gun down and shut that dog up, I'll let you bury the dead."

Sundance was baying for all he was worth. He knew where the hunter was; he could smell the man's sweat and he could see the moss-covered barrel of his gun. Fowler had him by his collar and was crooning into his ear, afraid for both of them.

Deckard, a few feet away, wasn't afraid. His mind was too busy calculating angles and distances. He had followed Sundance's eyes and now knew where the hunter was hidden beneath a partially downed tree—the question he wrestled with: could he aim his rifle in its current position well enough to kill the man in a quarter of a second.

Once, ten years before, one of Deckard's instructors had called him: *Scary-fast*. He was still scary fast, but he wasn't magically fast. Against another opponent, he might have tested that speed. Against a proven marksman, when his blood was up

160

and his finger already drawing back on the trigger, it wasn't a smart idea.

"I'm putting down my gun," Deckard said, slowly opening his right hand and moving it away from the trigger guard. Gradually, he laid the M4 in the dirt and stood again, his hands up.

"I didn't want to have to do that," the hunter said. "I really am sorry."

Deckard looked down at Wilson's corpse. His eyes were wide and his mouth was a round "O." He seemed puzzled by his abrupt demise. Deckard reached down and closed the eyes. "I'm sorry, too," he whispered.

2—Newark, New Jersey

Shannon DiGirorio, her grimacing face streaked with sweat and tears, pushed on the heavy desk with all her might. Across its expanse stood the door leading from her office to the hall—it was partially open. The lock had failed ten minutes before. The knob had just popped right out to bounce off the desk with a little "clang" of metal.

Since then it had been a battle to see who would control the door. On one side of the door was a desk and on the other side of that was Shannon, all alone. Beyond the door and straining at it with savage and unholy strength were monsters, some of them were monsters she had known and worked with when they had been people.

A few hours before, the hospital had been humming as it usually did, busy, but not overly so. Then, along came the agents from FEMA. Like fat, officious vultures, they had descended at dawn, snatching up doctors and nurses and anyone who they felt they would need—need for what was never exactly explained.

Shannon didn't think even the FEMA agents knew exactly why so many people were being "relocated." As far as the gossip went, anyone trying to leave the Quarantine Zone was being shot to death. So why were doctors needed?

"Typical bureaucratic nonsense," one of the elderly patients had answered, as he gummed a set of yellowing dentures. "Them government shits go by the book even if the book don't make any kind of sense. I seen it all my life."

Shannon was sure he was right. All of the FEMA agents had Emergency Preparedness booklets tucked under their arms which they would consult from time to time as they comman-deered not only staff, but also blood, IV supplies, bandages, drugs and all kinds of medical equipment. Things had gone from humming and mellow to frantic and rushed.

The understaffed hospital was in an uproar and patients were beginning to stack up in the halls by the time Mary Gainor and her six year old son, Caleb came in bleeding from the bite Donald Briggs had given him.

Both mother and son were smeared in a slick, black slime which Mary explained away as being "grease." She was afraid of what would happen to them if anyone found out the truth of how they had been attacked by a zombie right on the front lawn of their Newark home.

In the first minute that mother and son were in the ER, the "grease" was smeared on the handles of the main entrance doors, and on the reception desk, and all over the triage room. A dozen people were infected in no time.

The infection spread as a curious and playful four year old named Kenny, tried to engage Caleb in a game of hide and seek. Kenny was bored and filled with little boy energy that could not be contained. He had been in the ER for an hour ever since his older brother had cut himself while making toast. Sometime in that hour, his mother had given up on trying to keep Kenny in his seat, and now, he snaked back and forth through the crowded waiting room to visit Caleb. Every time he did, the four year old couldn't help touching, well, everything.

Kenny spread the Com-cells far and wide. Within an hour, seventy-eight patients and ER staff were complaining of headaches. Thirty minutes after that, the first violence occurred as Mary Gainor went berserk and attacked one of the "new" people in the ER.

The "new" ones were all so clean and snooty, and they made Mary's stomach grumble in hunger. Without a police presence, orderlies were called in. It took three men to subdue her and her son. The same three men were called back four times in the next forty minutes and, by then, the ER was a dangerous place and not just because of the layer of Com-cells that coated nearly every surface.

It was frightfully dark and shadowed as all the lights had been smashed. The endless caterwauling that echoed throughout the halls was like something out of an asylum for the criminally insane. People, staff and patients alike, huddled in corners or beneath chairs, moaning and crying in horrendous pain. They glared at those less infected than themselves and threw violent, volcanic tantrums at the least provocation.

People just coming in to the ER, turned and fled after only a minute or two, and, sad to say, many were already infected as they did so.

Mary Gainor, high on mega doses of *Percocet*, watched the mayhem overwhelm the ER while strapped to a gurney. She no longer cared about her son. All she cared about was keeping the pain away and figuring how to feed. Her belly growled, endlessly. She grew desperately hungry for fresh blood, but there was none to be had. In the two and half hours she had been in the ER, everyone there become infected. They all stank like rotted meat.

The smell of them was enough to drive her into a rage, but with the help of the drugs coursing through her veins, she held the anger in check long enough to plot and scheme. There was fresh blood nearby, she could smell it coming down from the duct work.

"It's upstairs," she growled, her voice grinding like rock on rock. "You," she barked at one of the stinking, mewling creatures crawling along the baseboards. It had once been human. It had once been a doctor. Now its rage was beginning to overcome its pain. "Untie me!" It listened and obeyed, though its once nimble fingers were now clumsy sausages that fumbled at the straps for what felt like an eternity to Mary.

When she was free, she set about closing off the hospital, blocking doors and pushing the infected into place so that there would be nowhere for the *others* to go. It took thirty minutes to seal off the lower floor and by that time the Percocet was wearing off and Mary's mind was beginning to revert to a primitive level where a need to kill vied only with a need to feed.

Grinning a madman's black grin, she headed up the stairs, followed by an assorted group of erstwhile patients and staff who were now slavering, hungry zombies.

The rest of the hospital was oblivious to what was happening. After FEMA had made off with half the staff, the various departments found themselves running around, completely frazzled. And when they weren't speeding from room to room and rushing through the all-important paperwork, they watched the endless loop of TV footage of the massive parachute drop and of the scores of giant planes rumbling over city after city, and they even ran to the window when the hundreds of Army Blackhawks buzzed over the city.

Marty Aleman had not erred in thinking that the country needed a shot of something to calm their collective nerves.

The sight of the planes had made a shoeless Shannon Di-Girorio almost wilt in relief. She had a brother in Providence barely sixty miles from the edge of the Quarantine Zone and she'd been worried sick for him, though in truth, for the last two hours she had been too busy to be worried.

She hadn't been a floor nurse in ten years, and three hours on her feet made her remember why she had given it up for a cushy job behind a desk. Her aching feet were the reason she was in her office when the first of the zombies from the emergency room came lurching up out of the stairwell to sow terror.

The hospital had been so well constructed and sound-proofed that the first few screams barely registered on her. They sounded like a distant steam pipe letting go and she only grunted as she watched television footage taken from a traffic cam. It showed what looked like a strange parade of stumbling people going past in an endless stream.

They were just showing the location of the traffic cam when a louder scream jerked Shannon around in her chair. The scream had been high and piercing. It was a scream of fear the like of which Shannon had never heard in her life. The sound froze her in place as she listened as more screams joined the first.

Instinctively, she knew that zombies were in the building and yet, in a moment of pure stupidity, she went to the door to peek out. There were dozens of black-eyed people going in every direction all with their mouths hanging open and their black gums looking slick with oil.

She hauled her door closed but not before she locked eyes with a man in scrubs. It was Dr. Reynolds, or, at least it had been. Now, it was a zombie with fine, white teeth in a dank mouth. It attacked the door, trying to tear it down with its clawed fingers. Shannon backed away, crying fat tears of terror, her heart suddenly racing so fast that it felt as though it would speed right out of her chest.

"Oh God," she whimpered, her hands fluttering uselessly in front of her face. "Oh God…I gotta get out of here." She spun in a circle, looking around for some sort of salvation. The window was the only way out and she ran to it.

It offered a straight drop of at least sixty feet to the concrete parking lot below. A narrow ledge of brick, three inches in width, just below the window was the only path to safety. It ran the length of the building and the only hope it offered was an insane path to the other windows that sat along it. It was a fool's hope.

No one could shimmy around the building on that thin of a ledge and even if they could, how would they get into any of the other windows?

Shannon turned from the window and her tears came harder than before. The door thrummed and shook under the blows of what had once been Dr. Reynolds. The door wouldn't last. The knob was already loose, going up and down instead of just turning.

Shannon began to blubber, but all the same she went to her desk and heaved her weight into it. She strained against it, finding just enough strength to push it against the door.

Two minutes later, the door knob popped off and its *clang* rattled in Shannon's heart. The door was thrust back and the desk along with it. Grey hands and arms reached through the gap of the door as she pushed against her side of the desk with all of her feeble strength.

The door *banged* suddenly and the desk slammed back into her, knocking her onto her butt. More tears rained down from her eyes as she scrambled to her feet and threw her weight into the desk. It barely budged.

Shannon realized right then that she was going to die. She had seen the videos on the internet of the zombies feasting on living people. It was a horrible way to die.

"They're going to eat me," she said, out loud. The thought sent her into hysterics and she screamed and shoved uselessly against the desk as the door opened inch by inch.

When a grey head pushed through the opening, its glasses askew, she knew that anymore struggling would be useless. She looked over her shoulder at the window and thought about the narrow ledge. It was narrow but then so were her feet; her shoes were size 6.

"I can make it," she whispered.

There was no way she could; however, the only other option was so ghastly that she turned to the window and saw the first obstacle she would have to overcome: the window didn't open. It had no latch or mechanism to lift or cant it.

"Then I'll break it," she said, forcibly. She wasn't a weak person. Mentally she had overcome a great deal in her life and now she told herself over and over again: "I can make it. I can make it." On some level deep inside of her, she knew she could scrape and claw her way to safety. First, the window had to come down.

She released her hold on her side of the desk and hurried across the room to a planter she had picked out the year before. With the sound of her blood rushing in her ears, she hefted it up and ran at the window, throwing it full force at the glass.

A hundred lines erupted in the glass, springing out from the point of impact. The fact that it hadn't blown straight out with the first strike wasn't a disappointment to her. It was strong glass; she knew that. She knew it had to be to keep the crazier patients in.

And that was okay because another strike or two would do it…but not with the planter. The pot had exploded on the first strike. "The chair," she whispered, her frightened eyes falling on the chair she had used for the last three years. It was a heavy hunk of furniture that normally would have caused her back to give out if she had tried to pick it up.

Now, she hefted it up in one move. It almost overbalanced her, but she recovered, tottering slightly before she ran at the window. She struck it with the sound of a gong and rebounded, falling on her ass with the chair on her chest, practically pinning her down. And that was okay, too.

There was a gaping hole in the glass now.

"One more," she whispered getting to her feet and lifting the big chair once again. She spared a moment to glance back at the door where two of the monsters were fighting each other to get into the room.

"One more," she repeated and then charged a second time. She willed herself through the glass and so strong was her charge that she almost willed herself and the chair all the way onto the pavement below.

The glass blasted out in a shower of crystal rain and the chair hung up in the falling glass long enough for her to disentangle herself from it and let it drop. Cut and bleeding, Shannon knelt on the edge of the window where the carpet met the glass and watched the chair fall. It seemed to take a long time before it crashed onto the face of the parking lot far below.

"Oh, God," she said, staring at the chair. If she fell from that height, she would splat onto the pavement with her internal organs shooting out of her ass and her eyes *literally* popping out of her head. She dragged her eyes from the chair and turned to the tiny ledge. It was so small that her heart began aching just looking at it. Shannon was no longer tough and confident. She was weak and cringing, afraid to stay where she was and afraid to risk the ledge.

Behind her, the desk was thrust back and the door opened even further. Four creatures—four zombies, scrambled over each other to get at her. One was the foul Dr. Reynolds, who was no longer handsome, one was a nurse in blue scrubs, her dark eyes empty of life, and two were children, who had been overcome by the virus in the ER—their eyes were sharp with cunning and their faces, hungry and feral, were nothing short of nasty.

One of the children moved left and the other went right, while the two adults clambered over the desk, coming right for her. They were like lions hunting and she was going to be like the buffalo who was pulled down and feasted upon.

It would take a long time to die. Humans did not have the jaws and teeth of the larger beasts of prey. They took smaller bites—many, many smaller bites. Each one a torture.

These thoughts had Shannon rooted in place, paralyzed by fear. She might have stayed right where she was until Dr. Reynolds fell on her, but then she caught one of the children signaling to the other. That wasn't right. They were supposed to be brain-dead monsters. They weren't supposed to be able to signal or communicate in any way.

For reasons unknown to her the idea that the zombies could think made everything that much more heinous.

But it also got her moving. She went to the hole in the window and without looking down stepped through and onto the narrow lip of brick. With no other handhold available, she clung to the razor edges of the glass with her right hand; it cut her flesh to ribbons and her blood ran like water, but she didn't notice. She was focused. She would make it and she would live.

The ledge was tiny and her feet, although narrow, were big compared to it. She could just grip the brick with the very tips of her toes and thankfully, she was barefoot, having come into her office to give her aching feet a rest. Had she been in her no-nonsense black wedges, she would have been forced to try to slide across the ledge with her feet pointing in opposite directions and her center of balance too far back. The slightest bit of wind would have plucked her right off the ledge.

Not that her current stance was all that much better. With her arms thrown out and her cheek pressed against the glass, she looked somewhat like a gecko on the side of an aquarium. She also looked like easy pickings for Dr. Reynolds.

He proved to be a true zombie by ignoring the hole in the glass altogether and launching himself at the window. He struck face first, cracking his fine white teeth and making a noise like a dropped bag of potatoes. The impact sent him flying back and caused the sturdy glass to vibrate beneath Shannon's cheek.

The nurse in the blue scrubs tried her luck next and threw herself against the glass as well. She was smaller and weaker and still Shannon could feel the vibrations which threatened to shake her off her narrow perch.

In spite of the pain, she gripped the edge of the hole harder and, had it not been for the two devil children, she might have been able to stay on the ledge long enough to frustrate the two adult zombies into leaving.

The children weren't fooled by the glass. They went right for the hole, forcing Shannon to let go of her only handhold and shuffle to her left a few feet. Now the only thing keeping her from falling was the blood leaking from her many cuts. Where her skin touched the glass, the drying blood formed a tacky bond —it was the weakest of bonds and felt to Shannon to have all the adhering strength of a dozen sticky-notes.

"You fall," one of the child zombies croaked as it stuck its head through the gaping hole Shannon had made.

The other zombie came to stand next to the first. With their lank brown hair and the deep circles beneath their dark eyes, they might have been brother and sister. Both were utterly fearless, standing with their toes hanging off a sixty foot drop as if they were balancing on a curb.

"You fall," the girl child agreed. She then flapped her hands at Shannon as if impatient and wanted Shannon to fall right then.

"Go away," Shannon begged. "Please, go away. I didn't do anything to you, I swear."

"You fall," the girl child said again and then nodded and pointed down. When Shannon didn't fall, the girl reached out towards her with fingers stained red. "You fall!" she cried, scratching at Shannon's outstretched hand.

With a whimper, Shannon took another two steps to her left, sliding across the glass, leaving a smear of blood and tears behind. She was crying freely, now.

"Please go away." She had been on the ledge for less than a minute and no longer felt so sure that she was going to make it. The two adult zombies were pounding on the glass for all they were worth, making the window vibrate. Her calves were already beginning to burn and her breath was so ragged that she feared that she would accidentally blow herself off.

Amazingly, the girl ducked back through the hole and disappeared inside Shannon's office. "You too," she said to the zombie boy. "You go away also. Please." The boy grunted something that seemed like a laugh and smiled an evil grin until the girl came back.

She held an armful of items: Shannon's stapler and her day planner and her keyboard. Seeing the items sent a shiver up Shannon's spine. "W-What are you going to do with that stuff?"

The girl answered with a demonstration: she threw the keyboard at Shannon, and even though it missed, Shannon screeched and nearly fell. Her hands came off the glass first, and then her cheek peeled away. For a moment she was perfectly balanced. Then a slight puff of wind pressed her back to the glass.

Foolishly, she sobbed against it.

With a flick of her wrist, the girl brought her to her senses. The day planner smacked against Shannon's face. This time, she didn't waiver or slip. Doggedly she clung to the glass and began to ease to her left inch by inch.

The stapler struck her in the head with a sharp *thunk* and still she kept herself moving, slowly shuffling to the corner of the building. Pens were thrown next, and an old rolodex she hadn't used in years. A desk lamp missed as did file folders.

The girl was running out of things to throw! "Fuck you," Shannon spat as she kept edging further and further away. She had developed a rhythm, one that she felt would take her around the building twice if she needed.

In ten minutes she made it to the corner of the building, where there was nothing but brick. She couldn't stick to the brick. In fact, the brick seemed to repel her flesh and now she wavered once again, but she pressed on until she got to the very edge and saw that the next section of the building was long. At least seventy yards of flat glass, sitting on a tiny ledge of brick.

But she didn't have to go all the way. She just had to go far enough to find an office with people in it. They would let her in. With her calves burning, she set off on her narrow path and luck was on her side again as she only had to take twenty-two shuffling steps before she peered through the glass into an office where three peopled were huddled behind a desk.

"Hey!" Shannon yelled, as loudly as she dared. She maintained her balance by a strict control of her body and yelling forcefully undermined that. The one word was enough to get their attention. All three stared in amazement for a few seconds before they shocked Shannon by waving her on, dismissively, as if she were a panhandler.

"Hey! God damn it, break the window!" she cried. Two of them lifted fingers to their lips to shush her, while the third waved at her with frantic gestures to "keep going."

"Fuck you! Open the window or I'll scream."

One crawled out from the desk and going to the window spoke at her ear level: "We can't. They're right down the hall."

"Please let me in," Shannon begged. The man mouthed the word: *S-o-r-r-y*, before crawling back under the desk. Shannon was all set to lash out when she felt a sudden pain lance up the back of her right calf. It was like someone had stabbed her in the leg and was now twisting the knife.

"Cramp," she hissed, tapping frantically with her right hand on the glass. The three people in the room did nothing and gradually Shannon came to realize that she was going to fall. Nothing could stop it now. Her right leg couldn't hold her weight and her left was beginning to weaken. In a second she lost her balance. She tried pin wheeling her arms, to no avail. Near absolute terror seized her, but so too did a sudden savage maliciousness.

Her heart turned to stone. She was going to die because of them! She filled her lungs and let out a piercing note that could be heard for a mile as her calf spasmed and the wall seemed to fall away from her.

Desperately, she clutched at it, but gravity had her and sucked her down—sixty feet straight down to concrete.

Chapter 14

1—12:49 p.m.
Hartford, Connecticut

The moment they cleared the line, Thuy had them turn course, heading northeast, hoping that if there were any pursuers they'd be thrown off by the move. Unlike Jerome, who thought that a thousand men would come rushing to blanket the area, Thuy didn't think that anyone would follow them.

Who would they be looking for exactly? No one had seen their faces, after all. And it sounded as though the 82nd had their hands full enough as it was. There were gun battles stretching up and down the line.

These generally weren't intense or sustained but Thuy figured they would hold the soldier's attention long enough for the three of them to make their getaway.

"How long before we're safe?" Courtney asked as she trudged along, her back bent under the weight of the radio. After she had used it to save them, she wouldn't think about leaving it behind no matter how tired she became.

Jerome squinted up at the sky before he answered: "Another couple of miles, I would say."

Thuy guessed that he had pulled that number out of thin air since he hadn't added any facts to back it up. She let it go, happy to finally be free, though in truth, she found this new freedom to be a tad oppressive. Everything was quiet on this side of the line. Quiet and dead.

Nothing moved on the streets or in the fields or in the air. They walked through Terryville just east of Bristol, surrounded by thousands of homes each one empty and dead.

"Hello?" Thuy called out, her voice rolling down the streets. There was no answer, but an echo.

Courtney got a case of the shivers and Jerome looked ill. "Don't do that anymore, okay?" he asked, his eyes darting around nervously. "It's not right…sorta like yelling in a cemetery if you know what I mean."

Having never yelled in a cemetery, she didn't know what he meant. Nonetheless, she noted her companions distress and agreed not to call out without cause. "I would like to find a change of clothes, some food and a vehicle," she declared.

"Find?" Courtney asked, raising an eyebrow.

"Okay, steal. Normally, I would be dead set against stealing, but I believe this is an emergency situation. And besides, I'm wanted by the FBI on terrorism charges. I don't think a petty little larceny will effect my prison sentence all that much."

Jerome stepped back, his face screwed up in puzzlement. "You are wanted for terrorism? You? What could you have possibly done to be on the FBI's radar?"

Courtney and Thuy shared a look. Courtney's came with a brief head shake but Thuy answered, regardless, her sense of guilt heavy on her shoulders. "This…" she waved her hands around indicating the entire town of Terryville. "This is all my fault. I started this. My work was sabotaged but I began it and…"

"It's not your fault, Dr. Lee," Courtney said, interrupting. "Like you said, your work was sabotaged. You're not to blame, but that reminds me that we need to alert the authorities concerning that one lady who has the virus. There's been so much going on that it just slipped my mind."

Thuy put both hands in her hair and pulled. "I forgot as well. And I also need to find John Burke. I left him behind. Damn it!"

"Who's John Burke," Jerome asked. "And what lady?"

Before answering, Thuy turned to look back the way they had come. "John was a patient of mine. The only one in the study who proved immune to the effects of the Com-cells. His daughter was at least partially immune as well. But now I've gone and lost them both, and John is probably dead. We left him back at the camp."

"Was he that skinny redneck?" Jerome asked and then held his hand up to his chin. "About this tall?"

Thuy's eyes narrowed. "Yes."

"Then I bet he's still alive. He was with me for a few minutes when we were trying to find soldiers who were willing to ditch Colonel O'Brian and get out of the camp. I had just convinced these guys on the line to join us and when I looked around, he was gone. Probably snuck off into the woods like a chicken."

"Do not be so quick to judge," Thuy said. "His seven year old daughter has been out on her own for two days now. John is just doing what he feels is right."

"As we should be doing," Courtney stated before pointing up at an ivy-covered two-story bungalow. There was an older Ford Ranger parked along the curb in front of it. "I bet we'll find the keys inside sitting on the credenza or hanging on a hook or something."

The three went to the door, but before they rang the doorbell, each took a few seconds to make themselves a touch more presentable: shirts were tucked in and buttoned properly. Jerome patted down his short hair, while Thuy raked her slim fingers through hers, somehow making it look as though she had just stepped out of a salon.

Courtney wasn't so lucky. Her curly brown hair was an unruly mane that only a shower and a proper brushing could tame.

Once they had made themselves look at least half-way presentable, Thuy rang the doorbell. She then stood back and waited with her head cocked, listening for the slightest noise from within. Thirty seconds passed and then she rang the doorbell three times in a row.

"I hope they have some food," Courtney whispered. "I am starving."

"Me too," Jerome said. "And I need a shower. Being around those guys with the black eyes was disgusting. I didn't even want to breathe when I was near any of them. Say, how does the disease pass from person to person, anyway? Can I get it just by breathing too close to one of them?"

Thuy, who was also hungry and, as she had dried urine all over her, was more in need of a shower than either of the other two, jabbed the doorbell three more times before answering. "I'm not sure how the transmission occurs in full. It's almost certainly blood-borne, meaning the pathogen is present in blood and other bodily fluids. Normally, for a person to become infected from a blood-borne disease he or she must have an open wound. In other words, there has to be a path into the person's system. But in this case…"

She trailed off for a moment, thinking about how quickly and thoroughly the disease had spread. Clearly, not every person who became infected was walking around with an open laceration and, just as clearly, not all of them had been scratched or bitten by one of the infected.

"In this case," she went on, "I believe we are dealing with a hardy, virulent pathogen that can be transmitted in more than one way. But don't look so worried, Mr. Evermore, you are young and fit. Your body's immune system is strong enough to deal with a *whiff* of the pathogen, you might say. So as long as an infected person doesn't cough into your face, or sneeze on you, or spit in your eye, you should be fine just breathing normally."

"What about touching stuff?" Courtney asked, looking down at her hands which seemed extremely dirty compared to how clean she usually kept them.

Thuy glanced down at her own hand for a moment before saying: "Try not to touch 'stuff' and if you do, then wash your hands as soon as possible afterwards. Speaking of washing, I want to get to it. Let's go around back. I don't like the idea of breaking into this place right here out in the open."

In no time, Jerome pounded in the back door. "Hello?" he called as he stepped in. "Anyone home?" The air was silent and the house as dead as the rest of the town. He waited only a moment before saying: "Dibs on the shower."

While he showered, Thuy and Courtney went through the house and discovered it had everything they needed: plenty of food, water in plastic jugs, clothing in various sizes, though all slightly too small for Jerome and slightly too large for Thuy.

They also found the key to the Ranger hanging on a nail in the kitchen. In thirty-five minutes they were showered, changed and loaded into the truck. They took all the non-perishable food and left a note apologizing for the theft.

"So, where to?" Jerome asked, as he tugged at the collar of a plain, white t-shirt which he wore over a pair of clingy, grey sweat pants that stopped just above his ankle bone.

Courtney had on a pair of loose black slacks and a man's button up dress shirt while Thuy had found a pair of blue jeans which she rolled up at the bottom and cinched tightly with a belt. A green t-shirt that hung, loosely on her slender form completed her outfit.

"Hartford seems like a sensible destination," Thuy answered. "It's the seat of government for the state. We should pass on the information to them concerning Anna Holloway and the vial she carries."

With zero traffic on the roads, the eight miles flew by and they sped up to the newly created wall in minutes. Jerome

174

stopped the truck a few hundred yards away and swore in amazement: "Holy fuck."

"Indeed," agreed Thuy. The wall that had been thrown up overnight stretched as far as the eye could see in both directions. It had been constructed with a nod to necessity and panic rather than to coherence or beauty.

In some places, mounds of furniture made up the barrier and in one place, thirty payloads of sand had been dumped to form a long pyramid connecting a jumbled mass of bed frames on one side to twisted hunks of scrap metal in the shape of an angular giant slug, on the other.

For the most part, the wall consisted of cars stacked on cars, which teetered on top of trucks or buses. In Thuy's eyes, it was a most unsturdy affair and she noted with some relief that it was still being worked on by seemingly endless teams of people who welded and buttressed and shimmed, and others who dragged yet more items to be layered on top of the last.

With a smile, Thuy said: "It seems that, as well as forgetting the basic laws of physics, they also forgot a gate within their wall." This was her version of a joke and so she was a little disappointed when neither of her traveling companions cracked a smile. "Or they just don't want visitors," she added. "Either way, let's go see if we can talk our way inside."

In short, they could not. The people of Hartford now consisted of two tribes. The first group were the people of the interior. They were the old and the weak and the fearful. They hid in their homes as zombies in ever growing numbers took over outside, lurking in the dark places and feeding until they were stuporous.

The second group were the people of the wall. They were the strong. They had spent all night building their wall and now they manned their wall and were prepared to defend their wall. They ate on the wall and slept on the wall and they pissed over the side of the wall—at least the men did, and yet, in a way, they were no less fearful than the first group.

Jerome eased the Ranger forward until he saw just how many guns were pointing at the windshield. He stopped the vehicle and looked over at Thuy. "I got your back."

She had no idea what he meant by that, but smiled at him nonetheless, before slipping out of the truck and walking up the highway to where it ended at the wall.

When she was forty paces away, she was stopped with a sharp word from one man, who was joined by three others who told her to: *Leave* and *Go back the way you came*, and *Get the fuck out of here*. She attempted to explain who she was, but a thrown beer can made her hop out of the way.

"No one gets in," said the oldest of the men present. He carried a deer rifle across his back and had on a black baseball cap, which he wore so low that Thuy couldn't see his eyes.

"I have important information for the governor," she said, speaking quickly before another can was thrown her way. The older man held out a hand, stopping a young man in mid-stoop who was undoubtedly going for another can. Thuy went on in a rush: "I know who is responsible for all of this and that person is currently on the loose outside of the zone and is carrying a vial of what are called Com-cells."

The older man looked at one of the people who had told Thuy to leave. They both shrugged. "That's great and all," the older man said, "but you still can't come in."

"May I speak to the governor, then?"

"She's gone," he replied. The fact that there were zombies within the boundaries of the city were just rumors that came to the wall in drips and drops, however the news that the governor had left the city had sped around the walls in two directions, the gossip meeting just south of where Thuy stood.

"Yeah," the other man spoke up. "She's gone to check the fortifications of the other cities and to try to reopen the border with Massachusetts."

"Reopen the border?" Thuy asked. "When was it closed?"

The man with the deer rifle and the low cap stared for a long time before answering. "You have all this supposedly 'important' information and you don't know that the borders are closed? *Yeah right* is all I gotta say."

"Keep movin'," cawed the other man.

Another can was thrown and the jeers recommenced, forcing Thuy to hurry away. "That didn't go very well," Thuy said in an understatement. After explaining what she heard and saw, she waited for Jerome's and Courtney's input. Neither knew what they should do.

"I say we go look for the governor," Thuy said. "If I had to guess, she went to Manchester first. According to the highway signs, it's not even thirty miles away and it's a fairly good-sized city."

They detoured north around the walled city and once again sped to their destination in no time. The walls of Manchester were smaller, but the people were no less fearful. Again, Thuy was greeted with pointed guns, and the faces that leered down on her had touches of paranoid madness to them.

This time, Thuy did not bother explaining herself other than to say that she had information for the governor that was "Top Secret" in nature. Her ill-fitting clothing did not add credibility to this claim and she was openly laughed at. At least the people of Manchester didn't throw things at her, and they did acknowledge that they had not seen or heard anything concerning the governor.

"Maybe we should try New London next," Thuy suggested to the others. "But first, I need a change of clothes. People aren't taking me seriously."

Clothes were found and time was wasted. Using a brick, they smashed open a shop window and Thuy found a serious looking grey pantsuit that fit her reasonably well. A note wasn't left this time when they climbed back into the Ranger.

Jerome drove southeast for a few miles but stopped abruptly, the tires leaving black streaks behind the Ranger as a Kiowa scout helicopter buzzed right up Route 2, flying just high enough to clear the power lines that occasionally crossed the road.

Behind it came a massive train of green helicopters that stretched beyond the curve of the earth. Each was crammed with men and equipment.

"Mr. Evermore," Thuy said, trying to make herself heard over the din, "why are those helicopters here?" It made no sense to her. The army had just had an airborne jump which had been mind-boggling in its scope, so why the need to bring in even more soldiers?

"It's the 101st, I bet," he answered. "But why they're here I don't know. Unless they have orders to…" The Kiowa suddenly dropped down to road level, coming to hover directly in their path. Behind it, one of the hundreds of Blackhawks landed, spilling out a dozen soldiers, who turned their guns on the Ranger.

"Oh shit," Jerome hissed and spun the truck around.

2—Washington DC

Three hundred and fifty miles southwest of Jerome's stolen Ford Ranger, Lieutenant General Phillips watched the little truck "flip a u-ey" and tear out of there. He sat in a high-backed leather chair, with a cup of tea at his elbow and a scone sitting on a hundred year old bone-china plate two inches from the cup.

The room—the Situation Room, beneath the west wing of the White House, was agreeably comfortable and warm without being hot. There was every amenity he could think of available with a snap of his fingers. He had access to technology that few people could ever dream of. Best of all, the air was scrubbed and filtered. It was unlikely that anyone had ever caught a cold from being in the Situation Room.

Despite all of this, Phillips wanted out of there as fast as he could. He belonged in the field with his men, not sipping tea with the president.

"They won't kill those people in that truck, will they?" the president asked his chief of staff.

Across from Phillips, his boss, General Heider rolled his eyes. Marty Aleman glared at the general before restoring his face to its near-constant state of bland pleasantness. "Of course not, sir. The original use of force orders still apply. The men can't shoot unless they are attacked."

"Good, good. I wouldn't want murder broadcast on live television. We've had enough bad press to last a lifetime."

Heider sat back and drummed his fingers on the table as he tried to control his temper. It was becoming more and more evident in his eyes that the president was a moron and an utter empty suit. He was leader of the free world simply because he had good hair and could read from a teleprompter in a convincing enough manner that people actually believed the words he was reading were his own.

"This is a secure feed," Heider eventually said, speaking to Marty. "We're the only ones who can see it."

Marty grinned at him—the mechanical movement of his lips never touched his eyes, which were dead cold. "Good. I think the time for pageantry is passed. Thanks to the president's quick action, we have given the news stations enough footage to keep them busy for a few days. Hopefully long enough for you to fix this situation."

"What is the situation, exactly," the president asked, pointing at the wall screen. "That map is for Connecticut and those markers say 101. I just got done telling the press that the 101st was going to reinforce the southern line in New York. What the hell are they doing in Connecticut? Don't we already have men in Connecticut? That was a real parachute jump this morning, wasn't it? That wasn't a fake, right?"

Heider leaned back in his chair so that the front legs came off the ground. He stared at the ceiling. Clearly, he wasn't going to answer. Marty said: "Those were real sir, but remember there was an outbreak in Hartford."

"Yes, but we have the 82nd in Connecticut already." The president then leaned in close to his chief of staff and hissed: "Do I need to explain how important New York City is? The rest of the state is just forest and hills and crap. New York City is vital."

Vital for your re-election? Phillips wanted to ask. Instead, he went to the map and tapped the city of Hartford, which was shaded in red. "There are infected persons in Hartford. We don't know how they got there or how long they've been there or if there are more of them in the suburbs. We can't pull the 82nd back to a new line because they would have to cross through an infected area to do so and we don't how the disease is transmitted. It could be that some of them are infected even now and have yet to show symptoms."

Heider blew out a long breath before letting his chair thump down. "This was all spelled out in the brief that we submitted. We don't write them because they're fun, we write them to make ignorant politicians less so—if that's possible."

General Phillips grinned at his boss, thankful that he was finally speaking out. The morning had been the single biggest cluster-fuck Phillips had ever been a part of, and it was all due to one man's need to look good no matter how much shit was being thrown around.

On the literal fly, with eight hundred copters in the air, Phillips had been forced to change the orders of the 101st Airborne Division. Instead of being dispersed on the southern perimeter of the Quarantine Zone, they were forming a new line east of Hartford.

From a logistics point of view this actually helped out greatly. The division would be able to move and fight as a proper division with its chain of command intact and its supply line unhindered and unpilfered by other units. General Milt Platnik of the 101st was the only general happy with the change of orders.

Ed Stolberg, commanding officer of what was left of the 42nd Infantry Division had, as expected, hit the roof. "I can't do it, sir. I can't hold the line with what I have left. You can court martial me if you wish but I'm pulling back ten miles to Highway 6. It'll shorten my lines and give us some breathing room."

"You'll do no such thing!" Phillips barked. "You will fight in position until help arrives, and it will arrive shortly. The 10th Mountain Division is on its way. The first units should arrive within about three hours."

That was a lie. Fort Drum was three hundred and fifty miles away on the other side of the state. They would have to drive at a hundred and twenty miles an hour to get there in three hours.

"I'll be out of ammo in three hours," Ed replied, his voice rising well beyond what would normally be considered insubordination. "I'm pulling back. That's all there is to it. I don't have any choice in the matter."

"What if I got you air support?"

Ed made a rumbly sound in his throat as he thought it over. "Yes. I could hold with air support. But where would you get the fuel? There isn't a drop of JP8 left in the state."

"There's plenty in Boston. Logan sits on a sea of it. I have a marine detachment and two destroyers heading to fetch it right this moment. And I have a good two hundred or so Blackhawks and two dozen Apaches that are now at my disposal. Most of them are practically empty after trailing their coattails along half the Atlantic seaboard, but we're scraping together all the fuel they have for a few sorties. You just have to tell me where to send the Apaches."

"What about the 'use of force' orders," Ed asked. "As far as I know, they haven't been changed. It's one thing when a governor orders National Guard units to disobey orders but you and I can't. They won't even let us use gunships."

Phillips knew this better than anyone but he also knew just how thin the 42nd was stretched. He needed the Apaches. His men would die without them. "The orders have been changed with regard to helicopters," he lied…again. "Collins set a precedent, one that we will follow."

"And did that order come from on high?" Ed asked, warily.

The corps commander waffled at that point, and unfortunately, he had an awful excuse to terminate the call. "We'll talk later on the subject. Right now I have to call Frank and give him the bad news."

Frank Frazer went silent for a full minute when Phillips told him that the entire 82nd was now trapped in the Quarantine Zone. Phillips let the silence spin out; there were just too many implications to rush right onto the worse news.

"We'll be resupplied properly?" Frank asked when he had run through a hundred nightmare situations in his mind.

"Yes, as will Hartford. It will take a few days for things to sort themselves out, but we plan on utilizing the full force of the military here."

Frank possessed a keen mind and read more into the response than someone as hot-headed as Ed Stolberg would have. "Hartford…full force…what are you getting at, sir?"

"It's been decided by the Joint Chiefs that Hartford will need to have a separate quarantine. A zone within a zone, you might say." Again, Frank remained silent for a long spell, digesting these new orders. When Phillips had let it sink in long enough, he went on: "We believe there are close to three hundred thousand people within the walls of Hartford. When they find out there are zombies among them, they'll attempt to break out."

"They'll do more than attempt," Frank said, "they'll succeed. I have just over eleven thousand men. It's not enough."

Phillips had expected this response. "You have just over eleven thousand *trained* men who have better arms and better communications than a mob of civilians. A 'whiff of grape' will disperse them."

"And then what? Do you think my job will get easier when it's a city of three hundred thousand zombies?"

"I hear you, Frank, but think what Connecticut will look like if we don't secure the city. Where will this tremendous mob go in search of safety and what will they do to get it? They'll attack other cities looking to get in and they'll attack the state's borders looking to get out. When that happens, how far will the infection spread? There are three and a half million people in the state. Think about that."

Dutifully, Frank considered the effect that a third of a million people roaming the state would have. It wasn't a pretty mental picture. "I will need the rules of engagement changed. It's as simple as that. I will also need all the mortars and machine guns that I was forced to leave behind back at Bragg. And lastly, I'll need massive air support at my beck and call."

"Consider it done," Phillips said.

Now, he had to come through with his promises. It wasn't going to be easy with the president and General Heider glaring at each other with Marty Aleman between them, trying his best to placate them both.

"We are done here!" the president said, pushing back from the table. "And Heider, your days are numbered in Washington. All of this mess can and will be laid at your feet. You said it could be contained. You gave me promises."

"I never made promises. I said the situation *could* be contained under certain circumstances and that I would need to have complete access to the full firepower of the military, which you denied me. As Commander in Chief, this will be all on your head. The voters are going to blame you."

Talk of voters blaming him turned the president's face beet red. "Wrong. With the massacres, I'm pretty sure I can prove that you couldn't be trusted with the power you did have. You forget, I have the press on my side."

"And I have the military on mine."

The president suddenly went cold. "Are you threatening me?" he asked in a whisper.

Heider realized he had used a poor choice of words. "No, at least not physically, but if I say the word, every one of the Joint Chiefs will resign. And, I believe many of your top generals will, as well."

For some reason, the other three men in the room turned to General Phillips as if to gauge his response. "I was already planning on tendering my resignation," Phillips said. "I can't fight this war under these conditions."

Marty knew what a corps commander's resignation at this juncture would mean. The press would be all over it and too many questions would be asked and too many honest answers would have to be given. It would be a disaster if the full scope of what was happening got out.

"You can't quit, your country needs you." Marty was a shrewd operator and knew that all these Army-types could be manipulated with patriotism.

Phillips chuckled, seeing right through Marty. "No, it doesn't. My country needs my soldiers to have complete use of the weapons they were trained to use. I will stay only on the condition that the rules of engagement are changed. Otherwise I resign and I tell you that a number of divisional commanders will as well. No one wants to be saddled with this mess."

"Maybe we can reach a compromise," Marty suggested.

The president wouldn't hear of it. "First they'll want machine guns and bazookas, and pretty soon it'll be tanks and artillery, and then it'll be planes and bombs and napalm. It'll be just like Vietnam all over again."

Heider laughed: "It already is! Inept leadership in the White House is ruining our chances of nipping this in the bud."

The president slammed his fist down on the table. "You are fired, Heider. And no, you won't be missed. There are plenty of generals who can take your place. Snide generals are a dime a dozen." He then turned on Phillips. "Your request is denied. We don't need tanks when we have enough brave soldiers to do what's right. I have already called up the Army reserve. Pretty soon you'll have half a million men in the battle. That will be more than enough."

Marty added the cherry to the top of the cake: "And we would need someone to run this *army*. What do you say to that?"

I would say that's quite a bribe, Phillips thought. They were offering him command of a fighting army—his dream job.

He sat back, his eyes straying to the map where the outline of the Quarantine Zone stood out sharply in red. With half a million men, the Zone could be held, easily. The reservists would come in dribs and drabs over the course of a couple of weeks, but that would be okay. If he gave Ed Solberg permission to retreat to Highway 6, that would buy time for the 10th to get into place and then he could begin the arduous task of rearranging his forces.

Or not. He could wait until the first reserve division was ready and lift the 42nd out of the line completely, which would allow…

"Phillips, take the job," General Heider said, "but don't allow these morons to run you or the operation. Do what is necessary, militarily, not politically." He started heading for the door, speaking over his shoulder: "I'll let myself out."

He didn't make it out of the room before a young man with a sharp part to his hair and an obviously brand new suit hanging on his lanky frame came bustling in. "Excuse me," he said in a rush and then, much to Phillips' amusement, bowed toward the president. "Sorry to interrupt, but Mr. Aleman said to come to him personally if there were any more developments."

When the young man didn't go on, Marty asked, "And?" The word hung in the air as they waited for him to spit out what he had barged in to say.

"Newark is under attack!" he cried out.

Although each person there knew exactly where Newark, New Jersey was, they all immediately yanked their heads around to stare at the map.

It sat smack dab in the middle of the most densely populated area of the country. Twenty million people lived within a ten mile radius of the city.

Suddenly, an army of half a million soldiers seemed dreadfully small—too small to deal with this. But it was all they had. "I'll take the job," General Phillips said. "And I'll take the tanks, too."

Chapter 15

1—1:51 p.m.
The Hartford Quarantine Zone

Suddenly, there were two Quarantine Zones. Three actually, if the not-yet-begun siege of Hartford counted as a separate zone.

Chaos reigned in all three.

The Governor of New Jersey immediately recalled every police officer, state trooper and national guardsman he had lent to New York. This represented about a third of the forces making up the 42nd Infantry Division. This move began a legal and political battle that raged in Washington, Albany, and Trenton, as everyone with any say in the matter claimed the soldiers and law enforcement officers as their own.

General Ed Stolberg knew he was in trouble when, instead of ignoring calls from grasping politicians, he had to begin ignoring calls from greedy lawyers.

Regardless of who eventually won, the governor's order had the unfortunate effect of leaving General Ed Stolberg in a terrible position as he tried to withdraw back to Highway 6. Many of the Jersey units found the move a prime opportunity to simply leave. Their family and friends were in danger and little was going to stop them from going home.

When they left, they carried off as much ammo as they could carry in as many trucks as they could steal.

The logistics quagmire became logistics hell. Units ran out of ammo in the middle of battle and suddenly the entire southern border disintegrated. Stolberg tried to regroup at Highway 6 as planned, but so many units just kept running past the new border that he could think of nothing better to do but let them run, knowing that they would tire eventually.

Air power alone stopped the majority of the zombie horde north of Highway 6. General Phillips stuck to his threat of resignation and received certain concessions which included the use of helicopters since they could be "snuck" in, buzzing at treetop level. He was also promised machine guns and mortars which could be dropped in by C17s.

Tanks, bombers, and artillery were ruled out as being too conspicuous. Although, General Heider— his "firing" forgotten by all—wanted to argue for more, Phillips took what he could get and ran with it, at least as far as he could.

The lack of fuel paired with the new logistical and rein-forcement demands spread him perilously thin. Thankfully, he was able to scrape together enough fuel to sortie fifteen Apache gunships. The Apaches, with their undercarriage mounted 30mm chain guns and their Hydra missiles, were some of the deadliest machines ever devised. He threw them in wherever the line was close to being overrun.

Dr. Lee had no conception of the full extent of the turmoil her Com-cells were causing. She only knew that it was impera-tive for her to report to the highest authority figure she could find and divulge everything she knew concerning the Com-cells and Anna Holloway. Finding a place of safety was secondary to this, although, thankfully, the two goals seemed to go hand-in-hand.

With the 101st forming a new barrier to finding the gover-nor of Connecticut, Hartford appeared to be the only logical des-tination. "Back to Hartford," she ordered Jerome.

"Why? They won't let us in," he groused. "We should try heading south and taking a boat out of this ridiculous state."

Courtney snorted: "You think no one else has thought of that idea? I guarantee that every boat that can float has been tak-en already and if there happens to be a few left, I bet the Navy and Coast Guard are patrolling the coast, night and day."

"They can't be everywhere," Jerome countered. "The navy is tiny compared to what it used to be. We only have a couple of hundred ships and they're spread out all over the world. We should be able to slip by with no problem."

"You would be correct if it were just ships we had to evade," Thuy said. "They also have planes and lots of them. No, going by boat might be the most dangerous thing we can do, especially during the day. No, we will go to Hartford. Their walls were the largest and they had the most people patrolling them. First, we need to get you two changed and we need to commandeer a new vehicle, one that fits the role we will be playing."

Jerome's eyes narrowed as he asked: "What role are you talking about? They've already seen us. Are we going to put on fake mustaches?"

"*They* haven't seen us," Thuy countered. "A few people on the other side of the city saw me. But as for mustaches, you're on the right track."

Thuy took them shopping in the suburbs of Hartford, where everything they needed was just sitting there. The fact that is was all sitting behind locked doors was becoming less of an issue for them.

Windows were broken with little fanfare and zero remorse. In no time, the three were "suited-up". Jerome and Courtney looked like the squeaky-clean, smartly turned out, young go-getters who always seemed to hang around up and coming politicians, which Thuy assumed the role of.

They ditched the Ranger for a black Yukon Denali they "found" at a dealership, and just like that, they were transformed from three desperate refugees to three people who were "with" the governor's team. Thuy assumed the role of chief of staff and cautioned the others to stick to their roles—Jerome as driver/bodyguard, and Courtney as personal assistant.

A new access point was chosen into Hartford and Jerome sped the Denali right to the wall that sat across Highway 2. As before, guns were pointed their way. This time Thuy ignored them completely as she strode up and announced: "The governor has sent us. We need to talk to the mayor." She hoped that the generic terms "mayor" and "governor" would suffice as she didn't know their names.

"About what?" called down a woman with a cascade of brown hair and what appeared, from Thuy's angle, to be a wide shelf of a nose.

"About things that shouldn't be discussed in front of so many people," Thuy replied glancing left and right at the hundreds of faces staring down from the wall.

The woman with the wide nose turned to a man next to her and hissed something. They had a conversation that consisted of a lot of whispering and shrugs and many bewildered looks. The building of the wall had been a spontaneous event and there was no one who could be called a leader among them.

They dithered as they tried to come to a decision. The governor represented authority, which they craved; however strangers represented danger, which they feared.

Thuy worried that the fear would win out and that they would be turned away and so she used their own fear against them. "I have been sent to discuss important matters with the mayor. Matters of life and death. Likely, your life and death," she said, speaking directly to the woman.

"Like what?" the woman asked, her voice rising.

"Your mayor will have to decide whether or not to inform the people of Hartford. My job is simply to deliver the information to him and him alone. If I cannot do that then, I'll have to go back to the governor, I'm sorry."

This hint of doom was enough to override any other fear. Ropes were cast over the side of the stacked cars and in minutes the three of them were pulled up to the supposed safety of the walls.

Even as Thuy thanked the "Warden of the Wall" as she thought of the woman with the wide nose, a mob of grizzled and grey-haired zombies from the SunRise Assisted Living facility, descended on a four-story brick apartment building. Although the rebooted zombies had been feeble in life, in their undeath they were wickedly strong. Doors were battered in and screams filled the air.

People tried to escape through a back door, but Jaimee Lynn Burke was waiting to ambush any who came that way. She knew the picking would be good and that the big people would be focused more on running away than fighting. She let three men go by because they seemed too large for her pack to handle. A woman laden down with two children was a different thing altogether.

Her pack rushed out from their hiding places in the bushes and dragged the woman down. Of course, she screeched but no one stopped to help. The others speeding from the building ran in a wide circle around her and her two children.

Jaimee Lynn ate the slower of the children. It was so soft and sweet.

Six miles away, Thuy was oblivious to any of this. She asked the warden to accompany her to the mayor's office and an awkward moment occurred when a car was found and the woman asked: "Where is it? I've never been to the mayor's office before."

"Downtown," Courtney threw out in a moment of panic.

Thuy's smile went thin at what she thought was a poor answer. "We rarely have dealings with the mayor and when we do, he comes to us, not the other way around. We're going to have to ask for directions, I suppose."

They headed downtown where the streets were practically deserted. No "one" was about, but there were plenty of "things."

The warden was slow to catch on that they were zombies. One of them, a limping horror that was naked save for tennis shoes and the remains of a pair of pants that were fouled up around one ankle, came roaring out from an alley, making the woman swerve to keep from plowing over it, nearly crashing the car into a lamppost in the process.

"What the hell?" she cried out. It was the first of its kind she had ever seen close up, and in her fear she had pissed out a few drops into her underwear. "How are they in the city?"

"This might explain the soldiers we saw to the east," Courtney remarked.

"And why the governor has fled her capitol," Thuy added. "We should deliver our information and get out of here as soon as possible. Ma'am? If you could get back on the road, we stand a better chance of escaping."

The warden had tried to make a U-turn and hadn't quite got all the way around and was now barreling up a sidewalk that only just fit the car. At the first opportunity, she drove off the curb and sent them bouncing back onto the street.

"Excellent," Thuy said. "We're in luck." She pointed at a sign which arrowed them in the direction of the Hartford City Hall, which turned out to be a brooding, heavy, grey-stoned building that looked dead from the outside. Inside was another story. It was a beehive of activity. The mayor was a busy man. He and a hundred and forty of his closest friends and family members were hard at work, not with the people's business, but with his own.

These friends were everywhere, hurrying about, stacking furniture, nailing windows shut and otherwise fortifying the building. They also kept anyone from getting past the doors to see the mayor. Thuy was not easily dissuaded and her story, told with such believability, bought her an interview with the mayor.

Mayor Donnie Perez, resplendent in a perfectly tailored, light grey suit, took one look at Thuy and before she even opened her mouth, said: "You aren't with the governor's office. I would have remembered you."

With her exotic looks, there was no sense lying. "You are correct; however I do have information that needs to be brought to the attention of the government."

Before she could go on, the woman who had driven them from the wall blurted out: "There are zombies in the city!"

"I know," he said, dryly, gently touching his jet black hair as if feeling for anything that might be out of place. "If that's all…"

"It's not," Thuy answered. "I need help finding some people. The first is a woman named Anna Holloway. She has more than likely escaped the quarantine. She is a corporate spy and is traveling with a Chinese national who…"

Perez put his soft, brown hand out so that his palm was inches from her face; it smelled of coconut-scented lotion. "I have more important things to do than hear about how one corporation tried to screw over another. But, you are pretty," he said, coming to stand very close to Thuy. He looked her up and down, giving her a wolfish smile. "Perhaps I could offer you some protection."

"I don't need protection. What I need is for you to listen to me. This stopped being about corporate interests when my work was sabotaged and all my patients turned into flesh-eating monsters."

The mayor stepped back, his soft hands drawn into his chest. "Your work? What work is that?"

"I worked for R&K Pharmaceuticals. I bio-engineered the cells that ultimately turned into this zombie disease, and right now there is a vial of those cells in the hands of two very dangerous people. They're outside the Quarantine Zone and they aren't afraid to release what's in the vial."

"Where are they?" Perez asked.

Thuy glanced back at Courtney, who paled and edged a step behind Jerome. "Th-the pilot of that B-Blackhawk said he let them off in Montrose." When the mayor only raised an eyebrow, she added: "Montrose, New York? It's about five miles north of Nyack, which is about five miles north of Yonkers, which is about four miles from New York City."

This information only added to the mayor's confusion. "A military Blackhawk gave a pair of saboteurs a ride? Why would they do that?" During the next five minutes, Thuy explained how the zombies came into being and the danger Anna and Eng posed. Surprisingly, Perez gave it all a shrug. "They were dropped off twelve hours ago? I'm afraid you're too late. I think they have already released the virus." A grimace creased his handsome features, aging him. "It sure explains what's happening in Newark."

Now it was Thuy's turn to look confused. Perez told her a stunted and twisted version of what was happening in Newark. When Thuy asked how he had come by the information with all the phones were down, he explained: "A little bird told me," trying to sound mysterious. His one link to the outside world was a CB radio which had once been part of the city's communications equipment that for some reason had never been thrown away.

"By 'bird' do you mean a two-way radio?" Thuy asked.

Before he could answer, Specialist Jerome Evermore broke his silence for the first time since entering the city. "How many people live in Newark?"

"Too many to count," Perez replied. He took a breath to go on, only just then a smattering of small arms fire erupted. "Find out how close that is!" he screamed. Then, in a blink, he was the calm politician again. "Like this woman said, there are zombies in the city, you know. Not a lot, just a handful."

His frightened reaction made Thuy's stomach drop. This was no leader. "It only takes one," she said and then glanced at Courtney and Jerome. "We should get out of here before it's too late."

"I'm afraid it's already too late to leave," Perez said. "The 101st has cut us off in the east and the 82nd is moving to surround us. They'll be here anytime if they aren't out there already. Either way, where would you go if you could get out? No, you're safer with me, and maybe we can parlay what you know and who you are as a way out of here."

2—The New York Quarantine Zone

Without a shovel, the burial of Dr. Wilson took nearly an hour. It wasn't a true burial at all. Deckard and Max Fowler used rocks to cover the body. It was strange to Deckard that the moment he wanted rocks he couldn't find them. Tired and aching, he went back and forth trying to find them and secretly begrudged the rest Chuck and Stephanie were getting.

The pair sat under an oak, leaning against each other, letting the shade of the tree cool them. They held hands—something that Deckard noted with a twinge of jealous.

Where, in all this mess, was Thuy, he wondered. She was never far from his mind. The night before, as he run an endless race and fought countless zombies, he had pictured her face. Now, he hefted a rock and trekked back to the body of Wilson with it on his shoulder, and there she was, still lingering in his mind.

"It's been ten hours, she's got to be long gone by now," he whispered. "Knowing her, she's probably in Washington, advising the president." A smile crossed his face as he pictured her raising a skeptical eyebrow at the fool of a man.

The smile slipped as he came up to the mound of rocks that covered almost all of Wilson. A man in fatigues holding an M4 with its barrel pointed Deckard's way, stood just across from the body. He was as tall as Deckard, but lean as a reed with a face as sharp as a hatchet.

"I wanted to tell him sorry," the man said. It was the hunter.

"Not a lot of good it will do him," Deckard said, as he came forward and gently laid the rock down. A few more would finish the job.

"I guess you're right," the hunter admitted. He jerked a thumb behind him. "I dug up a few rocks when I was making my hole. You're welcome to them. We're going to be shifting the line it seems."

"To where?"

The hunter took a long breath, before answering: "Hartford…it seems I killed that man for no reason. I-I don't know what to say. We were supposed to defend this line, but now there doesn't seem to be a line, or we're all on the wrong side of it. We're trapped in the Zone, same as you. That's what I was told."

"And there's no way out at all?"

"Who knows? There might be some ways to get out, but I don't know of them. If it was me, I'd strike out for Massachusetts, and hope to get lucky. But that's me. Sorry to say, your little group doesn't look to be all that lucky."

Deckard eyed Chuck and Stephanie, who appeared wasted and cruelly thin, and he thought of dead Dr. Wilson, and he thought of everything he'd had to fight for just to get here, which was basically nowhere. The hunter was right, they weren't lucky. "What if we were smart?" he asked. "Do you think a smart person could get out of here? Could they make it to Washington?"

"I doubt even a genius could. Planes aren't flying and the trains aren't running. Even if you could get a car out of the Zone, a lot of states have closed their borders. You might be able to slip out of the Zone on foot, but even then it'll be dicey. This place is crawling with zombies and you have soldiers surrounding you. Hell, even the coast is being watched day and night."

Fowler had come walking up with a rock of his own. He tried to joke: "So the only way out is by tunneling?" It fell flat as no one even cracked a smile.

Deckard barely heard the joke. His mind was taken up by the fact that maybe Thuy wasn't as far away as he had guessed. She had escaped the Zone the night before, but with the Blackhawks so short of fuel they couldn't have gone far. Probably not even to Hartford and that meant she was likely still in the Zone as well.

Knowing her, Hartford would be her primary destination. Anyone else would have raced out of state as fast as they could. Not Thuy. Her first thought would've been to alert the authorities concerning Anna and Eng, and, knowing her, she might have even tried to turn herself in.

"I need to get to Hartford," he said.

The hunter shook his head. "No you don't. There are zombies in Hartford, it's why we're going. Besides, they've put up a wall, so getting in is going to be an issue. And if you could get in, you won't be able to get out again. We're not letting anyone out, no matter what."

"What if I told you that the only person who has a shot at finding a cure and ending this plague is in Hartford? The woman…the *scientist* who invented the Com-cells is in Hartford and it's imperative that we find her."

This only brought a wry smile to the hunter's lips. "If you were to tell me that, I would ask the same thing my platoon sergeant would ask: Where's your proof? And then you'd turn out your pockets and tell me that you have none, and I would have to conclude that you managed to lose a girl you love and you might be willing to do or say anything to find her."

"You'd be both right and wrong," Deckard said. "She is a scientist and she did have her work sabotaged and…and I do love her." It felt odd admitting this to a stranger when he had only said it once to Thuy.

"Love is nice," the hunter murmured, taking a moment to think about Deckard's words. It made him sad. "Love or not, I'm sorry, but the outcome would be the same. If you go in, they're not going to let you out again. Either way, I wish you guys luck."

He left them staring at each other over the body of Dr. Wilson. Chuck Singleton, who was idly turning Stephanie's short brown hair around one callused finger, asked: "Whatcha gonna do?" Deckard was slow to answer and so Chuck answered for him: "If it was Stephanie trapped in that city, there isn't much that would keep me out."

Fowler seemed surprised at this. "According to that guy, getting in isn't the problem. Getting out is the problem. In fact, it looks like a huge problem."

Stephanie grabbed Chuck's hand and kissed it with pale lips. "I'm with Chuck on this one. I'd go in for him, even if I didn't have the strength for it."

"Do...do you have the strength left for anything?" Chuck asked; his worry for her making him choke on his words. She had dark circles under her eyes and her skin was like chalk. Even her smile was weak and short lived.

"Not much. I'm so tired I could fall asleep right here and maybe never wake up. But I can't. I can't rest. I have to go on and on and on. Maybe we'll escape and maybe we won't. Maybe we'll die, maybe we won't, but I'll be with you one way or another."

Chuck wiped the worry off his face with a genuine smile. "Then I figger we go to Hartford. If we have any chance at whippin' this cancer, it's with Doctor Lee. I like ta-think she might be able to brew up a new batch of them Com-cells."

Fowler looked as though someone had knocked him on the head. "All of you are going? Really? You don't even know if she's in Hartford. She could be anywhere. And you heard that guy, they won't let you out once you get in."

Deckard gestured at the forest surrounding them and said: "She's got to be somewhere and if she hasn't escaped the state, she's more than likely in Hartford. We're going and you should, too. Being out here isn't all that great if you ask me. We have limited ammo, and no food or water. It would be a miracle if we survived the rest of the day."

For a full seven minutes, Fowler stood, staring at nothing and really thinking of nothing. His body was one big ache and he was tired like he had never been tired before. Concentration came with difficulty, but he was sure of only two things: going to Hartford would likely be the death of him, and secondly he really didn't want to be alone. Being alone and dying alone scared the crap out of him. Finally, he said: "I'll go."

It took a few minutes to finish Dr. Wilson's burial and then it took a few more for Chuck and Stephanie to stand. It felt as though their bodies had turned to rust in the hour they had rested. Slowly, they began working the kinks out of their joints until they felt they could go on.

The men of the 82nd Airborne had double-timed it east to the city. For them, a four mile run was nothing. For Chuck and Stephanie, four miles was another torture to endure. They could not run. The best they could do was an excruciating tortoise-like pace that hurt Deckard as much as it did them.

He kept envisioning the thousands of terrible things that could be happening to Thuy while the minutes ticked by.

They moved so slowly that, once again, they were menaced by zombies coming up from behind. It became a race of cripples, one that Deckard couldn't win, even if he got to the city first. Ahead of them in Hartford, the multiplying zombies were beginning to reach critical mass.

Jaimee Lynn's pack had grown to thirty malformed children and adults who she could barely control. Not that there was much of a need anymore. At eight in the morning, the few hundred infected people creeping around in the alleys had seemed like few in such a large city. By eleven the number had grown to a couple of thousand; enough to be alarming to Thuy when she entered the city. Now, at one in the afternoon, the few thousand had become thirty thousand with hundreds more turning every few minutes.

The people in the center of the city: the old and the weak, were also the unarmed. Those who fought with bat or knife, died. Those who hid were unearthed, pulled from their hiding spots and eaten. Those who ran, went from one danger into the arms of greater danger.

As the big zombies battered down front doors, she and her pack would lie in ambush in the back. It was Jaimee Lynn's favorite method of hunting. When she leapt out to attack, frequently, her appearance alone was enough to make her prey freeze. She was a horror to look upon. She was so utterly caked in blood that she was a sight straight from hell.

Wet, red blood glistened over the tacky maroon of earlier kills. She had blood rimming her nose and in her teeth. Her blonde hair was now a dull brown and the black deposits beneath her nails had come from thirty different victims.

When people saw Jaimee Lynn, they inevitably screamed a lunatic's scream.

Eventually, the cries and shrieks of those being slaughtered became too much for those still in hiding. Filled with terror, they ran around assembling their belongings for a flight. Those fortunate enough to have garages, stuffed their cars with the obvious: food, water, jewelry, blankets, and extra clothes. They also loaded up on the not-so obvious: televisions, fine china, gravy boats, computers, make-up, and photo albums. Essential or not, not a cubic inch of car space was wasted.

People without garages were forced to grab what they could carry and make a dash for their cars. Sometimes they tried to run back for more; sometimes they didn't make it back.

The predictions of panic became a reality as tens of thousands of people in tens of thousands of cars made a mad break for freedom from a city that had been, not just walled off, but *sealed*. Every street that led to the outside world had been painstakingly blocked and there was no way they could be unblocked quick enough.

Every street that pointed toward the wall became crammed with cars as traffic jams bloomed and, when a few zombies from the center of the city came to investigate the fear-filled honking and the desperate yelling, people abandoned their cars and fled. This only made things worse and soon the streets were impassable.

It was in only three spots that the wall was taken down quickly enough to keep the traffic jams from forming and a total of eleven thousand people managed to escape, in a mad, helter-skelter rush. Another twenty-seven thousand climbed down from their posts on the wall. With nothing but the guns in their hands, they charged out into a state that simply crawled with the undead.

Once the 82nd arrived and plugged the holes, the civilians begged to be let out of the city, but their pleas fell on deaf ears and it wasn't long before desperate battles broke out between soldiers and civilians.

The soldiers were outnumbered twenty to one and at times they were close to being overrun by sheer numbers; however General Phillips proved correct in his assessment of both his men and his opponents.

Lacking a central command, the civilians made numerous unsupported and sporadic attacks. Although carried out with amazing vigor, each began and ended in a piecemeal fashion with the bravest going forward in a rush and fighting for as long as they saw fit. Rarely were these attacks driven home with the same determination that a trained soldier would show.

Demonstrating that communications and leadership were as important as firepower, General Frank Frazer shifted men from threatened point to threatened point. Calm and cool, more like a man playing chess in the park on a sunny afternoon than a blustering general, he concentrated his forces exactly where they were needed for exactly the right amount of time, and no more.

He broke the back of each attack and his line bent but did not break. His victories were not celebrated. He and his men were sickened by what they were forced to do. After one battle, Frazer glassed the carnage with a pair of binoculars. Sixty men and women lay sprawled in the street while another two hundred or so crawled back to the walls of their doomed city leaving trails of blood behind.

"In the short run, we've won a battle," he said to himself. "In the long run we've made it permissible for soldiers to slaughter the very people they were sworn to protect. Even in victory, we have lost."

In the five hours he had been on the ground there had been a change in his soldiers' attitude. They had been reluctant to kill— at first. Then, they killed out of duty to their brothers and their mission and to the people in the "real" world. Now, outside the city walls, they grumbled and cursed the people of Hartford for trying to escape what seemed like certain death.

Frazer felt the anger coming from his men and it saddened him

"*They're cowards!*"

"*They need to clean up their own mess instead of trying to pollute the rest of the world.*"

"*If you're not going to shoot the zombies, you should at least shoot yourselves!*"

The general turned away instead of reprimanding his men. As a student of history, he knew that civilization was the thinnest of veneers covering a dark and barely understood core. Humans had been little more than brutal beasts for two million years and it was only in the last three hundred years or so that the idea of civilization had come to take on a real meaning.

It wouldn't take much to turn back the clock.

Deckard led his little group through the empty suburbs right toward the sound of the inhumane savagery. The hard-fought battles could be heard for miles and the closer they got, the more Stephanie regretted her words from earlier. She hadn't expected such heated fighting.

In her mind she had pictured a slightly rosier scene: men sitting in foxholes outside the city, smoking cigarettes, chatting quietly and killing the occasional zombie that ambled by.

The sound of guns was very loud, when Chuck coughed and cleared his throat before saying. "We just gonna walk up on 'em? They sound a might bit trigger happy for that."

Deckard stopped under a shading tree, wiped a sleeve across his face, and asked: "What do you suggest?"

"Maybe if we had a white flag, they might be slower to shoot at us."

It was a sensible idea and quickly adopted. Sheets were easily found and a flag created. Deckard carried it, holding it high as they walked through the deserted neighborhoods just south of the city.

The buildings grew closer and closer and the houses smaller, the further they went. The wall of cars and cast off junk ringing the city had just come into view when Deckard saw movement in an upper-floor window of a tall Victorian home.

He stopped, the hairs on his arms sticking up. People were watching him and worse, people were pointing guns at him. He could feel them. Then came the audible "click" as someone flicked their rifle from safe to fire.

Chapter 16

1—2: 41 p.m.
The Hartford Quarantine Zone

"Don't make any sudden moves," Deckard whispered.

"Why?" Stephanie asked, feeling strangely nervous and not knowing why. "What's wrong?"

Deckard jutted his chin up towards one of the homes on the block. "Upper floor window at our eleven o'clock. Rifleman." The group stopped and stared, trying to pick out the soldiers in their camo against a suburban backdrop. Deckard could pick them out better than the others. "There's another cattycorner at our two o'clock."

Stephanie squinted mightily before she saw the outline of a man in green, squatting next to a bush. When she saw the gun pointed their way, her heart missed a beat and the sweat seemed to freeze down her back. Instinctively, she raised her hands as if in surrender.

A voice from the house hailed them. "Go back! You can't go this way."

Moving slowly and deliberately, Deckard placed his rifle on the ground and raised his hands as well. "We can pass!" he yelled back. "You're with the 82nd Airborne and we know that your orders are to keep people from leaving the city. They don't forbid people from wanting to go into the city."

"Why the hell would you want to go in?" the person in the window demanded.

Before Deckard could answer, Stephanie spoke up: "We need to find a woman in the city. Her name is Dr. Thuy Lee. She's a scientist. She has the cure for the disease."

Out of the corner of his mouth, Deckard whispered: "What are you doing? She doesn't have the cure."

"I know that, but he doesn't," Stephanie answered without turning her head. In her opinion, Deckard was too in love to lie effectively and Chuck was too honest to even make the attempt. Fowler seemed like a nice guy, but in her eyes he wasn't the smartest of men.

If they were going to lie their way through to Hartford, she would have to do it. She raised her voice again and called out: "We need to find her before it's too late. If the, uh, disease spreads too far, it might become unstoppable."

This last part wasn't exactly a lie, still it caused a whispered conversation to break out among the hidden soldiers guarding the street. Stephanie was able to track their voices and now saw them hidden in the shadows and beneath bushes and under cars. Eventually, one of them asked: "How do we know you're telling the truth?"

"Why else would we want to get into a city full of zombies?" Stephanie answered. The soldiers had no response to this. It was clearly something they hadn't expected.

As the soldiers whispered back and forth to each other about what to do, Deckard dropped his white flag onto the street and called out: "We're going to take the magazines out of our guns."

Slowly, deliberately, the four of them dropped their magazines and jacked out the chambered rounds. With their bolts back and their ports open, they slung their rifles across their backs and advanced with their hands up. Twenty feet from the house, a sergeant with a face that was stubbled and pock-marked stepped out from behind a minivan and ordered them to halt.

"There really is a cure?" he asked, unable to keep the hope out of his voice.

"Yes, there is," Stephanie lied, easily.

Deckard added: "If we can speak to an officer, I can give you proof."

"Why an officer?" the sergeant demanded, suddenly suspicious. "Why can't you explain it to me?"

"Because when I explain things to you, you're going to talk to your company commander and he's going to talk to the battalion commander and so on. I want to cut out as much of the crap as possible. We don't have a lot of time. Tell them we know where Dr. Thuy Lee is. She's wanted by the FBI, probably on their *Ten Most Wanted* list."

"Ten Most Wanted? Why would someone with a cure be wanted by the…" He paused at seeing Deckard's glare. "Right. Sorry. I'll make the call."

It took thirty-six minutes, seven calls and seven abbreviated explanations before General Frazer was reached. The name Thuy Lee was not a name he was likely to forget. Hours before, it had come up when he had been debriefed on the cause of the virus. A smirk had crossed his face at the idea that an evil scientist, as she was thought to be in some circles, would have such a cartoon name.

The name Thuy had come up a second time, thirty minutes before. Someone high up on the food chain had floated the question of whether or not it was feasible to rescue a person from within Hartford.

"Who's so important that I should risk my men?" he had asked his boss, General Phillips, thinking that good men would be killed trying to rescue the governor or some senator, or some filthy rich fat cat who thought he could bribe his way to safety.

Phillips surprised him by answering: "The Mayor of Hartford says he has the scientist who started the plague. A woman named Thuy Lee. The FBI is after her, too. Some people think she's valuable and others think she's dangerous. Either way, they want to know if you can zip in there and get her."

"Zip in?" Frazer pulled the sat-phone from his ear wondering: *Zip in? Was that a joke?* "No, sir. No one's going to be zipping in any place. Other than a few Apaches I lent to Ed Stolberg, all my choppers are grounded from lack of fuel. And I won't send men in on foot. The chances of one of them coming out infected is too great. I don't think one scientist is worth it."

But a scientist with a cure would be.

Frazer was on the other side of the city when his intelligence officer tracked him down with news about a possible cure. In a minute, he had commandeered a truck, hoping to "zip" around the city, but with all the zombies it was slow going. By the time he reached the little group, they were snoozing in the shade of a poplar tree, flinching every time a soldier gunned down one of the zombies that had been limping along in their wake. There was already a mound of them in the street.

The general conferred with the pock-marked sergeant for a moment and then cleared his throat, loudly. At the sound, PFC Max Fowler cracked an eye. In a flash, he hopped up and came to attention. "You a soldier?" the general asked in his slow drawling voice.

"PFC Maxwell Fowler of the 42nd, sir. I'm an MP, sir. My unit was one of the first guard units in place holding the perimeter of the zone. Unfortunately, the line was pulled back without our knowledge and we were left stranded."

"And your uniform?" Frazer asked.

Fowler hesitated, glancing down at the blue jeans and Led Zeppelin T-shirt he had taken from an abandoned home back in Gamet Corners. "Sorry, sir. I...I had to throw it away when it got zombie blood on it. That was hours ago, sir. We're not infected, I promise."

General Frazer had taken a small step back. This promise of not being infected had not been believed by the paratroopers, either, and the group hadn't been allowed to come within fifty feet of the line which, at this point happened to be a cross street called Jordan Lane.

"As much as I want to believe you, we can't take chances," Frazer replied, holding up a hand, just in case the soldier thought about advancing. "Perhaps you should tell me what you know about Dr. Lee. Does she really have a cure?"

Fowler glanced once at Deckard and then dropped his head. "No, sir, I don't think so." He paused as the soldiers around the general began to mutter and grumble, angry that they'd been lied to. "She might not have the cure, but I believe she could be our best chance at finding one. She's a genius. I've seen her in action. She's scary smart. I think it would be wise to find her and secure her."

"Scary smart?" General Frazer asked, showing his temper. "That's all you have? There are plenty of smart people in the world and I doubt that she's so much smarter than any of them."

"I'm willing to bet she is smarter than most people who call themselves geniuses," Deckard said. "But it's not her smarts that you should save her for. It's her knowledge of the disease that makes her valuable. She developed what's called a combination cell. It's a cell with regenerative powers—healing powers you might say. It was sabotaged during testing, but I bet she could find a way to use that same cell to cure the disease."

Frazer shrugged. "I won't hang my hat on a 'maybe.' I won't gamble the lives of everyone in the world on a 'maybe.' Because without a doubt if you go into the city you *will* come out as a zombie or someone on the verge of becoming one. I won't stop you from going in, but I will kill you if you try to get out."

"People have been trying to kill me for days now," Deckard said. "I'm not too worried."

"I am," Stephanie murmured.

The general caught her words. "Then don't go. It's a suicide mission. Listen to that." From the city came a steady *pop, pop,*

pop of guns firing. Beneath the sound of the guns were faint screams that went on and on. "Don't go to Hartford. Find a different town to hole up in. Mansfield is walled and is supposedly zombie free. Try there."

Stephanie gave him a tired smile. "Sounds lovely, but I don't think I can walk that far. No, I'll go into Hartford and we'll find Dr. Lee. I trust her and I trust Mr. Deckard. And you know what? I trust you, General. You'll do the right thing when the time comes."

He shook his head. "When the time comes, I'll kill you ma'am, and it will be the right thing to do. The disease spreads too easily. You know that probably better than I do." Her tired smile turned sad. She looked so done in that the general wished he could order her to stay, but he didn't have the authority. Instead, he turned to the sergeant. "If you have any extra ammunition, give it to them. And some food and water."

"See?" Stephanie said, her smile growing bright again. "You are doing the right thing already."

"It feels like a stupid thing," Frazer said.

As a few magazines, some MREs and a couple of canteens were reluctantly laid in the street, the general told them: "Your doctor friend is at the Hartford City Hall. Once in the city, go north. There's a road that cuts through the city on a diagonal. You'll want to veer right on that for a couple of miles. When it ends, there'll be a park on your left. City Hall is in there somewhere. Good luck."

"Thanks," she said, taking Chuck's hand and following after Deckard, who was in a hurry to get to Thuy.

The four person group scooped up the food and ammo and crossed through the thin line of men. Stephanie had expected there to be hundreds of soldiers, but there were only eight visible and that was counting the general. Once on the other side of the street, the men slunk back into the shadows, leaving only the general watching them. Stephanie waved and the older man waved back. He did so with his face set in grim lines. He didn't think he would ever see them again, in fact he was sure of it.

2—The Hartford Quarantine Zone

"We got through that line easier than I thought," Stephanie remarked. "I thought it was going to be much harder. Maybe Hartford won't be so bad, either." They had gotten in a good long rest while waiting for the general and now she felt as close to perky as a person with stage four lung cancer could.

"Let's hope so. Lock and load, people," Deckard said, pulling his rifle off his back, slapping in a magazine and letting the bolt *thunk* forward.

Ahead of them stood the makeshift wall which had been built only the night before. Brown stains—blood that had run down its metal structure and had dried—gave the wall a far older appearance. The bodies sprawled along its top baking in the sun gave it an evil feel. It was now deserted save for the crows that picked over the corpses.

In the end, the wall had proved worse than useless. Not only had it failed to protect them from the zombies, it had trapped them when they were most desperate to get out. Right then the wall appeared to be little more than a monument to man's desperation.

It stood roughly forty feet in height, though to Stephanie it might as well have been a hundred. She couldn't climb it if her life depended on it. Thankfully, the wall had been tumbled over in a number places as people had rammed it with their cars in order to break free. Usually that hadn't helped in any appreciable way. Cars still couldn't get past the wreckage.

But people on foot could.

Deckard, moving slowly with his head up and his eyes out, led them toward one of these areas. As they got closer, the air hummed with the sound of tens of thousands of flies as they gorged themselves endlessly on the corpses.

The gap in the wall had been the scene of one of the more intense battles. There were bodies everywhere—a few of them still moving, a few still groaning, a few pleading for help.

One man sat propped against the rear bumper of a Volvo that sported Utah plates. He had four holes in his body and a pool of blood around him that seemed impossibly large. By all accounts, he should have been dead.

"Give me water," he gasped, holding out a hand to Stephanie. The hand was red and shiny and slick.

She paused, but Deckard grunted: "Don't. It would be a waste."

Of course, it would be a waste of water, but that wasn't really the point in her mind. She *needed* to help the man. It was an imperative that came from the soul. Wouldn't she want to be helped if she was in the same position? Wasn't that the nature of the Golden Rule?

"It'll just prolong his sufferin', darlin'," Chuck said as he tried to ease her along. That at least made more sense. She didn't want to be the cause of more pain. Willing her heart to stone, she turned away from the man. Two steps later there was a loud BANG! from behind her and something that was akin to an angry bee zipped between her cheek and Chuck's.

Before she knew what was happening, Chuck threw her down behind a car that her shocked mind could only classify as "green," and it was a moment before she realized that she had just been shot at. Feeling a strange *zing* of electricity go through her, she stared around and watched as Fowler dove to the ground, dragging Sundance with him, while Chuck struggled to disentangle his rifle that had become fouled in the grill of the green car.

Amazingly, Deckard had not moved except to spin around. In a blink, his M4 was at his shoulder, his right index finger on the trigger. He had it aimed back the way they had come. Stephanie craned her neck over the green car to see who had shot at her: it was the bloody man.

He was struggling with a deer rifle, trying to pull back on the bolt with hands that shook and were as weak as a child's. He never got the bolt back. "Give me some damn water," he hissed. Almost as an afterthought, he spat out: "Please."

"I can't," Deckard replied, lowering his rifle. "We don't have enough for ourselves. Besides, if you're infected…"

"I'm not!"

A look of anguish crossed Deckard's rugged features. "I can't take that chance. There's too much blood. Sorry."

The man spat at him. "Fuck your sorry."

"Right," Deckard replied, backing away. When he came up alongside the green car, he gave Stephanie a once over. Satisfied that she hadn't been shot, he said: "Let's move. Things are only going to get worse the deeper into the city we go."

She was slow to get up. When Chuck had tackled her, she had cracked her knee on the pavement and now she couldn't bear to put her full weight on the leg. Chuck let her drape an arm across his shoulders so that she could keep up as they moved down the trash-strewn street.

Hartford had changed overnight. The city that had banded together in such an amazing display the day before was now a city without pride or joy. No longer was the city open and bright. It was now a dark and frightening place. The streets were a disorderly confusion of abandoned cars and dead bodies. Blood, both black and red, sat in congealing pools, or ran down gutters in horrific little streams.

Screams vied with gunshots for supremacy in the still fetid air while the smell of rot and death hanging over the city was enough to dizzy Stephanie's head. She clung to Chuck and his grip was like iron. He would never admit it, but he was frightened as well. She could feel his heart racing.

The shadows moved with the dead and the dying, with the infected and those who were clean and desperate to remain so. Their faces could rarely be seen. Usually there was just a glimpse of pale skin or a flash of hair as people ducked away out of sight.

They were the people from the wall who had run from it when they realized they were trapped. Two days without sleep, two days of hard labor, two days of fear that built up, greater and greater, had turned them paranoid. They hid from Deckard's little group, afraid to be seen by anyone.

After all, who could be trusted? Who was sick and who wasn't? Who was ready to eat your face off and who would put a bullet in your eye? No one knew. Many perfectly healthy people were shot to death for the crime of getting "too close" to someone.

Within hours the people of Hartford had become tribal in nature: those people on the inside of the group were to be helped and protected. Those on the outside were to be feared or killed.

The fearful, xenophobic people were dangerous; however, the zombies were worse, far worse.

Tens of thousands of them roamed the city at will, sniffing out the clean blood of the living. The undead were as voracious as they were strong and all but the stoutest doors could be ripped from their hinges.

When the doors came down, people fled into a city that no longer resembled a modern city. Fires burned out of control and dense black plumes of smoke could be seen rising in columns a mile into the air.

Deckard led his little group into this new hell. Within five minutes, everyone but him regretted their decision. They crept up Franklin Avenue, keeping to the shaded side of the street, praying to God that they would be able to make it at least to the diagonal road that General Frazer had spoken about, before they were attacked.

Their prayers were not answered. Three blocks into the city, a pair of black-eyed fiends stumbled onto the street in front of them. Deckard, followed by the rest, ducked behind the nearest parked car. "If they go the other way, we'll be alright," he said. They went the other way, but they were not all right.

The zombies were following a very light wind, breathing in the scent of fresh clean blood. They tracked the smell just up the block to a small mom and pop grocery store where a number of locals had barricaded themselves. The little group watched as the front door of the store was attacked.

Those inside climbed to the roof of the store and began shooting at the zombies. They had terrible aim. It took seven shots to kill two zombies and the booming sound of their guns could be heard up and down the street. In no time, more zombies poured out of the shadows and out of neighboring buildings— some coming from directly behind Deckard's group and if it hadn't been for Sundance and his keen sense of smell, they might have been caught unaware.

With just enough time to get away, the group ran down the closest street, one with quaint, little cottages and old trees that stood as silent sentries up and down the block.

The group was fresh meat and out in the open. In seconds dozens of the undead were pounding up the block after them. "This way!" Deckard said, crossing over the street. He hurried along the side of a house and into a backyard strewn with toys.

The fence surrounding the yard was a six-footer made of faded grey planks. Stephanie took one look at it and quailed. She feared she lacked the strength to pull herself over.

Chuck felt her hesitate. "Don't worry, darlin' I'll get you over."

"What about Sundance?" Fowler asked. "We can't just throw him over. If he breaks a leg, Courtney will have my balls."

Deckard had no intention of throwing a hundred pound dog anywhere. After giving the fence a quick once over, he took hold of one of the boards and hauled back on it with all his strength. It was only held in place by a few rusting nails and with a squeal of protesting wood, he pried back the board. A second board was yanked out, leaving a hole plenty big enough for them to get through.

The zombies were right on their heels as they slipped through the opening, but Deckard refused to shoot them. He feared giving away their position any more than they already had. Besides, the opening was barely a foot wide. The zombies stacked up at the hole as the first of them couldn't contort itself properly to fit through with ease.

Eventually, after peeling back its grey skin like a molded banana, it slithered through. By then, the group was across another street and zipping through a second backyard. This one was a jungle compared to the neatness of the first. It was so overgrown that the weeds had become shrubs, the shrubs had become bushes and the bushes had become wild, many-branched green monsters that could, and did, hide actual monsters.

An entire family of infected individuals had crawled into them to hide from the sun. Only in the last few minutes had they finished their transformation into zombies. Deckard hurried past them without noticing, but when Chuck and Stephanie hobbled by, leaning on each other, the creature that had once been the mother of the family suddenly burst out.

Stephanie screamed and as Chuck released his hold on her shoulder, her injured leg buckled and she fell, accidentally pulling Chuck down with her. The mother zombie rushed forward, her black mouth open wide in hungry, evil joy.

This time, Fowler was the quickest. He swept up his rifle and plugged the mother twice in the forehead before she made it five steps. Right behind it came the rest of the family: three youngsters with teeth sharp as razors, and their lumbering daddy that was a huge mound of jiggling grey flesh dressed only in boxers. Fowler incorrectly gauged the larger of the zombies as the more dangerous enemy and dropped it with two quick shots, while the children moved, quick as adders.

Instead of coming forward in blind hunger, they spilt, dodging left and right so that Fowler's next shot took off an ear, but otherwise did no damage. Deckard managed to get one of the little beasts with a three-round burst that spun it around like a top.

The other two were on Chuck and Stephanie so fast that no person could have saved them—only Sundance was quick enough. He flashed forward, his white teeth looking as large as daggers and his growl that of a wild beast. He stood over Chuck and Stephanie bristling in anger, and his sudden appearance stopped the child zombies, who could still remember an instinctual fear of large dogs.

They stopped long enough for Deckard and Fowler to correct their aim and fire. The two fell and, just like that, Sundance reverted from a hell-hound to a tail-thumping dog.

"That was close," Stephanie said, as Chuck pulled her to her feet. She tried to hold herself up, but her muscles were quivering and wouldn't stop. Her legs threatened to give out and she didn't think she could stand without help.

"It was," agreed Deckard, tersely. "Okay, if we're all good, we need to move. I'm sure those gunshots were heard from one end of this city to the other."

Stephanie tried to move, however, her legs wouldn't listen and the quivering had made its way into her arms and chest. "I just need a second," she said in a whisper to Chuck.

Deckard heard and turned on her. "You don't have a second. This isn't the time to get a case of the vapors. We have to clear the area before the stiffs descend on us like flies. Come on, suck it up."

She tried again and failed again. Deckard looked as though he were about to say something scathing, but Chuck turned on him with flinty eyes. "Y'all might want to shut yer mouth. This isn't a case of the vapors. This is what stage four lung cancer looks like after three rounds of chemo. You don't just suck that shit up."

The hard look on Deckard's face softened. "You're right. I'm sorry. How about I help her, Chuck, and you lead for a while. Just keep striking north until we get to that diagonal road."

Deckard slung his rifle and then lifted Stephanie to her feet. After the cancer and the chemo, she was as light as she was weak. He held her easily.

When Fowler had corralled Sundance, who had been sniffing over the bodies, Chuck set out, moving north, going through backyard after backyard. It took longer this way but it felt safer. They were less exposed except when they were crossing the streets in quick rushes.

Without Stephanie's weight on his shoulders, Chuck felt stronger and the entire group moved along at a quick pace for the next thirteen blocks until they reached the diagonal. It was Maple Avenue and it had been a main thoroughfare before the zombies; now it was a main thoroughfare *for* zombies.

By then Chuck was flagging, coughing little bits of lung up and spitting them in the grass. Since they had thrown off the pursuing zombies, Deckard decided a break was in order. They found a two story home to rest in that overlooked Maple.

After clearing the house, Deckard sat in a north-facing window, mindlessly chewing his way through an MRE as he watched the road, looking for patterns in the movements of the zombies and hoping they would be drawn off by something.

Chuck and Stephanie ate half an MRE between them before falling into a deep sleep. Fowler ate and rubbed Sundance's stomach. He too fell asleep with his headed cocked all the way over on his shoulder.

Full now, Deckard fought to stay awake. He had to get to Thuy before it was too late—this had been an urgent demand consuming his entire consciousness for the past twenty hours. But now, after three days of constant battles and crushing stress, he could barely think of anything but sleep.

His eyes closed at just after two in the afternoon. They all were so exhausted that they likely would have slept around the clock, but they were eventually woken by a low moan.

Deckard's first thought upon waking was: *A zombie got inside the house!* He sprang up, gun at the ready, and took one step toward the door when the moan sounded again—this time from within the room.

It came from PFC Max Fowler.

"My head," he said. Though he spoke in a whisper, they could hear the fear in his voice. "My head, it hurts. Deckard… my eyes, how are my eyes?"

Deckard moved just close enough to see the man's eyes properly: they were very dark.

Chapter 17

1—4:46 p.m.
The New York Quarantine Zone

Anna Holloway's head thumped just above her left temple, pulsing every second or two along with the beat of her heart. When the headache had first begun, she had felt a thrill of fear go through her. She had been frightened enough that, at the first opportunity, she had stolen away from the others, got down on her knees and begged forgiveness for the many inhumane acts she had committed.

She didn't even believe in God, but she was a woman who always covered her bets.

That had been two hours before, during their long march south, which had left her feet blistered and her level of exhaustion so great that she was on the verge of collapse. Their escape was not going as planned.

Killing FBI Agent Meeks and stashing his bloodied corpse beneath a pile of stove-cut logs back in Montrose had been easy enough, but getting the group to believe that he had just "run off" proved impossible. Suspicious looks darted among them and later, as the group of five hostages and four hostage-takers began a diligent search for a boat to take them down the Hudson, Anna caught bits of whispered conversations.

The group was afraid of Anna and Eng and had every right to be, but they also feared the unknown. Montrose was an utter ghost town. It was deserted in a way modern Americans with their chaotic, busy lives simply couldn't understand. The sound of their footsteps echoing among the empty buildings gave them the shakes. They clung to each other and kept to the center of the street in a little knot.

It was not a shock to Anna who overcame their fear first. It wasn't Bob and Allan, two grown men, or Renee, Meg, or Jenny, the three state trooper dispatchers, it was Jack and Alivia, the teenagers.

"We need to go after them," Eng whispered when the brother and sister left to use the bathroom and never came back.

"I don't think so," Anna answered. "They have a fifteen minute head start. They could be a mile away by now. You'll never find them, and even if you could, what would you do with them? Kill them? Chain them up? How do you think that will affect the others? Not in a good way, I'd be willing to bet."

Eng grumbled: "We don't need any of them. We should kill them all. What if they run away, too? What if they alert the authorities about who we are and what we have with us?"

Anna was a spy and that made her a high-stakes gambler. She had been impressed with Alivia and Jack from the very start —how many other teens had managed to survive the Quarantine Zone on their own? Anna was willing to guess that it was an awfully small number. On the flip side, Anna wasn't impressed with the adults. They were weak.

She addressed them, holding up the vial of Com-cells: "Two more runaways," she said, with a little shrug. "They'll probably be dead in a few days. Either they will starve, or they will get shot by someone thinking they're zombies, or they'll just die of exposure. I don't really care one way or the other. What I care about is if they do something stupid like telling someone about us and about this."

Anna held the vial higher, making sure that each of them could see it clearly. "If the police find out about the vial, they'll come looking for it and there will be a confrontation and the vial *will* get dropped. This is the virus in its concentrated form. If its opened, it could infect everyone within a mile. Think about how fast the disease will spread. It'll get to New York City in hours. Can anyone tell me what might happen if eight million people got infected?"

Renee, one of the dispatchers raised a small hand. "It would be the end of the world, I bet."

"Yes, exactly," Anna agreed. "My point to this is, let's get through this safely and silently. Together, we have a chance."

The speech kept more of them from running. It didn't help them get further from the Zone.

Taking a boat down the Hudson and out into the Atlantic, where they could go anywhere they wished, was their first idea. The problem was that they were the last people with this idea. In a stolen Ford Expedition, they went up and down the river bank, going to every marina only to find all the docks empty.

The people in that region had heard about the endless traffic jams tying up the roads all through New Jersey and so they jumped in their boats…and in other people's boats, frequently against the owner's will, and headed down river.

"I guess we drive, then," Anna said. It was a bad option. The traffic jams in New Jersey weren't the only obstacles they would face. First, they had to get to Jersey and if they could fight their way through the growing hordes, they would still have to get into Pennsylvania where the borders hadn't just been closed, the governor of the Keystone state had used the words: *utterly sealed.*

"Maybe there are boats further inland," Renee suggested. "My uncle kept his boat on the side of the house, not at some marina. I bet there might be a few still around."

Two hours were wasted driving around looking for a boat. They eventually found a little fishing craft that barely held the seven of them. After much cursing by all involved, it was hitched to the back of the Expedition and hauled out to a boat ramp that fed into the Hudson.

The engine was tested and the tank filled with gas. Despite the puny size of the boat, it seemed that nothing could stop them from getting as far from the Zone as possible. They made it only three miles before they were intercepted by a forty-five foot Coast Guard response boat that came roaring at them.

"The river is closed to traffic. Turn around now or you will be fired upon!" A pair of mounted M240 machine guns were all the authority the Coast Guard needed. Eng heeled the boat around so fast that Bob nearly fell in.

"Now what?" Eng groused.

Anna thought that was obvious: "We drive."

Driving didn't work, either. They went back to the ramp where they had left the Expedition and took it south on I-9. They made it four miles before they hit what they thought was their first traffic jam. Both lanes were backed up as far as the eye could see. In the distance, Anna could just make out flashing lights.

"An accident?" she asked. "With everything going on, you wouldn't think that the cops would bother showing up for an accident."

They sat there waiting until Allan noticed something about the other vehicles in front of them. "Are those cars even on? Are there people in them?" For the most part the cars were so filled with household goods that Anna couldn't see through the back windows. At Allan's question, everyone piled out of the Expedition and discovered that there wasn't a single person in any of the cars.

"Holy Christ," Bob wailed. "Where is everyone?"

"I'll go ask the police," Anna said. "All of you wait here." Eng wouldn't wait and so the two of them marched forward until they came to a road block comprised of two police cruisers sitting nose to nose. An even dozen men crouched behind the cars. They weren't police.

"Stop right there!" one of them barked. "Hands where I can see them."

Anna left the vial in her pocket, raised her empty hands and smiled sweetly. "What's going on? What's all this fuss about?"

Her charm was wasted on them. None of them lowered their weapons and when the first man spoke again, he wasn't any more polite. "What's going on? Everything's fucked up and you're on the wrong side of the line, that's what's going on."

Anna's heart sank in her chest. Had the Quarantine Zone been enlarged again? She pushed the smile back in place and asked: "What line is that? The perimeter of the Zone is still miles to the north, isn't it?"

"For now, yes. But the 42nd hasn't got their shit together, so we started a secondary line. No one crosses it. We're sending people to Chappaqua. Someone said there's a relief center there for you refugees. You need to go back to the 117 and take it northeast."

"But…" Anna began.

"There ain't no buts and there ain't no getting through here. All the roads south are closed, and we have orders to shoot anyone trying to sneak around. So for your sake, don't even try it."

A lie came quick from her lips: "Of course not. I wouldn't dream of it. Thanks so much for all your help." She gave the gruff men a little wave before she pulled Eng around for the long walk back to where they left the others. "We can't go to Chappaqua," she said out of the corner of her mouth. "It's too close. It's way, way too close to the Zone, especially if the military is having issues." Eng grunted something that sounded as though he agreed.

The others agreed as well. They didn't trust Anna and they loathed Eng, and yet, they had experienced the zombies firsthand. They knew they had to put as many miles as they could between them and the Quarantine Zone. They had talked about getting into Pennsylvania, but even that felt too close.

"We can't drive, so we walk," Anna said. "The men back there said they were guarding every road, and there are a ton of roads out here. That probably means they aren't guarding the forest. It looked like it was pretty thick to the east."

Going east seemed like a good idea and, at first, the forest was so thick they couldn't see thirty yards in any one direction. It was close and hot. The air felt heavy in their lungs. The further south they went however, it grew more and more open until they reached the demarcation line of the "Second Line," which happened to be Interstate 287.

It was a hundred yards of wide open pavement that was being regularly patrolled by young men in a pair of pickup trucks. They tooled back and forth, guns hanging out of their windows, looking ready to run anyone or anything down.

Everyone, except for Eng, appeared deflated at the sight of them. The group plopped to the ground in defeat while he stood with his hand against a tree and watched the road. Ten minutes went by and, while Anna and the others drank from water bottles, he stood there.

"We can make it across," he said, finally. "There's a pattern. Every few minutes they are out of sight of that bend for a good twenty seconds. All we have to do is sneak down close and when they are out of sight we sprint across the road."

The group watched the next pass of vehicles closely and there was indeed a brief amount of time when they couldn't be seen. It seemed very brief to the three dispatchers, who were all over thirty and soft individuals accustomed to sitting for eight hours stretches.

"I don't know if I can make it," Renee whined.

"Then you can stay here and die," Eng snapped. "The rest of us will make it out alive. Unless anyone else wants to be left behind?"

No one wanted to be left behind, not even Renee, who changed her tune and promised she would make it and begged to be given an opportunity to try. Eng wanted to tie her to a tree, but Anna convinced him to let her come along. She figured that she probably wasn't all that much faster than Renee and if they were seen, the boys in the pickup truck would go after Renee first, giving Anna a few more seconds to hide or run.

When they crept to the side of the road, they saw that crossing it was going to be harder than it looked—in addition to the hundred yard run, there were two eight foot tall chainlink fences that would have to be climbed.

The four women looked at the fences in dread, but none of them said aloud what they were all thinking: *We're going to get caught for sure.* Anna dragged her eyes from the fence and suggested: "Maybe we could climb this closer fence first and hide in the tall grass on one pass and cross the highway on the next."

"Women!" seethed Eng, with a roll of his eyes. "Fine, but I'll leave your ass if we're seen."

"Sure," Anna said, eager to please—eager not to be left behind.

With the group hidden just under the eaves of the forest, the trucks spun slowly by and when they disappeared from view, one going east, the other going west, the seven burst out of hiding and rushed the fence. Anna counted the seconds as she dug the toes of her new tennis shoes into the fence and pulled herself up.

It wasn't a large fence by any means, and yet it took seven seconds to mount the fence and three more to drop down on the other side. Anna and Renee were last and they both stared out across the hundred yards of open pavement with dread. They weren't sprinters. It would take them close to fifteen seconds to cross the road and they'd be completely winded when they got to the other side. How would they get over the next fence?

"Everyone down," Eng hissed. "They're coming back."

Anna could hear the trucks; she refused to pull her head up to watch them. What was the point? Fear ate at her heart and she tried in vain to steady her breathing as they waited.

Snake-like, Eng watched the truck from the tall grass. "Ten seconds," he said. "Five, four, three, two, now!"

Anna leapt up and began running, pacing herself. In seconds, she was left behind as everyone else went at a full sprint. At the twelve second mark, Eng was at the fence while she had only just crossed the median. Two seconds later, she passed Renee who was dragging badly.

Although Anna felt that she could make it most of the way to the top of the fence in the allotted time and *probably* wouldn't be seen by the men in the trucks who would be a half mile away at that point, she was sure that Renee would never come close. And she was sure that if Renee tried, they would get caught for certain.

Instead of attempting the fence, she tackled Renee just on the other side of the highway. "Don't try it!" she gasped, hauling the woman back to a drainage ditch that ran along the side of the road.

"Get down, damn it!" Eng said in a carrying whisper.

Anna crawled into the ditch and began pulling up the grass around her. She threw handfuls of it onto her back in a desperate attempt to blend in. Renee imitated her.

The returning trucks could now be heard. Their tires thrummed. Both women froze in place. They even held their breath as the trucks drew nearer and nearer from both directions—and then they drove past.

"Oh God," Renee groaned in a whimper.

"Save your breath," Anna shot back. "We still have to get over the fence." In a minute, Eng began his count down and when he called out: "Now," both women went at the fence like animals and cleared it with six seconds left.

Renee stumbled into the forest and began to cry, while Anna beamed in triumph as she lay hidden in the old growth. When the trucks came and went once more, the group fled deeper into the forest, thinking that they were now safe.

Again, they were so wrong.

Many of the streets south of the second line were being patrolled as well. Rumors were flying around. People whispered that there were zombies in Newark and that the Governor of Connecticut had fled and that the southern portion of the Quarantine Zone was on the verge of collapse.

The people in and around New York City were in a state of panic. They were hemmed in from all sides, with their backs to the sea. Most of the population of Manhattan fled to long Island, while those north of the Harlem River, the people of the Bronx, Yonkers, New Rochelle and Mount Vernon, set up their "Second Line" and decided they would fight for it.

Fortunately for Anna's group of seven, the citizens were untrained and ill-prepared. The further south the group crept, the further their vigilance waned. The little group kept off the main streets and didn't dare try to steal a car. It was a twelve mile hike and somewhere along the way, Anna's head began to pound.

In spite of the danger to everyone around her, she kept it her little secret. Eng would kill her if he found out. He wouldn't hesitate.

And so she marched along with the others, her fear building with every mile. She decided that when the pain got bad enough, she would shoot Eng in the stomach and drive the others away. She would incapacitate him, but let him live simply so he could be the first person she ate when she turned into a zombie—it was what he deserved.

She planned his death in minute detail and it was sometime before she realized her headache hadn't progressed. It had been an hour and she wasn't going mad from the pain. "Oh, thank God," she whispered at the realization. Not even a minute later, she cursed. "God damn it!"

They had reached the southern tip of the Bronx where the view south was open before them: Newark was in flames. The smoke from the fires turned the sky black. Closer, all along the waterfront there were terrific battles being fought over control of the Hudson River. There wasn't a boat in sight.

After a day of marching, they were just as trapped as when they had started.

2—The White House

The monitors in the situation room were plenty big; however, what they were trying to display was so immense that the president found himself squinting at the details and he wasn't happy about it. He knew that squinting played hell with his wrinkles and made him look older. He could have put on his glasses, only they made him look even older than the wrinkles did.

"You know what we need?" he asked, turning to Marty Aleman. "We need one of those giant floor maps like the Nazis had in all those movies. That way you can see everything at once. You know, where all our armies are and where the bad guys are. Seeing it like this…it's not so good."

Marty didn't think the largest map in the world would help him make heads or tails out of what was going on. "I'll look into it, sir."

"Good, good because these maps are awful. And those symbols the army uses, I don't get them." He leaned in closer and spoke in a soft tone: "It's almost like they're trying to confuse me. Do you think that's what they're doing? Trying to confuse me? I wouldn't put it past them, you know."

"I'm sure they're not, sir. They gave you a briefing on what the symbols mean, complete with a visual key. You just have to match up the symbols to the display."

The president would like to, only the font used on the key was tiny, meaning he would have to squint even more. "Why don't you just tell me what all this is about? Why does it look like we're being invaded from Canada? And what are all the red circles? Why are there some here in Washington?"

"Those forces coming down from the north are the different elements of the 10th Mountain Division, remember? And the red circles are sightings of Infected Persons," Marty said. He had to force himself not to roll his eyes when the president drew in a sharp breath. "Don't worry, sir. So far we have investigated over two hundred claims and not one outside of the Quarantine Zones has proven to be real. Usually, it's just the homeless."

"Right, good, good," the president replied with a little laugh of relief.

Marty pushed his bland smile onto his face, before pointing at the biggest of the monitors. "Now, about the map. See those boxes with what looks like a '1' on top? Each one represents a company of soldiers."

"There sure are a lot of them."

"Yes there are a lot," Marty agreed. "But we are going to need more."

Now that the 10th Mountain had joined the fight, there were indeed many companies in the area of the Quarantine Zone, but that did not mean each had their full complement of soldiers. Many of the companies, especially on the southern and western borders were down to a few dozen men. Desertion accounted for most of the casualties, but a good number had been killed out-right, or infected. There had been so many cases of infection that a number of battalions had created squads of executioners who walked along the lines, killing anyone suspected of having the virus, without mercy.

"We need more soldiers…because of what's happening in Jersey?" The president sounded like a child answering a teacher.

"Exactly. It's why we are calling up the Army Reserve and the National Guard." Marty's bland smile threatened to slip as he added: "And it's why you authorized a limited Martial Law in the northeast."

Marty had no idea how Martial Law was going to be enforced. The entire state of New Jersey was a madhouse. During the last eight hours, the zombie population in Newark had exploded, boiling over into Jersey City, Union, Bayonne, Hoboken, Elizabeth, Paterson…the list went on and on, and would continue to go on and on, because no one was even attempting to stop the zombies in Jersey.

Almost the entire population of the state—nine million people, according to the latest census—were attempting to flee along roads that had been snarled in traffic for the last twenty-four hours. The Governor of New Jersey hadn't helped matters by assuming command of the New Jersey National Guard and demanding his forces double time it back from New York.

With the roads clogged with abandoned vehicles, and virtually impassable, the New Jersey guard units were forced to walk. Urged on by desperate pleas, some companies completed heroic marches of forty miles in eight hours. Men and women fainted from exhaustion and others bled into their boots as they struggled to keep up.

Under these conditions, unit integrity broke down and it was a ragged couple of thousand men who pushed over the final hills north of the city of Paterson and looked down on the pall of smoke from a thousand fires that hung over the ruin of the Garden State.

At that point, many of the soldiers sat down and cried, refusing to go on. Others pushed forward, desperate to find their families in all the chaos.

Officers tried to corral the soldiers to form a brigade, but they followed their own conscience. Those who stayed did so either because they were too tired to go on or too afraid. In the eyes of many, the fire and smoke and the frequent gunshots coming from Paterson were proof that the zombies were unstoppable.

Fear was rampant among them. It was like a disease of the mind and when no one was watching, men began to slip away. A few at first, and then more and more, as a governor, who was in way over his tactical head, issued orders from Trenton that were based on hunches or hours old information.

Sometimes he was overruled by his brigade commanders and sometimes he simply changed his mind. Exhausted men were sent here and there, sometimes backtracking minutes after arriving at their destination. Sometimes they arrived to find a town overrun by zombies and other times they found ghost towns where the air was silent and dead.

New Jersey was a mass of confusion. There was no "line," no "boundary of the zone" save for the borders of the state. Hundreds of people who'd been infected in Newark had fled along with everyone else. They went in all directions and now there were flareups everywhere.

Thankfully, the Governor of Pennsylvania had defied orders from Washington. Taking a cue from Massachusetts, he had shut his borders like a steel trap and refused to allow his National Guard units out of the state. On top of that, he called on every able bodied man and woman who could shoulder a rifle to rush to the eastern border.

His call to arms was answered with a fantastic turnout. Out of the nearly thirteen million people in the state, just over a million of them came to stand at the border. They were all needed. Two hundred miles had to be covered, which equaled to one person per linear foot of border.

The situation was far worse in the east. Eighty percent of Connecticut had been lost to the zombies, Hartford was imploding and the 101st Airborne Division was being tested almost continuously. Sometimes the soldiers battled bands of men and women who had made the conscious decision to fight for their freedom. They chose to die in a hail of gunfire rather be torn apart by the zombies. And of course, the soldiers fought the zombies that showed up in ever increasing numbers.

New York wasn't in much better shape. The southern border of the Zone was being crushed under the weight of the zombies. Even with a handful of tanks and Apaches thrown into the mix, General Ed Stolberg of the 42nd Infantry Division had taken it upon himself to retreat.

Knowing that he would be denied permission, he hadn't even asked his boss, General Phillips. He had decided that if he was going to be fired so be it, but he wasn't going to let his men get butchered for nothing. Because of the mayhem going on all over the northeast, he had only received a fifth of the supplies he'd been promised and now his men were running low on everything, especially bullets.

Even with the retreat, the 42nd was pressed further and further south towards New York City, which he'd been told to hold at all costs. He would try, but he wouldn't make promises.

Explaining all of this to the president had Marty popping Tums every few minutes. It seemed to Marty that the "Big Man" was turning into a child as the day progressed. He had even whimpered: "Oh, God," when one of the Pentagon flunkies stepped into the Situation Room to announce that China had unexpectedly launched three intercontinental ballistic missiles.

General Heider had jumped up in shock at the officer's announcement. The look of shock turned to one of utter disgust at the president's whimper. He snarled to the flunky: "What's their trajectory?"

Speaking in clipped robotic tones, the officer recited: "The three missiles were launched from their fields in Xinjiang and at the moment they are heading east. By their launch signature, we know they are Dong Fengs. Each of which can carry a 2190 kilogram payload with a 3.3 megaton yield. Nominal range is 5,500 kilometers. This gives them sufficient range to strike targets as far away as Korea, Japan, and our American bases in the Pacific."

"They're going to Shanghai," Heider said, and sat back down, blowing out a long breath. "Okay, good…that's to be expected, I guess. But they should have warned us."

"Good?" the president asked in sarcastic disbelief. "It's not good that they're using nukes. It means they're losing and if *they* can't stop the zombies, then how can we possibly do it?"

Heider's eyes narrowed. "Are you really suggesting that a peasant army with crappy weapons is more capable than the most technologically advanced army in the world? That would be moronic if you were. Then again, you haven't let us use our most technologically advanced weapons, so…" He let the suggestion hang in the air.

"I gave permission for you to use your tanks," snapped the president. "Where the hell are they? Hmm? It's been five hours and I don't see any in action. And now you talk of technologically advanced weapons? Is that your way of saying you want to use nukes, too?"

The room grew stone quiet as each of the men at the table considered the possibility of a nuclear option.

Marty feared that if one nuke was used, it would open a floodgate that couldn't be controlled. He couldn't help wonder how long it would be before someone pointed a couple of nukes at the capitol? The president hadn't been popular with the military before the outbreak. Who knew the level of hatred they had for him now?

The president wished he could take back his words. He feared nuclear bombs, secretly thinking that if enough of them were used they could crack the earth's crust as though it were an egg shell. He tried to change the subject. "About those tanks…"

"You made us leave the tanks behind at Bragg and Fort Campbell," Heider said, secretly happy to get the conversation back to conventional weapons—he didn't trust this feckless president. The idea of him wielding nukes made Heider shudder. It also triggered some very inappropriate and treasonous thoughts which were a struggle to ignore.

The general could barely look the president in the eye as he went on: "We're getting the tanks to the battlefield but it takes time. Do you have any idea how hard it is to prepare thee hundred tanks for air transport when all their fucking drivers are in Connecticut? Fort Bragg is practically deserted. You wanted everyone to make the jump and you got everyone—riggers, mechanics, ammo specialists, fuel supervisors, everyone. Now I have Air Force pussies trying to figure out how to drive tanks when they don't even know how to put gas in them."

"So your inability to cross-train soldiers is now my fault?" the president demanded.

"For your information," Heider began, his voice raised and his eyes flashing angrily, "There are no soldiers in the Air Force! They have airmen and the last time I checked, they don't have tanks, so training with them would be problematic."

Marty was still so stunned by the missile launch and the idea that the Chinese were resorting to nukes as quickly as they were that he had forgotten his role as political manager. He had to calm the situation before Heider went too far.

"Enough, please. I'm sorry, General. If we could go back in time, we would have made different choices. We should be dealing with the immediate future. How do we save New York and New Jersey?"

"Whatever you do, don't say nukes!" the president warned. "They are off the table."

"Okay, if you insist," Heider answered, trying not to let the relief sound in his voice. "I think that saving New Jersey is impossible. Everything north of Trenton is already lost to us. I could send in a few battalions of Maryland reservists that I've managed to scrape up, but what would be the point? There are no lines, no natural barriers, no rallying points."

"What about south of Trenton?" Marty asked. "Maybe we can begin resistance in the state there."

Heider glanced at the map and said: "Again, what would be the point? There's nothing there. No, I think it's better that we preserve our strength. We should use the time we have to fortify the south side of the Delaware River. It's a natural barrier to the rest of the country."

Marty tapped a pencil on the table for a moment before saying: "Sounds like a good plan. But what about New York? We cannot let it fall. There's the political fallout…" Heider began to interrupt, but Marty put out a hand. "We have to consider the political ramifications, now more than ever. Trust me, General, there will be repercussions if things aren't presented properly. The people are going to want to blame someone, and the president and I are very, very good at shifting blame. When heads roll, and they just might, literally, you can rest assured they won't be ours."

"What are you saying?"

"I'm saying hold New York City at all costs."

At the cost of letting millions of zombies break out of New Jersey? Don't these two idiots see this is the far greater danger? Heider thought as his stomach went suddenly queasy.

He had to walk them back from the idea if he could. "Logistically, we've reached our breaking point. I already have units that aren't being resupplied, and our fuel situation along the entire east coast is atrocious. I can't sustain the men we have and if the IPs in Jersey get out …"

Marty stopped him. "I understand and I'm sure that they will understand that the supply situation isn't the best. And yes, sacrifices will have to be made. Your men understood this when they signed up and raised their right hands. New York is your top priority regardless of the costs."

The queasiness in Heider's gut turned to pain. More sacrifices? How many more soldiers could he sacrifice before the rest turned on him?

It's for the greater good, he said to himself as he glanced up at the map once again. His eyes fell on the little dot of Hartford. It would have to be the 82nd Airborne Division that he would hang out to dry. He would start there and if necessary, he would cut off the 101st next.

General Phillips would probably resign before he let two entire divisions perish, but in the great scheme of things, the loss of one general wouldn't even be remembered, not after Rhode Island and the last bit of Connecticut were overrun and utterly destroyed.

Heider reached out a hand to Marty. "Can I get some of those Tums?"

Chapter 18

1— 5:38 p.m.
The Hartford Quarantine Zone

Deckard backed away from Fowler and his dark eyes and low zombie moan until his heel struck the far wall. Even that did not feel far enough away. In the corner of his eye, he saw Chuck Singleton reach out a slow hand for the M16A2 that sat on the floor next to his thigh.

When Stephanie saw what he was reaching for, she said: "Chuck, no. It's not his fault."

Fowler looked over and saw the gun. "Oh, God," he groaned, grabbing his head, his face a perfect image of misery. "How…how did this happen? I haven't touched any blood at all, not even Dr. Wilson's. I made sure of it. I was always so careful."

"This city is full of blood," Deckard said. "It could have happened anywhere. One little drop is all it takes."

"But I didn't touch any!" Fowler suddenly yelled, his dark eyes blazing with rage. Chuck's hand continued its stretch for the rifle. Seeing this, Fowler's anger faded in a second, to be replaced by guilt and fear. "I'm sorry, I'm sorry. Hey, please don't be upset. I didn't mean it."

Chuck nodded. "I know you didn't, but that's the problem. Y'all's gonna do stuff. Mean stuff. It won't be on purpose, but y'all's gonna do it anyways. I think we need to figger out what *we* are gonna do." He gestured to Stephanie and Deckard as he said this.

"What do you mean, exactly?" Stephanie asked. "Wait! You're not thinking of…of killing him, are you?" In answer, Chuck's hand slipped up the grip of the M16. "Oh shit," Stephanie said, realizing that was exactly what he was going to do.

Fowler glanced over at his own rifle, which leaned against the wall two feet away.

Chuck warned, "Don't try it."

"I—I wasn't going to try anything. L-look, you can't just kill me. I didn't do anything wrong. All I did was touch something. Deckard, tell him I didn't do anything."

Deckard tried to give him a sympathetic smile, but it was hard to smile at a dead man. "Of course you didn't do anything wrong, but that's not exactly the point. We need to protect ourselves. If you could think clearly, you would understand."

After a long pause in which Fowler stared down at the tips of his boots, he said in a whisper: "I get it. You guys are afraid I'll do…something. And I will, won't I?"

"Yes," Deckard told him. "But we wouldn't blame you, just like I hope you don't blame us."

Fowler began to nod, but then his face twisted up in sudden anguish. "But not yet, okay? My head's not too bad and I can still be helpful. I can touch things now." He reached out and ran his hand over Sundance's belly, tears in his dark eyes. "Who's going to watch the dog? Who's going to take care of him? I told Courtney that I would bring him back to her."

"I'll do it," Stephanie said, "if I make it." Even with a two hour power nap, she felt exhausted to the core of her being. Still she thought that maybe the dog would help take her mind off her own pain. She clapped her hands and called: "Sundance, come here boy."

The German Shepherd's ears swiveled in her direction and his tail thumped, but with Fowler still rubbing his stomach, he wasn't going anywhere. Fowler had to give him a shove to get him moving.

"Good boy," Stephanie crooned as the dog began padding over to her.

He had only taken a few steps when Fowler cried: "Stop! Sundance, no!" The dog jerked in puzzlement, which was the least extreme action. Alarmed at the outburst, Chuck and Deckard gently squeezed down on the triggers of their guns, both within an ace of killing Fowler.

"Come here, Sundance," Fowler said, softer now, one hand on his forehead, the other held out for the dog. When Sundance came back and licked his hand, Fowler grinned, a miserable grin and said, "See, I am useful. I saved you, Stephanie."

"You did?" she asked, wearing a watery smile, afraid that he might yell again, or become violent. Chuck would shoot him for sure if he did. "I mean, thank you. That was kind of you."

With a high manic laugh, Fowler said, "You don't even know what you're thanking me for!" He pulled the dog down onto his lap, holding him in an awkward hug. Stephanie thought he was using the dog as a shield, but he rolled the dog over and held up one of his paws. There was something underneath his nails that looked like tar or dark dirt or…

"That's zombie blood," Stephanie said, as a shiver ran up her back. "You did save me."

Fowler ran a hand along Sundance's belly once more. "And he killed me. I was so careful. I was always so fucking careful. I walked around like the world was one big disease." He stroked the dog's head and added: "But I never thought you would kill me." Sundance heard the pain and the sadness in Fowler's voice and made a whining sound in the back of his throat.

They were quiet for a time as the sun dipped just over the horizon. Fowler and Deckard were each considering their mortality and dwelling on how life could be so easily yanked away. Chuck and Stephanie held hands, leaning into each other once again, not really thinking about anything. They had long before come to grips with their coming deaths.

Twenty minutes passed before Fowler let out a shaky breath that sounded as though he were blowing the ragged leftovers of his soul out of his mouth. He then nodded and made an odd noise that sounded like a cross between a laugh and a sob. "You're going to have to kill both of us. You know that, right? Sundance is just as much a danger to you as I am."

Stephanie and Chuck shared a look—shock, at first and then guilt. Fowler was right. The dog would have to die. "Well, shit," Chuck said. "This just gets crappier and crappier."

"Yeah," Fowler said, unhappily. There were tears—greyish tears—dripping down his face. "You should do him at the same time as me."

"Are you ready?" Deckard asked, surprised that the man had come to his decision so quickly.

"Yes. The pain is worse than I thought and there's no use waiting. It won't get any better. Nothing has been getting better. Tell my wife…never mind. You'll never find her. She has to have left by now and I don't know where she would have gone." He took another breath and then pushed himself to his knees, facing the wall. "Do it. In the back of the head. Make it quick."

"Shouldn't we say something?" Stephanie asked. "A prayer or some sort of eulogy?"

228

"Just do it!" Fowler seethed, turning to glare at her with mad eyes. "No one cares. Not God, not anyone."

Chuck and Deckard shared a look of discomfort. "You take care of the dog," Deckard said and brought his gun to bear. "On the count of three." He began counting slow and steady as Fowler's shoulders involuntarily hunched up and his face took on a grimace of misery and fear.

Almost too late Stephanie shoved her fingers in her ears and clamped her eyes down tightly. The twin shots came through, muffled but loud. Fowler's body flopping over sounded to her like a bag of laundry being dropped down the stairs—it made her want to retch.

Chuck turned her away. "Don't look." He led her out of the room and down to the kitchen, where he hunted around for cleaning supplies. The former occupants of the house had taken all the food but left the bleach. He added water and bleach to a bucket and began cleaning their shoes and hands.

A minute later, Deckard came down and did the same thing. He also cleaned his weapon and the extra ammo he had snatched from Fowler's still warm corpse.

"He was a good man," Stephanie said. "He and Doc Wilson were both good men."

Deckard grunted. He didn't want to think about Fowler just then. Killing an innocent man wasn't easy. It stole something vital from the killer even under the best of circumstances, even when it was absolutely necessary. "We should go," he said, wiping down his rifle with a clean dish cloth. "I'm sure the zombies heard those shots."

After the twin killings, no one wanted to linger in the house any longer than necessary, but they were kept from leaving by the zombies who had multiplied in numbers during their two hour nap. The monsters had indeed heard the gunshots but hadn't yet figured out what house they had come from.

The three of them were penned up and, with nothing better to do, they explored the house from top to bottom—all except the room in which Fowler and Sundance lay sprawled in unnatural and contorted positions. Deckard and Chuck refused to even look in the direction of the room, while Stephanie would constantly cast sad eyes at the door and sigh.

During their search they discovered backpacks, half a pantry worth of food, a pair of sleeping bags, two boxes of 12-gauge shotgun shells, but strangely, no shotgun. They took the shells regardless, thinking they would come in handy if they came across a shotgun at some point.

The only other item of value that was found were the keys to a hard-top Jeep Rubicon that sat parked on the side of the drive. It was a new model, red and shiny, and Deckard wondered why it hadn't been taken when the owners fled. He would have taken the Jeep to get away before practically any other vehicle, except for maybe a big SUV which could plow through a horde of undead with ease.

He took the keys to the living room window and gave the button on the fob a click. The lights blinked. It meant the Jeep was good to go.

Only, where would it go? There was no way to drive the thing out of the city. The streets near the wall were amazingly congested. "But the streets around here aren't," he said, feeling foolish. The interior of the city, save for a few crashes here and there and all the zombies, was relatively open—open enough for a sturdy Jeep to get through.

"Are you two ready to go?" he asked. Reluctantly, Stephanie nodded, while Chuck attempted to appear stronger than he was. It was obvious to Deckard that neither of them could go on much longer, but he knew they had to if they wanted to live. That meant getting Thuy and getting out of the city.

There were simply too many zombies in Hartford to stay and attempt to hide. Deckard knew the undead would eventually tear the place apart, house by house, looking for fresh blood.

How they would get out of the city would be left for Thuy to figure out. Deckard didn't have a clue how to get out, but he had ultimate faith in Thuy's mental powers. If there was a way out, she would find it.

Chuck came up, and after a glance out the window, gave Deckard a peculiar smile. "You want us to leave by the front door with all them zombies just strollin' around? You feelin' okay?"

"We're taking that Jeep. The roads are pretty clear...except for the zombies, that is."

"Yeah, except for them," Chuck said, trying to count the zombies in the street. He had counted over forty of them when Deckard swung open the front door and said: "Let's do it," and darted out into the early evening, carrying a rifle, two backpacks and a sleeping bag.

Stephanie followed after. She had a sleeping bag and an M4, and even that seemed like too much for her to carry. Her legs felt like they were weighed down with lead and, at the same time, her head seemed as though it was filled with air. Getting to the car, all of forty feet away, was a trial and when she climbed in the back seat her heart was pounding in her chest.

Chuck got in the front seat a second later and although he grinned at Stephanie, his normally tan face was a dead shade of pale and he brought up more hunks of grey matter when he coughed.

Without waiting for Chuck to even shut the Jeep's door, Deckard backed into the street, thumping solidly into a burly man who wore the shredded remains of a policeman's uniform. The Jeep bounced as its heavy-treaded tires went over him and the crunching of bones added to Stephanie's woes as her stomach lurched.

Deckard mumbled: "Sorry," but whether he meant the apology for Stephanie or the zombie, she didn't know. The bouncing continued as they shot up the street. Deckard did everything he could to avoid the zombies and that meant jumping over curbs, blasting through fences and tearing up lawns, none of which helped Stephanie's stomach.

"Oh God," she moaned, her words lost under the howl of the engine. There was nothing to do except grit her teeth and hold on. She certainly wasn't about to complain or ask Deckard to take it easy. Slowing down would likely mean being surrounded and then there'd be more crunching of bones and black blood spraying everywhere. The blood scared her the most.

It scared Deckard as well. The way Fowler's body had jerked when Deckard had shot him had been ugly. He had flopped over, like a slab of rubber, and the memory clung in Deckard's mind. *How easily that could have been me*, he thought as he slalomed up the block, dodging in and out among the creatures that charged out into the street when they saw the Jeep coming.

He had petted Sundance at least twenty times in the last day. It amazed him and frightened him in equal measure how such a simple thing had put him so close to death. It had him second guessing everything. Was the steering wheel contaminated? Had the door handle been covered in Com-cells? Was the air polluted with spores? Was he sucking in disease with every breath?

A cold shiver struck him.

"As long as we have a vehicle, we should carry bleach," he said. "And gloves, masks, and all that kind of stuff. You never know…Christ!"

The sun was setting on the third day of the apocalypse, making the shadows of the buildings long and deep. A man covered head to toe in layers of black blood had come stumbling out of one of these shadows and Deckard had to choose between side-swiping a van parked on the side of the road or running him over.

He chose the van. There was a jarring, screeching crash that crumpled the cover of the wheel housing and smashed the side mirror into the passenger window, which exploded all over Chuck.

Metal tore against metal for a second, and then they were past both the van and the monster. "Sorry," Deckard said for the second time.

"Ain't nothin'," Chuck answered, brushing away little diamonds of glass from his blue chambray work shirt. "What's a little attempted murder between friends?"

Deckard wanted to spit out a snappy comeback, only the image of Fowler's rubbery body flopping to the floor appeared fully formed in his mind. Fowler had been a friend and Deckard had blown his brains out onto the floor. He hadn't just attempted murder, he had succeeded.

For the remainder of the drive, he kept silent. Only when he finally saw the Hartford City Hall did he speak. "Shit," he said.

Although the interior with its tall, glass-ceilinged atrium was beautiful, the exterior: a three-story rectangle made of grey stone, was rather dull in comparison. What made it horrible were the thousand zombies climbing all over it, trying to break in through the many windows to eat the people trapped inside.

2—The Hartford Quarantine Zone

Dr. Lee heard the ruckus below her. It had grown in tempo over the last half hour, ever since the mayor's wife had foolishly pulled back one of the curtains on a lower floor window.

Thuy had given strict instructions. She had even carried out a class in light, sound and aroma awareness. All for nothing, it seemed. The attack commenced minutes later. They went for the one window, at first. Thankfully, its lower panes stood six feet off the ground and the beasts were stymied.

Then they began pyramiding, clawing over each other to get at the clean-blooded people inside. When one fell, others crushed him under foot and then they were inches closer to the window. More fell, or were pulled down, and soon the beasts were at the glass, and minutes later they were fighting their way inside.

Thuy had advised building a secondary wall of furniture around the office, which was being attacked. "A passive defense based on using their weaknesses against them is the proper course of action. Fighting them with guns, at this point, will only bring on a general attack."

"What the fuck do you think is already happening?" the mayor demanded. "*They* are attacking, already. We need to hold them off long enough for your friend to arrange a rescue."

He meant Courtney, who had taken over the communications room—it was actually the Communications/ Community Initiatives/ Legislative Affairs Room and the only real piece of communications equipment in the room that worked was the newly reinstalled CB radio. Still, she claimed the room as her own and had been hard at it for three hours trying to enact some sort of a rescue.

When talking with this or that government official, she used Thuy's status as "the only scientist" who could possibly come up with a cure for the zombie disease as her opening bid in her quest for a rescue. When that didn't work, she wasn't above trying to parlay Thuy's position on the FBI's Ten Most Wanted list to the same effect.

When it came to a rescue attempt, the State Department gave her a guaranteed "maybe." From FEMA, she got a: "We'll put you on our list." From the Department of Homeland Security, she got a: "I'll have to get back to you when we can arrange that, but it won't be before tomorrow afternoon." And from the FBI, she had her worst response: "Tell her: she's not going anywhere and should just sit tight."

Thuy found it all so ridiculous that she decided to find her own way out of Hartford. The only problem was she couldn't find her own way out of the Hartford City Hall building.

Gunshots began to ring out on the floor below her as the zombies breached the window. Emotionally wrung out, Thuy had retreated to what she knew: books, data, research. She had been sitting behind a desk, poring over maps in the Records Office, but at the sound of the guns, she turned off the lights and went to the window. Carefully, she pulled back the layers of material which kept light from escaping into the evening and appraised the attack on the building.

Perhaps a hundred zombies had been trying to force their way into room G3-Human Recourses. Now, with the guns blazing away, hundreds more of the monsters were charging from all over. "I told you so," she said to herself with a sigh.

She went to find Courtney, who was red-faced and bristling into the CB mike: "No, I am not the Chief of Staff. I am his secretary. Yes, Marty Aleman is my boss. This isn't so tough to understand. He's requesting a helicopter…" She paused as Thuy shook her head.

"It'll be soon," she told Courtney. "Twenty minutes, maybe thirty if the mayor's people don't panic."

"Then it'll be twenty," Courtney said taking the mike and knocking it against her forehead in frustration. "Son of a bitch… no, I'm not talking to you, sir. Let me call you back. I have a situation here." She clicked off the radio, sighed, and stared at the wall across from her. "What are we going to do? How are we going to get out of here?"

Thuy's lips drew down as she said: "I haven't been able to come up with anything beyond the most primitive: a fire. We might be able to escape in the confusion as the building burns down."

"It would take a pretty big fire and that would mean there's a good chance that we will die from smoke inhalation or be overcome by the heat." Thuy's only answer to this was a barely perceptible shrug, which caused Courtney to lean back in her chair as she realized Dr. Lee thought death by fire was an acceptable risk. It didn't say much for their chances.

Courtney's heart sunk. "How do we do it? Start the fire I mean?" she asked, listlessly, unable to get excited over the prospect of participating in something that would likely lead to her death.

"It won't be hard. We will need to gather all the flammable material we can, pick a door and light it up." It sounded like a crappy plan even to Thuy. "We should find Mr. Evermore and enlist his aid."

Jerome was neck-deep in the battle in room G3 where the bodies of the undead were piling up like cord wood and the scent of spent gunpowder could be smelled down the hall. In a lull in the fighting, Thuy explained her plan, only to be greeted with outrage by everyone present.

"Why the hell would we want to burn down our only refuge?" the mayor demanded. "In case you haven't noticed, we're winning this fight." Everyone present, including Jerome, nodded in agreement. The mayor, buoyed by this show of support, went on: "And I, for one, don't think it's wise to chance those streets." He pointed out into the growing darkness, where the moans of the undead hung in the air as if the wind itself was in agony.

Thuy stepped closer to the mayor and whispered: "It seems like a bad bet now, but it'll be worse soon when you run low on ammo. Have you done a count of your ammo and have you seen how many of *them* there are?"

The mayor hesitated, appearing, just for a moment, like a scared little boy. The moment passed and he said: "We'll save burning down the building around us as a last resort."

"That's a decision arrived at through fear," Thuy remarked, loud enough for everyone to hear. "I will prepare the combustibles for when you come to your senses. Mr. Evermore, I will need your help."

Jerome hesitated. He thought that Thuy was crazy for even considering torching the place. First off, the building was made out of stone! Sure, there was framing and dry wall and carpets and such, but he couldn't picture the fire being big enough to amount to much. And even if it did, fire was an unpredictable weapon that would burn friend and foe alike.

"No, I don't think so," he told her. "They need me here. Sorry." He twitched out a quick smile and then bent to the task of reloading his weapon, taking his time as if it were more complicated than it really was.

Thuy wasn't used to being told "no" by people she knew. Strangers were one thing, they hadn't yet experienced her brilliance, but Jerome should have known better. They had spent the better part of the day together, plenty of time for him to realize her intelligence outmatched that of the mayor's by a significant margin.

"If your only talent is in pointing a gun, then by all means stay," she said, with ice in her voice. "Is there anyone here with the foresight to help me?"

No one said a word. Thuy threw her hands up in exasperation and stormed out of the room. When she found Courtney grunting and straining as she hauled a rolled Persian rug that weighed almost as much as she did toward the west side entrance, Thuy said: "It looks like we're on our own. The *men* seem to think they know better. That looks extremely heavy. It is a cylinder. It can be rolled with far less effort."

"Oh," Courtney said, dropping the hefted end of the carpet with a thud. She went to the center of it and gave it a shove with her foot. The carpet rolled a few feet on the polished tile. She shoved it again—moving the carpet was easier, but it still wasn't easy, especially without help.

Thuy seemed above physical labor. She walked slowly along next to Courtney with her eyes fixed on the far wall. "We will do this on our own," she said. "It might take a little more time and effort, but the end result will be the same. You continue here and I will secure weapons and as much ammo as I can get my hands on. Remember, breaking out is only the first step."

"I remember," Courtney said with a grunt. "I just wish that woman hadn't left us. We could have used her car." She meant the "Warden of the Wall" who had stolen away when the zombie threat had begun to increase.

"I agree. It was short-sighted of her. After I get the weapons, I will see about transportation, though I fear getting keys to one of the cars in the parking lot will prove most difficult."

Thuy was so fixated on the problem of acquiring carefully guarded keys that she missed the sarcasm when Courtney said: "Yeah, probably as hard as moving this hundred and thirty pound carpet."

"Mhm? Yes, the carpet. Get it in place and don't be shy about getting more. I'll see you in a bit." Thuy left her, heading back to down to the ground floor, where the battle was in full swing. As she had predicted, the number of windows being attacked had multiplied.

So far, the mayor's people were holding their own; however, the pile of ammo in the center of the floor was noticeably smaller. Thuy went to it first and, when no one was looking, she grabbed three thirty-round magazines and shoved them into the waist of her pantsuit and hid them under the jacket.

When they were secure, she went to room G3. She didn't stride to it with her usual self-important air, she walked along the wall, hoping that she looked "casual."

Casual did not come easily for her, yet everyone was either too busy or too frightened to notice her. It didn't really matter. There were no weapons just lying around and nor were there car keys left sitting out on desks. She went to room after room with no luck.

Eventually, she made her way to the west entrance where Courtney had built a substantial pile consisting of: drapes, carpets, paper and pieces of a desk that she had destroyed by hand.

Courtney wiped sweat off her brow and asked: "No luck with the guns?"

As Thuy showed up empty-handed, the answer was obvious. Out of deference to the situation and Courtney's ramping fear, Thuy swallowed an acidic retort and said. "No, on both fronts. We might be able to get out of the building but we'll be unarmed and on foot."

"Crap!" Courtney seethed, kicking a drawer from the desk and sending it skittering across the tile. "What the hell are we going to do?"

"We can't wait for them to run out of ammo," Thuy said, slowly feeling the weight of decision heavy on her. "Our only choice is to light the fire. Unfortunately, we're going to have to tell the others or they'll be trapped."

A grimace crossed Courtney's face. "They'll stop you if you tell them. You know that."

"But they won't stop you. I want you to light the fire while I go tell them. If they try to do something to me, something not so nice, promise you'll leave regardless."

Courtney said she would and then bent to the task of lighting the fire, starting with the reams of paper she had collected. They went up quickly and so Thuy hurried away, rushing to the other side of the building where the sound of gunfire was a storm of noise that pierced her ears.

She had to yell to be heard. "I'm lighting the fire! You're running out of ammo. You know that. You know it won't last. So come with us and make a break for it, now before it's too late."

One of the men near the window pointed outside where the lawn of the building teemed with the undead. He cried: "We can't go out there! Don't you see them all? There are too many, you stupid bitch!" An angry murmur of agreement accompanied the outburst.

"Grab her," the mayor said to one of his men. At a hundred pounds, she was literally half the size of the man who took her arm in an iron grip. "Get her lighter," the mayor added.

Thuy didn't have a lighter, but she still had the three magazines tucked into the back of her pants. They were quickly discovered. The man who had a hold of her growled: "What the fuck is this? Look what she had." He held up the magazines.

The mayor's face went stony. "We're running out of ammo? Really? Or did you just hide it all? Someone find the girl she was with and bring her here." Two men left and the rest eyed her coldly. Their animosity seemed to give the mayor permission to give in to his anger and fear. He came up to Thuy, grabbed her face in one hand and then shoved her back so that she fell hard to the tile.

This naked aggression stunned the men and the shooting grew less. Beneath it could be heard the faint sound of a horn blaring. Every head turned to the window. "There's someone out there in a Jeep," Jerome Evermore said. "He's turning circles, getting the zombies to chase him."

Thuy knew right away who was driving the Jeep: "Deckard, oh my God." It had to be him. Who else would brave the city streets? And why? The mayor didn't strike Thuy as a person anyone would risk their life for. It was egotistical, she knew, but she hoped she was that sort of person to Deckard.

She was correct in her assessment. It was Deckard who had the Jeep's high beams flooding the night, its hazards flashing, and the horn blaring. He was a one-man parade and those zombies who weren't already at the windows turned toward him, eager to feed.

With the room's attention away from her, Thuy jumped up and tried to run; however, the mayor snagged her arm. "You know who they are?" he demanded. "Are they here for you?"

"They are and if you even think about getting in their way, they'll carve you up." She yanked her arm from his suddenly limp grasp and sped out of there. In the middle of the hall, she found Courtney and two of the mayor's men. "Let go of her!" Thuy demanded using the full power of her authority, which was basically nonexistent and yet the men let Courtney go.

Thuy thought they had reacted to her, but it was the mayor standing behind her waving them away. Once more he grabbed Thuy and whispered: "Take me with you. I can…" he stopped as the first true billows of smoke mushroomed up out of the fire

Courtney had made. In seconds the great atrium that stretched sixty yards long was filled with dark clouds.

"There's not enough room for you and your family," Thuy said. "You saw the size of the vehicle."

"I meant, just me. I can help you. I know people…people in high places. You'll need someone with my clout in order to get out of the city."

A spasm of disgust that couldn't be helped slipped across her face. The foul man clearly didn't care if his wife or his friends got eaten alive. It was sickening and there was no way she wanted him anywhere near her.

"No. You can stay here and run your city."

His eyes blazed in fury and she thought for a moment that he was going to punch her, but suddenly searing black smoke enveloped them. He began coughing, while she dropped to the ground and scooted across the floor on her knees where the smoke was still only a haze.

She went to Courtney, who was also hacking and coughing, and dragged her down where the air was still at least partially breathable. There was no need to talk. They both knew their only chance was to head toward the fire and get outside before the smoke killed them.

The only question: how many zombies would be waiting to attack them? Ten or fifty, it didn't matter. One would be enough to infect them if it got close enough.

They crawled toward the source of the appalling heat, where a murky and shifting orange light showed the pile of odds and ends that Courtney had built into an inferno. Fearing that their faces would blister away to bone, they turned to the side and skirted it, heading for a door that had been locked and blocked. Efficient and hardworking Courtney Shaw had seen to fixing that hurdle as well and she produced a key.

One turn of the handle and they burst out, knocking back a *thing*. Zombie was too kind of a word to describe the fleshless horror that dragged its intestines behind it like horrid, fly-covered streamers. Courtney was shocked by the sight and backed away, stepping on Thuy's feet.

"No! This way," Thuy said, grabbing Courtney and yanking her to the side. Together, they plowed through a run of bushes that lined the walk. The creature with the hanging intestines was quickly on them, but as Thuy had foreseen, the bushes snagged on its guts and held it back. It snapped at them like a dog on a leash.

They backed away only to find more zombies coming at them. Most were partially eaten and exceedingly lame. A few were faceless and blind. The stench of the smoke and the dark baffled them, making it easy to dodge around them.

"God!" Courtney whispered, mesmerized at the wretched sight. Thuy pulled her on, her mind already onto the next obstacle before them: seventy-five yards of zombie infested city streets between them and the Jeep.

Deckard was doing turns in a parking lot down the block from them. He had the zombies' attention, perhaps more so than he had bargained for. His plan was to draw them away and then zip back, only they moved at different speeds and were strung out. There was no way to zip anywhere. He needed another minute, but the faster monsters were on him too quickly, and he had to race onto a west-bound street to keep from being attacked.

Thuy watched him go with a sinking heart. Their only shot at safety had just driven away and now there were hundreds of stirred up and snarling zombies in front of them and a burning building behind them.

Unarmed as they were, the building was safer. She turned to go back, but that was when two dozen shadowy forms rushed out of the bushes, cutting them off. Like most of the creatures, they were grey-skinned and black-eyed, they snarled and flashed broken teeth. But they did not attack. They seemed to Thuy to be waiting on a command from their leader.

She had kept them well fed. *She* had kept them safe. *She* was smart. *She* stepped closer. Her pale hair was streaked with blood and her bloated belly hung with a half-gallon of congealing black blood, pushing out the dirty hospital gown she wore.

Thuy recognized the gown before she recognized the girl. "Jaimee Lynn? Is that you?"

Jaimee Lynn grinned an evil black grin.

Chapter 19

1— 6:23 p.m.
The Hartford Quarantine Zone

The circle of little zombies began to close in. They were feral, horrid creatures, though some were only half-creatures, missing limbs, and sometimes the flesh from their faces. Thuy recoiled in fright, stepping back into Courtney, who made a whimpering sound. The sound seemed to egg on the small pack of monsters and they came closer, showing fearsomely sharp teeth.

"Stop!" Jaimee Lynn ordered and, to Thuy's utter amazement, the pack closing in stopped. Jaimee Lynn moved toward Thuy, stepping slowly, warily, like a tiger cub seeing a Sambar deer for the first time. Instinctively, it knew it was food; however, caution was instinctive as well.

Jaimee Lynn had forgotten her own name and the sudden reminder brought with it strange memories. Pictures in her head. This woman, with hair the color of night and her warm golden skin, was in one of them. She was pretty and Jaimee Lynn knew her mommy was pretty. Everybody back home always said so. She could remember that much.

Thuy held up open hands as Jaimee Lynn came within arm's reach, looking as though she couldn't make up her mind whether to launch herself at Thuy or not. If she did, Thuy saw that there would be nowhere to run, she was surrounded. Nervously, her eyes kept shifting side to side, taking in the other foul little children. They hadn't moved. They hadn't been told to move. But as they kept licking their lips like a dog would when a steak was dangled just out of reach, Thuy knew it was only a matter of time before they did move.

Jaimee Lynn was her only chance. She was the only one of them with a spark of intelligence still in her eyes and she was the only one who seemed able to focus on anything beyond the demanding hunger.

Forcing calm into her voice, Thuy said: "Hello, Jaimee Lynn. Do you remember me?"

The filthy little blonde squinched up her face as she tried to piece together where she knew this familiar looking lady from. Finally, she asked: "Are you my mommy?"

"No, Jaimee Lynn. I-I am Dr. Lee. I am a friend of your father's, remember? Do you remember the hospital where you got that gown you are wearing? Your father was with me at the hospital. I was trying to help him feel better. Your father and I are friends. Do you remember that?"

"I remember the fire," the little girl zombie said.

"Yes, there was a fire, a big, scary one, but your father lived through it. I helped him." Thuy tried on a disarming smile, but she knew she couldn't hide the fear in her eyes. Now that the Jeep was gone, the hundreds of zombies had turned back toward the most obvious sign of humanity, which, in truth, wasn't Thuy and Courtney.

They were two rather small people, lost in the dark, their human scent mostly covered by the stench of the monsters surrounding them. No, what drew the mass of zombies was the building going up in flames. There were very human cries emanating from it, and there were gun shots ringing out, and what really got their tummies rumbling was that there were people clearly silhouetted in the windows as they battled other zombies or simply fought for air.

It was they who drew the horde back from chasing after the Jeep, but from Thuy's perspective, it looked as though the zombie horde was heading right back for her. "Can you help me, Jaimee Lynn?" Thuy begged in desperation. "If you do, I can help you find your father."

"My father?" she asked, her faced lined in puzzlement. "Y'all keep sayin' that. Y'all mean ma *daidy*?"

Jaimee Lynn spoke the short sentence so quickly that to Thuy it sounded like: *Y'allmeanma daidy,* and it took her a moment to realize that *Y'allmeanma* were three separate words; however she couldn't fathom the meaning of the last word. "What do you mean when you say: daidy?"

Courtney, who had been standing so close to Thuy that a stray particle of light couldn't have found its way between them, said: "Her daddy, her daddy!"

"Yes, right. Of course I mean your daidy, Jaimee Lynn," Thuy said, catching on. "I can help you find your daidy if you can get us away from here. I know where he is and I know that he has been looking for you. In-in fact, that's why I'm here. I came to find you, Jaimee Lynn."

"Ya did?"

Thuy was about to answer when the Jeep suddenly raced back into view, barreling down the street, its headlights like two huge dragon eyes. The zombies all around the City Hall building turned for the Jeep once again, charging as best as they could.

Most could only stumble along, but in their eagerness, they made out a surprisingly fast stumble. In a minute, there were only a few zombies around Thuy and Courtney, not counting the pack of children, which was still too many in number for them to handle.

"So, Jaimee," Thuy said, drawing the girl's attention back to her. "Can you tell your friends to move aside so we can go. It should just be you, me and Courtney. We don't want to scare your daidy."

A glint of suspicion touched Jaimee Lynn's dark eyes. "My daidy ain't scared of nuffin. Y'all even know him at all?"

Before Thuy could answer, a man streaked by, racing for the Jeep which had broken away from the mob chasing it and was parked a block away, blaring its horn. In between the honks, Thuy could hear her name being yelled.

It was Deckard's strong voice and that should have filled her with great elation; however she was still surrounded and what was worse was that the man who had run by had been the mayor. The sharp angles of his grey suit stood out in the dark and, despite the fact that there was very little light, his perfectly styled hair glinted.

When he got to the Jeep, there was no guessing what he would say or do.

"Of course I knew your daidy," Thuy assured the little girl zombie. She tried a carefree laugh only it came off sounding fearful. "He was tall and tan with rough hands, remember? And he always needed a shave, right? He asked me to find you, but only you, Jaimee Lynn. So please tell these other children to step aside so we can go to him. You want to go to him, don't you?"

"Course I do," Jaimee Lynn said. She really wanted to see her daidy, only the longer she stood there in front of this soft, soft woman with her beautiful scent, the more Jaimee Lynn wanted to eat her. She wasn't hungry, but that didn't mean she didn't have room for a few bites.

It didn't help matters that Thuy kept turning to look at the Jeep with her head twisted around, showing off the perfect lines of her neck. It made Jaimee Lynn drool.

Thuy couldn't help herself. The mayor waved the Jeep over and, as she watched, he jumped in. *Why'd they let him in?* she wondered. What was he saying to them? What if he told Deckard that she was dead? The answer was as easy as it was heart-wrenching: the one man she loved would drive away, simple as that.

She saw it perfectly in her mind's eye: Deckard would be stunned by the news. He would sit back behind the wheel in shock, but only for a few seconds. Then he would recover, consider his possibilities, as the mayor spoke more lies and promises into his head, and then he would do the smart thing and leave.

In spite of their predicament, Thuy couldn't help herself and watched the Jeep, waiting for it to peel away. As she did, Jaimee Lynn watched her, the string of black drool reaching her collar as her pack closed in. Only Courtney kept her wits.

"Let's get Jaimee Lynn to her daidy," Courtney said, grabbing Thuy's arm and squeezing it, digging her nails in until Thuy winced. "Don't you think we should get going, Dr. Lee?"

"Right, yes, of course." Reluctantly, Thuy pulled her eyes from the Jeep and looked for somewhere where there weren't crowds of zombies. The only place was to their right at the Wadsworth Museum of Art, which seemed to be an ideal place to go. The front of it resembled a castle, complete with tall turreted towers and narrow, easily defended windows. If the mayor had been smart, he would have chosen to defend that building instead of City Hall.

"We need to go that way," Thuy said pointing at the building. "Jaimee Lynn if you could move them, please. We can go find your...Jaimee Lynn?" The little girl zombie was eyeing her neck. Subconsciously, Thuy touched her throat with her left hand; the other she put out towards Jaimee Lynn, as if telling her to stop. "Tell them to move, Jaimee Lynn if you want to see your father. You do want to see your father, don't you?"

"Yeah, I do. It's just..." She paused to swallow. "I'll also wanna eat you. I just don't know which I wanna do more."

Thuy could guess which she wanted to do more as Jaimee Lynn's stomach suddenly growled and her pack of mini-zombies came even closer.

244

2—The Hartford Quarantine Zone

Deckard spun the wheel hard left and gunned the engine, dancing the Jeep Rubicon through the zombies, trying to draw them all towards him so that he could zip back to the front doors of the building. Chuck would take over driving then as Deckard ran inside to find Thuy.

That was the plan, however the Jeep was a blocky vehicle and the "dance" Deckard had it doing was without rhythm or grace. He nearly hit a fire hydrant and had to slam the brakes to keep from crashing into a parked UPS truck. As he yanked the transmission into reverse, a man suddenly jumped into the back seat.

Stephanie Glowitz, who sat in the other back seat, gaped for a precious second, before trying to shoot him. The sun had set, and night time in the zone was dark and scary as hell. She didn't know if this was a full-on zombie, ready to start eating them, a partial one looking for revenge, or just some dude—she couldn't chance it being "just some dude."

She had an M4 which she tried to yank away from the window and point the man's way, but it was an unwieldy weapon in such close quarters and he spoke before she could kill him.

"Thanks so much for rescuing me. Your kindness will not go unrewarded."

He had a fluid way of speaking: clear, precise and silky smooth. Stephanie stopped trying to kill him; however Deckard was of another mind. "Get out," he ordered.

"You don't understand. My name is Danny Perez, I am the Mayor of Hartford." Thinking that this was all the introduction or explanation that was called for, the mayor gave Deckard a toothy, white, confident smile. The sort of smile a movie star would have.

Seeing the smile, Stephanie was even happier that she hadn't killed him. Deckard only modified his stance slightly. "Get out, now!"

"He'll prolly die iff'n you kick him out in the middle of this," Chuck drawled, sounding as though he didn't care one way or the other. "Maybe y'all might want to drop him off over there by that castle-looking building."

Deckard grunted—his way of agreeing when he didn't have time for much talk. And with hundreds of zombies converging, he had said all he could. He floored the Rubicon around the hydrant, bounced them back onto the street and raced for the odd building that did, indeed look like a castle.

"Look," the mayor said. "I'm not getting out. You can't make me. Besides, you should want me to stay. I can be useful. I have friends in high places. If you stick with me, we can get out of the Zone. Don't you want to get out of the Zone?"

Because of a sudden surge of zombies charging up out of the dark, Deckard was forced to loop around to the building, giving him time to ask the mayor: "If you're so high and mighty, where are your friends? If you're the mayor, why are you bumming a ride instead of catching the next helicopter out of here?"

"An interesting question. I was asked by the governor to remain here to keep order until the city has fallen. Clearly, it has. And I would have had a ride, except things fell apart quicker than I thought they would. So, if you would be so kind as to point this...this..." He waved his tanned hand around, indicating the Jeep.

In Chuck's eyes, a man who didn't know what a Jeep looked like wasn't much of a man. He snorted laughter as Deckard said: "It's called a Jeep. And we aren't leaving without a woman named Dr. Thuy Lee. She's in the City Hall building."

"Dr. Lee?" the mayor asked, his smile faltering. "I'm afraid she was bitten not too long ago. I'm sorry, but she's done for. She's not going to make it."

The Jeep began drifting, its engine quieting as Deckard took his foot off the gas. He suddenly so weak he didn't think he had the strength to drive. Next to him, Chuck stopped laughing, his lean face suddenly looking haggard and tired at the news. "Y'all might want to goose the gas a bit," he said quietly to Deckard. He then asked the mayor: "What about the people who were with her? John Burke? Courtney Shaw?"

After a moment's hesitation, the mayor lied through practiced lips, "There was no one with her." He was so smooth and easy a liar that he almost believed it himself. "She came alone. Sorry."

Deckard's eyes narrowed at the hesitation and his foot went back on the gas. He could usually spot a lie from a mile off and though he hadn't spotted the bald-faced lie the mayor had told, on some level, Deckard marked him as someone not to be trusted. The man was too smooth when he didn't have to be. It didn't make sense and it didn't add up.

He turned the Jeep toward the City Hall building, running up on a curb and shooting across the lawn, carving two wide tracks in the grass. His headlights picked out the circle of small zombies, but he missed the two women standing smack in the middle of them.

Stephanie saw them, however. It was Jaimee Lynn's hospital gown that she caught sight of first. It made the little girl appear ghostly and her eyes had lingered long enough for her to pick out the blonde hair and the sharp angle of her thin face.

"That's Jaimee Lynn…John Burke's daughter!" she cried, pointing. "And that's…that's Dr. Lee and that other woman from the trooper station. We should…" She couldn't finish her sentence as Deckard spun the wheel so hard that Stephanie was thrown onto the mayor in a tangle of arms and elbows.

Deckard curled the Jeep around in a short arc, careening into the group of kid zombies and crushing five of them beneath two and a half tons of rubber, glass and metal. Jaimee Lynn and the rest scattered.

"Get in!" he yelled to the two women.

The Jeep had come on them so quickly that Thuy thought it had been aiming for her. She had nearly gone running out into the dark along with Jaimee Lynn and the other children. Thankfully, in her fright, Courtney had clung onto her, holding her in place. She was like an anchor even when Chuck reached around and opened the back door.

The dome light displayed the oddest scene. To Thuy it seemed as though Stephanie Glowitz and the mayor had been caught in some sort of romantic moment. They had been sprawled all over each other and now, as if found in the middle of a guilty act, they were trying to rearrange themselves properly.

In spite of the odd sight, neither woman needed to be told twice about getting in where it was safe. Thuy darted in first, followed by Courtney who tried, but just could not shut the door; there was no room. "Move over! I can't get the door shut!"

The back seat of the Jeep was not designed to hold four adults and so Stephanie ended up sitting on the mayor's lap in order to free up enough room to allow the door to shut.

As Deckard roared the Jeep onto the street again, Chuck flicked on the dome light, staring into the back seat with flinty eyes. He seemed rather angry in Thuy's opinion, though for what reason she didn't know.

"Hello, Mr. Singleton," Thuy said, giving him a worried smile—what if he had been bitten? What if he was on the verge of turning into a zombie? "I want to thank you and Mr. Deckard for rescuing us."

"You ain't been bit," he growled. That she was not bitten seemed to cause his puzzling anger to deepen.

As Thuy knew all too well, sudden, inexplicable anger was a telling symptom in someone afflicted with the Com-cells. She gave Courtney's leg a stiff squeeze in warning, but the woman had already made the connection and was easing her hand back to the door she had just locked. Things were going from bad to worse.

"No, I have not been bitten," Thuy said. "You are very perceptive, Mr. Singleton. How...how are you doing, Deckard?" Seeing that his jaw was clenched as if he were gritting down on a piece of steel and his large hands had the steering wheel in a death grip, she was afraid of his answer.

"A little pissed off, if you must know."

He sounded it. "Is that right?" Thuy said, feeling weak. She was tired of the constant motion and the constant battle, and she was sure that if Deckard and Chuck were infected, they would be a hundred times more dangerous than Jaimee Lynn.

"Yeah, that is right," Deckard answered. "It means I was lied to. Care to explain yourself before I kick your ass out of this Jeep?"

They were doing about forty miles an hour, shooting northwest on a street that was dotted with abandoned cars and crawling with zombies. Even if he slowed, there was nowhere to get out. The sight out of the window had Thuy's stomach in a knot and all she could say was: "Uhh..."

The mayor started saying the same thing: "Uhh...I don't know...I thought she was bit. It looked like she was, you know. Perhaps I made a mistake. It was dark and everything was happening so quickly."

Thuy's confusion evaporated in an instant and now it was her turn to grow furious. "He told you that I had been bitten? You snake! You...you...jerk-shit!"

Her attempt at cursing, although it stemmed from a place of volcanic anger on her part, actually diffused the situation to a degree. Eyebrows were raised and Chuck had to turn away to hide a sudden smirk.

"I'm sorry," the mayor begged. "It was an accident. Y-you were surrounded and it was dark. How was I to know you weren't bit?"

"You could have helped us," Courtney snapped. "Like you said, we were surrounded and you ran right by like a fucking chicken-shit."

The mayor began nodding, eager to please. "Yes, you're right, I did. It was a mistake. I should have…"

"Oh, shut up!" Courtney yelled, right across Thuy's face. There was a silence after this that lasted a block and a half, then Courtney realized something was not right. "Where's Max and Sundance and that doctor?" Deckard and Chuck shared a look, one that had her stomach dropping. "They can't be dead."

"Yes, actually," Deckard said, in a sad voice. "But they went quickly and they were both brave right down to the end." Another silence gripped the Jeep seeing them almost to the wall. Deckard stopped just short of the dark, brooding mass of tangled steel. A few zombies ambled around, not enough to get their hearts racing.

Chuck sighed, a phlegmy, wet sound, and asked: "What about you? Where's all y'all's friends? Them dispatchers an' all? Where's John?"

"Some died," Courtney answered, her eyes shifting down to rest on the pumps she had stolen hours before. Her friends never had a chance. They hadn't been geniuses like Dr. Lee or warriors like Deckard. They had just been people…just like Courtney. It was a wonder she was still alive, just like it was a wonder Chuck and Stephanie had made it. They both looked awful.

In truth, the only one who didn't look worn from their ordeal was the mayor, who was even then in the process of patting down his shiny hair.

"What are we going to do with him?" Courtney asked, pointing, distastefully the mayor's way, as if even looking at him would coat her with the invisible slime that he seemed layered with.

Deckard's glare returned. For the last few minutes, he had been concentrating on driving which was a far better alternative than thinking about the last moments of Max Fowler's life. "He doesn't deserve our protection, but I can't just kick him out. Not out there." He lifted his chin toward the window where the zombies were angling closer, limping along faster now that the scent of fresh, clean blood had hit them.

The others either grunted or nodded in agreement—all except Thuy. "If he stays, it'll be as a corpse." Her words were ice and her dark eyes were full of hate. "Mr. Singleton, will you please shoot him if he doesn't get out of the car in the next minute?"

"I think that might be murder," Chuck said, with a glance at Deckard, which was almost a cry for help.

The mayor nodded and pointed Chuck's way saying, "That's right. It would be murder. You can't let her do this. I didn't do anything wrong."

"Nothing wrong?" Thuy demanded, outraged. To everyone's astonishment, she grabbed the gun from Chuck's surprised fingers. "You were the one who attempted murder. Two counts of it. Get out now, or I will shoot you."

3—Montrose, New York

Three blocks from the motel where Anna and Eng had held their hostages the night before stood *The Hound's Tooth*. It had been a honky-tonk where, in a grand tradition that was as old as time, people danced and drank, fought and sang. At the bar, men spilled their beer on the girls they were one-lining, while in the bathroom others were mixing puke with urine in the foul smelling toilets.

General Phillips, the newly promoted commander of the newly designated 7th Army, sat at the bar. It was empty except for the three shots of cheap whiskey lined up in front of him. Though he could have upgraded to a slightly higher grade such as *Johnnie Walker Black* or at least *Makers*, he had chosen the cheapest whiskey because he didn't feel as though he deserved anything better.

The surface of the amber liquid shook gently as the air pulsed. A thousand rifles were going at it a mile away, while overhead, Apaches and Blackhawks buzzed. There was even the thrum of seven artillery pieces mixed in—all he had managed to airlift in.

He watched the whiskey dance as his staff of fifteen men waited for him across the street in an abandoned diner. They didn't know it, but they were waiting to hear that their fearless leader had decided to give up on Connecticut altogether. Already, the 82nd had been hung out to dry. For the last eight hours, he had given them excuses instead of the supplies they had begged for.

They were dead men in his eyes and dead men didn't need supplies—and yet they still had a mission to complete. They were the first line of defense against the wave of creatures that had begun pouring out of Hartford. The 82nd had been buying time for Phillips to gain control of the situation. It was why he had lied over and over to Frank Frazer, telling him that he was doing everything he could, and that it would be just a matter of time before help arrived.

There was no way he could have told Frank the truth. If Phillips had told ol' Frank that the President had ordered him, in essence, to cast aside the division, he would have pulled his men back, circled them as if they were in "indian country," fought in an ever-shrinking perimeter, and, knowing him, would have lasted out the remainder of the war. That was the kind of man Frank was. He would have done it, knowing that if he lived he would have been court-martialed and shot for treason…to him that would have been a tiny price to pay for saving his men.

Phillips wished his choices were so simple. Gallantry was an easy thing when the choices were so obvious. What wasn't obvious was the "big picture." The big picture was horribly frightening. Quite simply, nothing was working the way it was supposed to, starting with the very concept of a federal government.

The president had begun the day forcing patriotism down the country's throat. No matter what channel a person turned to, they were inundated with scenes of planes and paratroopers, helicopters and tanks, fierce camo-covered men and stern women in uniform. Perhaps it had been necessary at first, then it had become cloying to the point a person could piss red, white and blue.

Sometime after the first fires began in Newark, it became menacing. Marty Aleman had leaned on his contacts in the media to keep what was happening in Newark quiet, but, amazingly, they had gone from lapdogs to attack dogs in a matter of hours. Fearless reporters were suddenly all over TV demanding answers—what they got instead were guns shoved in their faces.

Just when Phillips was finally getting his fuel situation under a tiny bit of control, priorities were changed. Hundreds of desperately needed helicopters and thousands of his best soldiers were "re-assigned" to a new combat group, operating under orders directly from the White House.

This force, composed of about three thousand Rangers and Special Forces personnel, literally descended from the skies like dark angels of an evil god to enforce the President's notion of unity and brotherhood. At the cost of wreaking havoc with Phillips' tenuous supply line, the seemingly countless cable TV channels were brought to heel at gunpoint and in no time—once the bodies were removed and the blood cleaned up—the news shows were back to running what felt like endless loops of the morning's parachute jump or delivering prewritten statements that spun everything in a positive light.

"Goodbye freedom of speech," Phillips said and took one of the shots with a shaking hand. The cheap whiskey burned going down. "Goodbye freedom of the press." He took another shot and grimaced, the long age lines on his face becoming ruts in his flesh.

For over a minute he stared at the third shot, wondering what he would do with it if it were poison. He liked to think he would have downed it without hesitation. Slowly, he reached for it, brought it to his lips, and whispered: "Goodbye 82nd."

It was a doomed division. In spite of his promises of a second "Berlin Airlift," it had been impossible to keep them supplied. Their expenditure of ammo was fantastic. For the last five hours, they had been using a wall of lead to defend themselves and, although it had worked so far, bullets were being used up at an unsustainable rate.

Phillips had admonished General Frazer and ordered him to restrict the number of rounds carried by each soldier, but he had been politely told to go fuck himself by his subordinate. Frank was catching on and now Phillips' empty promises carried the same weight as his threats.

Thankfully, General Milt Platnik of the 101st, still had hope in spite of the trickle of supplies getting through to him. Of course he had begged for more, but there wasn't any more of anything to be had.

It wasn't just ammo that was an issue, it was everything. The amount of supplies needed to sustain an army in the field was amazing and yet, of all the thousands of items that were necessary, Phillips would never have guessed that plain old water was what would break him. In this land of disease, no water source could be trusted.

In their haste to do the president's bidding, Phillips' divisions had been forced to leave certain things behind and that included every water purification system in every single division.

This put them in tough straits. Boiling water in mass quantities was out of the question in the middle of battle and there was a strange lack of iodine tablets. Phillips guessed they were being hoarded. One way or another, the lack of iodine meant clean water had to be flown in—along with everything else. Because the northeast was basically closed to ground traffic, supplies were being air dropped where they were needed. And this too was unsustainable.

The president thought he had an original idea when he said: "Just parachute what you need in." As if the army had an endless quantity of thousand linear foot chutes just lying around. They had many but over half had been used in the last ten hours of the operation and they couldn't risk using up the last of them on an isolated division.

The 82nd was withering on the vine. Logistically, they were screwed. There were only so many planes and only so much fuel and there was just too much need. Priorities had to be made and the 82nd was not a priority.

According to the president, the last strip of Connecticut wasn't a priority either. He was fixated on New York City almost to the detriment of the other fronts, forcing General Phillips to begin "shading" the truth in order to help the Pennsylvania National Guard hold back the growing menace from New Jersey. Thankfully, it wasn't difficult to fool the president since the man had zero military sense and not much in the way of common sense either.

Phillips simply could not understand what purpose there was trying to keep New York City safe when the wide open land north of the city stank of disease and decay and to the west New Jersey was a giant walking graveyard, while to the east, most of Connecticut was barren devastation surrounding little pockets of humanity.

"No good at all," Phillips said, the whiskey poised at his lip. "Fuck New York." Losing New York City would be hard on the war effort, but it wouldn't mark the end; however, if the Pennsylvania border was compromised, that would be that. The Keystone State was simply too big to contain. There were thirteen million people in a state with a border that was almost a thousand miles long. How could that possibly be defended with so few soldiers?

"It can't be," the general whispered and downed his third shot. With a sneer at the bitter taste, he pushed back from the bar and headed across the street before the alcohol kicked in. He didn't seem to matter much in the great scheme of things, but appearances were appearances and it wouldn't do to stumble into a meeting.

The men in the room snapped to attention as he strode in. "At ease, at ease. Let's get on with it." The diner had been chosen because the grill was still operational and there was plenty of grub. One of the many lieutenants, who seemed to always flutter about his staff, had been busy whipping up a steak dinner, and a plate was set in front of Phillips seconds after he sat.

The steak wasn't bad, which only made his guilt all the heavier. There were men of the 42nd who hadn't eaten in the last 48 hours.

As he ate, sitting across from a seventy-two inch retractable screen, his staff gave him their evening report—they would give him another one just before taps. He doubted if he would sleep that night. The men in the field certainly wouldn't.

"The good news first," LT Colonel Granderson stated, and pointed to the northern border of the New York Zone. "The 10th Mountain Division has fought off every threat and, unless there is some wholly unexpected development, should be able to maintain their lines through the night. As per your suggestion, we have explored the idea of transferring men from the 10th to help shore up the Pennsylvania Guard, unfortunately the numbers are suggesting that a shift would cause more problems than it would solve."

He flicked to another screenshot, this one a picture of the Adirondack Mountains. "The 10th is holding the entire northern portion of the NYZ. It's a hundred and fifty mile length of the Zone. It is all forest and mountain with very few surfaced roads, so shuttling men from one hot spot to another is a slow, complicated affair. General Renalt has created a number of small reserve groups but that's at the cost of a dangerously thin line. They only have about one man for every seventeen meters of front."

Granderson switched the image on the screen to a scene of a highway that was blackened, pockmarked, and strewn with corpses. "Now, for the not so good news. This is Highway 202, approximately a mile and half north of here. According to General Stolberg, he will abandon it in about forty-five minutes. He has prepared a fallback point here…"

Another image, that of a map showing the lower third of New York State. The colonel pointed at a lake that crossed a good portion of the map. "That is New Croton Reservoir. It stretches almost nine miles and, according to Stolberg, it will cut his front in half."

"Yes, but it also puts them a mile and a half closer to the city," Phillips said.

The colonel made a face as if what he was about to say next pained him. "Yes sir, it is, but at the same time, the general has finally given us a casualty list. He only has forty-two hundred men left and they are dog-tired. Most haven't slept in two days."

"Forty-two hundred," Phillips said, breathing out slowly, wearily. At one point, he'd had eleven thousand soldiers, police and civilians fighting for him. "Tell Ed he has my blessing to shorten his lines. Alright, what crap do you have for me next?" He tried to smile as if the false face would lessen the blow he knew was coming.

A second colonel stood. His name was Evert Lloyd and he had drawn the worst assignment as liaison between the 82nd and the 7th Army staff. "General Frazer is again asking for supplies and reinforcements. Attacks out of Hartford have picked up. He is also reporting an increased tempo from IP attacks from the suburbs. He has built lines of circumvallation and contravallation, but says that it's only a matter of time before his lines are breached in one direction or another. He's requesting permission to pull back."

Lloyd didn't need to add: *Again*. Frazer had been begging to save his men for three hours now.

"Tell him that with the dark we will be able to get him more air support. The president has agreed to carrier strikes."

In truth he had agreed to *limited* carrier strikes. The president's precise words had been: "They should be used to knock out bridges and such." The words "And such" were so ambiguous they could mean anything and for Phillips that included bombing runs against the zombie hordes.

Lloyd went on with his report: "Things are picking up with the 101st, which is making the planned withdrawal a might bit touchy, but General Platnik says the first phase, the shift to

I-395, should be completed by midnight and the move into Providence completed sometime by tomorrow morning."

Pulling the 101st out would be the death knell, not only for Connecticut, but also for most of Rhode Island. Still, the move would hopefully save Providence and about a million people, as well as the 101st Air Assault division. What was better was that Providence had a fine seaport which would allow Phillips to shift some of his logistical burden onto the US Navy.

"And New York City?" Phillips asked. "What's going on there?"

Chapter 20

1— 7:22 p.m.
New York City

The packed subway car rocked side to side, lulling Anna into a stupor, her eyes growing heavier and heavier until it was a struggle to keep them open. Desperately, she wanted to sleep. She wanted to give in to the demands of her exhausted body and her stressed out mind.

Only she couldn't. She had to go on. It was survival of the fittest now, and in spite of her two broken fingers, her slowly healing burns, her many cuts and her multi-layered bruises, she vowed to be one of the survivors in all of this.

"This is all Thuy's fault," she mumbled. She was so tired it felt as though she had been drugged. It was hard to keep her eyes open and hard to care where they were going. Across from her was a map of the New York City transit system. Just at the moment, it was mostly a blur.

She squinted at it trying to makes sense of the colored lines and the little letters and numbers that stood for the different trains. If she hadn't spent two years in the city after graduating from Cornel, she would have been hopelessly lost. As it was, she had to trace the red line on the map that represented the "1" train as it plodded south along Manhattan's west side. It was going to Brooklyn where they hoped against all odds to find a boat.

The subway car held Anna's group: Eng, Bob and Alan, as well as the three dispatchers, all of whom were suffering from an advanced case of Stockholm Syndrome. They had been threatened repeatedly by Anna and Eng, and still they had begged not to be left behind. They were idiots.

Besides the hostages, there were seventy-six other people crammed shoulder to shoulder in the car. Earlier it had been even worse, the trains had been outrageously stuffed with people, each with their one allotted suitcase. Those who couldn't find a spot on one of the many trains were forced to walk. During that long day, upwards of two million people had crossed over one of the four bridges that connected Manhattan to Long Island. Now,

Manhattan, a hundred feet over Anna's head, was freakishly empty, at least the center of it was.

All along the near side of the Hudson River were grim-faced marines in camouflage, pale sailors in dungarees, nervous airmen who were gently holding rifles as if they were made out of bread, and a mishmash of scraped together army units. With some states practically in open rebellion, refusing to let even federal troops cross their borders and other states holding back their best units, General Phillips had to use what he could.

His orders were to fortify New York City and he had. He was doing it with the rear echelon: men and women from the laundry services and oral hygienists, and mechanics who had never been out of the motor pool. He had pencil-pushers, cooks, computer analysts and glorified flight attendants.

They were a frightened lot, standing shoulder to shoulder with New York City police officers and firemen and a few thousand civilians who all seemed to be carrying what looked to everyone to be absolutely tiny and useless pistols.

The east bank of the Hudson River along Manhattan was a fourteen mile strip, guarded by nearly ten thousand men and women. Ten thousand wasn't many, making it just another of the very thin lines expected to hold back the hordes.

If it wasn't for the width of the Hudson River, the line would've caved long ago. The water was calm and black, drifting gently past, lit only by the dying fires that raged throughout New Jersey.

With the dark, the zombies could hardly be seen until they got close to shore, and even then, they were mere formless lumps in the shadows, usually indistinguishable from the regular corpses that floated downstream. Thousands of precious rounds were wasted on bodies that were already bullet-ridden.

Still there were enough zombies to rattle frayed nerves and cause bursts of panic among the untried warriors. The gunfire was constant, making it seem as though the fight for the river was in full swing, while in truth, it had yet to truly begin.

After crossing over into Manhattan, Anna had taken her group straight away to the river, hoping to get astronomically lucky and find a boat just sitting there ready to be stolen.

Of course, there hadn't been a single boat in sight, but what she had seen of the odd conglomeration of soldiers, sailors and airmen made her realize that New York was doomed. They were afraid. All of them. From what she had seen it was only a matter of time before someone screwed up and touched something they shouldn't or let themselves get bitten and not tell anyone.

In other words, it was only a matter of time before the disease would overwhelm Manhattan and from there it would travel across to Long Island, where twenty million people were huddled like sheep. Twenty million soon to be zombies. Anna gave them two days…three at the most.

This was why she squinted up at the transit map, trying to make out where to transfer to the "R" train. The R ran along the west Brooklyn shore where there were dock after dock, and piers and wharves of all sorts. If there was a boat to be had, Anna liked her chances there.

With a great screeching of brakes, the train came to a slow grinding halt. Anna glanced around, saw the sign for Times Square/42nd Street, and squawked: "This is us! Get up, this is our stop!"

Her little group had fallen asleep and was slow to get moving. Eng was the first up and after stepping onto the platform glanced back. "We should leave them. They're dead weight."

"I'd give you up before I gave them up," Anna told him. It was true. It was dangerous traveling with Eng. Not only was he a snake that couldn't be trusted, he was also wanted by the FBI, the same as her. If it were just the two of them going about, they would stand out. The group provided them with cover.

They also did everything Anna asked, something she appreciated in a group of morons. As she held the subway door from closing, they filed by, looking spent. She had nothing to fear from them. They were too tired to think and that meant they were too tired to rebel.

The R train was as packed as the 1 had been. It ran out to the "island" as the New Yorkers called Long Island and the last holdouts were making their way east towards the illusion of safety.

Anna got her group off early, raising a few eyebrows among the other passengers. She didn't care, knowing that the faceless masses only saw other faceless beings when in crowded situations. She would be forgotten in minutes.

As the train began pushing down the tracks, Bob looked around, slowly coming to the realization that they were still in Brooklyn.

"We should have kept going further inland," he remarked. "We're not that far from the harbor here."

"That's the point," Anna replied. "The harbor is where they keep the boats and we need a boat. It's simple, really."

Bob began nodding, but it was with a troubled expression on his face. "But why do we want a boat? We made it through the lines. And there were soldiers. We should be safe now."

"We should be, but we're not," Anna said, speaking over her shoulder as she headed down the platform towards the stairs. "If a zombie makes it onto this island and starts spreading the disease, where do we go? Sure, it's named 'Long Island' for a reason, and it's plenty big, but it's still an island and a boat is the only way to get off of it. Why wait until the last second to find one?"

Bob answered with a tired: "I guess that makes sense."

Anna paused as she got to street level, gazing around at the strangely darkened city, trying to get her bearings. Nothing looked familiar. The twelve story buildings all around them blocked her view of the harbor and hid any other landmarks that might have clued her in.

Slowly, she spun in place, saying: "And we have to find a boat tonight before the Navy really tightens its grip on the northeast. Son of a bitch! Does anyone know which way west is?"

Eng snorted. "That way. Do you know anything about the stars?"

"I know enough," she lied. "Let's go." They headed in the direction Eng had pointed, and as they walked, Anna glanced up at the few visible stars overhead, wondering if one of them was the North Star. If it was up there, it wasn't obvious. She was still looking up when Eng nudged her and pointed.

New York harbor stretched before them. A few miles to their left across the water was Staten Island. It rose up, a dark mass against a dark horizon. Its long west coast, so close to New Jersey, had been considered indefensible and now it was nearly completely abandoned. Pretty much the only people remaining were the forgotten remnants: the very old, the homeless, the violent inmates who were considered just as deadly as the zombies.

Directly west was New Jersey. The night was so still that the screams and gunshots from the city of Bayonne could be heard drifting across the water. To their right was Manhattan, many of its buildings still lit. Seeing them gave Anna a touch of hope.

Seeing the empty piers right in front of her dashed that hope. There wasn't a single ship in sight. No yachts, no barges, no sailboats… not even a dinghy.

"We keep going," Anna said. "Something will turn up."

They trudged along for an hour until they came to the Belt Parkway which curved around the southern edge of Brooklyn. Here, the docks gave way to a protective sea-wall where men and women with an assortment of guns stood guard. They were stationed every thirty feet and it was no wonder they were jumpy as hell

Anna had a light shot straight into her eyes as she came up to the first. "Will you please stop that," she asked, using a far nicer tone than the one she really wanted to use. "We aren't zombies."

"Then what are you doing here?" The voice was a timid whisper coming from an uncertain shadow.

"We're checking on things," Anna answered, stepping closer. "Our job is to make sure security is tight. We have to make sure no one's run off."

The shadow wavered even greater, as if it were about to dissipate from pure fear. "Has anyone?"

Anna had no idea. "No, not yet. We're just checking. There aren't any boats around here, are there?"

The shadow bobbed slightly, which Anna took to be a shrug. "No, I don't think so. The last boat I saw was just before sunset. It was crazy full. I'm talking like two hundred people on a thirty foot sailboat. I thought it would sink, but it didn't."

"Okay, good," Anna said, her stomach knotting up. "What about cars? You see any of them?" So far they had come across a few, locked and keyless.

Another bob. "No. None driving around...except for a few Humvees. The soldiers come around every thirty minutes or so, doing what you guys are you doing."

Had there been a touch of suspicion in the seemingly innocuous statement? "We're, uh, with the mayor's office," Anna replied, thinking quickly. "He wanted someone to check on things and sent us. And, you know what? We should be getting back with our report. Thanks."

She had taken three steps away when the shadowy figure hissed: "Wait." A chill went up Anna's spine as she turned with a smile that glinted in the darkness. The shadow hurried up to her and leaned in so that his hot breath was in her face. "Can you tell me what's happening? Wasn't there supposed to be some big military thing this morning? It was all over the news. What happened to it?"

The little group had been asking themselves the same thing. They had seen the hundreds of planes and the clouds of helicopters. At first, Anna and Eng had watched the display of military power with some trepidation, figuring that if the army got into the swing of things too quickly the apocalypse would falter before it got going. If that happened, at best they would be caught up among the fleeing refugees. At worst, they would find themselves stuck in yet another Quarantine Zone. But, as the day wore on, so did their worry about the military being too effective.

"The army is trying," Anna said, patting the man on the arm. "Unfortunately, what happened in Newark kind of took us by surprise, but I think we've got it contained."

"What did happen?" he asked, his relief at getting answers evident in his tone. "They say that the zombies got to Jersey by way of the river. Is that what happened? Do you think they can get up here?" He pointed a shadow-blurred hand at the sea-wall which rose four feet straight up out of the black water.

She couldn't imagine a zombie getting up it, and at the same time she wouldn't put it past one of them to somehow climb straight up out of the river like a spider on a thread—it was just how the last few days had been going, everything horrible had become not just possible, but likely.

"Stay vigilant," was all she could say. It seemed to disappoint the blob of a man. Anna didn't care, she was already stalking off into the dark heading further along the edge of the harbor, afraid that she was wasting their time. Anyone with a lick of brains would have grabbed any available boat and gotten the hell out of there long before.

Still, she had to try. The alternative was simply to pray for a miracle and she knew there wasn't a god worthy of the name who would ever answer one of *her* prayers.

Doggedly she went on, not caring if the others in her group kept up or not. She was determined. If there was a boat to be had, she would find it and she would kill to get it if that's what it took.

This mindset carried her and the others for five miles along the Belt Parkway. They moved slowly, frequently stopped by patrols of army personnel or gangs of civilians who were ready to shoot anything that moved if it was in the least bit suspicious.

Their story of being "with the mayor's office" was never questioned, though just as with the first man, it elicited many questions from people who had been living on a steady diet of rumors since the sun went down. Anna developed pat answers that were designed to end conversations—once she had asked her own question that is: Where are the boats?

No one knew.

Seven minutes after nine, they were nearly run over by a Humvee. It came out of nowhere and before they knew it, the group had three rifles pointed at them while flashlights turned them temporarily blind.

"Who the fuck are you?" a soldier demanded.

Anna didn't hesitate: "My name is Miranda Morgan. We're with the mayor's office."

"Who was the second president?"

Now she faltered, "Huh? What?"

One rifle shifted her way, turning her blood to ice in her veins. The soldier asked again: "Who was the second President of the United States?"

Lieutenant Eng of The People's Liberation Army answered: "John Adams."

He was waved to the side. "Step away from the others. You, blondie, who was the third president?"

She understood now what was happening. "Thomas Jefferson," she said calmly, "but you are wasting your time, we're not infected."

"We'll decide that. Get over here and shut up." The soldier turned next to Renee, one of the dispatchers.

She started to blubber. "I don't know history. I never knew history. C-can you ask me something else?"

The soldier had a sheet of questions. He chose a math question: "What's thirteen times thirteen?" Renee blubbered some more as she floundered through numbers. When she threw out the wrong number, the soldiers started looking back and forth at each other, but the leader said: "She gets a third question. What do you get when you mix the color blue and the color yellow?"

"Green?"

"Yes," the soldier said to everyone's relief. Now blubbering in relief, Renee went to stand next to Anna and Eng as the others were tested. Bob acted as though he had a heart attack when he missed his first question, but he rallied for the second. The others passed their IQ tests, and just like that, the soldiers were climbing back into their Humvee.

"Hey, wait," Anna said, coming to the door of the vehicle. "What about the guys who were in that building?" She pointed at a warehouse that stood across the street, silent and grim. "There were three guys in there acting all strange."

"Really?"

Anna nodded exuberantly and almost went too far with *honest to God!* but changed her reply to: "Yes, they were a little scary." She was thanked by the soldiers who hurried towards the warehouse with their guns at the ready. When they were out of sight, she pointed at the Humvee and whispered: "Everyone in!"

She had to find a boat and after the long night and the little question and answer session, she realized she was never going to find a boat on foot.

They clambered into the Humvee with Eng driving. He was a fine driver and the roads were eerily empty. They made great time zipping from cove to cove and to every bay on the island— all for nothing. There was no getting off the island, Anna realized, except by plane or helicopter, and these were controlled by the military.

And there was only one way to get them to part with an aircraft and that was by blackmail on a massive scale.

2—The Hartford Quarantine Zone

"Stop being melodramatic," the mayor said to Thuy, trying not to stare at the gun in her small hands. "You won't shoot, we all know it. You're not that kind of person, so put the gun down."

"I *wasn't* that kind of person," Thuy corrected. "I am now. Get out while you have a fighting chance, which is more than you gave me."

"I didn't…" the mayor began, but stopped when Thuy jabbed the tip of the assault rifle into his leg.

"You are a snake and a liar," she accused. "You left your friends and family to die. You left us to die in a manner that can only be described as attempted murder. For that I judge you. Get out whole and healthy or get out bleeding."

Outside the slim metal walls of the Jeep, the city was filled with the dead roaming everywhere, killing and feasting. Seeing them made the mayor's tan face turn white. He spoke through lips that were unnaturally tight: "Shooting me would be murder. Are you a murderer?"

In answer, Thuy pulled the trigger of the M16. The sound was loud, but not as loud as the mayor, who began screaming at the top of his lungs.

"Ho-lee shit," Chuck drawled, eyeing the blood. "Deck, y'all better take this machine down a few blocks before we let *His Highness* out or we'll have an issue ourselves."

"You aren't going to let me out!" the mayor cried. "She's the one who's shooting people. She's the one…"

Thuy jabbed the gun again, this time into his chest. In a clear, calm voice she said: "Get out when the Jeep stops, or I will shoot. I want to impress upon you that I am serious. Do you believe that I am?"

They stared into each other's eyes until the mayor looked away and said in a dry voice: "Yes." For the first time he wore an honest expression. For the first time he wasn't a snake of a politician. For the first time he was a real person in real pain.

Even Thuy softened. "We'll find him a better spot to let him out," she said.

Only, there wasn't a better spot. Fires had begun in many buildings where people were out of ammo and desperate. Where there weren't fires there were screams and gunshots, and the streets were filled with roving battalions of dead. With so few actual people left, the zombies were now suffering from ferocious hunger and their strength and speed seemed to have increased, something Thuy didn't think was possible.

Deckard's face was hot with sweat as he jerked them all over the road. "Does anyone have any ideas on how to get out of here? I can't drive around all night." He glanced into the rearview mirror at Thuy when he said this, knowing that if anyone had an idea of getting out of the city, it would be her.

"You're going the right way," she told him. "Keep on this road until you come to Scarborough Street. We'll get out there."

"Out?" Stephanie asked in a whisper. "I thought we were just talking about the mayor getting out. Y-you don't mean all of us, right?" She certainly hoped that it would be just the mayor. With the setting sun, the streets had become a nightmare, and judging by the mass of shooting going on beyond the wall, the 82nd was still in place, holding back the hordes.

Thuy patted her leg, hoping to calm the woman. "Unfortunately, Ms. Glowitz, we can't drive this vehicle out of the city.

We will be killed if we do. However, there are ways out. I suspect these ways are still available to us unless the military is far more thorough than I have given them credit for."

"But you know these secret ways?" Stephanie asked, trying to remember if Dr. Lee had been from Hartford. As far as she could remember, Dr. Lee had gone to school in New York City. "How can you possibly know any secrets about Hartford?"

"Simple. While I was trapped within the City Hall, I put my time to good use. There is a records room that contains detailed plans of the city and in the northeast of the city, near the University of Hartford, is the north branch of the Park River. As it routinely floods every decade or so, a series of drainage tunnels were built to conduct the overflow on towards the Connecticut River."

Stephanie felt the fading hope within her begin to swell. There was only one problem. "How big are these tunnels? Are they pipes that we'll have to crawl through? Or are they bigger?" *Please say bigger, please say bigger!* she begged internally.

"They have an aperture with a four foot diameter. It's going to be a bit cramped but we will be able to walk."

Just as Stephanie began to breathe a sigh of relief, the mayor said: "Those openings are barred. We'll have to cut them in order to get through and that'll take time, I mean like twenty or thirty minutes with a hacksaw."

"Shit," Stephanie said, spitting out the word in a whisper as hope died within her. They wouldn't last five minutes out there.

Chuck reached back and put his hand on her knee. "It'll be alright cuz I will be right next to you. 'Sides, this flashy piece-a-crap don't know dick. A gas-powered reciprocating saw can rip through a hunk of rebar in a minute."

"But we don't have a gas-powered reciprocating saw, do we?" the mayor asked, throwing his bloody hands in the air. "We don't even have a normal saw. We'll never get out that way."

Thuy glared at him until he sat back. "Don't make me regret not killing you, because I can remedy the mistake very quickly." The mayor dropped his gaze and went back to gripping his bleeding leg. When Thuy saw he had been sufficiently cowed, she said: "We passed three hardware stores on the way here. We'll get saws and flashlights in one of them."

That was so much easier said than done. It wasn't as if they could stroll up and down the aisles, picking out whatever they wanted. It was more of a mad scramble mixed with a panicked flight.

The front window of the first hardware store consisted of either jagged razors sticking up in the frame like teeth or thousands of particles that glittered across the pavement when the Jeep's headlights swept over them. The moment they pulled up, all four doors of the Jeep sprang open. Thuy and Deckard ran for the store, glass crunching under foot, while Chuck went to the driver's seat and Courtney ran around to bookend the mayor between her and Stephanie.

A second after the rear door closed, Chuck went heavy on the gas, spinning the tires in reverse—already zombies were lurching in towards the store, attracted by the lights and the noise.

Deckard and Thuy stayed low, hiding behind the shelves. Not all of the creatures had given chase. Some were lingering, the sound of glass giving away the fact that they were drawing closer. "This way," Deckard whispered, pulling her deeper into the store. As they went, they passed all sorts of interesting and necessary items that Thuy paused to grab: painter's masks, latex gloves, lighters, 16-function hand-sized multi-tools, flashlights and lastly, the reciprocating saw.

It was a bulky thing and heavy. Deckard took it, accidentally knocking over a precariously balanced display of socket wrenches. They came down with a clatter that seemed to go on and on. In seconds, five zombies came charging and Deckard leapt out to meet them.

He had a rifle across his back, but he had less than twenty rounds left in it. As well, he knew it would be loud, only attracting more of the creatures. Besides, he found himself in a building filled with tools perfect for zombie killing. He snatched up a long-handled framing hammer and was ready to start swinging when Thuy stopped him.

"One moment," she said as she reached up to slip a mask over his face. He wanted to stop for an even longer moment to kiss her, but they were out of time. The first of the creatures was on them. It was a woman…or it had been. Her breasts had been chewed off, along with half her face and most of her fingers. She'd been a big woman and her death had not been easy.

As a zombie she came on, grunting and licking the torn flesh around her mouth where her lips had been. Deckard timed his swing and sunk the head of the hammer an inch deep smack dab in the middle of her forehead. What would have killed any man wasn't enough to put the zombie down. She wobbled slightly and came on again her fingerless hands stretched out for him, the ends of them ending in shards of bone as dangerous as any tooth.

Leaving the hammer sticking out of her head, Deckard reached for a larger weapon: a four-pound hand sledge. This was overkill and when her head blasted apart under the force of the blow, he was splattered with sloppy wet tissue, all of it squirming with disease.

"Son of a bitch!" he seethed, dropping the hammer, which made a solid *clunk* on the floor. He needed a weapon that was longer, but just as heavy. He gazed around the dark shop looking for something that would kill with one strike but would also keep him at a safe enough distance to keep him from getting zombie crud all over him.

Shovels hung from the far wall and he was just hurrying to grab one when Thuy presented him with a pick-axe she had found in the gardening section. It had been designed for home use and wasn't exceptionally heavy and nor was it too long and unwieldy. He gave it a try on the next zombie that came up and was satisfied when the pick went three inches deep into the thing's cranium with hardly any effort.

It got a little stuck on the way out, but over-all it was a fine weapon for the conditions. With it, he dispatched two more zombies, making a pile at the door over which others began to struggle.

"Hurry, take off your shirt," Thuy commanded. As he did— going very slowly to keep from touching any of the ugly wads of brains that clung to his clothing—she took one of the shovels off the wall and jabbed it as hard as she could into the chest of one of the struggling zombies. Then she set the butt of the shovel against one of the checkout stands. The zombie pushed harder and harder against the shovel until the metal had torn through its heart and both lungs. That finally slowed it down and gave them a few minutes of peace.

After spotting another item that would be needed, she hurried back to Deckard and said: "Close your eyes," then, without waiting for more than a fraction of a second, she began spraying him in the face with an anti-microbial. The chemical smell was horrible and yet, he didn't complain. In fact, he relished it, hoping the worse the smell, the more effective it was at killing the Com-cells.

When he was wet with the chemicals, she took a paper towel and wiped him down and just when he thought it was safe to breathe, she sprayed him again as an extra precaution.

"Ok…good…thanks," Deckard said through a chain of coughs.

"I have to be thorough," Thuy replied, taking his pickaxe and handing over a sweatshirt she had found on a shelf. It had some sort of sexual reference to hammering and nailing printed across the front. "You can't die, Deck. I'm not going to let you. If you die, I die."

She smiled up at him, still pretty after three days of fighting. He was certain he looked as sorry as he felt but it was dark and she was leaning closer and closer. He bent down into her and kissed her deeply until she started coughing, waving a hand beneath her nose.

"It's not you. It's the chemicals. The fumes are…" She stopped in mid-sentence, her head cocked. The rumble of the Jeep could be heard growing louder. "We are going to finish that kiss, I promise, but survival comes first."

With a last touch of his arm, she hurried, not toward an exit, but to the far wall, where she took down a new and unbloodied pickaxe and handed it over to him. He took it with a sigh. "I suppose as a consolation prize it could be worse."

Hitching it over his right shoulder, he led her to the back door just as the Jeep returned, this time running without lights, trying not to arouse so much attention. Stephanie, who wasn't expecting Thuy and Deckard to come from around the side of the building, almost shot them when they came rushing up grabbing for the doors with blue gloved hands.

Unperturbed by a gun pointed her way, Thuy calmly shoved it away, saying: "It's just us and we have the saw and more." Deckard had carried the saw and the pickaxe, while Thuy had lugged two baskets of goods. For a few minutes, the mood in the Jeep was lightened as the group eagerly coated themselves with the anti-microbial spray and munched away on the dozen candy bars Thuy had grabbed.

Everyone received a flashlight, a pair of gloves and a mask. There was even a first aid kit which had very little in it that was much help with the mayor's wound. Still, the two rolls of gauze and the small stack of 4x4 absorbent pads was better than nothing.

The mood was still running high when they saw the dry ditch that ran to one of the many entrances to the drainage system. Although there were a few of the more dreadfully maimed zombies trapped within the ditch, there wasn't a single one near the barred entrance.

"A good omen," Thuy said, despite the fact that she didn't believe in fortune telling, omens, clairvoyance, or superstition of any sort. Then again, she didn't believe in the phenomena of zombies, but no matter how many times she called them "infected persons" they were still zombies.

To make a go at the bars, the group decided to change the order of attack: Courtney would drive while Chuck and Deckard went down into the ditch with the saw and the pickaxe. Stephanie and the mayor would conserve their strength in the back of the Jeep, while Thuy would hold one of the M4s trained on the mayor. She didn't trust him, no matter how pale and listless he had become—earlier, she had aimed the weapon with precision and the wound in his leg, though painful had only gone through muscle and not much muscle at that.

They ghosted up, went through what kids called a "Chinese Fire drill" with everyone switching places. Courtney barely waited for Thuy to get in the front seat before she drove off in a screech of tires and flashing lights. What followed next was harrowing for all of them.

The creatures went for the Jeep. It was shocking to see how many there were. Hundreds just popped up out of nowhere. They came draining out of buildings and crawling from beneath cars. Two minutes before there had only been a handful, now it was a mob scene of the dead.

Seeing them sent a chill up Deckard's spine and the saw was suddenly slick with sweat. Chuck lifted his head just up over the height of the grass and let out a low whistle. "That's a shit-ton of zombies. Least ways that Courtney can drive."

Courtney was banking the Jeep all over the place, doing her best to draw the zombies away without getting cornered and that meant she had to take the Jeep off the smooth streets. Too late, everyone scrambled for their seat belts. In seconds, they were being bounced around so much that Thuy cracked her head on the roof, biting her tongue.

The Jeep drew further and further away, until at last it disappeared. Chuck pointed at Deckard. "It's now. I'll keep them off y'all."

Deckard pushed himself into a squat and hurried forward, bent over at the waist until he reached the opening. Luck seemed to be with them: the bars were spaced eight inches apart; he would have to remove only one. The engine of the saw was loud and the action of the blade on the metal, a howling screech, was even louder.

The zombies heard this and the ones that had been left behind came on in a rush. Deckard could hear their moans even above the saw.

"Y'all better hurry, Deck!" Chuck hissed before he raised the pickaxe and swung at the first of the beasts charging down on him. There were a dozen of them coming at him and if it hadn't been for the drainage ditch funneling them into a line he would have been overwhelmed and overrun. He swung the axe over and over again. His leathery hands felt the bite of the axe, but they were used to the feel of hard labor, it was his lungs that began to fail him. It wasn't long before he was gasping for breath.

Deckard glanced once behind him, cursed loudly and then turned back to the saw. He could not cut any faster for fear of snapping the blade. A steady rise of smoke was already coming from it and he knew that if he pressed too hard the blade would break and although he had extras, they would take time to replace.

"Slow and fucking steady," he said. But he couldn't go too slowly. Already the Jeep's horn had gone quiet—Courtney was coming back.

The blade finally ate its way through the upper cut a minute later. By then Chuck was swaying with each swing of the axe and the Jeep was just down the block and finding the street still surprisingly full of zombies.

Without rest, Deckard started making his second cut on the bar as low as he could go. Again, smoke drifted up. The heat generated by the friction of metal on metal slowly warped the blade and Deckard's fear of breaking the slim metal became reality when the top third of it made a *twunk* noise and went whirring off into the darkness when he still had a quarter inch to go.

Chapter 21

1— 8:44 p.m.
The Hartford Quarantine Zone

For a good three seconds, Deckard stared in disbelief at the saw before Thuy said softly into his ear: "I have another blade." He hadn't known she was there and he nearly jumped out of his skin. Shaken, he glanced back to see the mayor a few feet away, standing on one leg, supported by Stephanie, while further up the ditch Courtney stood just a few feet higher up from Chuck. She had an M4 at her shoulder and was aiming it at the flocking zombies. When she pulled the trigger, it seemed tremendously loud.

There were still hundreds of zombies in the area and at the sound of the gun they came charging even faster, zeroing in on the ditch.

"There's no time to replace it," Deckard said, dropping the saw and grabbing the bar with both of his blue-gloved hands. He heaved back, using all the strength in his back, legs, and arms.

"That'll never wor…" Thuy began, but stopped as the bar began to bend. The heat of the blade had softened the metal. Still, it took all of Deckard's prodigious strength to bend it.

When it was bent, pointing straight at Deckard's chest, he called to the others: "We're clear! Pull back."

They gathered at the entrance, ready and desperately eager to go in. Thuy stood in front of the small opening, blocking it. "I will go first into the tunnel," she told them. "Try to keep up because I'm not going to slow down. Ms. Glowitz, if the mayor becomes too much for you to handle, leave him behind. Also, you may shoot him if he asks you to or if he becomes a danger."

The mayor began to splutter noises of indignation, but Thuy didn't have time for what she considered nonsense. "Chuck, carry the saw and go next. Courtney, I want you after him. Deckard, I want you to take up the rear. Any questions?"

Besides more bluster from the mayor there were none and so Thuy placed the two baskets she had hauled from the Jeep just inside the entrance to the tunnel. She grabbed one of the flashlights and one can of disinfectant, before hurrying down into the pressing dark.

Behind her, Stephanie and the mayor moved awkwardly along because of his wound and her draining strength. To make matters worse, they were both tall and had to walk with a pronounced hunch, which slowed them down even more. In half a minute, Thuy was far ahead, while behind them, practically stepping on their heels were Courtney and Chuck, hissing for them to hurry. At the very rear was Deckard who was stood at the bars shooting into the mass of grey flesh that filled the entrance of the tunnel and crushed up against the remaining bars.

He had no idea what he was shooting at. The creatures blotted out the little light there was from the outside world. The tunnel was black except for the flash of his gun. From its meager source, he saw the last flashlight in the baskets. He snatched it up and beamed it into the mass and was so shocked he took a step back.

Like a sausage grinder, the zombies were being pressed through the bars. Sometimes their heads exploded from the pressure, sending up a geyser of black brains, but a scary percentage came through with their heads elongated or misshapen, but otherwise unaffected.

"Fuck," Deckard whispered, before he turned and ran, bent almost in half. Far too quickly, he caught up with the others. It wasn't just the mayor slowing them down. Chuck was laboring and struggling to draw air. When he pulled his mask off in order to catch his breath, Deckard saw that his normally tan face was stark white. Under the weight of the mayor, Stephanie was also struggling. They kept falling into one wall or the other.

"Courtney, switch with Stephanie," Deckard ordered as he changed out his second to last magazine. "Chuck and Steph, I want you two to just sit here for a minute and rest. Let them get a little ways ahead. I'll hold off the zombies." This wasn't easy. The zombies came in a wriggling grey wave, filling the tunnel, falling all over themselves, crawling over those in front, their bodies twisted and warped from the pressure of coming through the bars.

Shooting into such a mess was almost a waste of their limited ammo, but they had no other weapon. The axe had been left behind in their haste to flee. Chuck and Courtney barely got thirty seconds to catch their breath before Deckard was pushing them on again.

Three hundred yards ahead, Thuy was a bare speck of light, standing at the juncture of two more of the larger tunnels. From her studies, she knew that there was a maze of tunnels down below the earth. Most were small, no more than pipes that drained water out of street gutters, but there were larger ones the same diameter as the one she stood in. The idea was that if one became blocked, the water would flow around it to the next.

This redundancy made for a very dark and frightening puzzle. Thuy had memorized one section, just enough for them to escape and she knew there would be two more sets of the larger tunnels between her and her first turn. She wanted to get to them as quickly as possible but the others were far back.

Their flashlights looked like matches being waved about and the echo of Deckard's gun rolled down the cement tunnels toward her in an eerie manner. It was as if she were hearing a gun being fired from another time and it made her feel even more alone.

She was suddenly struck by a bad case of goosebumps. It felt as if every inch of her skin was tented up by them. Beneath the sound of the gun, there were low moans and the patter of feet. It could only mean one thing: there were zombies in the tunnels and not just behind them.

For now, they were not in sight which was good since she was weaponless. Between the six of them, they had two M4s and an M16, and not enough ammo to last a ten minute fight. Thuy sank low in the cross-section of the tunnels and shot her light back and forth from tunnel to tunnel, afraid that one of the beasts was creeping up on her.

When Courtney and the mayor finally reached her, she wanted to give in to her relief and rush into their arms. Instead she took a steadying breath and looked them over. "Where's Ms. Glowitz?"

"Back there," snapped the mayor, jerking his head to the rear. Just then, he didn't care about Stephanie or really any of them. He wanted out of the tunnels as fast as possible. The dark and the weird noises were creeping him out. "They'll catch up. We should go on. Is that the way out?" He pointed down the tunnel they'd been following.

"Does it matter? There's no getting out without the saw," Thuy answered. "That means we wait."

Three minutes never felt so long. The sound of the zombies drew steadily closer. They were coming on faster than Chuck and Stephanie. Thuy could just make them out at the range of her flashlight when the others joined them. She didn't bother pointing out the obvious danger they were in, she only plowed ahead.

In the very rear, Deckard retreated slowly, letting the others get a good lead. Every few minutes he fired his gun, dropping the closest of the zombies. He would then run to catch up—though "run" wasn't very accurate since he could only move in an odd squat-waddle that was terribly ungainly and far slower than his normal sprint.

Still the zombies were slower, at least the ones behind were. The ones coming up on them from the sides seemed way too fast. Every time he came near one of the larger openings, he could hear their moans…and sometimes he could hear high-pitched laughter that made even a veteran like him get a queer case of the shivers.

When they reached the intersection of tunnels that marked their turn, Thuy stopped again. Now, she hid her light and asked the others to hide theirs as well. It attracted the beasts and she didn't have any way to fight them.

Stephanie reluctantly gave up the M4 she'd been carrying when Thuy asked for it. No one wanted to be defenseless, but she at least had Chuck, who, tired though he was, was a man who knew how to fight.

As Deckard came up to the group, sweat pouring from his brow, Thuy told them: "We have only about a half mile to go. Just a couple more turns and then…"

A warbly cry suddenly drifted down the tunnel: "Doctor Leeeeee? Doctor Leeeeee?" Thuy gasped, realizing who it was calling her name. It was Jaimee Lynn Burke.

She was completely mystified at how the girl could have possibly found her and when the child answered the unspoken question, it nearly caused the scientist to come unglued. "I can smell y'all Doctor Lee. I can smell y'all's clean blood. It makes me hungry, Doctor Lee."

Thuy felt a new fear that was unlike anything she had felt in the last three days. She was being hunted. She was being stalked. She was being hounded and if she had known the cunning little monster that Jaimee Lynn had become, Thuy would have guessed she was being driven into a trap. This new terror of being hunted was so all-encompassing that Thuy froze, her back to the curved wall of the tunnel.

Deckard shoved the mayor aside and crawled to Thuy. In a whisper, he said: "Lead us out of here. You have a gun, she doesn't. She's just a child."

"Sure, okay," Thuy answered, with just a ghost of her earlier confidence. "We go right from here. We go to the third intersection and then left again."

Thuy wasn't the only one freaked out by the sound of the child's voice and the laughter that kept coming to them from out of the darkness. They moved in a clump, slower than before, Thuy held the M4 held out in front of her, the trigger almost halfway pulled.

It seemed to fire on its own when they ran into the first of the child zombies. Unlike normal zombies that would have come on relentlessly, the children scattered at the bright light and the flying metal, leaving three of their number behind.

The group carefully moved around the bodies, doing their best not to touch the black blood that coated the walls. Once passed they hurried on until they came to the first intersection. Thuy roved her flashlight down each of the four tunnels. There was nothing in sight, but what they could hear was unnerving to all of them. The laughter was back and so close.

"Ignore it," Thuy said. "We can leave them behind if we hurry."

That was wishful thinking on her part. The kid zombies were faster in the cramped tunnels and they were tireless in their pursuit—and yet they didn't close in as Thuy expected.

She pushed on, faster now, toward the next intersection. Seventy more yards taken at a run, her body bent oddly. Her legs burned from the cramped conditions, but because of her height it was nothing compared to the pain the others were feeling. Stephanie and Chuck were limping from the cramps in their legs and Deckard thought it would have been easier to crawl.

At the intersection, high laughter coursed down each tube, save for the one to the right—they needed to go to the left. The group was no longer clumped, as it had been. They were spread out, in danger of being cut off from each other. Thuy was desperate to push on, but feared an ambush from the sides.

"I'm going on," she said to Courtney and the mayor when they caught up to her. "I'll go slowly, I promise. You two guard these tunnels until the others catch up."

276

The mayor looked down into the black nothing on the right and wanted to piss himself. "Guard them with what? We don't have guns."

"Just alert us if anything comes your way. I'm sorry, but we can't wait for the others and we can't go on without them. Stay here and do your duty." Thuy glared into the mayor's eyes until he nodded, she then left the two and moved forward into the left tunnel.

If she could remember the map correctly, there was barely two hundred yards to the tunnel that emptied into an overflow point out in the real world where there would be stars and fresh air and maybe no zombies. They'd be beyond the city limits and beyond the lines of the 82nd.

She pressed on despite the fear eating her insides up. She walked slowly towards where the laughter was loudest.

Behind her, Courtney kept watch on her tunnel. The light in her hand shook, making the shadows jitter. There were whispers now in the dark. There were plots and plans, and death was on the air. She thought her chest would explode in fear, but at least she had someone watching her back.

Desperately needing a touch of humanity, she glanced behind her, expecting to see the mayor sitting in his tunnel. What she saw was simply a black hole. He was gone.

2—Long Island, New York

"There's no way off this island, agreed?" Anna Holloway asked her partner in crime.

Eng glanced over to where the others sat in the Humvee, looking like abandoned kittens waiting to be bundled in a sack and tossed in a river. They were parked just up from the hundredth yacht club they had visited that night. Just like all the rest, there wasn't a boat in sight.

They were all exhausted, but Anna had a plan brewing behind her blue eyes. "As far as I can tell," Eng agreed, "but I'm guessing you have something in mind?"

"If we can't get off on our own, then we'll need help and the only way we can get help is by twisting some arms. We need to be able to cow the authorities into submitting to our demands, completely. They have to fear us. They have to be so afraid that they'll let us break quarantine, and this time, five hostages won't cut it, but maybe five million will."

After a sly look back at the others, Eng whispered: "I'd say we have enough of the Com-cells to create five human bombs. Do you think that'll be enough? It doesn't seem like a lot."

"First off, all it takes is one zombie to turn Long Island into fifty miles of death. Secondly, if we do this right, the authorities won't know how many we have. If we place the five we do have here and there around the island, with the suggestion we have more, they would be a real threat and a real bargaining chip."

Eng's eyes almost disappeared as he thought over the idea. Involving the US military would make things extremely dicey. It was well known in China that their technological capabilities were fantastic. Even then planes were cruising overhead and there was no way to know if the pilots were somehow listening in on their conversation. At the same time, the military was clearly stretched perilously thin. Eng had noted the rash of different units they had run into that night. When combat engineers and signalmen were standing guard over empty stretches of seawall, it suggested things weren't going well. Perhaps the military was so overwhelmed that they would suspend their rule about not negotiating with terrorists. It was worth a shot.

"So how do we proceed?" he asked. "They have been docile so far, but they won't remain that way if we start jabbing them with needles."

Anna wondered if he was right. The little group had been pathetic to the point of being apathetic to their fate. Even then they could have wandered away into the night and there would've been little Anna or Eng could have done about it.

Still, it didn't hurt to err on the side of caution. "A little subterfuge will do the trick," she whispered. "Follow my lead."

She sauntered up to the group. "I think we should take a break. We've been running around like crazy. But first, Bob can you help us down at the docks? There was some equipment that looked interesting, but I'm not strong enough to help Eng."

Anna had to hold back a cruel laugh when Bob puffed up his chest as he stood—ego stroking was the first step in getting a man to do what you wanted. She had figured that out in the first grade.

The docks, so close to the pounding of the surf and filled with so much rope, were the best place to subdue their hostages. Bob went down to a little boathouse, cracking his knuckles and warming up his back. He looked stupidly surprised to find it empty and his mouth came open when he saw the guns pointed at him.

"Just turn around nice and easy or Eng will shoot you in the gut," Anna said. "This is just a precaution."

"A precaution against what?" Bob asked, obediently turning.

For some reason a lie wouldn't come to her just then and she started fumbling out words. Eng saved her. "There's a traitor among us. One of you is thinking about running off."

"That's right," Anna was quick to agree. "We don't think it's you but you are the smartest so we figured we should hold you here until we figure it all out."

Bob allowed himself to be trussed up by Eng. He even gave them helpful hints as to who he thought it was who was going to run off. "If I had to guess, I'd say it was Renee. She's always going on about how…hey, what's with the gag?"

"Just a precaution," Anna said. "Open up." It was a little sickening to Anna that he didn't argue. He opened his mouth and accepted his fate.

With Bob incapacitated, it was Alan's turn, then Renee's and then Meg and Jenny. Soon the five of them were lined up on the floor, all in a row. Since proper bio-hazard equipment wasn't available, Anna and Eng improvised, using fisherman gear. Rubber boots and hip-waders covered them from the waist down, while windbreakers, hoods, and scarves covered the rest. Even rubber gloves were found. Squinting over the top of her scarf, Anna loosened the cap off the top of the vial and moved toward Bob.

Too late, he tried to fight back, but there was little he could do. Eng knelt on his chest while Anna dabbed a small amount of the Com-cells just under his nose. The only thing his struggling did was to cause him to hyperventilate, sucking in more of the Com-cells than if he had remained calm.

The same was true for all of them. Renee tried to roll around to avoid her fate, while Alan blew air out of his nose as hard as he could until Anna held his nostrils clamped shut until he couldn't take it and when she finally released his nose, he sucked in a lungful of the disease.

Then he cried. They all did. Anna only rolled her eyes, restoppered the vial and then cleaned the outside of it with pure ethyl alcohol.

"Now we wait," Eng said after he had stripped off his outer layers.

"Wrong," Anna said. "Now, I wait. You need to scout some locations where we can hide these guys. They should be close to major concentrations of humans, but not so close that they'll be easily found. While you're doing that, I need to figure out how to contact someone in charge in a way that won't get us caught."

This was the harder chore by far. Finding and killing bad guys was what the army did better than anyone. It was nothing for them to track cell phones and radios, basically the only two ways Anna had to communicate.

For an hour, right up until Renee started thrashing on the floor, Anna wracked her brain, trying to come up with some way for them to make their demands known. Minutes later, they were all squirming on the floor like caterpillars on a hot frying pan. The pain was the first sign that the Com-cells had taken root.

Anna went outside just as Eng came driving up in the Humvee. He made a face at the noise coming from the boat house. "You should tell them to shut up," he snarled. "If someone walks by our goose is cooked."

The idea of telling five people afflicted with the zombie disease to "shut up" was so asinine that Anna spat out. "Why don't you go tell them? It would do you some…" Her words faltered mid-sentence. Suddenly, she realized how she could communicate with the people in charge.

"We need more rope and we're going to need something to make blindfolds out of. And I need a person, preferably military." The idea wasn't foolproof and communication would lag, but they didn't need to discuss much and they weren't about to try to negotiate.

Over the next hour as the five hostages became five zombies, Eng gathered the needed supplies, including a soldier he snatched at gunpoint as he squatted in a bush not far from his post.

3—Long Island, New York

His name was Private Second Class Andy Wagner of the 67th Brigade Support Company, Indiana National Guard and if he wasn't already in the process of taking a dump, he would have shit himself when he heard the sly steps coming his way.

Andy was no warrior. He hadn't joined the guard out of a sense of patriotism, he had joined so the army could pay for his college. Now, he was filled up to his chin with regret.

He had been sitting alone for hours, frightened half out of his wits, with only terrifying rumors and wild guesses leaking down the line as his source of information. The monsters of his imagination were truly horrible creatures: huge, undead fiends that were more demon than human. The one thing he hadn't imagined them to be was sinister and quiet.

"Hey…who is that?" he asked in a whisper. When the person didn't answer, but only kept moving forward slow and careful, Andy looked around for his gun. It stood, leaning against a tree, eight feet away. He leaned forward, his ass sticking out behind and was just about to waddle over to it when a shadow broke away from the surrounding darkness.

"Just stay where you are and finish up there," the shadow said. "You don't want to meet your commanding officer stinking like shit do you?"

The shadowed man was so frightening to Andy that he mistook the words "commanding officer" to mean God. He honestly thought he was about to be killed right there with his pants down around his ankles. He started babbling: "I-I d-didn't do anything. I-I'm just a records specialist. I-I didn't do anything."

"Wipe your ass," the shadow said. "You stink." Andy did what he was told, going through the motions hastily before pulling up his trousers. The man stopped him from buttoning them. "Not yet. Step away from that pile of crap. Good, good. Now put this on your head."

It was a black ski hat. Andy put it on, knowing that he would then be asked to yank it all the way down so that it covered his face. He suddenly realized he was being kidnapped. "I think you have the wrong guy. I don't have any money or anything. I-I'm just a regular guy."

"You'll do. Now pull down the hat until it covers your eyes. Good. Get on your knees with your hands behind your back."

Andy had his wrists and arms bound and then he was frog-marched to a Humvee. He knew it was a Humvee by the smell and the sound of the engine. Did that make this man a soldier? When he tried to ask, he was punched in the face.

His head thumping from the punch, he was driven just long enough to get carsick. It was a fight to keep down the MRE he had been nibbling on for half the night. Even though the hat only extended just past his nose, he didn't want to puke, afraid to upset his captor.

When they stopped he forgot his stomach as his fear reached a peak. He began to hyperventilate and make whiney sounds in the back of his throat—he was sure he was going to die and he never imagined he would die like this, tied up and blubbering. The more he thought about it, the more he couldn't stop himself from freaking out.

The shadow man punched him the gut, knocking the air out of him. As Andy lay on the ground, desperately trying to breathe, the man leaned down and said in a whisper: "You need to be quiet. There are zombies nearby and if they hear you crying like a bitch, they'll get hungrier than they already are."

Zombies? Zombies, here on Long Island? How was that possible? These thoughts seemed to shock his lungs into compliance. Suddenly, he could breathe again, though he did so with all the strength of a mouse, taking little wisps of air though he craved more.

What if they heard him?

The hat was torn off his head and he found himself standing in front of a house. It was small, no bigger than a cottage. On the side was a driveway that led to a detached, single car garage that seemed like something out of a haunting. The dark hung on it heavily so that it was hard to make out.

"Don't make a sound," the man told Andy as he pulled him by the arm. They were thirty paces from the garage when something inside thumped heavily. Andy couldn't help himself and stopped, his legs unwilling to go forward.

"Is that a…" He couldn't bring himself to finish the sentence. The man nodded, putting a finger to his lips and then dragged Andy on. He was pulled right to the side of the garage where the man shoved him up on his toes so that he could see through the cracks of a boarded over window.

At first he couldn't see a thing and then a grey face smashed against the boards right in front of him. Its eyes were black as coal and from them what looked like oil dripped steadily. It snorted over and over again, its breathing growing more and more excited until at last it started scrabbling at the wood.

"It's got your scent, now," the man said with a smile. "We should leave." Andy tried to run, but the man forced him to move at a walk. "That was a zombie," the man said. "My friends and I created it."

"Why? Why on earth would you do that? That's crazy!"

The man shoved Andy, knocking him to the ground. "Right now your job is to listen. It's not to talk. That will come later. I have a dozen zombies just like the one back there. They are all getting very hungry and pretty soon they're going to break out and we both know what will happen then. The disease will spread and then everyone on this island will get eaten. Sad isn't it?"

Afraid that it still wasn't his turn to speak, Andy nodded. The man went on: "Luckily, you can change that. All you have to do is give your commanding officer a message for me. Do you know who's in charge on the island?"

"No, but I can find out," Andy answered, eager to please, eager to get the hell away from the zombie which was still scrabbling at the boards. "I can ask my captain. He knows."

The man smiled. His face seemed dark and Andy incorrectly pegged him as hispanic. "Good. Get this up the chain of command as fast as possible." He held up a slip of paper. "That's the address to this house and a list of demands. If you aren't quick the zombie will get out and then…" He shrugged, as if to say: *What can you do?*

With the hat thrust down again, Private Andy Wagner was sped back to where Eng had picked him up. Right away, Andy raced down Flatbush Avenue to where his C.O. had set up his command post and, without the least nod to military protocol, he burst in and began babbling his story.

"This really happened?" Captain Heverson of the Indiana National Guard asked, gazing down at the letter Anna had drawn up, his brow creasing and his lips disappearing into a line that went across his face. He didn't want to believe this private whose name he could never remember.

The day before, Heverson had been standing on his bathroom scale, looking over his paunch and sighing when he first heard a couple of overly peppy radio DJs making jokes about zombies in New York. Now, he and his Brigade Support Company were apparently on the front lines, something he had never expected.

Andy Wagner hadn't expected it either. He was on the verge of crying and his emotions overcame his common sense. "Yes, damn it, I fuckin' saw…" He stopped himself before he could make things worse. "I mean yes, sir. I saw it with my own eyes and it saw me. It *smelled* me. It has my scent." Andy's fear was so palpable that it became contagious and nervous eyes began to dart around the tent.

According to the newly revised SOP on possible Infected Person sightings, Captain Heverson was supposed to inform the battalion executive officer without hesitation, only Heverson didn't reach for the sat-phone. He was overcome with indecision. What if this was all in Wagner's head? The young man certainly seemed on the verge of a breakdown.

Or what if this was a prank? Heverson looked quickly around at his staff, searching for the jokester among them. They were all deadly serious. *No,* Heverson thought, *if this was a prank it was being played on Wagner.*

"So help me," Heverson growled, "if this is some sort of joke, people will be going to prison."

"It's no joke," Andy pleaded, miserably desperate to get the captain to believe him. "I saw it, sir. We have to hurry before it gets out."

The honesty in his eyes scared Captain Heverson, but he still didn't initiate proper protocol. New York City was being held at "all costs," which meant that over a hundred thousand civilians had been called to arms to guard the shores of Long Island. Many of them were on the verge of panic and there had already been a number of shootouts between perfectly healthy people. Heverson could imagine the carnage and the chaos that would ensue if word got out that there were zombies already on the island.

"I've got to see this for myself," he said.

Fifteen minutes later, his Beretta hot in his hands and his ears still ringing from the six shots he had put into Bob the zombie, Heverson made his call and Anna's plan was put into action.

Chapter 22
1—9:26 p.m.
The Hartford Quarantine Zone

The mayor of Hartford, Connecticut was desperate to get out of his own city. Danny Perez was mayor of a city of the dead. He didn't think he would be missed.

Certainly, he wouldn't be missed by Dr. Lee and her band of idiots. She had scampered down a tunnel straight to where the crazy laughter had been loudest. That had been lunacy.

Going back to where the other three, Deckard, Chuck and Stephanie were slowly coming up was also a bit nuts. They kept shooting over and over. Didn't they realize that all they were doing was drawing the zombies right towards them? Didn't they realize that they were probably being surrounded even then? The idea of being surrounded in the dark tunnels made him want to piss himself and it made him want to run screaming, only he couldn't. He'd been shot and even if he hadn't been, the tunnels were too cramped to run. He could only limp slowly along, dragging one leg, bent so far over that the hump of his back kept scraping the low ceiling.

Going off on his own, with only a flashlight for protection, was its own form of crazy, but he told himself that he could always go back if he ran into trouble. So far, however, he hadn't heard a thing, and that was because he was smart.

Zombies were clearly stupid creatures attracted by sight and sound…and maybe smell, if the voice in the dark was to be believed. He couldn't do anything about his scent, but he could do something about how much noise he made, which was why he crept along trying not to make a peep. He kept the flashlight turned off. So far it really hadn't helped him except to give him peace of mind that something or someone wasn't right in front of him in the dark.

He told himself that if there were zombies nearby, he would have heard them, and so far, the tunnels had been dead quiet except for the wicked laughter and the gun shots and Courtney Shaw whispering: "Mayor Perez? Mayor Perez?" All he could think was: *Keep drawing them to you.*

Slowly, he drew away from all the sounds, and after maybe a hundred yards, and passing six or seven of the smaller tubes, he came to his first intersection. As mayor of Hartford, he knew his city intimately, both the good and the bad. He knew exactly where each construction project was taking place—one such project was in progress, digging up a road, coincidentally to repair the very drainage system he was creeping through.

It would be a long trek underground of at least a mile, but he hoped that with each step eastwards he would leave danger further and further behind.

He crossed through the intersecting pipes and hadn't gone ten feet before he heard a whisper ahead of him. It hadn't been a whisper of voices, it had been the secretive sound of a tennis shoe scraping on cement—there was someone, or something ahead of him.

Just like that, his heart became a mad thing in his chest, running so fast that he was afraid that it would seize up from the strain. Moving slowly and deliberately, he turned in the tunnel and started heading back, placing each foot carefully, making sure he stepped as lightly as he could, holding his breath pent up in his lungs.

Sweat ran into his eyes and he blinked as if he were sending out some sort of signal. It made more sense simply to close his eyes, but he couldn't force them shut. They were wide open searching endlessly in the black nothing for the slightest shape, the slightest motion. He held the flashlight against his chest, ready to blast light at the first new sound. He made it back to the intersection. Ahead of him was the pipe that led to the others.

From it he heard shouts and gunshots and…and another sound that turned him cold. It was a slapping thud, similar to the noise a small child might make when tripping and falling on a sidewalk, only there wasn't an ensuing scream. The mayor could picture little zombies slithering down out of the feeder pipes, and dropping uncaringly onto their faces.

The sound repeated twice more. He couldn't go back. Without thought, he turned to his left and hobbled down this unexplored pipe for a few steps when he heard the snuffle of a creatures picking up a scent. Now, they were ahead of him.

His fear had him by the throat and before he knew it, the flashlight in his sweaty hands was on and pointing at a squiggly mass of zombies. They were children. Disgusting, horrible, dead children.

A scream ripped from his throat as he turned and ran in a squat back to the intersection, the light going in all directions. To his right were grey faces and sharp teeth. In front was a girl, pale and blonde, wearing a blood-stained hospital gown. Behind her was a regiment of monsters straight from hell.

The mayor flicked his light to the left up the tunnel where he had abandoned Courtney. Here, there were only three of the kid monsters, each one just tall enough not to scrape their heads on the top of the pipes.

It would have been smart to go in that direction. He could have used his bulk to rush right over them, only he couldn't do it; they were grinning such wicked malice that he could easily picture them latching on to him with their pointy little teeth and suckling on his flesh like giant diseased remoras.

Four seconds of pointless hesitation went by as he turned from one direction to another. It was enough to doom him to a very bad death. Had he charged the three, he would have been infected, but he might have gotten away with only a few bites. Instead the mass of children converged from all sides and in the cramped space there was nowhere to go and no way to fight.

2—The Hartford Quarantine Zone

The mayor's screams ran down the pipes, causing the fine hairs on Courtney's neck to stand up. The others had caught up and had paused to catch their breaths. Now, they were almost paralyzed in fear. Deckard pushed them on. Thuy was far ahead and all alone. There was no telling what terrors she was facing by herself.

He pushed them on as fast as they could go. Behind them came a gibbering mass that nipped at their heels and ahead—far ahead was Thuy's light bobbing, always moving, seeming to float on its own. He couldn't understand the courage it took to forge ahead like that, especially given the fact that she was completely alone.

They pushed on until Mayor Perez screamed his last. Though the scream was high and piercing, he was actually still long minutes from death. His fingers were raw bleeding stumps, his belly was wide open and there were mouths slurping in his guts. There was such a mass of bodies on him, pinning him down that he couldn't move. All he could do was cry. It was a blubbering noise that was worse than any scream. It was the sound of utter despair.

Not long after the blubbering started, there came a new scream, this one filled with fury. It was taken up by dozens of high voices that shook the pipes. A mother might have understood what was happening: a terrific tantrum was taking place. The tunnels had been too small for everyone to feed. Only nine of the little kid zombies had gotten in to the yummy soft spots and they had gorged themselves until their bellies sloshed and then they wallowed in hot blood, spinning and spinning in the hot, liquid copper.

Jaimee Lynn Burke had been too slow to get at the mayor and no matter how much she had ordered the others away, they wouldn't budge. They were in a blood frenzy and nothing short of a knife stuck in the base of the skull would have budged them.

Thankfully there were others with clean blood. "Dr Leeeeee!" she screamed.

A hundred yards away, Thuy paused, her back slightly bent, one hand on the curved wall of the tunnel and the other shining her light. Not for a second did she consider answering and the pause lasted for only as long as it took for her to take a single breath, and then she pushed on.

She could hear the others behind her and, although she hadn't glanced back once, she knew exactly what was happening. It didn't take a genius to piece together the events that had transpired. Nor did it take a genius to know that it was going to be a race to the end of the pipes. More than one emptied into the North Park and whoever got there first would have the advantage.

Thuy rushed on, knowing that Deckard would hate the idea of her going off alone. He would push the others on at their best speed…even if it killed them, and with Stephanie and Chuck that was a real possibility. They had fought a good fight, but it couldn't last.

They would be two more deaths on her conscience to add to the millions. Her feet slowed as she pictured the faces of the people she knew who had died. How many of them were walking around grey and awful? How many would still be alive if it wasn't for her? That answer was easy: all of them.

She trudged on, her back bent not simply from the tunnel. The weight of guilt pressed down on her and it was some minutes before she saw the bars that blocked the end of the pipe. With relief she saw that there was nothing between her and them.

"Thank God," she whispered. Thinking she was safe, she turned and waved her light up and down in exaggerated motions, hoping that Deckard would understand that all was well. But all wasn't well.

"Dr. Lee?" A child's voice from behind.

Thuy spun and saw a girl, pale and scrawny, standing on the other side of the bars. It was Jaimee Lynn Burke and behind her were leering hungry faces.

"Yes, Jaimee Lynn?" Thuy asked, fighting to keep her voice even. She had slung her M4 across her back and now it felt a million miles away.

"Weren't y'all gonna to help me find my daidy?" The idea of finding her father held some appeal to Jaimee Lynn, but it was nothing compared to her hunger. Running around in the black tunnels had spiked her appetite something fierce and the scent being given off by Dr. Lee was almost sexual in its power over Jaimee Lynn.

"Of course, I will help you find your father," Thuy answered, with a smile on her face. Thuy had not been fooled in the least by the question. She heard the lie in Jaimee Lynn's words and saw the hunger in her twisted face. "I know you want to find your father, but wouldn't you want to make a stop first? I have friends you could meet. Older people, soft people. Would you like to go see them?"

An image of plump, middle-aged, white meat, brimming with blood took over Jaimee Lynn's mind. Dr. Lee would make a fine meal, but only if she wasn't shared. She was small and skinny. How much blood could she possibly have? Not enough for two and Jaimee Lynn had a lot of mouths to feed.

The idea of soft, easy to catch old people had Jaimee Lynn salivating, "Where are they? Are they close?"

She hoped Dr. Lee wasn't referring to the others hurrying up behind her. Two of them, Stephanie and Chuck, were rags of flesh hanging on bone, while Deckard was a tough, mean thing that would put up way too much of a fight. He would be dangerous and not worth it. Out of the lot of them only Courtney was truly succulent—but she was just one person.

"They're very close," Thuy told her, "but all of your friends are in the way. If you can move them out of the way, I could show you."

Jaimee Lynn knew it wouldn't be that easy. The mutilated kids around her couldn't understand the concept of delayed gratification, especially after they had heard the wonderful sounds the mayor made as he'd been eaten. Their blood was up and pumping. They were primed and ready to feast.

Only there was still the matter of guns. They knew enough to fear the guns the grown-ups carried. And they knew the tunnels weren't good places to be around guns. The tunnels were good for picking off loners like the mayor had been, but they restricted movement. Jaimee Lynn's pack could only come at the grown-ups from four directions and already they had seen how easily the others had been shot down.

For the moment, both sides were at an impasse and it hurt Jaimee Lynn's head to try to think beyond it.

"Just move them back for a moment," Thuy said. "Just a minute and then we'll lead you right where you need to go. There'll be lots of people. You want that right? So just move them back."

Jaimee Lynn guessed that she would be able to move her pack away from the tunnel entrance, but she wouldn't be able to hold them back once the grown-ups came out. There'd be a fight and lots of them would be killed—and maybe that was okay with her. Her pack ate too much and they were greedy and never shared. She had set up the trap to get the mayor and hadn't tasted a drop of blood to show for her efforts.

"Alright, just give me a sec," Jaimee Lynn said with a black-gummed smile. She then started pushing the other zombie children aside saying: "Move, darn you! Git back. All y'all git."

Thuy watched, noting that Jaimee Lynn hadn't moved them far. When they got out of the pipe, there was going to be trouble. Then again, they were already in trouble. Deckard's gun had not let up. They were being pressed from behind by worse creatures than Jaimee Lynn's pack.

Courtney came up while Thuy was still trying to think of a plan to save them. She took one look at the children being pushed around and said: "We can't go this way."

"We don't have a choice. To go back means we run the risk of getting lost in the maze. And all indications suggest that the tunnels are flooded with adult zombies which are infinitely worse."

As always, Dr. Lee astonished Courtney. Here she was the smallest and arguably the weakest of the group, and yet she still had her M4 strapped to her back and clearly she thought that the kid zombies would simply let them pass through the force of her will. In Courtney's eyes, her bravery had become hubris—foolish hope based on extreme over-confidence.

"But there's no way they'll simply let us by without…" Courtney began, only just then, Chuck and Stephanie appeared out of the dark, each looking ready to pass out.

There was no time for passing out or even resting and Thuy ordered: "Here, step back. Let Mr. Singleton through. Don't worry about those little zombies. They…they are under control. Just get to cutting one of the bars away, if you please."

Chuck squatted down at the entrance and eyed the feral children through the bars as they slunk back and hid themselves like kids playing a game of hide-n-seek. Beyond the bars, the drainage pipe ended at a tumble of rocks that sloped down to a small creek. Up and down its banks were reeds and weeds standing chest height; the children slipped down in the growth and in the shadows, Chuck could see their dark eyes glinting.

"Fuuuck," he said, probably for the hundredth time that night. The exclamation was all the time he allotted to himself for rest before switching out the broken blade on the saw and getting to work on the middle bar. Sparks flew, lighting up the dark, blinding his night eyes. He couldn't see more than two feet away. The beastly children could have come right up and he wouldn't have known it. Thankfully, Stephanie crouched behind him, one hand on his shoulder, guarding him as he worked.

It was slow going. Soon his muscles were quivering and the blade slipped repeatedly out of the groove he had made, forcing him to start again. He didn't complain and he didn't stop. If he stopped, who would take his place? Deckard was fighting and Thuy was thinking. Stephanie was so sick she could barely stand, and Courtney was especially weak in the upper body. Chuck went on because he had to.

Behind him, Deckard heard the saw wailing like a banshee and stopped his slow retreat. From the flickering of the sparks, he observed the tunnel piling up with the grey bodies of the undead. There were hundreds, if not thousands, and the only thing stopping them from sweeping down on his friends and eating them alive was his M4.

Knowing he was low on ammo, he knelt with his weapon at his shoulder and waited to fire until the first creature crawled to within ten feet. He pulled the trigger and it dropped. A second beast crawled over the first a moment later. Another pull of the trigger and another limp body.

Deckard had to stop up the tunnel and the only material he had to work with were corpses. He shot methodically and with utmost precision until the stacked corpses couldn't be crawled over and almost no light could filter past. He had corked the tunnel, but it was a temporary fix. The raging howls of the zombies could be heard for miles as they pushed forward until the pressure became too great.

Gradually the mass of dead bodies was thrust down the tunnel, something Deckard hadn't foreseen. If it kept coming, his little group would be crushed against the bars until their bones were ground into a pulp and they slithered through like so much flesh-colored goo.

"You better hurry!" he yelled down the tunnel as he backed up, step by step.

A light struck him from behind and a woman's voice cried, "What the hell is that?"

There was no way to answer the impossible and there was nothing he could do but hope that the wall of bodies would collapse. It would mean he would have to retreat and start shooting again and risk running out of ammo, but it was a better alternative to this.

He stepped back slowly as the grey wall came on and then suddenly, happily it just collapsed and out spilled living corpses once more.

"Thank God," he whispered, suddenly grinning over the idea of facing a roiling mass of zombies. There were so many, the grin dried up and the next five minutes were the longest of his life as the number of rounds in his gun dwindled and the number of beasts grew and grew.

He was twenty steps from the bars and was down to his last four bullets when the screech of the saw suddenly turned to a loud *whirrr*, as the blade bit on nothing and the bar dropped with a clang of metal.

Seconds later, Thuy came to stand next to him, holding a can of disinfectant spray of all things. Germs were the least of their problems and he was about to say so when she abruptly ordered him to lead the group out.

"What about you?" he asked. She seemed so small and weak. At some point in the last few seconds she had given her M4 to Chuck and now she was armed only with the spray can.

"Someone has to go last. Don't worry, I'll be fine." In her other hand she showed him a lighter she had taken from the hardware store. "Fire and ethanol don't mix. It should keep them back until everyone gets through the bars."

A grin crossed his rugged features. "It should, just make sure you keep close to them and keep them off balance. Don't let them get a lot of momentum. If they get moving, no fire in the world will stop them."

"Got it," she said, advancing on the crazed tangle of the undead, the dead, and the dying. One beast was just crawling out of the pile. Without hesitation or remorse, she thumbed the lighter and sprayed liquid flame into its face in a short burst. It didn't even blink and now it was blind. A second one got the same treatment, only this one had been a woman with long black hair—her head became a torch, the smell of which was astounding and made her stomach do flips.

For a minute, until the others had shimmied through the tiny opening, Thuy stood within arm's reach of the horde, blasting flame at every face that came through the pile.

"Now, Thuy," Deckard called. "We're through." In an instant, she turned and ran for the opening. It was small and the cut pieces of metal were longer than before. She felt her jacket catch as she went through and for just a second she panicked.

Courtney came to her aid as she flailed. "You need to go back a few inches and then go forward. There you go." When Thuy looked up, she saw they were now beyond the lines of the 82nd, in some unknown suburb, but they weren't safe. Dozens of gleaming, evil eyes stared at them from the tall grass, while further on, beyond a little brook, there were shadows lurching in their direction.

"Jaimee Lynn?" she called. "Remember what I promised you? Soft bodies? If you want them then you're going to have to give us some room."

There was no answer. Deckard waited for only a moment before he said: "I got point, Chuck on my left, Courtney on my right. Thuy and Steph use the spray cans and remember, don't let them close on you. And, I almost forgot, who's got ammo?"

Three extra magazines were all that was left. "Make them count," he advised, once he had switched his out for a full one.

He expected trouble right off the bat and knew it was best to take the offensive instead of waiting to be caught unaware. With a low growl, he headed straight for where the child zombies were gathering in the brush. Two turned on him and he shot them both. The rest fled, but didn't go far.

The group could hear them whispering to each—they sounded like snakes. No words were used, but somehow they understood the hissed commands. Before the group could make it to the other side of the brook, the children attacked from all sides.

Beside Thuy, Stephanie suddenly screamed, and there was a whoosh of flame and a splash of light. Three guns went off in a string of shots as the reeds waved back and forth. Out of fear, Thuy lit off her can. In the light she saw they were surrounded by lithe bodies. The greedy, upturned faces shied away from the heat and the flame.

She was shooting flame when, unexpectedly, Deckard yelled: "Run!" And like some unthinking herd animal Thuy took off, blundering forward and sprawling right over Courtney, who had tripped with her first step and had fallen in the brook. The water was icy and the rocks were painfully sharp, but Thuy didn't even pause to sputter. The feral children weren't exactly smart, however, they were cunning and they could sense weakness.

They closed in for the easy kill with Thuy flicking, flicking, flicking her lighter and seeing nothing but a spark.

"I call the dark one," a voice screamed in glee. It was Jaimee Lynn racing through the tall grass at them, pushing the others aside. "No one touches her. She's mine. I called…"

The lighter finally caught, spouting a little golden flame. Thuy pointed the can straight across it and turned the little flame into a big one that caught Jaimee Lynn square. Her wispy gown went right up as though it had been soaked in gas and her hair was a torch that lit the night.

She howled in pain; however, the sound was obliterated by the crash of Courtney's M16 as she fired five times right in a row, spraying bullets and sending the children scrambling for cover. In seconds the children, including Jaimee Lynn seemed to have disappeared.

"Now!" Thuy screamed as she jumped up, pulling Courtney to her feet. They splashed across the brook and up the other bank where they had a fine view. To their left was the ugly back end of a strip mall: dumpsters, lazily stacked pallets, receiving docks stained with oil, trash…lots and lots of trash. A heavy screen of bushes hid the sight from the perfectly aligned backyards of a pretty row of suburban houses on their right.

In front of them was an overgrown field and right at the edge, only feet from getting clear was Deckard…and a mass of zombies.

Not realizing that his group had been split, Deckard had been rushing headlong towards the houses, but at the sound of the gun fire he turned and raced back, leaving Chuck and Stephanie half-surrounded.

"No!" Thuy yelled. "We'll catch up. Go! Go!" With that, she and Courtney plunged down the slope and into the thicket of tall grass where they couldn't see more than two feet on any side. Here and there, grinning faces would suddenly appear like shadow ghosts, seeming to float in the dark.

Courtney's fear was at a fever pitch. She couldn't stop herself as she shot bullets left and right, missing wildly. Thuy had to grab her gun to keep her from wasting the last of her ammo shooting at nothing.

"Wait until we're out in the open," Thuy told her. "We're close. Just keep running." Around them, the weeds swished with the passage of the undead children running on either side of the two, looking for an opening, hoping that one of the women would trip and then they would converge and feed like piranha.

In spite of the dark and the panic numbing them, Courtney and Thuy burst out into the open going at a full sprint. They had gotten turned around slightly and were forty yards to the left of where Deckard, Chuck and Stephanie were fighting off two dozen adult zombies.

With the children hanging back, lurking in the reeds, the pair of women were all alone and could have made a run for it. The thought never crossed their minds. With a single look towards each other, they ran at the zombies who seemed so much bigger and stronger than the children.

"Hey! Hey!" Courtney screamed, waving her M16. "Look over here." Of course they looked and of course they charged. Not all of them, but enough to open a lane for the others and enough to have Courtney screaming and running for her life with Thuy right behind.

They ran for the nearest house, jumped up on the porch and rattled the doorknob uselessly. It was locked and the house was dark.

"Shit!" Courtney cried, and then turned, only to see zombies coming up the porch stairs. Thankfully the steps were not easy for the clumsy creatures, giving the two women enough time to leap over the side railing. They landed in a bed of tulips, crushing them underfoot, and then took off again.

They caught up with the others and ran down the street, their feet slapping pavement, their breath hucking in and out, their movements a dead giveaway. Even in the dark of night it was obvious they were human.

Zombies streamed from out of every shadow, forcing the little group to run on and on. Thuy had a stitch in her side and to Courtney the air in her chest felt as if it were on fire—but that was nothing compared to what Chuck and Stephanie were feeling. The tumors in their lungs were like hunks of glass and every gulp of air came with a searing pain deep inside where the soul sat pressed up to the core of the body.

After a hundred yard sprint, they couldn't go on. Deckard saw it and pointed them at the nearest house. Its front door was locked, but he shouldered it in with one blow. After a quick glance to make sure there weren't any zombies inside, he led them through the house and out the back door. They crossed through the back yard to the fence where Stephanie collapsed and had to be lifted over.

"We can't go on," Thuy whispered to Deckard, once they were on the other side. "Find us somewhere safe."

He grunted a: "Sure," that was part sarcasm because obviously nowhere was safe anymore. The house just in front of them seemed as good as any and so he hurried to a basement window, pulled off his jacket and used it to break the glass which tinkled softly when it fell.

The group heard it as if it was an explosion of sound and they hunkered down, their eyes staring out into the night, their hearts thundering in their ears, certain that the hundreds of zombies they had just escaped from would come flocking.

None did, but that didn't stop them from scurrying down into the dark basement like a pack of rats. They feared risking a light, so they bumbled about knocking into things until the staircase was found. Once more Deckard led, his M4 at the ready, his eyes wide, his muscles tensed and ready for anything.

What he found was an average, upper middle-class home. Disregarding the *Pier 1* decorations and the *Ethan Allen* furnishings, he went straight to the front room, creeping up on the bay window from the side. Slowly, he closed the heavy curtains. Next he went to the front door and checked that it was locked.

To be on the safe side, he and Chuck heaved a leather couch in front of it.

Only then did he relax. He glanced back at the others trying to make out which one was Thuy in the dark. She was the smallest. The next smallest was Courtney, and then Stephanie and then…there was another shadow!

Sudden fear tore through Deckard. It wasn't Chuck, who had collapsed beside him, breathing in a wheezy rasp that sounded as if he had just climbed from his death bed.

The shadow meant there was someone in the room with them, someone who had come out of a back room or perhaps in from the back yard. No one had checked that door. Instead of clearing the rest of the house as they should have, the others had stood watching Deckard.

Just then a soft, hungry moan escaped the shadow. Thuy jumped and Courtney flinched back. Stephanie turned slowly, too spent even for fear. Chuck went for his weapon which he had set down on a coffee table.

Only Deckard could react. His rifle seemed to come up on its own, but there was no sighting it. His target was a black shape against a black background with only a suggestion of a human form. *It couldn't be human*, Deckard told himself as he pointed the rifle at the center of the shadow and blasted it twice, knocking it back.

Had it been human, it would have fallen or at least cried out, but it only stepped back two paces before staggering forward only to be met by Deckard, who rushed up and at point blank range, where he could finally see what he was shooting, blasted the zombie's head open.

It had been a woman and before Deckard had shot it, there hadn't been much to it but rags of flesh, cracked bones and a few barely working organs. In the dark, he had no way of knowing how harmless it was and so he erred on the side of caution, only now that error had deadly consequences.

The gun's blasts had been heard and the countless zombies they had just escaped from charged the home.

"Out the back!" Deckard cried and once more took the lead. He raced through to the kitchen, where he hauled back on a sliding glass door only to come face to face with two half-dead creatures. There were dozens more pouring through an open gate at the side of the house. There were too many to fight and with Chuck and Stephanie so exhausted, there was no room to run.

In the three seconds Deckard gaped, his escape was cut off. He'd had a chance to escape—alone. None of the others could have kept up, not even Thuy, and there was no way he could leave her behind.

"Back inside," he hissed, pushing them through the sliding glass doors and then hauling back on a long curtain, cutting off the little light the night afforded. He pushed through them and sped for the front door, only to be brought up short when it thumped, heavily, rattling on its hinges.

"Look out," he hissed in a whisper to Chuck who was standing in the middle of the living room, seemingly frozen in place. Dodging around the cowboy, Deckard hurried to a small office off the living room. One window faced the east side of the house, glancing out he saw there were zombies there as well, seven or eight, too many to try to rush by in secret.

Deckard came back into the living room and turned in a small circle, slowly realizing that they were trapped and that they were going to die very soon unless someone came up with a plan.

"Thuy? Tell me you have a plan. Please. Can you make some sort of bomb or something?"

She shook her head, her black hair somehow shimmering even though there wasn't any light. "I can...I can check in the kitchen or the garage...wait! The garage!"

"We can use a car," Stephanie cried, catching Thuy's sudden excitement. A second before, salvation was an impossibility, now it likely sat in the garage just waiting for them. With the last of her energy, she practically ran to the garage door that sat just off a small hall leading from the kitchen. Ignoring the moans and the banging on the doors and windows, she threw open the door and froze half in and half out of the garage.

Right away, Deckard knew there wasn't a car.

Hoping to find something of use, he pushed past her, squinting into the dark, looking at the shelves for something that could be used to create a fire or a bomb or, or...anything. Unfortunately, the people who had lived here had not been handy in the least. The shelves held some unused gardening equipment and the impeccably clean workbench sitting in the corner had only a few items on it: a hammer, two screw drivers, and a blue jug filled with windshield washing fluid.

"Where's the car?" Stephanie asked in a hollow whisper. She felt as though she was living a nightmare. The night had that slow motion, doomed feeling of a horrible dream that she couldn't wake up from.

"We'll figure something out," Deckard said, once again pushing past her. He hurried to the kitchen, knowing that if there was a way out of the trap he had accidentally led them into, Thuy would figure it out. He found her down on all fours with her head beneath the kitchen sink and a flashlight in her mouth. Already there was a pile of cleaning products next to her left leg.

He stooped to pick up one of the bottles just as there was a crash of glass from the far side of the house. Forgetting the bottle, he sped through the house and found Chuck bracing the door to the laundry room with his stick thin body.

"What's the plan, Deck? Tell me she gots a plan." Chuck was with Deckard when it came to an estimation of Thuy's intelligence. Chuck had never met anyone smarter. It was a fact, at least in his head, that she had more brains than the entire population of Norman, Oklahoma combined.

"I'm sure she's got something clicking," Deckard answered, clasping Chuck on his frail shoulder. "We just have to hold things together until she sets it in action. You guard this door. Courtney!" he yelled. With the zombies attacking the house, and the noise building, there was no sense creeping about as they had been. "Courtney, station yourself in the living room. I'll watch the kitchen door. Steph…" His words caught in his throat as Thuy stepped out of the kitchen, holding only a couple of spray cans in her hands.

By her expression, he knew something was wrong. "Hey Thuy…it's going to be alright. Just tell us what the plan is."

She shook her head and then shrugged. "I don't have one," she admitted.

"Yes, you do, you just need some time," Deckard assured her.

"No, time won't do it. We have nothing. There's nothing in the house and there's too many of them. Look," she pointed at the front door which was shaking and vibrating under the blows of the zombies tearing at it. "Time is what we don't have."

"I have a plan," Chuck said, with a strange smile on his face. "It's sure all queer that you didn't think of it, Dr. Lee."

Thuy's eyes shot wide and eagerly she asked: "What is it? What's the plan?"

"Simple. We gots to sacrifice one of us."

Chapter 23

1—10:17 p.m.
The Hartford Quarantine Zone

Eyes shot around the room. Each of them looking back and forth from one to the next, stunned and frightened by Chuck's statement. He was right. The only way out was for one of them to cause a distraction so the others could escape. But who? Who would be left behind to get eaten?

Stephanie knew she was the obvious choice. She was the sickest and the weakest and the worst fighter and she wasn't smart like Dr. Lee or resourceful like Courtney and she didn't have Deckard's endurance and strength or Chuck's toughness.

She was useless—except in this. In this one thing she could be greater than all of them. She could be a hero, if only she could find the courage to open her mouth or raise her hand, or do anything besides shake like a leaf and hope that someone would come up with a better plan.

When no one did, she tried to force herself to say something. She even went so far as to open her mouth but words refused to come. She could feel them in her chest ready to come bursting out, only her throat locked up and she couldn't get a squeak out.

It was up to Chuck to speak for her. He smiled suddenly at Stephanie and said: "I'll stay. I'll open the garage door a bit and make a ruckus. I'll bang some pans and such, enough to get them on me good, while y'all go out through the study window. It's got a screen on it that y'all can pop right off. Just whatever you do, don't shoot y'all's guns."

Unexpectedly, Thuy balled a fist in front of Chuck's face as if she was going to hit him. She only shook it in complete fury. "No! This is unacceptable. There's got to be another way."

Just then, one of the hinges on the front door gave way. There was a *crack!* and the sound of metal bouncing on hardwood floors. Calmly, Chuck squinted toward the door as if it was just one more sunset, adding to the net of wrinkles around his eyes.

"If there's another way," he drawled, "we've wasted all the time left to us in order to find it. Y'all better get going. Hurry now." Gently, he pushed Thuy's fist down and then pointed to the study door.

There was no time for words and so Deckard simply gave Chuck a nod and began pulling Thuy away.

"But…" was all she could think to say.

Courtney was just as speechless and walked past Chuck with a strange, blank look on her face as if she had been knocked on the head.

Next was Stephanie and she seemed as thunder-struck as Courtney. Chuck pressed the M4 he carried into her numb hands. "Be careful how many bullets you use, darlin'. There ain't a lot left. Just a touch over half a mag."

"All I'll need is two," she said as she slid the magazine out and thumbed a couple of brass bullets into her palm.

Chuck gave her a strange look and said: "Sorry, darlin' but y'all's shooting ain't all that good. Yer gonna need all them bullets and then some."

"Nope, just two. Hey, Deckard, catch." She tossed the magazine. It arced gracefully, but he was so surprised that he fumbled the catch.

"What the hell are you doing?" he asked. The answer was so obvious that he didn't know why he asked it. Stephanie had been a weakling since he had first laid eyes on her. Now she was strong.

"I'm helping you escape, now get going." Her words were sharp as glass and her eyes were hard. When Thuy hesitated, Stephanie shoved her bodily into the study and shut the door in her face to keep her from asking another time-wasting and pointless question.

Now, they were alone.

Chuck knew what she was doing and was incensed; however, before he could say a word, she strode past him. He caught up to her in the kitchen, staring around in the dark, trying to figure out which cupboard held the pans. "You need to get yer ass with the others! Go on. If you need a goodbye kiss, well ok, but then you need to git!"

She ignored his blazing anger and opened the first cupboard. *Bingo*, she thought and snatched two pans. When she straightened, Chuck grabbed her shoulders and brought his face within an inch of hers. "I am trying to save you."

Her courage peaked as she said: "You can't save me, just like I can't save you." She could see his pain, both physical and emotional. It was a mirror of hers. They were both going to die very soon, one way or another, and the one thing she had learned in all of this was that she didn't want to die alone. If she was going to die, she wanted it to be in the arms of the man she loved.

He understood, but the truth hurt so badly that he fought the inevitable and with a roar he turned his size 13 shit kickers and put a whomping big dent in the front of the refrigerator. "Son of a bitch! You go with them or else." Laughably, he had his fist raised.

It made her love him even more. Ignoring the rock hard fist and the clamoring of zombies breaking through the windows and hammering down the doors, she pulled him in close.

"You can only put off death for so long," she said, looking up into his eyes. As hard as his fist was, his eyes were wet and soft, and his lips trembled.

He was afraid, only she didn't realize what he feared until he asked: "You're gonna make me kill you, aren't you?"

She nodded. "I'd kill you, but I know you won't let me. You're too much of a gentleman." For some ungodly reason, these words struck her as outrageously funny and she brayed laughter and smiled up at the man who would kill her two minutes later. "Come on! Let's do this right!"

Taking one of the pots, she hammered it with sudden anger and strength on the side of the stove. Bam! Bam! Bam! She turned to him, her soft face wet with tears, her smile manic and at the same time endlessly sad.

"You got to try it," she said and held out her dented pot.

He took it and looking into her eyes, said: "Aw-right." It was his way. The one word confessed his love and told her that this was the right thing to do. They would go out together as lovers should.

With the pot in one hand, he went to the garage and flicked on the light. They both blinked at the glare and they both tried to hide the fear in their faces. Stephanie was ghostly white and so thin that it hurt Chuck to see what the last three days had done to her.

With a show of bravado he didn't feel, Chuck laughed aloud as he marched to the aluminum double door and beat it with his pot. The metal on metal was a storm of sound—it was also completely cathartic. The two of them pounded out their frustrations.

It was over all too soon. In half a minute, they both sagged back, their exhaustion overwhelming them. Chuck took Stephanie by the hand and led her back into the house, nearly running into a zombie who had slithered through the shattered glass of the sliding kitchen door and was now getting to its feet.

With nothing left to lose, Chuck waited until it had lurched within arm's length before clanging the now dented pot off the thing's head with all of his might. The zombie's black eyes crossed momentarily. It was stunned long enough for Chuck to plant his boot dead center in its chest and send it falling back into the others that had invaded the house.

"Upstairs," Chuck said, tossing away his pot and taking Stephanie's hand. She flicked on the light switch as she passed it. The light gave life to the place. The faces in the pictures hanging from the walls were of happy smiling people. Stephanie liked that. She took one off the wall and studied it as they went.

It was easier to find happiness in those still photographs than in the horrors coming up the stairs behind them. The house had filled with the dead, but she didn't want to think of them.

"In here," Chuck said. They stepped into the master bedroom and again she turned on the light. They had been in the dark for three straight days, afraid to live like people should. She didn't want to die like that.

Chuck shut and locked the door, and for good measure he grunted and groaned a dresser in front of it. The door was solid, but no more than a million other doors that had been torn apart by the beasts. They would get in, and it wouldn't be long.

"Do you think they got away," Stephanie said, going to the bed. For some reason, she laid the M16 down on the blanket, straightening it, carefully, so it lay exactly centered between the two pillows. Chuck gave it a glance and went to the window. The view was altogether frightening. The front lawn of the housed was ringed by zombies, fifty deep.

"Yeah, they got away. We woulda heard them if they hadn't. There woulda been shootin' and stuff."

The bedroom door shivered from the first attack. She wanted to ask: *Do you think they're coming back to save us?* but she was afraid of the answer. What if he said: no? "I wish we had music," she remarked, pushing her mind away to something else besides an unlikely rescue.

Chuck grinned. "Mood music?"

She laughed, but without any force now. "Just something to drown them out. They're so ugly." They both stood on opposite sides of the bed and stared down at it…and the gun. "Do we wait?" she asked. What she meant was: *Do we wait for Thuy and Deckard to get back with their guns and whatever rescue plan Thuy had managed to cook up?*

He considered, glancing towards the door that trembled under meaty blows. "I don't think so. If we wait we might be rushed and things might go wrong."

A shiver wracked her as her subconscious painted ghastly pictures on the surface of her mind. She forced her mind away from the images and her thoughts got hung up on a simple declarative statement: *This is really happening.*

"I wish we had a pistol," she said in a whisper. "I want to be with you. I want to hold you even…even in death. Is that gross?"

"Naw, it ain't. And we can still do this proper." He went to the closet and came back with a handful of coat hangers which he twisted and bent to form a stiff braid. "There…" He had just proudly displayed his handiwork when the door cracked. As they watched a panel split and ugly faces leered in at them.

"We better hurry," Stephanie said, but didn't make a move for the bed. She was suddenly afraid to lie down. Her courage had evaporated.

Chuck went to her, kissed her once and laid her down as if this was their wedding day. "It'll be nothing, darlin'. Close your eyes and listen to my voice." He tried to lay down next to her but she struggled suddenly, digging in her pocket.

"Bullets," she said. "We can't do this without bullets. Ha-ha." Her laugh was forced and her smile strained—the crack in the door was wider now. Soon it would come apart and the dresser would be heaved over. There couldn't be a rescue, now. It was too late—too late for everything except death, one way or the other. "Let's do this. Okay? I love you Chuck…do you love me?"

She was on her back and the tears in her blue eyes pooled and spilled down her temples. "Of course I do."

"Then it'll be okay." With him so close, her courage flared enough for her to pick up the rifle and lay it on her chest between her breasts, the muzzle up under her chin touching her porcelain skin.

304

He found he didn't need the coat hangers, his arm was plenty long for the job. "I'll be right behind you, darlin'. You just make sure to wait for me on the other side. I'm gonna need a good word to get through the Pearly Gates."

She tried to nod, but the bore of the gun stopped her. She was afraid to move and afraid that the gun would kick and only shoot her face off and she was afraid that the powder in the bullets had gotten wet and it wouldn't fire—above all she was afraid to die. She found herself trembling from head to toe.

"We never had a chance, did we?" she asked.

"I had the chance to fall in love with you," Chuck whispered. "I woulda done all of this over again just for that chance." He leaned over the barrel of the gun and kissed her lips. The touch of them were eternally imprinted on his mind.

"Me too." The door broke nearly in half. She tried to turn her head, but he held her chin in place. "I'll wait for you," she said and closed her eyes. It was a promise she would keep even if it meant forever haunting an undead world.

He brushed her lips once more, felt his stomach lurch as if he were going to throw up and then pulled the trigger.

It was a surprise that she didn't die right away. There was a hole in her, up under her chin, but her eyes were open and fixed and her mouth was slack. No air went in or out, yet her heart still beat. He refused to kill himself with her heart still beating. With gentle hands, he shut her eyes and kissed her again and listened with his ear to her chest.

At first her heart was like a hammer against a post, but gradually it became a hammer against velvet, and in seconds the sound of her heart grew less and less until it stopped completely.

The zombies were in the room by then and he only had time for one more kiss and one more pull of the trigger.

2—The White House

One man had sat in the situation room all night in complete silence. He had taken a corner seat and hadn't budged and yet his presence had grown steadily as the hours passed until he felt that if he sneezed everyone would cry out in fear.

His name was Lieutenant Colonel Oliver Manzetti and usually he was part of a rotating five man team who carried the "Nuclear Football," but as they were in the Situation Room, the football was unnecessary. The president had everything needed to launch a nuclear attack at his fingertips.

Everything except the ridiculously named "Biscuit." Before any order pertaining to the use of nukes could be processed by the military, the president had to be positively identified using a special code issued on a plastic card. To Oliver and really, to everyone else, such a precaution was smart.

The president, however had such a strict no-nuke policy that, from his first day in office, he had refused to even carry the plastic card around on his person as every one of his predecessors had done since Eisenhower. He told people that he counted on "smart diplomacy" not on arms to keep peace in the world. So far that "smart diplomacy" had taken the form of ignoring anything threatening and hoping that nothing truly awful would happen while he was in office.

Now, the president gave a glance behind him at Oliver whenever the latest bit of bad news came.

With each glance, the twin pit-stains under Oliver's arms advanced. He was appalled at the very notion that this windbag who was leader of the free world simply because he had won a popularity contest in which he had promised the most "freebies," could order a strike that could obliterate half the eastern seaboard.

The latest news had Oliver almost shitting himself.

"Are they terrorists?" the president asked after a quick backwards glance at Oliver. The president had this strange fear that the man in control of the nukes, as he thought of Oliver and the others like him, would be suddenly gone right when he was forced to use the big bombs.

Marty Aleman shrugged. He was so tired that he could barely lift his sagging shoulders. "It's hard to tell. Their demands aren't in keeping with what one would expect from traditional terrorists. If I had to guess, I'd say no."

"But they want to bring the virus here!" the president cried, his voice shrill. He had been going back and forth in the last few hours, from a frightened boy to a screaming tyrant. Now he was a mixture of both. "Surely only a terrorist would suggest such a thing."

"Or they're desperate," Marty replied, picking up Anna's handwritten letter for the fifth time and for the fifth time, he went through it line by line.

To Whom it may concern,

Because the military has not been able to control the spread of the "zombie virus," my comrades and I do not believe we are safe on Long Island. By chance we have access to "zombie" blood and have used it to create a dozen infected persons. Each of these persons is being held in separate homes behind locked doors, but as you know, doors and locks will only hold against them for so long, meaning you are on a time crunch to respond.

Our demands are simple, we would like to have safe passage arranged for the ten of us. You will provide two helicopters for our use. The first will convey a small group of us to Washington D.C. where we will be freed at a destination of our choosing. Once the first group is safe and outside of government control and surveillance, the second will follow.

Yes, each of us will have the virus on our persons and yes, we will make zombies within the capital. None of this is open to negotiations. Once we are safe, the location of each zombie will be released.

We do not wish to spread the disease any further than it has been. Our only goal is survival. Our safety and the lives of twenty million people are in your hands. If you agree to our demands broadcast the words: Lord Abraham's Revival on ISR channel 12 in the following locations: Garden City, Brentwood, West Hampton, and Riverhead. We will reply with Morning Glory Blinders and instructions for the first pickup. It is advisable for you to hurry.

Yours,
Professor X

"Professor X?" Marty mumbled. "Why on earth would they sign it Professor X?"

Three seats down from the president was the useless FEMA director, whose agency had done nothing but get in the way of everyone. "Maybe they're trying to impress us with the fact they're in academia."

"Maybe they are comic book nerds in over their heads," suggested the Secretary of Health and Human Services.

"Maybe it doesn't matter," General Heider groused. "We have ten people on Long Island threatening the lives of millions. We don't have time to play junior detectives or for guessing games. This message is twenty two minutes old. We need to decide right now if we're going to give in to their demands or if we're going to put our efforts into finding and killing them."

Everyone looked to the president who quailed under the weight of the eyes on him and turned quickly to Marty. The chief of staff touched the clean paper that had been printed minutes before, his fingers barely caressing it. "Are we sure it was a zombie that was found?"

Heider nodded. "Completely sure. We have seven eye witnesses, all of whom saw the thing get shot five times without flinching. The area for a mile around has been cordoned off."

Marty blew out a breath and took in the FBI director's hard-lined and heavily browed face. "If we go after them, how long before you can get men on this?"

The director didn't hesitate. "In a New York minute, but I wouldn't expect a miracle. Even if the person who wrote this left fingerprints, what would it matter? It'll be hours before we could give you a name. In the meantime, what do we have to go on? The only description we have is of a dark man, possibly hispanic, dressed in black. It's useless or perhaps worse than useless. If it gets out that we're looking for a 'dark' man on an island crammed with people on the edge of panic, there'll be blood in the streets."

"So you suggest letting them go?" the president asked. "You suggest letting the virus come here?"

"I'm saying you might not have a choice about letting them leave Long Island, but it doesn't mean we can't track their moves once they're here. We have at least a dozen drones we can station around the city. We can be on them in no time and track them without their knowing. Once we have all of the terrorists together, we can swoop in and snatch them."

Marty liked the plan, however the president looked like a confused child. "But the virus...here!"

"It seems like our only choice," Marty said, soothing the great man. "If the virus gets out on Long Island where there are an estimated fifteen to twenty million people...I don't think the army would be able to contain them."

"I know we can't," Heider told them. "My men in the New York area are already spread thinly. If the virus spreads there as fast as it's spread everywhere else, there would be only one option." His eyes darted to Lieutenant Colonel Manzetti.

"Oh God," the president groaned.

Marty patted him on his liver-spotted hand. "Don't worry, sir. We are going to put that off as long as possible. I think we can all agree on that. Okay, it's agreed, by the president's order, we will allow the perpetrators to leave Long Island and we will catch them here."

The president wavered for a second and then nodded. Immediately, Heider picked up a phone and said: "It's a go on two. Repeat: it's a go on two."

A heavy silence followed this as everyone at the table began to visualize the dreadful possibilities of bringing the virus to Washington. Eventually, the president broke the quiet by asking in a timid voice: "When do we...you know." He jerked his head at Manzetti.

Heider looked puzzled by the question. "You aren't even letting us use air power to its fullest and you're talking nukes? That doesn't make the least bit of sense."

"Maybe Heider's right," Marty said. "Maybe it's time we let loose the dogs of war completely."

"Okay, sure," the president said, caving in on his principles, "But what about the nukes? At what point do we let them loose?" He made it sound as if they were caged dragons apt to turn on their master if he wasn't careful.

Marty and Heider shared a look, each hoping the other would answer. Heider had more to lose and so he sat back with an expectant raised eyebrow that said: *Go ahead, be the bearer of bad news.* Marty hid his sneer as he turned back to the president and said: "General Heider believes that the time is not far off. Please, tell him, General."

Marty had danced aside and now the president's unpredictable glare was back on Heider. Slipping a smile on his face to hide his anger, General Heider said: "Mr. Aleman and I have decided that the time for nukes is dependent on whether the lines hold in southern Massachusetts and the eastern Pennsylvania border, with the Penn border being the more important of the two. If it falls, there's no major force or natural barrier for a hundred miles."

He went to the monitor, enlarged Pennsylvania and tapped the capital: Harrisburg. "We'll lose half the state, with our fall back point here along the Susquehanna River in the south and our ass hanging wide open in the north."

"And our army? Where the fuck are they?" The president's voice was like ice. "We spend trillions every year on them and for what? Where are they?"

"You know where they are," Heider said, slapping the monitor with the flat of his hand. "Right here you have units from as far away as Virginia and Indiana and it took a colossal effort to get them here in the time it did. We'll have more units in place tomorrow and more the day after that, but if you look at this fucking map you'll see how huge an area they're covering and if we lose the Penn border that area is going to double."

The president's anger perished like a soap bubble, leaving behind only the slime of fear that coated his mind. "Then we use the nukes. We have to."

"Not just no, but hell no!" General Heider said. "We have to give our soldiers a chance to win."

"What about the rest of us?" the president asked, once more glancing back at Manzetti as if he were a devil perched on his shoulder, tempting him with the power to end all of the mess in one go. "Where's our chance?"

3—The Hartford Quarantine Zone

They ran to live. They ran, going light with two rifles between the three of them and only 28 rounds of ammo.

Thuy had a few odds and ends, a knife, a lighter, some string. What weighed her down was the anchor of her conscience. Chuck and Stephanie. Young lovers, dead because she wasn't as smart as she had always thought she was. She'd made mistake after mistake and as a result the corpses were piling up in the millions.

Her feet stumbled. Deckard caught her, moving as quick as a cat. "We're almost safe." He was being kind which was why she didn't call him a liar. They weren't anywhere near being safe. They had escaped the city of Hartford, not the much larger quarantine zone that surrounded it, which teemed with the undead.

The beasts were everywhere, dark shadows that moaned and moved, seemingly always coming right at the three as if drawn in by a giant magnet. Time and again, they broke away from a suburban street, dodged through back yards and climbed fences, only to find themselves in almost the exact same position.

"We need to get indoors," Deckard said.

"No!" Courtney hissed, her eyes huge, like twin lamps. "We'll be trapped just like before."

Thuy didn't have an opinion. Inside or outside didn't seem to matter. Sooner or later, they would die like everyone else.

Deckard didn't wait for her input. Ignoring Courtney, he grabbed Thuy's hand and headed right up the front steps of a ranch house. With a crash, he threw himself against the front door.

Listlessly, Thuy followed him in. She thought she was beyond caring or even surprise, but when Deckard flicked on the living room light, she stopped in her tracks, and was knocked into by Courtney who was staring at the chandelier that hung from the ceiling in utter horror.

"Turn it off! Turn it off!" Courtney was almost blubbering.

Deckard calmly said: "No. We want them to come. In fact…" He began flicking the switch up and down like a toddler making the mental connection between the switch and the light coming from the ceiling fixture. Deckard flicked a good twenty times until he heard the moans drawing closer to the house.

Leaving the light on, they slipped through the house to the back door and then ghosted out into the night. Another fence was hopped, but this time they didn't go on. They leaned against it, listening to the zombies tearing up the ranch house, looking for the people.

The light and the noise made by the rampaging zombies only attracted more zombies. Soon the yard was filled with them. Deckard grunted out a: "Let's go," and began crawling through the grass. He kept low when he reached the front of this new house, but did not cross the road where he could be seen.

Using parked cars and low fences and whatever else they could for cover, they went up the block to the corner house and paused in front of it. "Stay here," Deckard said. "I'm going in through the back door…"

"Why go in at all?" Courtney said, interrupting in a voice that carried in the night.

Angrily, Deckard shushed her. "Are you trying to get us killed?" he hissed. "I'm getting the keys to this vehicle." He patted the dark hunk of metal that Thuy leaned against. "Stay here and be quiet for fuck's sake."

Courtney mumbled: "Sorry." Unlike Thuy, she didn't sit back. She squatted with her M16 held to her chest, as her head went back and forth, looking up and down the block.

Thuy didn't bother looking. "I failed them," she said in a whisper. "Just like I failed everyone else."

Unexpectedly, Courtney grabbed the jacket of Thuy's torn pantsuit and growled into her face: "Shut the hell up. You don't get to be like this. You need to be…I don't know, focused or something. You got to keep it together and help get us out of here."

"I don't know if I can," Thuy answered in a voice so low that Courtney could barely make out the words from four inches away.

"Yeah you can. All you got to do is concen…shhh! What is that? Oh, it's Deckard. Oh, thank God." Thuy saw that Courtney was shaking, and every once in a while, when she turned her head, the tears on her face could be seen glistening.

"Get in," Deckard said, easing up to the vehicle—a 2011 RAV4—and opening the passenger side doors. Once the women were in, he scampered around to the other side, hopped in and flashed a grin when he saw the fuel gauge in the green. "Where to?" he asked as he started the car.

Next to him, Thuy only shook her head. She was normally beautiful but so reserved that her beauty seemed more like a picture an untouchable one held behind the clearest glass. Now she was beautiful, but broken. "I don't know where to go," she said. "Someone else is going to have to think of something."

Deckard began driving. He went straight, not knowing where to go or what to do. Normally he thought of himself as resourceful. Right there on that dark street, drifting at a steady fifteen miles an hour as they passed dead houses and dead people, he could think of nothing…or at least nothing that constituted a workable plan.

Driving out of the zone was impossible. And so was walking or riding a bike. A boat sounded nice except he was sure they had all been taken, just as he was sure the Navy and Coast Guard were patrolling the shores looking for any stragglers.

If there were a plane around, Deckard figured he had an even fifty-fifty chance of getting it airborne, but landing it was a pipe dream that would end in a crash and an explosion. And even if he could land one, he was sure that he wouldn't be allowed within ten miles of an airport. The Air Force would shoot them down.

What about parachuting out of the zone? he wondered. It took very little training to pull a rip-cord. Anyone could do it.

"I need a map," he said, leaning well over Thuy and digging through the glove box. "We can fly a plane out of the Zone and then parachute to safety."

Courtney's excitement flared up and died in the course of seconds. "That won't work."

"It's not all that scary," Deckard told her. "Especially after everything you two have gone through. Sure the landing won't be the softest, but…"

"It won't work because there aren't any planes," Courtney said. "The order came from FEMA. I heard it yesterday morning. The government ordered all planes within the Zone to be… what's the word, not seized. Scuttled? I don't know, but they were to be destroyed."

Deckard sat back behind the wheel and began coasting again, unsure what to do or where to go. A bank would be a good place to hide out in unless the power went out and the air stopped circulating. They would be safe right up until they died of asphyxiation. And what would they do for food? And what about water?

Deckard drove for thirty minutes and the car's engine was the only sound. Thuy stared out her window without seeing anything, her eyes completely blank. In the back, Courtney fidgeted and tried to come up with some idea to get them out of the Zone. Although she still had contacts in the outside world, she had no way to reach them and even if she could, she didn't have any leverage. She had no reward or threat that was compelling enough for anyone to risk letting them out of the Zone.

Eventually, Thuy spoke: "I deserve this."

"You don't," was Deckard's knee-jerk response.

"Then why is everything so hard? Why can't we ever get a win? If I don't deserve this then how else do you explain Chuck and Steph…" She broke down, fat tears rolling down her high-arched cheekbones. "All of this is my fault, and I suppose, our current situation is apropos. I should be fated to endlessly drive through the hell I created."

Deckard immediately pulled over. He opened his mouth to tell her that there was no such thing as fate when he spied the pink balloons tied to a mailbox, not three feet from Thuy's window. A sign in the front lawn read: *It's A Girl!* His eyes tracked up the sidewalk of the house—he cringed at what he saw: blood across the battered in front door, shattered glass in the flower bed, and something small and pink cast away in the lawn.

He pulled his eyes away from the small pink thing, hoping to God that Thuy hadn't seen it. Her eyes were dead on it.

"That's not your fault," Deckard said, in a voice gripped with emotion. He put out a hand to pull her face away, but she bared her teeth and stormed out of the RAV4, heading for the pink bundle. "Thuy, no," he said, in a whisper as he jumped out and rushed out after her.

She beat him to the bundle and fell down in front of it, her sobs loud in the night. Courtney, who had come up behind, took one look at the bundle, and had to choke back her own tears.

"My fault!" Thuy suddenly shrieked, her words smacking hard against the abandoned buildings and coming back to her softer and softer. The pain inside her was like a volcano that threatened to explode. She wanted to scream it out, but Courtney wouldn't let her.

The one-time dispatcher tackled Thuy, sending her sprawling within inches of the dead baby. Stunned, Thuy found herself on her back with the younger woman straddling her. "Okay, it's your damn fault," Courtney yelled. "Who cares? Wallowing in pity isn't going to fix anything, and you know what? No one wants to hear it. What we want to hear is how you're going to fix the problem."

"I can't fix it," Thuy answered.

"You can't or you won't?" Courtney demanded.

That answer wasn't so easy. If Thuy could fix the problem that the Com-cells represented, of course she would, but she was stuck in the Zone with no way out...or at least no way they had yet discovered.

"I can't," she said. "I would, but I'm stuck here, just like you."

"You're not stuck here like me," Courtney said. "I'm stuck here because I've reached my limit. You understand? I think of myself as pretty smart, but that can only get me so far. But you...you haven't reached your limit yet. I know it. You've just got to stop fixating on all of this." She waved her hand to indicate the neighborhood and the sad house and the heart-breaking pink lump.

"Can you do that?" Courtney asked. "Can you take it one step at a time and get us out of here?"

In the corner of her eyes was the baby, a broken pink horror, while staring down was a living woman. One deserved Thuy's entire soul in payment for what had happened to her and the other deserved all of Thuy's mind.

"Yes, I can."

Courtney helped Thuy to her feet and before she could look one last time at the tiny, broken body, Courtney pulled her away, heading for the car. They got as far as the mailbox when Thuy dug in her heels and stood still.

"No," she said, shocked. "It can't be that easy."

Deckard and Courtney shared a look over Thuy's head. "What?" Deckard asked. "What's so easy?" His eyes went to the mailbox, while hers were on the balloons.

Before he knew it, Thuy broke away and raced back to the house with Courtney and Deckard begging in hushed voices for her to come back. She ignored them. Stepping over a pool of blood, she entered, and by instinct, made her way to the kitchen. On a counter, right where she expected it, sat a black, punch-button phone. She left it unperturbed on its cradle and went for the drawer just below it, and, triumphantly, lifted out a phone book.

"Please be a thing. Please be a thing," she chanted over and over as she flipped through the yellow pages.

It was a thing. The quarter page, color picture was proof. "We can get out," Thuy said and held up the book.

"By hot air balloon?" Deckard asked, feeling as though he had stepped into some sort of low-tech time warp. "But you can't steer one of those. They just…they just go where ever the wind takes them. Right?"

"Who cares?" Courtney cried, throwing herself into Thuy's arms. "They fly and that's all that matters!"

Chapter 24

1—11:03 p.m.
The Hartford Quarantine Zone

There was an address for *Ray & Pearl's Hot Air Balloon Rides—Open Sundays!* staring them right in the face. Deckard tore the page out of the book and took Thuy by the elbow, steering her out of the house before she found another wild hair growing out of her ass.

A hot air balloon? The thought gave him the heebee-jeebees and he knew why: control. Really, it was the lack of control that bothered him. His was a type A personality, and type As didn't leave their lives in the hand of fate. Really, this was worse than giving control over to the capricious nature of fate. It was far worse. This was him putting his life on the line with only the *wind* deciding things.

There was one thing he knew for certain, there was nothing more fickle than the wind. And yet, he didn't have a better plan and so he gunned the car in a U-turn with a hard smile on his face, the stress of the night culminating in this unlikely plan, finally showing through.

Thuy saw the smile and knew that it didn't stem from an abundance of joy at the plan she had worked up. "It should be just fine," she said. Hers was also a type A personality, however, she figured she would have enough control of the balloon to get them to safety. "Have you never heard of the 'prevailing westerlies?' All we have to do is transport the balloon close to the Massachusetts border, send it up…"

"And hope we don't get shot down," Deckard said, interrupting. The eagerness alight in her face darkened and he immediately regretted his words. "Sorry, I'm sure we won't be shot down. It's dark and no one's going to be looking up. Chances are we're going to float right by the line without a problem." He gave her a smile that was ninety percent lie. A hot air balloon was such a big fucking target that it hurt to think about how easily it could be shot out of the sky.

Courtney was all for the idea, anything to get away. She asked for the advertisement, saw the little map and the address, and began directing them. Although she had never been to Connecticut, her work with General Collins the day before had given her intimate knowledge of the road system.

"Take a left," she instructed, squinting out the window at darkened road signs. "We want to head west to Canaan. If you turn on your lights we could be there in half an hour."

Turning on the lights was the smart, but terrifying way to drive. It was one thing to putt along with the shadows moving in their periphery, it was quite another to light up the undead and see their endless numbers and their grey hungry faces and the ribbons of flesh hanging from their putrid bodies. Next to him, Thuy stiffened and he put a hand on her thigh and squeezed gently.

Her hand covered his and he drove like that down haunted roads, both of them uplifted by the touch. In the back seat Courtney didn't have the warmth of another person to calm her and she grew increasingly nervous. "Jeeze!" she exclaimed when she saw a hulking zombie that looked as wide as the RAV4, "Fuck," she whispered when she saw a line of soldiers in helmets and armored vests coming at the car—not one of them had a face left.

When she saw a pack of weasels, their whiskers dripping blood, eating the remains of a toddler, she vomited up a croaking, acid-tasting burp and asked: "Can we turn off the lights? We're pretty close and there's no need to attract any more attention, right?"

Deckard snapped them off and drove blind for a while until his night eyes regained their focus.

They were very close at this point. The address was on Copperton Street, which began smooth and paved in a suburb of Canaan. A few miles later they were stuttering along a dirt road that hadn't been properly leveled in years. The damage to their kidneys was offset by the fact that the zombies were far fewer in number.

As should have been expected for a place where hot air balloons were launched, the land was flat and open. For miles in every direction, the earth had been freshly turned in preparation for a planting that would never occur. In the middle of one field stood a barn, looming like a mountain of shadow. The signs for Ray & Pearl's pointed them right at it.

"Courtney and I will clear the area first," Deckard said as he eased up. "Thuy stay here until I tell you to get out. Not before, understood?"

When she nodded he stepped out, his black boots kicking up a bit of dust. It made him think of Chuck and the faded, down in the heel cowboy boots he always wore. Melancholy seized him and he made a wide circuit around the barn with only half his mind on the idea of danger. The other half dwelt on his own guilt.

Thuy hadn't done anything wrong. Chuck and Stephanie were dead because of him, not her. He was the one who had led them into that house and he was the one who had shot one of the least dangerous zombies he had yet seen. And he was the one who hadn't said a word when the concept of sacrifice had come up.

Deckard stopped at the corner of the barn, ran a hand through his dark hair and then spat on the ground. "That's it," he whispered, meaning: that was all the time he would waste on guilt. He'd done what he'd done and there was no use beating himself up for it. If he lived, he would deal with the guilt then.

He had led them into the house because Chuck and Stephanie would have died in the backyard if he hadn't. He had shot that zombie because in the dark there had been no way of knowing how weak it was. And he had not volunteered to die because it didn't make sense. He was the strongest. In a perfect Darwinesque world, he should be the last to die.

With the guilt pushed back into his subconscious, he moved to the partially open front door of the barn and peered inside. The darkness made the interior seem immense, as if it went on for miles. "Hello?" he called out. "Any zombies in here?" He waited, listening intently. Louder he yelled: "Hello!" After half a minute, he relaxed.

"Anything?" Courtney asked, creeping to the doors. She had her rifle pointed uncomfortably close to his midsection. Easing out a hand, he pushed the tip away.

"We're clear, at least for now. Get Thuy, I'm going to find the lights." The barn was "newish" and windowless. When he found the switch for the lights, they blinded him and he was quick to shut them off again.

In that fraction of a second, he had seen enough. A flatbed truck sat directly in front of him, while arranged along one wall were the gondolas that hung suspended from the bottom of the various balloons. Sitting in folded piles were great lengths of multi-colored fabric—these could be none other than the balloons themselves.

Thuy came in with a flashlight that seemed like a candle in comparison to the large overhead arrays. She hauled the main doors shut behind her and then proceeded to go around the room cataloguing everything and making little noises in her throat.

She didn't want to admit it, but hot air balloons were a little more complicated than she had reckoned. To start with, there were two massive gondolas made of a light wood and two smaller "baskets" made of wicker. These would have to be attached to one of the six immense balloons that were folded and set on wooden tables that were sturdy enough to bear the weight of a car.

Next, there were the sandbags that would assist in moving along the vertical plane—how many should be carried aloft with them? And how many tanks of fuel? And which of the four "burners" was to be used in conjunction with which basket or gondola and with which balloon?

Needless to say there weren't any instructions sitting about for her to peruse. She had to settle for something far simpler: pictures. On the walls of an office were dozens of poster-sized pictures of the balloons in action. Although two dimensional, she was able to extrapolate the number of tanks and sandbags to be used with the smallest of the wicker baskets.

Since all of the balloons were striped in red, white and blue, it was hard to tell which of them was the smallest. She walked around them for a few minutes before she threw out a guess.

"This is the one," she said, feigning confidence. "Okay, first things first. Ms. Shaw, I need you to check the fuel status of that truck and find us the keys. Deckard, I will need the truck loaded with six sandbags, two fuel tanks, the smallest of the baskets, the burner on the far left and this balloon." She tapped an arrangement of nylon that weighed five hundred pounds.

"Is that all?" Deckard asked, under his breath as Thuy went back into the office to look for more pictures. She needed close-up pictures in order to figure out how to get the balloon up in one go. With the zombie menace so unpredictable, they weren't going to have time for second or third attempts.

Luckily, she found a scrapbook that showed a balloon stretched out on the ground with the basket tilted on its side. If she hadn't seen the picture, she would have attempted some sort standing arrangement and likely torched the balloon in the process.

While she was doing her research, Deckard found a pulley and winch system attached to an overhead beam and was able to move everything onto the flatbed except the balloon itself. It was trussed up like a seventy foot burrito. "Court, I need your help," he said when she had come back from scrounging up the keys to the truck.

The two of them manhandled the balloon up into the back of the truck, only to have it slither off the side. It took two more tries before they had it in place and strapped down.

"Pretty easy so far," Thuy said, not noticing the sweat glistening on Deckard's and Courtney's foreheads. She laid out the scrapbook on the hood of the truck and showed them the steps that would need to happen. "When we get to the launch point, the first thing we need to do is prepare the balloon. It needs to be spread out completely flat with the top pointing away. Next we need to attach the burner to the basket and attach the gas tank to the burner. We turn this conglomeration of parts on its side and, as one of us gets the fan going, the others begin attaching the hang ropes using the carabiners. Total inflate time should be about five minutes."

Deckard's frown deepened as her explanation went on. "That's going to be a long five minutes. We're going to be out in the open, and we're going to make a lot of noise and the flame is going to attract every zombie within miles."

A nod from Thuy. "For these reasons, I will be taking the smaller vehicle and will act as interference if we run into any zombies."

"I don't know," Courtney said. "What if we come across a problem with the balloon?"

Thuy's brow creased. "Then I expect you will fix it. Courtney, I may have more book smarts in certain fields than you, but you have a fine mind. There is nothing concerning a hot air balloon that is truly mysterious. Hot air rises. Trap it within a balloon and the balloon rises as well. It's pretty simple. I will be the distraction because I am smaller and weaker than either of you. The balloon will call for a certain amount of muscle, of which I have very little."

Courtney saw the wisdom in Thuy's words and after a single nod, went to the passenger side of the truck.

"I'll get the door," Thuy said.

"Not yet." Deckard grabbed her around her slim waist and pulled her close. He didn't try to kiss her. He wanted to breathe her in and stare into her eyes, afraid that there weren't going to be many more opportunities to do either. "I hate the idea of you in another car. I hate the idea of us being separated."

"Hey!" she said, punching him in the chest and forcing a grin onto her face. "Aren't you supposed to be reassuring me? I'm the damsel here."

He chuckled at the idea. "You? A damsel? That'll be a cold day in hell." Perhaps it was the reference to hell or the doom hanging over their heads, but either way, their smiles faltered and when they did kiss it was with surprising force rather than subtle intimacy.

Neither wanted to end the kiss. However, with her guilt still heavy on her, making her feel as if she didn't deserve Deckard, Thuy pulled away first. "I'll get the door," she repeated.

"And then stay right on my ass. If we get separated, we meet back here." Thuy answered him with a thumbs up and then pulled back the sliding door. He drove through, stopped and tossed something that glinted in the night. "You aren't going to get too far without keys." He grinned at her, wanting to say the words: *I love you*, but fearing to as well.

They almost felt like cursed words, as if there was a horrible finality to them. In his mind, saying *I love you* was equivalent to saying good bye—forever.

"Thanks," she said and her throat constricted down on her own words of love. *When we're safe, I'll tell him*, she thought and ran for the RAV4.

A twenty minute drive west along deserted roads brought them to the New York State border. From there they went north for a while until Massachusetts sat a few miles to the east. Then it was just a matter of finding a deserted farm, blowing up the balloon and floating west.

Of farms, there were many. Of deserted farms, there were none.

Zombies seemed to be drawn to the humanity beyond the border and many could be seen traipsing through fields, heading east. Deckard was getting frustrated when Courtney suddenly said: "The Titans!" He gave her a quizzical look and she went on, quickly: "The Taconic Titans. It's a high school a few miles from here. I've been there for a football game. They have a great stadium. It's kinda new and completely fenced off, we should be fine."

She pointed the way and the miles slipped quickly by. When they got close, Deckard turned off his lights. It was just as she had said: a wide open and empty area completely surrounded by a ten foot fence. The only hole in the fence was where Deckard plowed down the gate. Once in the stadium, he chugged the flatbed truck straight to the fifty yard line and leapt out with Courtney right behind him.

Instead of untying the ropes, he slashed them with his knife and then began grunting the immense nylon balloon down to the ground. Thuy joined them seconds later, and with all three hauling, the balloon came off the truck with much more ease than it had going on. "Courtney and I will get this," Thuy said. "You get the basket ready."

Like old hands, the three carried out their duties with amazing speed. The balloon was unrolled and stretched, the burner and the gas tank were fixed to the basket and then the hang ropes were attached.

In two minutes, Deckard had the burner going on low heat and maximum fan. The air spewing from it was hot, but not blistering, and quickly the nylon began to inflate.

Thuy and Courtney grinned at each other from opposite sides of the balloon—then Courtney's grin dimmed when she saw a halting parade of creatures stumbling in their direction. Zombies were at the gate in platoon size. "Thuy!"

Thuy ran for the RAV4, but as she passed Deckard who was hefting a fifty pound sandbag, she slowed and said: "Don't leave without me!"

"I won't," he called after her. "Be back in three minutes."

She felt that two minutes would suffice right up until she saw the size of the horde she was dealing with. A dozen or so were at the gate. A thousand were beyond it. They were heading to the stadium where the burner glowed bright enough to light up the night.

In an effort to keep them away, she turned on her brights and leaned on the horn. Immediately the RAV4 was surrounded and she was forced to blast into them before they tore off the doors or hammered in her windows. Hoping that they would chase her, she took off toward the school. At least eight hundred followed after—the rest went for the stadium.

Deckard saw them coming. "Get that thing ready to fly!" he yelled as he stalked toward the zombies with his M4 at his shoulder. He marched right up to the first and plugged it between the eyes. It fell and another took its place. He took two steps back and one to his right and fired again.

He led the undead away from the balloon, firing slowly, heading for the bleachers on the home side of the field. When he reached them, he ran up four of the odd steps and looked back and saw the balloon slowly filling up with air. Soon it would begin lifting from the ground.

"Two minutes," he muttered, his words lost in the din of the hundred zombies arrayed all around him. Awkwardly, they scrambled up the bleachers to get at him. In response, he went higher still and then ran thirty yards down one, in order to give himself more room. They gave chase and he was forced to go practically to the top. From there he had a great view of the school grounds and could see the headlights of the RAV4 in the furthest parking lot of the school—she was too far away!

The mob came at her from all angles, driving her further and further away. Deckard knew he had to buy her time to get back, but he was in a hard spot, himself. He couldn't go any higher and there wasn't much more room to retreat. He was almost to the far end of the bleachers with a hundred stumbling corpses coming after, when he heard a scream and a gun shot from the field.

The inflated balloon seemed to fill half the field and Courtney looked small standing just beside the basket as it began to lift off the ground. In one hand she held her M16 and in the other was one of the anchor lines—and it wasn't tied to anything but the balloon. It was about to take off without them!

"Son of a…" Deckard began cursing as he raced, with wild steps, straight down the bleachers taking them three at a time. Then he was on the track that surrounded the field and was sprinting through the crowds of zombies for all he was worth.

The inflating balloon and the fire seemed to mesmerize many, however, the girl just underneath drew more than she could handle. She shot her gun one-handed from point blank range, mounding up the zombies as they came.

Deckard got to her just as she ran out of ammo, with three of them charging. Using the balloon's tether rope, she leapt up and lashed out with her feet, flailing and kicking, holding them back until Deckard shot them properly. Then, with eight perfect shots, he killed those around them, giving them the tiniest window of opportunity.

They needed it. The burner was going full force and soon, Deckard had to throw the M16 over his shoulder and pull with both hands on the anchor rope to keep the balloon from flying away. Heaving with all his might as more zombies bore down on them, he pulled the basket low enough for Courtney to climb in.

Without wasting a second, she turned the tank's knob, slowing the burner to a hissing simmer, but the balloon kept rising. "How do I stop it?" she yelled, staring around at the small basket as if she had overlooked an anchor.

Deckard had no idea. He didn't think you could stop a hot air balloon once it got going. And this one was moving. The wind had picked up and in a second, he was being lifted and hauled along. Only by happenstance was he able to reach out with one foot and catch the open cab of the truck, hooking it with his toes. Then he was being stretched, his hands burning where the rope bit into them.

He cursed and grimaced in pain, trying to hold on because Thuy was finally coming back. The RAV4, its front covered in black blood and zombie parts, raced onto the field making straight for the balloon, only to be intercepted by a throng of the undead.

She detoured around them and in those few seconds, the strain became too great and Deckard's foot lost its feeble hold. Before he knew it, he was twenty feet in the air with the balloon shooting west toward the far end of the stadium.

"Don't leave me!" Thuy screamed at the top of her lungs, racing the vehicle down the field, one hand on the steering wheel, one hand waving desperately. For a moment Thuy was below Deckard and could see him fighting to climb the rope with bleeding hands. He would know how to stop the balloon, she thought, or at least lower it by bleeding off the hot air.

He would never leave her…these were her last thoughts as she came skidding up to the fence that surrounded the stadium and watched, helplessly as the balloon sailed over and out of reach. In seconds, it was gone, hidden by the night and then she was alone—except for the thousand zombies charging after her.

Epilogue—Garden City, Long Island
Midnight and Beyond

Anna Holloway and Lieutenant Eng strode across the open grass, mindful of the eyes on them. Of course it was too dark to see anything, beyond a few feet. Even the thrumming helicopter was nothing more than a dark, shapeless lump in the night.

They couldn't see out past their noses, but that didn't mean soldiers weren't out there. More than likely there were men with high-tech, low-light cameras hidden in the trees, filming their every move, trying to catch a glimpse of their faces—in vain. With all the contraptions the army had these days, Anna knew the dark wouldn't hide their identities and so she had them cover their faces in scarves, hide their hair under skull-tight hats and bundled themselves in heavy coats that made it hard to tell their true size.

Less likely, and far more frightening, was the idea that there were snipers perched up in one of the buildings that ringed the park. She had chosen this particular park as the extraction point simply because it was surrounded by apartment buildings, each teaming with people. The idea was that the government would be less likely to assassinate two seemingly defenseless people while there were witnesses about.

Neither was close to being defenseless. Each carried a Beretta stuffed into the waistband of their pants and hidden by their coats. And they each carried a vial of blood in their fists.

It was real zombie blood.

Eng had thought it would be a good way to remind the military who was in charge—*and* he wanted to be on an equal footing with Anna. He absolutely hated the idea that she'd had the upper hand this entire time with her vial of Com-cells. Now she could fall to her death or get accidentally shot, or get eaten by some stray zombie, or be strangled with her own panties after one last good fucking, and Eng would still be able blackmail the world.

The vials went unnoticed when they were stopped by a soldier who was armed to the teeth. He gave them a long look. "Get the fuck out of here," he said in a shout to be heard over the helicopter. He had been told to expect between four and seven people, all of whom were armed and dangerous. The two people in front of him looked like curious hipsters who had wandered over to see what the fuss was about.

"Morning glory blinders," Anna shouted back to the soldier. The man twitched as if shocked and then took a step back, raising his gun, the barrel looked as though it was shivering. Next to Eng, Anna stiffened and she too stepped back.

Eng was the only one of the three who was unafraid. He guessed that if the military was going to arrest them or kill them, they wouldn't have sent one man, and if they had, he would have been more prepared. "Morning glory binders," Eng repeated. "Now let us on the helicopter."

The soldier looked confused. His gun wavered, the bore switching from Eng to Anna then back again, only to finally point at the ground. "Uh, is this all of you?" he asked, looking over their heads.

"Yes. Step aside or else." Eng held the vial up higher so the soldier couldn't fail to see it.

The man edged further away, holding his hands in the air and letting his rifle hang from its strap. "Okay, okay. I-I was just told there would be more of you. That's all. Everything is how you asked for it, okay? We have been instructed to let you board without interference." He pointed with one of his raised hands at the helicopter.

Eng marched toward the helicopter and Anna had to hurry to catch up. When they were out of earshot, the soldier keyed his mike. "This is Papa-two. I have two headed for the bird. I say again, two heading for the bird and they are carrying vials right out in the open."

"Roger that," the pilot said, feeling something twist in his gut. He turned his bulky helmet to the right and picked out the pair moving slowly forward. His night vision goggles gave him excellent night-sight, but he still couldn't pick out the vials of blood, though he was sure they were carrying them—why else would each of them hold their hands out like they were?

"Call it in," the pilot ordered his co-pilot.

The co-pilot didn't reach for the radio. He was half turned in his seat, watching Eng and Anna come up to the Blackhawk. His goggles were perched on the brim of his helmet and he had no problem seeing the glass vials reflecting the glow of the instruments.

"Shit," he whispered. "They've got the vials just sitting in their hands. Are they stupid? What happens if they drop them?"

The pilot flipped his goggles up and blinked until he could see things in their natural hues. Under the dim interior lights, he could see Eng climbing into the bird, one-handed. The other was still held out.

"Stow that shit, damn it!" the pilot barked as Eng sat down. When it was obvious that Eng couldn't hear him, the pilot keyed his mike: "Bill, get a helmet on that one so I can talk to his dumb ass."

The helmet was offered and the pilot started in immediately: "We aren't going anywhere until you and your friend stow those fucking vials. We're not going to risk you dropping them."

"Actually, you're going to do as you're told," Eng explained.

After a moment in which the pilot gritted his teeth, he came back on, saying, "Look, you have free passage to Washington. No one is going to do anything to you. Those are the orders. The only time we can do anything is if we believe you are going to use the bird to spread the disease. With the vials out, we aren't leaving."

Eng hesitated, but Anna made a show of putting the vial in her pocket—she kept her hand there as well. Eng did the same. "Safe and sound," he said. "Now we can go."

The pilot stared back at him for a moment and then faced forward, gripping the stick a little too hard. "Call it in," he growled.

Word was relayed from channel to channel until the president heard it thirty minutes before midnight of the third day of the apocalypse. He sat back in the plush seat absolutely uncaring that it had cost taxpayers thousands of dollars. "Okay, that's that. How many drones to we have in place?"

"Fourteen at the moment," the FBI director said, glancing at his notes. "But we'll have three more ready to go by the time they reach DC."

The president turned his bleary eyes to General Heider, the Chairman of the Joint Chiefs of Staff. "And Pennsylvania?" The president longed to look back at Colonel Manzetti to confirm that he hadn't disappeared, but he'd been told by Marty Aleman that it was beginning to creep everyone out how often he let his eyes linger on the man with the nuclear codes.

Heider had his glasses off and was rubbing his face with both hands, up and down, pulling his old man's flesh around like it was a mask. "It's up in the air still…but it's going to be close."

"I gave you the damned planes," the president snapped. "You wanted planes, I gave you planes. You wanted tanks, I gave you tanks. What more do you need?"

"Honestly, I need time," Heider replied. "You only federalized this mess this morning. Given enough time, we can hold, I know it." He needed time to catch his breath, to figure who was where, who was alive, who was dead and who was only sort of dead.

Marty picked his head up from the desk where he'd been resting. "Time is the one thing that's not ours to give. The people won't stand for any of this much longer. This morning, when this was only an up-state New York issue, we had people murdering each other over loaves of bread. What do you think it's like out there now?"

Heider honestly didn't know. His focus was on the battle and it had been enough to keep him so busy that he had forgotten to eat or drink and now his head was pounding.

At his shrug, Marty said: "I'll tell you how it is, people are at each other's throats. The number of murders has skyrocketed since yesterday. It's up over twelve-hundred nationwide and the numbers of lootings is reaching epidemic levels. I don't need to tell you, General what that's doing to your ability to mobilize."

It's killing me, Heider thought. Every state had called up their guard units, but none had turned them over to the federal government. What was more, many of the governors had illegally appropriated reserve units, if not their men, then their equipment. It was a huge mess that only added to his woes.

And yet…"Twelve hundred?" Heider said after a moment when the number reached his groggy brain. "In a country of three-hundred million, that's not a lot. I would have thought it would be more."

"You don't know these people like I do," Marty said. "They're sheep right up until the shit hits the fan and then they turn into blood-thirsty…" It took him a moment to come up with the right word: "…Jackals."

Heider sat back from the table. A large part of him wanted to get up right then and walk away. "That's how you think of the American people? You're wrong."

"The numbers don't lie, General." Heider thought Marty's snide look needed to be punched right off his face, but there were three Secret Service agents in the room and the general remained seated. "Good," Marty said, thinking he had won some point when he had only further cemented his distaste for the very people he helped to lead.

He gave the general a smarmy, shit-eating grin, never realizing that his *doom and gloom* outlook was nowhere near accurate. He saw things through the very narrow tube offered by the media, who fixated on anything negative. The truth was that *most* people weren't looting and very, very few were committing murder or even considering it. In fact, many crimes had dropped to almost nothing. Arson, pedophilia, burglary and rapes simply weren't occurring.

The people had seen the news and were properly afraid. The great majority of them did as they were told: they remained indoors, they made lists of their supplies, they began rationing and they began hoarding water in tupperware containers and pots and even in bathtubs.

They also began to look out for one another in a manner that was almost unheard of in twenty-first century America.

On their own they began trading with neighbors, and on their own they gave what they could to those who were in need, and on their own they looked out for one another and on their own they took up their weapons.

Milo Musial, a recent graduate of Brentwood High in Pittsburg, Pennsylvania was one of these. Just nineteen, he took up the Winchester 30.06 he had been given as a birthday present two years before, and headed east. Next to him on the bench seat of his Dodge truck, was a backpack that held seventy three rounds of ammunition and a lunch packed for him by his tearful mother.

He drove east until at sunset he was ten miles from the New Jersey border. There he was slowed by a line of cars and trucks, many of them sporting the Stars and Stripes. The line was four miles long and before five minutes had passed, thirty more cars joined it behind him. An hour later, he was pointed to a field that had once been planted with turnips but was now a three hundred acre parking lot.

As if he were pulling into a concert, civilians with flashlights directed him to a spot and then hustled him out of his truck, asking for his keys in the process. "We may need them," was all the explanation given and was all the explanation needed. He understood: they might need the truck or just the gas. Either didn't matter to him.

The truck was simply a conveyance. He was there to fight. He was there to die. He was there for God, family, and country. He was part of a voluntary crusade that had sprung up out of nowhere. If the gas or the battery from his truck were needed for the cause, then so be it.

He left the keys, slung his pack and shouldered his rifle. With hundreds of others, he marched for miles and then was placed on the line. Around him were men and women in camouflage, and in overalls, and in jeans that hung so low that half their asses were open to the cool night air.

Milo expected to be afraid. These were zombies he was facing and he had watched enough television to know that it wasn't going to be pretty. But his fear wasn't any greater than anyone else's. In fact, two seconds after arriving he found himself comforting a soldier in uniform: a pretty young thing named Ginny Kinna.

All day, Ginny had kept hold of her MOPP gear and her gun and a few bullets, and all day she had marched until her feet were filled with blister-pus and her muscles ached. They were retreating, which, in Ginny's mind meant they were losing. At sunset, the line had underwent a major shift. Again to the west. West, west, west.

At least, with this last shift, she had been able to ride in a truck. They rode to the Pennsylvania border and for some reason she thought that since she was a New Yorker, she could be done with the fight. But no…more marching, deep into the night and then an actual fight with real zombies that came out of nowhere.

It was dark and Ginny could hear their moans long before she could see them. She could hear the moans and the sound went right up her spine and made her shiver and the shivering never stopped. She was still jittering when the first monster came crashing out of the forest in front of her.

She froze, her gun stuck on her shoulder as if she had sprung some useless, rigid growth. Thankfully, she wasn't alone. There were real soldiers around her who knew how to shoot and weren't afraid and hadn't peed themselves. When Milo Musial came on the line and was pointed to a spot next to Ginny, the first thing he noticed was the cute girl. The next thing he noticed was the dark stain spreading from her crotch.

"You okay?" he asked. Before he knew it, she had buried her face in his chest. She sobbed and made blubbering noises. She clung to him and he was still trying to dislodge her when he heard his first zombie let out a long, low sound that sent a shiver right up his spine. The zombie wasn't alone. The first hungry moan was accompanied by many more. How many, Milo had no idea, but the forest shook with the sound, and the passage of their feet was an immense crackling of leaves and snapping of twigs.

"Get off," he said, reaching for his rifle.

She wouldn't let go. He fired his gun right across her face. At first it was impossible to see what he was shooting at, but then the night was lit by flares which showed the forest in front of him crawling with the undead steadily coming forward.

He fired and his rifle, normally as loud as a cannon, was drowned out by the thunder of a thousand guns. A storm of lead flew, ripping into the creatures—they didn't seem to care, they kept coming despite the horrible destruction wrought.

People began to scream. Some in terror, some trying to rally the line: "Aim for the head! We've got this! Stand your ground!"

The voices were drowned out when a pair of what looked like enormous grey dragons streaked overhead with a roar that swept all noise aside. A half-second after they passed, the hill just down from Milo erupted in ear-shattering explosions.

Some of the men and women cheered, others were too stunned and could only stare as the flames shot into the sky. Milo was too busy fighting to do anything else. When the dark descended upon him once again, he had to wait until the zombies closed within ten feet before he could shoot. To do otherwise meant a waste of ammo and he was running through it fast enough already.

More explosions and more flares. People were screaming and the zombies were stacked six deep in front of Milo. He and dozens of others stood on a long hill with a stack of felled trees before them slowing the zombies down. It was a good position and could have been held for some time except the zombies were massed too close and in the dark it was hard to tell friend from foe.

By accident, the next bombing run was directed on the hill itself and just as Milo stooped to reload the world around him went white and his head felt like it was turned inside out by the concussive force of the explosions.

Ginny had been huddled in a ball, and when the world erupted in flame and smoke and screams, she did the only thing she could think to do: she ran. Her flight was helter-skelter and the panic that poured off of her was a contagion that ate into the will of others. In no time, soldiers and civilians were pelting away as fast as they could.

Many of the civilians had been untried and unprepared, and their fear had ramped up beyond their control. The soldiers who ran were either like Ginny, ill-fitted for the demands of battle or they were the flip side of the coin. They were men and women who had braved the horrors of the undead for hours. They had fired and fired and fired their guns until their ears rang and their shoulders ached and their hearts trembled.

During the long night, their courage had slowly eroded and now, people were running and bombs were falling on the living and nothing seemed right. They ran, thinking that the whole line was pelting away.

Officers could not stop the retreat of so many. General Phillips' staff received thirty calls in three minutes from up and down the line, everyone saying the same thing: *The center has fallen!*

Phillips didn't need a radio to know his soldiers were in trouble. He had stepped out of his command post to watch the bombing runs and now he could see little figures sprinting across the road below him.

"Son of a bitch!" he shouted, hurling down a long dead cigar he'd been munching on. "Someone call off the Air Force! Are they fucking blind!" He went on a tirade that used up every curse word in his vocabulary.

When he paused to take a breath, a major raised a hand. "General Heider wants an update."

Quieter, Phillips hissed: "Son of a bitch." He took the phone and said: "This is Phillips."

"Tell me the line is holding," Heider answered. It almost sounded like an order to Phillips, as if he wasn't looking for an update, but a lie.

"Can you repeat that, sir?"

Back in the Situation Room beneath the White House, where everything was in chaos and time seemed to be speeding up, Heider turned partially away from the president and repeated: "Tell me the line is holding."

"I don't know if I can say that in all honesty."

Heider grinned as if he had just heard good news and then gave the president—the now wild-eyed and slightly unhinged president, a thumbs up. "Everything's good, sir," he said.

In his ear, Phillips said, "Things aren't good. We just had the Air Force bomb the shit out of our own position. I have soldiers and civilians running away right now. The center of my line has just disintegrated and we don't have a reserve force to plug the hole. I used the last of them twenty minutes ago. I don't think we can hold…"

"Thanks for the report, Phillips," Heider said interrupting. "Remember, hold that line at *all costs,* or…or, well never mind." His voice was tweaked—the fear in it came through over the cell phone.

Phillips went suddenly cold. "Are they thinking nukes," he asked, pitching his voice low and covering his mouth with his free hand.

The grin on Heider's mouth broadened until he looked almost jovial. "Yes, of course. Thanks so much, ha-ha. I'll look for another update in about thirty minutes."

Heider hung up the phone on a stunned General Phillips. Then, like everyone else, his eyes slipped to Lieutenant Manzetti sitting in the corner. The man looked like he had taken a sweat-shower. The talk of nukes had flown around the table in the last few minutes after Anna Holloway played her final card in her bid to escape. Unexpectedly, she had ordered the pilot of the Blackhawk to set down in the middle of Baltimore—not Washington DC.

There wasn't a drone within fifty miles and the moment the Blackhawk had landed, she and Eng had just ghosted out into the night taking their deadly vials with them.

The president lost it over this. He came unglued, shouting: "They're out there with the virus! They're out there! They could be anywhere. They could be making zombies left and right." As this was patently obvious, no one said anything. This only set him off further. "Someone do something! Heider, get some of your men…no, get a lot of your men. We have to contain Baltimore before they can get out."

The idea was absurd. "Sir, I don't have the man power for that."

The president's eyes twitched suddenly as a thought struck him. "You would if we just used the nukes. Everyone knows we're going to have to use them sooner or later." The president said this blithely as if it had been discussed and agreed upon already.

It took the breath from Heider's chest. When he could speak, he said: "We have to give my men a chance. Please."

"One chance," the president shot back. Marty tried to say something but for once, the president was his own man. "I said one chance. If the line falls once more, then…then that's it. We drop the bombs." Heider tried a second time to plead for his men, but the president only held up a single finger. "One chance."

A hundred and sixty miles northeast, Phillips stood in the dark, staring down at where his men had been fighting, not just for their own lives, but for the life of the country. If nukes were dropped in thirty minutes, how many could he save?

"A mere handful. A few thousand." He didn't have the logistics to move any more out of harm's way, not so quickly. "Fuck," he whispered.

A colonel came up out of the dark to ask: "Do we fall back to the next line? I have brigade commanders looking for answers. They're afraid of being flanked."

"Fall back?" he asked as if the idea was new to him. "Do we have a choice?" It was a rhetorical question, one the colonel tried to answer only to be waved *quiet* by Phillips. "Yes. We will fall back. We need to move as fast as…" he stopped as his ears caught the sound of a gun going full bore. He went to the lip of the hill and stared down into the dark where the flashes of a single gun could be seen.

Someone was still on the line, holding the center against all odds.

During the bombing run, Milo Kostas had been struck by a flying hunk of burning tree. The world had gone black and he had only just regained consciousness to find himself in his own special hell. Around him the forest was on fire, lighting up the bodies. There were dead bodies everywhere, hundreds and hundreds of them—at least he thought they were dead.

Some began to pick themselves up. Their moans seemed to awaken more, and soon the land before him was coming alive again. Without a thought of running away, Milo looked around for his Winchester, but it seemed to have evaporated with the explosion. He found instead Ginny's M16.

It was a wonderful weapon, light and accurate. All alone in a scarred landscape, Milo held the center of a two-hundred mile line, firing one bullet at a time. The idea of running never entered his mind. He was there to fight. He was a son and a brother and a young uncle to a tiny baby. People depended on him to stand like a man.

Above him, higher on the hill, Phillips watched for long seconds as his flesh flared with goosebumps. "Who do we have to send down there? Do we have any medics? Clerks…anyone?"

"There's just your staff up here," the colonel answered. "Though, I think there's part of a division HQ about a mile up the road. They were asking for fall back orders as well."

How far could they go to escape nuclear weapons? Not far enough. "Tell them…" Phillips stopped in mid-sentence, thinking of General Horace Collins, who had died the night before in a vain attempt to save Connecticut. *Could I do less with the entire country depending on this one fight?* he asked himself.

The answer had to be no.

He turned to the colonel. "No one falls back. Tell them this is where we make our stand. We fight here and we might die here, but we don't retreat. Make your calls and then gather everyone from the staff and order them to get down to the line as fast as possible. No exceptions."

The colonel paled under the starlight, but ran off to do what he was told. For a few moments as the single gun kept up its lonely chatter, Phillips watched to make sure the colonel followed his orders, as he watched, he took out his cell phone and dialed Heider. "Sir, the line is going to hold. Do not send the nukes. I repeat, do not send the nukes."

"Thank God," Heider said, breathing out heavily into the phone. "Listen, Phillips, I'm going to need you to brief the president in person concerning the likelihood of holding…"

Phillips interrupted: "That's going to have to wait. I don't mean to be rude, but I have a battle to fight." He hung up on his boss and grinned, feeling a sudden burden lifted from his soul. For too long he had kissed ass, doing whatever it took to further his career. That time was over. Now he would do whatever it took to win.

With a ringing shout, Phillips pulled the Beretta from its holster, jacked back the slide with a flourish and ran down the slope as his eighteen year old self would have.

He ran straight into battle and for the first time in many years he felt not only like a soldier, but like a warrior, and as a warrior, he would fight for his people, and he would die for them as well if that's what it took. The End

Author's Note

Thank you for reading The Apocalypse Crusade, War of the Undead Day Three. I sincerely hope that you enjoyed it. If so, I'd like to ask a favor: the review is the most practical and inexpensive form of advertisement an independent author has available in order to get his work known. If you could put a kind review on Amazon and your Facebook page, I would greatly appreciate it.

Peter Meredith

Now that you're done with Crusade 3, you're probably wondering what to read next. You could go with my *Undead World* novels that have, collectively over 2,000- five star reviews. A lot of people seem to like them. Or you might try my new series: *The Gods of the Undead*, but be forewarned: there is an obscene amount of blood spilled and skin flayed and love lost and all sorts of sadness. On the other hand there's also heroes and heroines, bravery and sacrifice. And there's adventure that spans the world as two people fight the undead from New York to darkest Africa.

As many stories do, it starts small with just one man.

The Edge of Hell

Gods of the Undead, A Post-Apocalyptic Epic

Prologue
Alex Wilson

Officer Alex Wilson had to pull his cruiser over. He didn't need to, he had to. It didn't matter that he was in the middle of a south bound lane on the FDR Drive. He had to see and he had to hear for himself what was happening.

He pulled over and cut the siren; the lights he left on, whipping around, cutting the night in blinding red and blue. At first all he heard was the insane babble of the dispatchers—in three years on the force he had never once heard fear in their voices. Normally, they spoke in lackluster tones that suggested they were bored to tears with their jobs.

Now, they were screaming into their mikes, ordering units from all over the city to converge on the bridges that spanned the East River, connecting Queens to Manhattan.

"What's happening?" someone demanded over the radio. "Dispatch, say again, what's happening?"

"I don't know…I don't know. I'm not supposed to tell, but…but they're monsters, I think," was the strange reply the unknown officer received.

Alex flicked off the radio and sat still with his head cocked. Even through the heavy glass, he could hear the pop, pop, pop of gunfire, only it wasn't just: pop, pop, pop. It was a thousand pops going off all at once. Feeling a sudden churn in his guts, he climbed out of the cruiser and the sound of the battle assaulted him. He was a mile away with a wide river between him and the fire-fight and still the sound was frightfully urgent.

He didn't rush off, however. The churning in his guts intensified, and only slowly he climbed back into the cruiser. "Son of a bitch," he whispered and then stuck the car in gear. Gradually, he built up speed and far too soon for his liking, he was at the Queensboro Bridge and being directed to heel his cruiser in next to a row of forty others.

Even as he pulled in, another cruiser squeezed right up next to him and another pulled up next to that one. He slid out of the car feeling his stomach twist, going beyond churning; it was a curdling sensation that made him feel sick.

The officer in the next cruiser beat him out, rushing to pop his trunk. "What is it?" he asked as Alex reluctantly opened the trunk on his cruiser.

Alex couldn't answer at first; the sound of the guns firing was now mingled with screams. So many screams. "I-I don't know," he said after taking a gulp of air.

"They said monsters," another officer said, a little, fake laugh in his voice. It was a high, oddly girlish sound as if someone had a good hold of his balls and were giving them a healthy tweak.

Another officer, further down the row of cruisers was screaming: "Masks! Get your damn masks on! Come on, damn it!"

Masks meant there were germs in the air…zombie germs. The idea that just breathing could turn him into one of them was horrible and Alex dug in his trunk for his protective mask. It came in a pouch that he buckled around his waist. It took three tries to snap in place and as he struggled with the simple buckle, the sound of the firing came closer and the screams grew evermore urgent and loud. People were dying right on the bridge and yet Alex felt as though he was moving in slow motion. He couldn't seem to get his feet moving despite then urgency in the air.

Some of the officers were pulling on their mask and others were hauling out shotguns or Colt M4s. Alex only had his 9mm Sig Sauer P226 and it felt altogether puny, certainly too puny to use against an army of undead.

He needed something bigger: a machine gun or a grenade launcher. Anything would be better than the pistol. "Hey," he hissed to the officer who had pulled in next to him. "You don't happen to have a…"

Just then, someone turned him around and screamed in his face: "Get to the line! Hurry!"

Alex was pushed and shoved onto the bridge where his fellow officers were lined up. There were forty or fifty of them, all looking green, all sweating and scared. Alex was sure he looked just as terrified. His hands shook as he tried to check on his second magazine. It dropped, clinking on the cement. Frantically he scrambled for it. He was deathly afraid, but of what exactly, he didn't know. He had no idea what they were facing and yet he was practically pissing himself.

Questions ran up and down the line: "What's going on? What's happening? What are they? Are they really zombies? Really?"

No one knew, but it wasn't long before they found out.

The bridge stretched east toward Queens. Normally, a person could see across the half-mile span without a problem but just then, the far end couldn't be seen. A swirling black cloud engulfed it. And it didn't just hover over it, it advanced against a gentle westerly wind.

Within that unnatural black cloud were creatures masquerading as people. They shambled forward, bringing with them a horrid stench of decay. It was so bad that even the veterans of a hundred murder scenes ripped their masks out of their holders and pulled them on.

Gagging from the stench, Alex held his mask to his face, but didn't put it on. The mask would cloud his vision and he needed to see what he was dealing with. Monsters was what the dispatcher had said. Seconds later, he saw that she had been wrong. These weren't exactly monsters—they were zombies. They could be nothing else.

The creatures stumbling though the swirling darkness had been people at one time, only now they were the living dead. They were corpses somehow imbued with life. They limped along, dragging ropes of intestine and leaving long trails of blood and pus behind them. Their decayed and rotting flesh hung in ribbons off their bleached bones.

They were horrors that had no right to live and there were thousands of them.

Someone yelled: "They-they're zombies! Aim for the head!"

Alex was way ahead of him. He had the mask in one hand and the Sig Sauer in the other. He peered down the iron sights, waiting until the leading wave of monsters was within thirty yards. He couldn't miss from that distance.

A captain screamed: "Fire!" The line of officers let loose with a ragged volley, some using handguns, some shotguns and some M4s. Those zombies in the first line were staggered, many falling, causing the wave of undead to slow as it stumbled over them. More shots created more mayhem and the bridge became an obstacle course of black blood and rotting limbs which slowed the attacking monsters even more.

Alex shot his Sig Sauer dry and in the three seconds it took to reload, the zombies were ten yards closer. Strangely, the thunder of the guns going off all around him and the acrid stench of the spent gunpowder calmed his nerves to a degree.

It didn't last.

A foul creature, grey and stinking of death, pushed itself over the mound of wriggling bodies and came for Alex. He aimed and fired, certain that he had hit the zombie in the head; however, it didn't fall or even slow.

"What the hell?" he whispered and then took aim again and now at twenty yards he knew he was a good enough marksman to plug the bitch dead center. He caressed the trigger, there was a shock that ran up his arm to his shoulder, and then he saw the thing's head rock back, bone and brain and unknown crap flying onto the bridge.

Again it didn't fall. It just kept coming closer and closer, close enough that Alex could see a gaping hole just off center of its forehead.

Alex wasn't the only one just realizing that things were far worse than they realized.

"Oh, my God!" someone screamed. "They're not dying!"

That wasn't possible. In the course of two hours the world had turned on its head and yet these were zombies, flesh-eating, brain-chomping, undead zombies and everyone knew that you could kill a zombie with a head-shot. That was supposedly a fact, and yet the zombies kept coming, seemingly impervious to any bullet. Even the creatures that had collapsed earlier, were fighting their way to their feet.

Movement out of the corner of his eye had Alex turning. Some of the men were running away! Everything was suddenly chaos. A few men ran, a few fired their weapons, a few stood there not knowing what to do.

Alex glanced down at his Sig Sauer for a brief moment, tempted to toss it away and run, but he managed to swallow his fear long enough to empty the gun into the corpse that was now only ten yards away. The 9mm blazed with orange flame as Alex hit the zombie with every round. It jerked with each strike, coming to a standstill almost within reach. Then the two just stared at each other; Alex trying to come to grips with this new reality, and the zombie trying to stand with a body that had been torn to shreds.

An officer next to Alex stood with his head wagging side to side, saying: "That ain't possible." His pistol sat useless in his hands.

Another officer, this one a round-bellied sergeant who had been too long at the desk, yelled: "Keep Firing! Keep firing!" He had a shotgun and when he pulled the trigger, the zombie in front of Alex flew back, its head coming off its shoulders. Every time the sergeant squeezed the trigger on the gun, his belly would jiggle and a zombie was blasted back.

Alex watched him with one thought in his head: I'm going to die. There were too many zombies and not enough men with shotguns. He started backing away. With only a pistol he didn't

340

think he stood a chance. A second later, it rattled on the pavement as he turned to run. The sergeant caught him.

"Stand your ground!" he roared into Alex's face.

"Give me your gun and I will!" Alex yelled right back. It was suicide to stand there with only a pistol. Already a dozen officers were screaming with zombies latched onto them, tearing them to pieces with their teeth alone. Those officers with shotguns and M4s were able to hold back the flood of walking corpses, but anyone with only a pistol was already running or dead.

The sergeant hesitated, seeing the truth of the situation around him, but somehow he found the courage to hold out the shotgun. Alex eagerly snatched it and began blasting the walking dead. The shotgun was like a cannon, it thundered and flashed with every pull of the trigger, throwing body parts into the air.

Over and over he fired, his hands growing numb, the corpses piling up in front of him in a mound. When his gun ran dry, he fed shells from the bandolier on the strap, he had twelve shots left—they went in less than a minute. He turned to yell for more ammo, only to realize that he was all alone.

The line of officers had fallen. Some men had run off and some were being fed on by the creatures. The lucky ones had their throats torn out, the unlucky ones were being eaten alive, screaming at the top of their lungs.

Alex spun, desperate to escape; however, before he could take his second step, a grey hand with bloody fingers reached out from the pile of corpses and grabbed his ankle. He went down, the empty shotgun flying from his grasp. He tried to pull away, only the zombie had a grip of iron and a strength that was irresistible.

Slowly, Alex was dragged to the mound of corpses and pulled under, his screams growing more and more muffled until he was buried entirely and the teeth of a dozen zombies tore into him.

Fictional works by Peter Meredith:

A Perfect America
The Sacrificial Daughter
The Apocalypse Crusade War of the Undead: Day One
The Apocalypse Crusade War of the Undead: Day Two
The Apocalypse Crusade War of the Undead Day Three
The Horror of the Shade: Trilogy of the Void 1
An Illusion of Hell: Trilogy of the Void 2
Hell Blade: Trilogy of the Void 3
The Punished
Sprite
The Blood Lure The Hidden Land Novel 1
The King's Trap The Hidden Land Novel 2
To Ensnare a Queen The Hidden Land Novel 3
The Apocalypse: The Undead World Novel 1
The Apocalypse Survivors: The Undead World Novel 2
The Apocalypse Outcasts: The Undead World Novel 3
The Apocalypse Fugitives: The Undead World Novel 4
The Apocalypse Renegades: The Undead World Novel 5
The Apocalypse Exile: The Undead World Novel 6
The Apocalypse War: The Undead World Novel 7
The Edge of Hell: Gods of the Undead Book One
The Edge of Temptation: Gods of the Undead Book Two
Pen(Novella)
A Sliver of Perfection (Novella)
The Haunting At Red Feathers(Short Story)
The Haunting On Colonel's Row(Short Story)
The Drawer(Short Story)
The Eyes in the Storm(Short Story)
The Witch: Jillybean in the Undead World

Printed in Great Britain
by Amazon